CONNE
WEDDINGS

THREE-IN-ONE COLLECTION

KIM O'BRIEN

All scripture taken from the Holy Bible, New International Version ®.
niv ®. Copyright © 1973, 1978, 1984 by International Bible Society. Used by
permission of Zondervan. All rights reserved.

This book is a work of fiction. Names, characters, places, and incidents are either
products of the author's imagination or used fictitiously. Any similarity to actual
people, organizations, and/or events is purely coincidental.

Cover Design: Kirk DouPonce, DogEared Design

Published by Barbour Publishing, Inc., P.O. Box 719, Uhrichsville, Ohio 44683,
www.barbourbooks.com

*Our mission is to publish and distribute inspirational products offering exceptional
value and biblical encouragement to the masses.*

 Member of the
Evangelical Christian
Publishers Association

Printed in the United States of America.

Dear Readers,

A long time ago I became estranged from a very good friend. We'd been roommates in college, maid of honor at each other's weddings, and seen each other through a lot of tough times. I never understood what happened, but our conversations became more and more infrequent until they stopped all together. I was devastated. Every year I sent her a Christmas card, but in my heart of hearts, I knew our relationship was over.

So you can imagine my amazement when, at the surprise fiftieth birthday party my husband and kids threw me for me, there she was, standing in the back with her husband and a handsome, grown-up son. It had been fifteen years since I'd seen her. She and her family had traveled hundreds of miles to be with me. We hugged. I cried. We talked. She lifted a burden that had been on my shoulders for years.

To me, this was the ultimate example of God fixing things that seemed impossibly broken. I had lost faith that this friendship would ever be healed. The lesson to me was never to stop believing—that God can heal all things, and His timing is always perfect.

I hope the following stories will inspire your own faith. That you will laugh with my characters as they struggle to overcome their challenges, and rejoice as they discover, as I did, what God can do in their lives.

Thank you for reading.

Kim O'Brien

LEAP OF FAITH

Dedication

Special thanks to Jenny Chang, MD, for answering my questions and generously allowing me to visit her laboratory at the Baylor School of Medicine, and to Melissa Landis, PhD, who gave me my first view of a cancer cell. These are extraordinary women doing extraordinary work. Any factual errors in the book relating to breast cancer are mine.

Chapter 1

S tacy, what in the world do you think you're doing?" Dr. Deena Bradley stared down at her sister—seven months pregnant, plopped on top of a bulging suitcase. The lid had caved in under Stacy, and clothing protruded from the gaping sides.

"Packing." Stacy tugged impatiently at the zipper. "Or trying to, but it won't shut. Packing these maternity clothes is like packing parachutes."

Deena reached out her hand to pull her sister from the suitcase. "The only place you're going is to bed. Remember what the doctor said."

"Get away." Stacy slapped Deena's hands away, and her pointed chin lifted a notch. "Evie's camp starts in three days."

Blue eyes met blue eyes. When her sister's chin came up like this, Deena knew she was sunk. While Deena had two years and almost six inches over her, Stacy had inherited the genes for stubbornness.

Deena put her hands on her hips. There had to be a few genes for stubbornness in her DNA chain. And even if there weren't, she knew the one sure way to get Stacy back in bed. "Don't make me call Jeff."

Stacy's features changed abruptly at the mention of her husband's name. "Oh, Deena. You can't do that. Please don't ask him to come home from work early. He thinks his poetry is soothing, but it's driving me crazy. One more ode to our unborn child and I'm burning his rhyming dictionary."

Deena hid a smile. Jeff had a great heart but wrote terrible poetry. His last work, read at Thanksgiving, dealt with grief over a man's inability to become pregnant. "I won't call him, but you've got to get back in bed." She closed her fingers around Stacy's petite wrists and leaned backward, helping her up from the suitcase.

Tucking Stacy into the king-size bed, Deena perched on the edge. "You know, bed rest isn't the end of the world."

Stacy stared at her as if she were crazy. "I can't just lie here for eight weeks."

"Yes, you can. School's out, remember?"

"Yeah, but I'm snack mom for Jack's soccer camp. And I'm chaperoning five girls at Camp Bald Eagle, remember?"

"I'll buy snacks for Jack's team, and you can send Evie to camp without you."

"Send Evie alone?" Stacy shook her head. "No way. She'll just get into trouble."

"So keep her home, then."

"Not an option." Stacy's chin came up. "She needs this camp."

"So send her, then. How much trouble can a kid get into at a church camp?"

Stacy just lifted her brows.

"She's twelve. You have to let go sometime."

"And sometimes you've got to know when to hold on." Stacy pleated the fabric of the embroidered ivory bedspread. "She's got the hormone thing starting. One minute she's happy, the next in tears. Everything I say to her is wrong, and then she just wants to cuddle."

She pushed the covers back, but Deena pulled them up just as firmly. "Stacy, stop it."

"I appreciate you coming and all." Stacy pushed the covers off again. "But I know how busy you are with your lab and your experiments. There are some snickerdoodles on the counter. You ought to take some when you go."

"I'm not going anywhere." Not that she hadn't had one eye on the clock. "And neither are you."

"If I back out now, the church is going to have a hard time finding someone to replace me."

Deena stared at the hollows under her sister's eyes, the paleness of her skin, the fingers so swollen from pregnancy that she couldn't even wear her wedding ring. "They'll find someone. It isn't something for you to worry about."

"I'm her mother, Deena. It's my job to worry."

The unspoken "If you had children, you would understand" hung in the air between them. Just as it had when Stacy had dropped out of graduate school just credits shy of her master's degree in physics. And before that when Stacy had traded her fitness club membership so her son could play on a fancy sports team.

Rising, Deena crossed the room to pull back the lace curtain. Like everything else in the house, it was old but lovingly cared for.

She peered into the backyard. No, she didn't understand how someone could love others so much and always put herself last. But then again, Stacy could never seem to accept Deena's choices either. "You bury yourself in work," Stacy always accused. "You have no life."

A stockade fence in which no two posts stood the same height surrounded a yard desperately in need of a good mowing. Jeff had built the fence, just as he had Jack's tree house, which Deena always referred to as the Leaning Tower of Pizza. That thing just couldn't be safe.

Her world was completely different. Instead of tree houses, backyard baseball games, and kids, Deena had her laboratory at the University of Connecticut Health Center. Her cell culture room might not seem very cozy to other people, but Deena loved the small room with an incubator keeping tissue samples cold and the sterile work area behind a plate glass hood. She felt at home among the glass pipettes and trays of subculture plates. Deena might not be good at reading bedtime stories, but she was very good at reading the story the cell samples told her as she studied them beneath her inverted microscope.

Jack walked into the backyard along with Godzilla, their harlequin Great Dane. Where was Evie? Deena wouldn't have put it past the girl to be planning another prank. The other night Stacy had called her in despair because Evie had gotten on the intercom at the local supermarket and announced a half-price doughnut sale at the bakery. "What am I going to do with her?" Stacy had said.

The pranks were harmless but seemed to be escalating. Stacy wouldn't send Evie alone to camp, and if Evie stayed home, she'd make it impossible for Stacy to rest. There was only one solution.

Deena let the curtain fall back into place. "I'll go, Stace. I'll take your place at the camp."

Stacy laughed. "You're kidding, right?"

"No."

"You're brilliant, Deena, and you'll probably cure breast cancer someday. But when it comes to kids. . ." Stacy shook her head sadly. "Let's just say you aren't Mary Poppins."

Deena lifted her eyebrows. "I may not have children, but I have Mr. Crackers. I understand regular care and feeding."

"These are kids, not a parrot. You'd have a nervous breakdown within three days. You have to build up your endurance before you can be around kids full-time."

"I made it through Christmas and Easter, remember?"

"Holidays are different. Besides, this is a Christian camp."

"I'm a Christian."

"You need to be able to model your faith, Deena, pray with the kids, and help them understand how much God loves them."

"I can do that." Deena lifted a photograph off the top of the mahogany dresser. The picture was an old one now, taken when her mother was still in good health. Before the breast cancer.

In the picture her mother was the exact age Deena was now, and the similarities were striking. They had the same arched black eyebrows, fair skin, and light blue eyes. Their smiles matched, as did the single freckle on the left side of Deena's mouth. The only difference was their hairstyle. Evelyn had worn hers in a wavy, shoulder-length shag; Deena preferred a modified pixie cut.

"I have to drag you to church," Stacy pointed out.

"I have a very busy schedule," Deena hedged. "Mine isn't a nine-to-five kind of job."

Stacy pulled herself higher against the pillows. "Exactly. You haven't taken a vacation in years. Are you telling me that you would take a week off?"

What would her mother have looked like now? Deena set the photograph back on the dresser. She'd have to clear it with Dr. Chin, but she thought Olson and Papish, both highly trained researchers, could fill in for her. "Yes. I'll take my laptop and keep tabs from the jungle."

"Not a jungle, Deena. Northwestern Connecticut. The foothills of the Berkshires."

"You know what I mean." Deena swallowed. "So what do you think?"

"I don't think you can do it."

Deena feared her sister might be right, but she was more afraid of losing her sister than failing as a camp counselor. "Stacy, I'll take good care of Evie. I promise."

Stacy's face turned very red, just as it always did when she was about to cry. Her sister had inherited not only the stubborn genes but also the emotional ones. Her nose turned red at the tip. Her lips trembled, but her eyes held a mixture of relief and gratitude. "Are you sure?"

Deena looked around for the box of tissues. "Yeah, Stacy, I'm sure."

Stacy sighed. "I know Evie can't stay here, and I can't go to camp. So thank you, Deena. I'll call Pastor Rich first thing in the morning."

Chapter 2

Deena was bent over unpacking her suitcase when she felt a thump on her shoulder. Screaming, she spun around, ready to battle whatever monster had jumped onto her inside this awful, musty-smelling cabin. It was only Evie, though, who stood behind her, grinning broadly. The other girls were laughing, too.

"Got you, Aunt Deena," Evie said. "Got you good."

"That you did." Deena struggled to take the prank with good humor. Her nerves still jangled from that two-hour bus ride. All that screaming—and if she heard one more rendition of "Ninety-nine Bottles of Root Beer on the Wall," she'd have to be institutionalized. What had she gotten herself into?

She forced a smile. "I thought a bat landed on my shoulder."

"Bats are nocturnal," a small girl with Clark Kent glasses and honey-colored hair said. Her camp T-shirt, the same one Deena and the others wore, looked about six sizes too big for her.

"Yes, they are," Deena agreed. "Unless they're rabid."

This of course turned out to be the completely wrong thing to say because it immediately caused all the girls to flutter around in girlish horror, requiring Deena to assure them the possibility of a rabid bat flying into their cabin was practically nonexistent.

"Well, if one came in," said a pretty blond-haired girl wearing way too much makeup, "I'd, like, spray it with my Freeze and Shine."

"You can't kill a bat with hairspray." A red-haired girl, also wearing heavy eye makeup, punctuated her sentence with a huge pink bubble. Deena watched in fascination as it grew to the size of the girl's head before shriveling and then disappearing back into her mouth.

"Maybe not kill it," the blond agreed, "but it'd stun it for sure. Spray enough of it and Freeze and Shine could, like, plaster that bat to the cabin wall."

Deena sat down on the bed. This wasn't going as she'd expected. Not at all. Somehow she'd pictured the kids more like her grad students, respectful of her professorial status and eager to learn from her. She'd pictured herself showing them the constellations at night, not debating the holding power of Freeze and Shine hairspray. She deliberately pushed Stacy's voice to the back of her mind. Stacy didn't think she would last three days. Deena would make the full week even if it killed her.

And it very well might. The cabin smelled musty and wasn't air-conditioned. The bunk beds had mattresses that felt like they'd been stuffed with straw, and

11

she hadn't seen a single power outlet for her laptop.

"Hey." A dark-skinned, heavyset girl with gorgeous curly black hair peered down at the cage at Deena's feet. "Is that a bird?"

The girl tried to peek beneath the cloth covering, but Deena moved the cage protectively closer. "He's an African Grey. A parrot," she clarified. Stacy had been very specific that she needed to speak like a person and not a scientist.

"What's his name? Can I see him? Does he bite?" The questions came faster and louder, overlapping. It seemed the girls didn't want answers as much as they wanted to be the one voice that would be heard above all others.

Before she could stop it, someone lifted the cloth covering. A big "ooh" went up as Mr. Crackers flexed his back.

"Hello," the dark-haired girl said. "Polly want a cracker?"

Mr. Crackers looked terrified. He said, "Shake your groove thing."

Music was one of Deena's guilty pleasures, especially pop rock, and the bird had picked up a lot of lyrics as a result. She jerked the cloth back in place. "Let the bird rest, okay? You can see him later."

She could have left the bird home with one of her grad students, but Deena hadn't been able to bring herself to do so. Having adopted Mr. Crackers from a former colleague, she suspected the parrot had abandonment issues complicated by low self-esteem.

She ran her fingers through her hair. *Think, Deena. This is just like when you were a graduate student and Dr. English handed you that stack of data and asked you to make sense of it. And it was an impossible mess until you sorted it out, broke it down into categories, and organized it.* Possibly the same technique could be used with kids. First she would gather data.

Deena pulled out her clipboard. Just holding it in her hands made her feel more like herself. "Okay," she said loudly, drowning out the voices eagerly swapping information about what pets had been left at home. "I'm going to take roll call. Please tell me a bit about yourself." She looked at the first name. "Alyssa Rossi?"

The small, honey-colored-haired girl raised her arm. "Here."

"You want to tell me something about yourself?"

Alyssa dug into her shorts pocket and pulled out a folded piece of paper. "My uncle said to give you this."

The list was a duplicate of the one Deena had in Alyssa's file. Prior to coming to the camp, Deena had been given information about each of the girls. Alyssa was the allergy girl—dust, mites, pollen, mold, pine, pet dander, bees, grass. . . . The girl also had moderate asthma, mostly triggered by pollution, anxiety, or intense physical activity. Deena was supposed to carry a rescue inhaler and EpiPen on her at all times.

"Anything else? Special interests?"

The girl shook her head. "None."

"Okay, then," Deena said. "Evie Matthews?"

"Present and accounted for." Evie saluted her.

"What do you like to do for fun?" Deena tried a more specific question this time.

"Play video games and listen to my Zune."

"Oh, what tunes?" Deena asked, genuinely enjoying the opportunity to get to know her niece better.

"Not tunes," Evie corrected. "Zune. It's sort of like an iPod, but Microsoft makes it and you can download videos and squirt music."

Deena had no idea what squirting music meant. In fact, it sounded kind of gross. She didn't want to look stupid by asking more, so she turned to the next name on her list. "Thank you, Evie. Now, who's Lourdes Sanchez?"

The heavyset girl with the gorgeous black hair raised her hand. "That's me." The minute she opened her mouth, Deena spied a full set of braces complete with purple and red rubber bands crisscrossing in an elaborate pattern. "I play the guitar and like writing. My dad is the music minister at our church."

"What kind of writing?" Deena prompted, thinking she might be on more familiar ground here.

"I blog, mostly."

"Are you on, like, MySpace or Facebook?" asked the pretty blond who had brought the Freeze and Shine hairspray.

"MySpace," Lourdes informed her.

"You're Britty, right?" Deena smiled encouragingly at the blond. "Britty Trekland?"

"Yeah. I like hanging out with my friends." Here she paused to grin at the red-haired girl next to her. "Taylor and I are cousins."

Taylor Anderson, the redhead, also wore a copious amount of makeup and chewed vigorously on a wad of gum. "Britty's parents and mine are going on vacation to Switzerland for a week, so they sent us here. They said it was a good deal."

"Well," Deena said bravely, "I'm sure we're all going to become good friends."

There was general agreement, and Taylor sealed the deal by unveiling half a suitcase full of candy. Each girl took a piece of chocolate, except for Allergy Girl, who reluctantly settled on a Life Saver after carefully reading the ingredients list. The girls held up their candy as if they were making a toast. "To friends," Taylor said. The others echoed her and popped the candy into their mouths.

"Okay, then," Deena said. "What's next?"

Evie was already in motion. "Explore. We want to explore the camp!"

∽

Hours later Deena turned off the cabin lights and climbed into the top bunk. The mattress, lumpy as it was, felt like heaven as she settled herself beneath the cool sheets.

Below her Alyssa stirred, gently shaking the boards of the wooden bunk. No problem—an earthquake couldn't have kept Deena awake. She put her hand under her pillow in her sleeping position.

She smiled. It had been a good day. They'd seen the archery fields, the pool, and the stables. They'd wanted to see the boys' cabins, but she'd talked them into a nature walk instead. The hike had been hugely successful. They'd watched a family of white-tailed deer bound through the woods, picked flowers in a field full of daisies, and pretended a fallen log was a balance beam and practiced leaping dismounts. After dinner, Pastor Rich had led an upbeat praise and worship time that had included a guest appearance by a Christian magician.

"Miss Deena?"

She opened one eye, listened, and then closed it again. Just that one little motion seemed to take all the energy she had. "Miss Deena?" the voice whispered in the darkness.

Good grief. It was past midnight. Where did anyone get the energy? Deena rolled to the edge of the bunk and peered over the edge. "You okay, Alyssa?"

"I think I need my allergy medication."

"Oh, honey," Deena said sympathetically. The girl was probably homesick. This wasn't particularly surprising. "You took your allergy medicine right after dinner."

"I know." A pause. "But I think I'm having an allergic reaction."

An allergic reaction? Deena opened both eyes. "What are your symptoms?" It was entirely possible there'd been something in those sloppy joe sandwiches. Deena hadn't digested them very well herself.

"I itch." In the darkness Alyssa's voice sounded small and youthful. "My arm is super itchy."

Deena felt for the slats of the bunk ladder with her feet and crawled down the side of the bunk bed. She nearly tripped over a pair of sneakers as she retrieved the flashlight from the night table. "Show me."

The girl, pale and elfin-looking in yet another man-sized T-shirt, held out a thin white arm.

It was red where Alyssa had been scratching, and Deena could just make out a few small red bumps. "I don't think it's an allergic reaction, honey. I think you got bit by a couple of very hungry mosquitoes." She patted the girl's shoulder. "We'll put some Benadryl cream on it and you'll feel much better."

"Maybe I should use my rescue inhaler."

"Are you having trouble breathing?"

The girl shook her head.

"Then let's try the cream first."

As she shuffled her way through the darkness to her first-aid kit, Deena felt her legs begin to itch. And a spot on her arm, too.

The beam of light found her medical supplies. She searched its contents as quietly as she could, all the while trying to ignore the way her skin itched.

Tube of Benadryl in her hand, she journeyed back to Alyssa. Halfway there, another small voice spoke out of the darkness. "Can I have some, too? My legs really itch."

The voice belonged to Lourdes. Deena turned toward her. "You got bitten, too?" Deena had read all the guide books that Stacy had recommended, even spent time at the local sports shop, peppering the salesperson with questions about camping and hiking. She'd thought she was prepared for anything, but evidently she hadn't counted on the mosquitoes here being so aggressive. From now on she'd make them wear the heavy-duty repellent, not the one that had looked chemically safer for everyone.

"Me, too," Evie said. "My legs really itch."

"And me," Taylor called out.

"Count me in," Britty added. "I would have said something sooner, but I didn't want to wake everyone."

Deena turned on the lights. The girls all gathered around her and extended their arms and legs, all dotted with bite marks and red from scratching.

She began dispensing the Benadryl cream and sympathy. It was going to be a long, long night.

Chapter 3

The small room they'd given him was no bigger than an oversized closet. At six feet four inches, Spencer Rossi was pretty sure he could lie down and span the length of the room.

He wasn't used to working indoors or having an office, and certainly not being called a nurse. None of these really mattered, though. He'd packed up the house, kenneled his dog, and driven a hundred miles with a kid who had barely spoken to him the entire way. Now he prayed God would do the rest.

He put down the MCAT study guide and took a sip of coffee. Six thirty in the morning. Miss Miriam, the retired nurse who had also volunteered to help at the camp, would be in at eight. Until then, he'd enjoy the solitude. Soon the kids would trickle in for their daily medications. The number of kids on everything from antidepressants to allergy medications amazed him. It hadn't been that way when he and Evan were kids.

"Hello? Are you the camp nurse?"

Spencer looked up as a tall woman with spiky black hair walked into his room. His first thought was that Wonder Woman herself had landed in his clinic. She had light blue eyes and skin the color of fresh cream. Her long legs looked capable of running down the fastest villain, and her waist looked about the size of his watchband.

"Yes. Spencer Rossi." He extended his hand. "How can I help you?"

Wonder Woman shook his hand. "I'm Deena Bradley. We've been up all night itching."

For the first time Spence allowed himself to notice the small group of girls peering around the doorway.

"I thought we'd been bitten by something yesterday," Deena said, "but it's getting worse. Benadryl helps, but it doesn't really stop the itching."

"Let me take a look." Spence bent to pull a pair of latex gloves out of a drawer, and when he straightened, he found himself looking into his niece's large green eyes. "Alyssa?"

The girl produced her arm unhappily. "Hi, Uncle Spence."

"Wait a minute," Deena interrupted. "You're her uncle?"

"And guardian," Spence stated, wanting to make it perfectly clear to Wonder Woman that he wasn't just a relative. Alyssa was his child, and whoever failed to take good care of her would answer to him.

As usual, though, he could tell he'd said the wrong thing. Alyssa stepped back from him and would have moved farther away except he was holding her arm.

"It started last night," Deena explained. "You think maybe it's chigger bites? Bedbugs?"

Spencer turned his niece's arm over and examined both sides. "Nope. Poison ivy."

"Poison ivy?"

"Poison ivy—as in that shiny green plant with three leaves and a red stem."

"I know what poison ivy looks like." Deena riffled her hand through her short hair, making it spikier than ever. "I can't believe I missed it."

Deena didn't look like the kind of woman who spent much time outdoors. "Lots of people wander right into it. What we need to do is make sure we wash all the oils off your skin and under your fingernails so you don't spread it to other parts of your body."

"Girls, I am so sorry."

Spence shrugged. As a wilderness paramedic, he'd seen his share of people baffled by nature. Weekend warriors who thought it would be fun to climb Mount Washington and then the weather turned. Or thrill seekers who found out the hard way that the great outdoors wasn't one big theme park.

He examined Alyssa's legs and the backs of her arms. "You have this rash anywhere else, honey?"

"No."

His niece looked even more awful than usual. Extremely pale, she had huge purple shadows under her eyes and a pinched look around her mouth. Small for her age, the camp shirt which admittedly he'd ordered in the wrong size—all but swallowed her small frame.

Spence reached for the Tecnu gel and tried to hold his worries in check. With all Alyssa's allergies, she might get a really bad case of poison ivy and need steroids, possibly a trip to the emergency room. He'd hoped this camp would bring them closer together, not add another brick in the wall.

"So where'd you run into the ivy?" Spence rubbed some Tecnu gel on an arm so thin it all but disappeared in his hand.

"In the woods." This came not from Alyssa or the woman, but from a tall girl with copper-colored hair. "We saw deer and found a cool meadow."

Spence frowned. "Did you check yourselves for ticks? I know it seems like it's fun to explore the woods." Here he paused to give Deena a significant look. "But if you don't know what you're doing, you should stay on the path."

Deena's cheeks reddened, and her lips pressed more tightly together. Good. She got the message.

He led his niece to the tiny sink. He washed her arm, dried it, and then smoothed calamine lotion over the area. She let him take care of her, but it was as if they were nothing more than doctor and patient. He wondered if it would always be like that.

He finished with Alyssa and started to work on the next girl, a pretty blond with a high ponytail and a lot of eye makeup. She had a good-sized patch of poison ivy on both her legs, which she probably got, she said cheerfully, when they'd found a fallen log and taken turns jumping off it into the grass. "We, like, had a contest to see who could jump the farthest. Evie won," she said, pointing to the tall, copper-haired girl.

The next girl, except for the red hair, was almost identical to the first in clothing, hair, and makeup. In his six months of parenting experience, Spence had visited the middle school enough to know that girls this age wanted nothing more than to look exactly like each other. Same straight hair, heavy eye makeup, jeans, and those open-buttoned shirts with the tank—no, that cami thing—beneath.

Spence cleaned the redhead's poison ivy, all the while wondering if any of these girls would become friends with Alyssa. If Alyssa would let them get close. If his niece would let anyone get close.

He finished with a Hispanic girl with large brown eyes and braces and the copper-haired girl named Evie; then it was Wonder Woman's turn to perch on top of the exam table.

She extended a lily white arm that looked as though no SPF sunscreen would be able to keep it from burning. Spence figured she'd be back in his clinic within the next forty-eight hours, wondering why her skin was lobster red.

A huge red bubble, about the size of a half-dollar, covered the soft skin on the inside of her arm. It probably itched like the devil, but the woman met his eyes without flinching when he doused it with the gel.

"That one is going to burst open and ooze," he warned her. "I'm going to go ahead and wrap it up now."

"Thank you," Deena said.

He pulled out a Coban bandage and some gauze pads. It occurred to him that this was a perfect opportunity to talk to Alyssa's cabin counselor, just to make sure she was on top of things.

"Girls," he said, "I need to talk to Miss Deena in private. Why don't you go next door to the commissary and get some candy. Ask Miss Suzie to put it on my tab."

The girls shot out of his clinic like sprinters out of the blocks. Good. He wrapped the gauze around the blistered patch on Deena's arm. "So—you have much camping experience?"

"None," Deena said.

Spence slowed his work as another red flag went up. "But you have a lot of experience with kids, right?"

"Not really."

He stopped bandaging her arm. "But you have some experience with kids."

"Well, I was a kid a long time ago. And I'm an aunt."

Spence frowned. Until six months ago, he'd been an uncle—a rather uninvolved uncle—so this didn't build credibility in his eyes. "So how did you happen to end up being a camp counselor?"

"Oh, it's a long story."

"I have time."

Deena raised an eyebrow. Not one of those overly plucked eyebrows that a lot of women favored, but a real eyebrow. A strong, arched eyebrow. "What is it, exactly, that you want to know?"

"I'm just trying to get to know you a little better." He cut the Coban and pressed it flat. "It's just that my...well, Alyssa, she's been through a lot." He hesitated, dreading this next part but knowing he had to tell her for Alyssa's sake. "She lost both her parents in a car accident six months ago." He kept his voice steady and ignored the sharp prick the words made in his heart. "It's been kind of rough."

Deena nodded sympathetically. "I'm so sorry. Pastor Rich discussed this a little with me when he went over cabin assignments." A trace of a smile softened the corners of her mouth. "If it eases your mind to know more about me, I'm thirty-five years old and have a PhD in pharmacology. I work at the University of Connecticut as a researcher in the Health Center. Breast cancer is my field. I'm not a medical doctor, but I'll take good care of her."

Spence cleaned the blistered patch on her leg and tried to sort out his thoughts. He respected Pastor Rich but still felt a bit uneasy with the camp director's decision to place Alyssa with Deena. He liked that she had a PhD but worried about her lack of experience with kids. "Alyssa's fragile. She's got moderate asthma and a list of allergies a mile long. Sometimes she forgets to take her medicine, so please be sure she comes to see me twice daily."

"Twice daily," Deena repeated.

"And keep her out of the pool today so the poison ivy has a chance to start drying up. Oh, and make sure she stays hydrated and wears sunscreen. She's quite fair-skinned."

"Got it." Deena hopped off the table. She had to be close to six feet tall, and when she put her hands on her hips, he couldn't help but imagine her in the red boots and Wonder Woman corset. He had to stop thinking about her like that. "Anything else?"

"No." *Yes.* A hundred other things flashed through his brain. Things like Alyssa would eat the treetop of her broccoli spear but not the trunk and no other vegetable. Like she was half blind without her glasses and not especially good-humored in the morning. She disliked his choice of music and sneezed when his dog entered the room. In short, Alyssa hated him, hated living with him, and did everything in her power to let him know it.

He stared at the woman in front of him, wanting to lay this knowledge at her feet in the hopes that she could somehow fix things, but he knew it would do absolutely no good. Unfortunately, Deena had even less experience with kids than he did.

"You're staring."

Spence pulled out his best grin. "I was just thinking that before you leave I should print out a picture of what poison ivy looks like. You know, just in case you happen to see it again."

Deena stiffened slightly. "I may be rusty on classifying plants, but I don't need a photograph." Back straight, she marched from the room in a huff.

When he'd insisted that Alyssa attend this camp, he'd been picturing someone else entirely in the role of cabin counselor. In his mind's eye, he'd pictured a woman with the godliness of Mother Teresa and the maternal skills of June Cleaver.

Instead, he'd gotten Wonder Woman meets Madame Curie. He struggled to conceal a wave of disappointment. Just what was God thinking, sending a scientist into Alyssa's life?

Chapter 4

Deena bit into a slice of leathery bacon. She and the girls were sitting on the long, hard benches in the cafeteria. They'd been late to breakfast, and as a result, everything had been left under the food warmers far too long.

"Please pass the syrup, Aunt Deena," Evie asked and proceeded to flood her plate with the sugary liquid.

Deena considered warning Evie of the dangers of eating too much sugar but instead put a forkful of cold and rubbery scrambled eggs in her mouth.

Her arm itched, her new shorts were giving her a wedgie, and she had the beginning of a headache. Plus she felt like an idiot. How could she have led the girls through a patch of poison ivy? Here it was, only day two, and already she'd landed herself and the girls in the clinic.

She jumped as the sudden blare of a loudspeaker urged the campers to the amphitheater for morning devotions. She glanced at her half-eaten plate. No big loss. She could always ask Taylor for some candy. The girl had everything from Tic Tacs to Godiva stashed in her suitcase.

Following the crowd of boys and girls, Deena marched out of the building into the warm June sunshine. They passed a courtyard area with pots overflowing with geraniums and baby's breath. Several benches were situated beneath leafy green trees. She would love to bring some medical journals and spend hours in the shade reading. Not this morning, though. She followed the kids down a flagstone path to an outdoor theater.

Rows of rough-hewn benches lined a gentle slope that led to the shores of Lake Waramaug. In the early morning sun, the surface gleamed like polished silver. She could see the boathouse on the left-hand side and rows of kayaks laid out on the beach area.

Two teenagers with hair curling around their ears took their places on the wooden platform in front of the lake. Deena looked at their electric guitars and expected a slightly jazzed-up version of a traditional church song.

However, the first chord—played at a volume that made her teeth vibrate—told her there would be no rendition of "How Great Thou Art."

She gripped the edge of her seat as the music blasted through the outdoor stage. The pounding bass hummed through her like a heart resuscitator as the teens belted out a song that consisted of basically one lyric: "I will wait upon the Lord."

The kids around her began to clap and sing. When Deena had been their age, she'd loved being in the church choir. But then her mother had gotten sick and there hadn't been time or energy to bring Deena to practice. Afterward, Deena had not had the heart.

The song ended and Pastor Rich stepped onto the stage. His bald head gleamed in the sunlight. "God, we thank You for bringing us to this place where we can learn more about You. We ask Your blessing on this camp, that during this week we may see You. May we know Your presence with a depth and intimacy that we have never experienced as an individual and as a camp family before."

As the pastor continued to speak, Deena's chest tightened. She hadn't expected this. Hadn't expected that the sight of all these kids bowing their heads in prayer would make her skin tingle and her heart ache. They were so young and so beautiful, these kids, and she could almost feel the purity of their faith rising off them. It reminded her of what she had been like at this age. Her mother had been recently diagnosed with cancer, but Deena had been so sure God would cure her mom that it hadn't bothered her much. She had bent her head, just like these kids were doing now, and confidently thanked God for the healing He was about to bestow on her mother.

The pastor kept talking, but Deena couldn't focus. She kept remembering, fast-forwarding in her mind the course of her mother's illness and the strength with which Deena had held on to her faith. Right up until the week before her mother passed away, Deena had been convinced that God would spare her. When He hadn't, she felt like something had died inside her, right along with her mother.

She'd been to services since then. Not as often as she should have and mostly to please Stacy. She had not, however, asked God for any more miracles.

She couldn't bear to be here another second. It just hurt too much. Hunching over so as to draw as little notice to herself as possible, Deena left the benches and walked away.

Seeking the solace of an empty cabin, she had to put on a good face when she discovered she wasn't the only one who had skipped out on the morning service.

Allergy Girl lay on top of her bunk, her hands behind her head, her eyes closed.

"Alyssa? Are you okay?" Deena hurried to the girl's side. "Is it the poison ivy?"

"I don't think so. I think it's my allergies." The small girl coughed dryly, but the sound had a fake, forced quality to it.

Deena studied the girl's face. It was pale, and dark shadows rimmed her eyes, a classic sign of allergies. However, all Deena's instincts were telling her the girl's problems had nothing to do with dust in the cabin or the pines around them. She needed to draw the girl out and find out more. But how? Alyssa looked like she wanted to take a nap, not have a heart-to-heart.

What would Stacy do? Probably pull out her mixer and bond as they made chocolate chip cookies. Deena didn't have a kitchen to work in, and even if she did, she couldn't bake.

"Well," Deena said, "maybe you just need to rest for a bit. We all had a bad night."

The girl turned her head toward the wall. Deena studied the curve of her back. Stacy would probably sit beside the bed and rub the girl's shoulders.

Deena crossed the room to the dresser and pulled the cloth cover off Mr. Crackers's cage. The African Grey looked at her. "Good morning, Mr. Crackers," she said. "Welcome to Camp Bald Eagle."

The bird stretched his wings and shifted on the perch. He seemed to have traveled well—only a few extra feathers at the bottom of his cage suggested any stress. Deena opened his cage and pulled out his water container.

"You want some fresh water?"

Silence.

"Okay. You're giving me the silent treatment," Deena said, rinsing out the water dish in the bathroom sink. "Well, you could have been left at home. Andres wanted to take care of you, you know."

She gave the parrot the water. "Come on," she coaxed. "Shake your groove thing," she sang.

The bird just looked at her.

"Is that the only thing he knows how to say?"

Surprised, Deena turned to find Alyssa watching them. "Oh no, he knows a lot of words. But right now he's sulking because I kept his cage covered up most of yesterday."

"He's so pretty."

"Pretty bird," Mr. Crackers said.

Alyssa almost smiled but quickly scowled instead.

"Pretty bird," Mr. Crackers said, cocking his head from side to side.

"He likes you," Deena said, turning back to the bird. "He only talks to people he likes." She hesitated. "You want to help me feed him?"

"I guess," Alyssa said. Although her voice suggested she couldn't care less, she lost no time getting out of her bunk.

Deena had saved some fresh fruit from breakfast in her fanny pack. Pulling out a bunch of grapes, she handed one to Alyssa. The girl carefully pushed it through the bars of the cage. For a moment, the parrot and the girl studied each other, and then the bird gently pecked the fruit from the girl's fingers.

She handed Alyssa another grape, and again the bird delicately took it. Alyssa turned to her, solemn as a judge, and said, "I've read that African Grey parrots are really smart."

"They are," Deena replied. "Mr. Crackers knows hundreds of words. He even speaks words in five languages."

"Out," Mr. Crackers said, fixing his gaze on Deena as if he were hoping to establish a telepathic connection.

"Oh, all right." Deena opened the cage and offered her arm to the parrot, who promptly hopped onto it. She withdrew the bird so Alyssa could stroke his feathers.

"He's so soft."

"He likes it when you stroke his back. Like this."

Alyssa repeated the gesture carefully. "Knee-how," she said. "That's 'hello' in Chinese."

"*Weintraube,*" Mr. Crackers said. "Weintraube."

Deena sighed. "That's German for 'grape.' I should have left him at home, but he has abandonment issues complicated by low self-esteem." She looked at Alyssa for the first time. There were twin spots of color on the girl's cheeks. "Hey, would you like to hold him while I clean his cage?"

"I guess," Alyssa said and then immediately reconsidered. "I mean no. No thanks. What exactly do you mean, abandonment issues?"

"Well," Deena said and fed the parrot a grape. "I adopted Mr. Crackers from one of my colleagues who took a field assignment in New Zealand. Mr. Crackers was very attached to Dr. Carnado, and after he left, Mr. Crackers got very depressed." Alyssa stroked the bird. "He started acting out—saying inappropriate words and pecking and clawing."

"So what did you do?"

"Well, I wore gloves whenever I worked around him, and I tried to give him a lot of positive reinforcement. Boost his confidence."

"And he came around?" There was no disguising the interest in Alyssa's voice.

"Yes, but slowly." Deena faced the girl. "He has two large cages, one at work and the other at home." She touched the metal bars of the travel cage. "I take him back and forth in this one. He still gets afraid, though, about being abandoned again. That 'shake your groove thing'—if he's scared, he likes to sing that."

Alyssa edged closer and held out her thin white arm. "I guess I could hold him, Miss Deena. Just while you clean his cage."

The arm didn't look strong enough to hold a sparrow, much less a big bird like Mr. Crackers, so Deena settled the parrot on Alyssa's shoulder instead. As she worked, two sets of eyes followed her every movement. "I want to tell you," Deena said slowly, "that when I was sixteen, I lost my mom to cancer. My dad had a heart attack five years later. I know what it's like to lose your parents. If you ever want to talk about it, Alyssa, I'll listen. Anytime, day or night."

Alyssa frowned and studied her hands. Deena feared she'd said the wrong thing, but then Alyssa looked up. "Everyone wants me to talk about what happened, but I don't know what they want me to say."

Deena nodded. "My sister and I used to say the same thing. Some people seemed more curious than sympathetic, but either way, we just ended up thanking whoever it was for asking about our mom and then changing the subject. I'm telling you about my mom, Alyssa, not because I want you to tell me anything. But I want you to know that I'm here for you, and I've been through losing a parent. Sometimes it does help just to talk. Having my sister was a huge help to me."

Silence.

Deena changed the position of one of Mr. Crackers's toys in the cage. "Day or night. You can come to me. Now, do you want to see Mr. Crackers solve his puzzle ball?"

Behind those Clark Kent glasses, Alyssa's eyes blinked furiously. She seemed surprised by the change in topic and took a moment to gather her thoughts. "Why did you ditch the morning devotional? Were you checking up on me?"

It was Deena's turn to feel her thoughts tumble and toss about in her mind. She could tell Alyssa that cabin counselors weren't required to attend morning devotions or say that Mr. Crackers had needed her attention. But one look at Alyssa's bright green eyes and she knew the girl would instantly recognize an evasion. She held the girl's gaze. "I wasn't checking up on you. I wanted to be alone for a bit. But I'm really glad you were here."

The girl's brow wrinkled as she considered Deena's words. "You think we'll get in trouble for ditching?"

Deena shook her head. The cage was clean now, but she wanted to give Mr. Crackers and Alyssa a little more time together. "No. We have about an hour or so before we're due at the zip lines."

Alyssa's gaze slid past Deena. "I think I'd rather just stay here in the cabin. My allergies are really bothering me."

"You can't stay here alone. But if you want, I could drop you off at the clinic. I'm sure your uncle wouldn't mind if you spent the rest of the day with him."

Alyssa pushed a strand of hair behind her ear. "Actually, Miss Deena, I'd rather do the zip lines."

Their eyes met. Alyssa seemed to be holding something back. Deena was intrigued but sensed now wasn't the time to push. Earning the girl's trust would require a lot of patience. Fortunately, in Deena's line of work, she had learned that some answers, no matter how badly you wanted them right away, took time.

Chapter 5

W eren't the zip lines totally cool, Miss Deena?" Britty asked with a flip
of her long blond hair.

It was midafternoon, and they were waiting for their turn on the
Leap of Faith, which, from the looks of those twin telephone poles and safety
netting beneath, promised to be as scary as the zip lines had been.

Deena fanned her face and pulled her bottle of sunscreen from her fanny
pack. They'd all been sweating, and there was no shade whatsoever. "Cool?" She
shook her head. "More like terrifying."

Squirting a bit of the lotion into her hand, Deena insisted the girls all reap-
ply. They grumbled, especially Britty, who claimed it kept getting into her eyes
and messing up her makeup. "You'll thank me when you're thirty-five and have
beautiful skin," Deena pointed out.

"You didn't look scared on the zip lines," Taylor said. "You were smiling the
whole way."

"I wasn't smiling. I was gasping for air and dealing with the worst wedgie of
my life. That harness was not meant for women my size."

The girls laughed. The line shuffled forward as another child successfully
completed the jump from the top of the first telephone pole to the hanging
trapeze.

"I can't wait to try the Leap of Faith." Next to her Evie practically vibrated
with excitement. "Look how high up it is. It's going to feel like flying. You gonna
do it, 'Lyssa?"

The small blond nodded. "Yeah. It looks like fun."

Fun wasn't the word for this activity, but it got her thinking. When was the
last time Deena had done something just for fun? Last Christmas Dr. Chin, her
boss, had a pizza party for the lab, but Deena had been staining some cells with
a new batch of inhibitors and had missed half of it.

"Hey, 'Lyssa," Evie said. "Isn't that your uncle?"

Deena looked behind her, and there, indeed, was Spencer Rossi walking
toward them. Just the sight of him set Deena's teeth on edge, although she wasn't
quite sure why. Maybe because he needed a haircut. His blond hair curled over
his ears, and he hadn't shaved this morning. Golden bristles, these a shade darker
than his hair, covered his jawline.

"Hey," Spence said. "A girl jammed her finger on the volleyball courts, and
I just finished taping it up. I saw you over here and figured I'd see how you guys
were doing."

More like he was checking up on them. On her. Deena stiffened. "We're doing fine."

To Deena's surprise, Alyssa inched closer to her. She had the feeling the girl wasn't moving closer to her as much as she was moving away from her uncle.

"The Leap of Faith looks cool, doesn't it?" Spence said enthusiastically. "Would you guys mind if I did it with you?"

Deena watched Alyssa's face go so completely blank that she figured it had to take enormous effort to make it look like that. "Don't you have to get back to the clinic?"

"Miss Miriam is covering for me." He patted the cell phone strapped to his belt. "She'll call if she needs me."

Deena didn't understand the dynamics of the relationship between Spencer and Alyssa and figured time together might enlighten her. "The more the merrier."

The line moved forward. Taylor blew a bubble with her gum and dodged Evie's efforts to pop it. Lourdes speculated with Britty whether one of the rubber bands on her braces had snapped free during the zip lines or if she had swallowed it. Alyssa studied the ground as if the packed earth was the most interesting thing she'd ever seen.

"This doesn't look hard, Alyssa," Spence said gently. The girl didn't reply. Her gaze remained fixed on the ground, and she gave no indication that she had even heard him.

"Alyssa," Spence said. "There's nothing to be scared of."

"Well, you go first, then," Deena told him, trying to lighten the moment. "That way I can see if the pulley system is strong enough to hold you. If it doesn't collapse, it'll hold me."

The other girls laughed. "That's so cool that you do stuff like this, Miss Deena," Taylor said. "The only thing I do with my parents is shop or go out to dinner."

Britty said, "Your point?"

Everyone laughed again. Everyone but Alyssa, who had begun tracing a half circle in the dirt as if she wished she could dig a hole and simply disappear.

Soon it was their group's turn. True to his word, Spence went first. He climbed the telephone pole hand over hand, rung by rung, not hesitating as he pulled himself onto the top. For a moment he balanced on top of the pole, silhouetted by the pale summer sky, impossibly tall and athletic, his blond hair shades lighter than his deeply tanned skin.

Deena felt her stomach tighten at the sight of him up there—like a big, tawny lion about to spring. She didn't like this feeling, not at all. She'd made a rule not to date anyone she worked with and then made sure she didn't meet anyone outside of work. The rule had worked well, or so she'd thought.

She could see now that all those pesky little dating hormones had been collecting, building up in her system, and just waiting for the worst possible moment to make themselves known.

He waved down at them, and then like a competitive swimmer, he dove off the top of the pole. He soared though the air, arms outstretched like Superman. He caught the trapeze easily, and everyone cheered. Well, almost everyone. Deena didn't know whether to ignore Alyssa's shutdown or draw her out.

As Evie began her climb up the telephone pole, Spence rejoined them in the line. He wasn't breathing hard, but his face was flushed and there was a hint of sweat around his hairline. "It's really, really fun," he said. "Just don't look down, Alyssa, and remember there's a safety net under you. There's no way for you to get hurt."

"I don't want to do this anymore," Alyssa stated matter-of-factly. "I want to go back to the cabin."

Spence placed his hand on the girl's thin shoulder. He used his other hand to point to Evie. "Just look at Evie. She's having a great time, and so will you."

True enough, Evie seemed to be making steady progress up the telephone pole.

"I just don't want to do it." Alyssa's gaze found Deena's. "Do I have to?"

"Of course not," Deena said.

Spence shot Deena a dark look. "Just try it," he urged. "If you climb up partway and change your mind, you can always come right back down."

Alyssa shook her head. "I don't like heights."

Deena didn't think this statement was entirely true. The girl had shown no fear on the zip lines. Also, Alyssa seemed to have been looking forward to trying the Leap of Faith until her uncle had appeared. She decided to follow an instinct. "Well, I don't like heights either. In fact, my stomach is still woozy from the zip lines. Every time I burp, I taste cheeseburger. Maybe I'll just sit this one out with you, Alyssa."

The girl looked at her gratefully, but Spence shot Deena another look that all but shouted she should stay out of this. "Sometimes the best way to get over a fear is to face it. That's what this exercise is all about—finding out how to let go of fears. There's no way you can get hurt, Alyssa. I promise you. And I'll be right here. Just try, honey. Please try."

"No!" Alyssa's face flushed, and her breathing quickened. The change happened quickly. One minute she seemed fine, just a little upset, and then the next, every breath seemed short and ineffective, as if her lungs were full of holes. Even before Spence's voice barked out an order to get the rescue inhaler, Deena's hand was inside her fanny pack drawing out the albuterol. She handed it to the girl, who stuck the plastic nozzle into her mouth and sucked the medication into her lungs.

Deena studied Alyssa's face more closely, frightened by what she'd seen and uncertain if the treatment was working and what she would do if it didn't. Fortunately, it did seem as if Alyssa were breathing a little more easily.

"Aunt Deena! Aunt Deena!"

She straightened slowly and turned. Her niece dangled from the trapeze, staring straight down at her. "Did you see me?" Evie yelled. "Did you see me? I did it!"

Unfortunately, Deena hadn't. She'd been too busy taking care of Alyssa. "I'm sorry." She wanted to explain that Alyssa had an asthma attack, but shouting it to the world would be embarrassing to Alyssa. She couldn't very well ask Evie to redo her jump either.

"I'm sorry," she said again. "I bet it was a really great jump."

"Yeah," Evie said in a voice that almost, but not quite, masked her disappointment. "It was."

Chapter 6

Deena dreamed of her mother. And in the dream, like so many others, Deena promised to use her life to help other women with breast cancer. She leaned over the hospital bed. *"I'll miss you,"* she said. *"I won't forget you. And I'll always love you."*

In the dream, her mother pushed back the long strands of Deena's hair, strands Deena had been hoping would soon grow long enough to cut and make into a wig for her mother. *"My special, shining girl,"* her mother whispered. *"So brave and so smart. God has blessed you so you can bless others."*

Deena jerked awake. For a moment, she didn't know where she was—if she had been dreaming or if something had actually brushed against her forehead. She sat up as high as the bed would allow in the low-ceilinged room and strained to see in the small amount of moonlight streaming through the window.

For a moment she saw only the dark outlines of the bunks and the boxy shadow of Mr. Crackers's cage atop the dresser. And then. . .her heart skipped a beat when something cold and clammy brushed against her calf.

She jerked her leg back and swallowed a scream. Fumbling in the darkness, she pulled out the flashlight tucked next to her pillow.

Clicking on the beam, she lifted the covers. A pair of small black eyes stared out of a fist-sized lump. Deena relaxed. A frog? Someone had put a frog in her bunk bed?

How old was that prank?

She spotted another one. It crouched near the first one. Poor thing. It looked scared to death. She reached to rescue it. Her fingers closed around the plump, moist body. She didn't want to crush it, so she kept her fist loosely closed.

Too loosely closed, it turned out. The frog slipped through her fingers and leaped into the darkness.

Seconds later a single scream, as shrill as a whistle, pierced the darkness. And then everybody was screaming.

They were the loudest, most ear-piercing screams Deena had ever heard. Anyone who heard the girls would think something awful was happening, like they were being chopped to pieces by an ax murderer.

Scrambling down the rungs, Deena nearly fell in her haste to get down. "Take it easy, everyone." Her words were lost as another wave of screams shook the cabin walls. "It's only a frog."

"Frogs!" Lourdes screamed, tossing her pillow and blanket off the top bunk bed. "In my bed!"

"Eww," Taylor shrieked. "Mine, too!" The girl leaped from the top bunk and landed with a loud *thump* on the wood floor.

"Mine, too," Britty hollered. "Help!"

"Calm down, everyone!" Deena screamed as pillows and bedding sailed through the air.

Something crashed. Someone grabbed her around the waist and screamed in her ear. Deena lurched toward the light switch, hampered by the girl with the death grip around her waist.

"It's okay," Deena shouted and winced as someone stepped hard on her foot. "You're making it worse by screaming." She doubted anyone heard that either.

Dragging along the girl clinging to her middle, she made it to the front wall and flicked on the switch. What she saw almost made her want to turn the light off.

Total chaos.

Girls screaming. Frogs jumping up all around them like popping kernels of corn. Pillows and sheets everywhere.

"Get it off me!" Taylor yelled, shimmying wildly as Britty whacked her back with a pillow.

"Hey, don't hurt it." Deena stepped forward to help. Too late—the frog sailed through the air and landed with a heavy *plop* in front of Alyssa.

The girl opened her mouth and froze. Deena couldn't tell if she was breathing or not.

She lurched toward Alyssa, hampered by Lourdes, who continued to hang on to her, begging her not to move.

"Calm down, everybody!" Deena knew she didn't sound so calm herself. She couldn't help herself. Things never got out of control in her laboratory.

I am so over my head, Deena realized. *So very over my head. I never should have come here. What was I thinking?*

Britty climbed onto the dresser, only to leap off shrieking. Mr. Crackers's bag of gravel overturned, and she heard the contents spill onto the floor. Mr. Crackers began to screech.

"I'll help you, Alyssa," Evie yelled, surging forward in an attempt to capture the frog that had Alyssa pinned against the wall. Her movement, however, only caused the frog to leap toward Alyssa, who shrieked in horror and then promptly burst into tears.

Deena finally reached Alyssa's side and tried to pull the girl's hands away from her face. "Alyssa, are you okay? Talk to me, honey!"

Alyssa looked up, her face chalk white. "I'm. . . Inha. . ."

"Hang on, honey," she said, "I'll get your inhaler."

She was halfway across the floor and picking up speed when suddenly the door shuddered under the force of someone pounding it with fists. A man's voice shouted, "What's going on in there? Is everyone all right?"

Deena grabbed Alyssa's albuterol inhaler. "We're okay," she yelled.

"I'm coming in!" the man yelled again.

She recognized that voice. "Don't. We're fine!" Deena placed the inhaler in Alyssa's hands and supervised as the girl brought it to her mouth, pushed the button, and inhaled.

"I'm counting to five," the man yelled.

"Girls," Deena ordered, "get dressed—fast. The cavalry's here!"

Chapter 7

The door opened. Deena, wearing navy sweats and a pair of pink bunny slippers, stood illuminated in the backlight of the cabin. "Hello, Spencer," she said cheerfully as if she'd run into him at the grocery store. "Nice to see you again."

" 'Nice to see you again'?" Spence narrowed his gaze. "Deena, it sounded like something terrible was going on here. Is everyone okay?"

"Everyone is fine." Her gaze strayed past him to the small group of camp counselors and campers that had gathered behind him. "Thanks for coming, everyone," she said, "but everything is fine. Sorry for all the noise."

She started to close the door, but Spence put his hand on the frame. "You can't do that—scare everybody like that and then just say it was nothing." He gestured behind him. "You worried a lot of people." Including himself.

He'd just been finishing up treating a kid who had spiked a fever of 102 in a nearby cabin. But even if he'd been in his own cabin halfway across the camp, he would have heard those screams. He was only surprised that more people hadn't come running.

"I'm sorry," Deena repeated more loudly this time. "We had a small problem with frogs, but it's completely under control now. Thank you for coming to see if we were okay."

"Told you it was something with either bugs or frogs," exclaimed Jenny, the counselor in the cabin nearest to Deena's. "Okay, everyone," she announced. "Time to get back to our cabin."

Deena murmured good night and again started to shut the door. Before it closed, another scream ripped through the cabin.

"Everything is not okay. I'm coming in," Spence said.

"Okay. But be careful where you step. I don't want you to squish one."

She was concerned about frogs when the girls were screaming bloody murder? Still, Spence moved carefully, shuffling his feet as he entered the cabin. He took a deep breath and released it. Frogs had done this?

The room looked as if a small tornado had swept through it. Every bed had been tossed, and pillows and bedding covered the floor, not to mention what looked like a bag of gravel had spilled everywhere. His gaze rose to the top of one of the bunks where the five girls huddled, peering at him over the top wooden slat.

He counted heads. Everyone looked okay. Thank God. His gaze lingered on Alyssa, white-faced and breathing a little too fast. He saw the rescue inhaler in her hand, and his jaw tightened.

"Look out, Uncle Spence!" Alyssa called. A scream, so shrill that Spence's eardrums seemed to swell in his head, filled the room.

Three more frogs hopped past him. Another one sailed overboard from its hiding spot in one of the upper bunks.

Broom in hand, Deena was carefully flushing them out from beneath the beds and dresser. "Get the door," she shouted. He couldn't actually hear the words above the shrieking, but he read her lips. And he moved. Fast.

⁓

It was about two in the morning before the cabin was straightened and officially declared frog-free. Even then the girls still seemed unsettled, reluctant to go back to bed, fearing that more frogs would come out of hiding.

Only after Spence promised to sleep on the front porch and keep watch did the girls allow themselves to be resettled in the bunks. He prayed aloud for them and let each girl add to the prayer if she wanted. To his disappointment, but not surprise, Alyssa remained silent.

He was still thinking about this as he settled himself on the front step on the porch. High above, bright stars burned in a pitch-black sky. Alyssa had shut herself off not only from him, but also from the Lord. Was he pushing too hard? Or not hard enough?

He breathed more deeply and more slowly and listened as hard as he could. Sometimes, and he could never force this, he would get a feeling, a stirring in his heart, and it would tell him what to do.

He sure wished it would speak to him now.

Instead, the screen door creaked open, and Deena joined him on the step. "You don't have to stay," she said. "They're all asleep."

Under the porch light, her blue eyes were black as onyx. She still reminded him of Wonder Woman, though. Only her eyes had shadows under them, and they reflected a vulnerability that wouldn't exist in a superhero. Superheroes didn't wear fluffy pink bunny slippers either.

"I told them I'd stay," he said. "I don't mind."

"You won't be very comfortable out here."

"Had worse."

"'Had worse.'" Deena gave a poor imitation of his voice. "You can stop the macho thing," she continued in her normal voice. "The truth is you're a softie. You don't want the girls to wake up and not find you keeping guard outside."

He shrugged. Alyssa needed to know that when he gave his word, he kept it, whether it was convenient or not. Trust was something you earned, and sleeping on the porch was a price he was more than willing to pay.

"Nice slippers," he said.

"Evie gave them to me last Christmas. In case you didn't know, she's my niece."

"Thought she had to be related. Looks kind of like you. Has your eyes."

Deena sighed. "That she does. Look, I'm sorry you had to come out here tonight. Things got out of hand."

It was exactly as he'd feared, but he found little satisfaction in being correct. Oddly, he wanted to reassure her. "I don't think you're the first cabin counselor who has ever dealt with a prank involving frogs."

Kids could be challenging. In his six months of parenting, he had a whole new appreciation of the art of raising a child. Especially twelve-year-old girls. He remembered the first day he had arrived at Alyssa's house to live with her, how the very sight of him had turned the girl's face ashen. Even before he opened his mouth, he'd been doomed to say the wrong thing. She'd run for her room within minutes. He'd thought it would get better. Prayed it would. So far it hadn't.

He was beginning to wonder if Alyssa would be happier with someone else. Her maternal grandparents had offered to raise her, but they lived in Texas—a long way from Connecticut. Besides, Evan and Mattie had made him Alyssa's legal guardian. He'd been honored, but baffled when they discussed their decision with him. "Why me?" he'd asked, thinking himself the least likely choice.

"Because you're her favorite uncle," Evan said and patted his shoulder. "And you've got the biggest heart of anyone in the family."

Before the accident he and Alyssa had enjoyed each other's company. Now, however, she wouldn't give him the time of day.

"My ears are still ringing from the screams," Deena said.

Spence smiled. "They were pretty loud."

This close Spence could see her nose was slightly too long and her mouth too wide for classic beauty. But it was a striking face. She was not the kind of woman who walked into a room and faded into the background. She probably scared off a lot of men with that straight, frank look. He wasn't intimidated, though. But then again, she was wearing pink bunny slippers.

"Who did it?" Spence traced a crack in the wood step. "Who do you think released all those frogs?"

She shrugged. "Does it matter?"

"Of course it matters. This sounds like a prank a boy would play. I'll check with the other counselors and see if we can figure out who did it."

"I don't think you need to do that."

"You saw someone?"

"Not exactly." Deena pulled her knees more tightly to her chest. The sweatpants rose, revealing a very trim pair of ankles. He moved his gaze back to her profile.

"But you think you know who did it."

"I think it was Evie. The wild child." Deena sighed. "That's why I'm here. I'm supposed to make sure Evie stays out of trouble."

Great. Not only did Alyssa have a counselor who had no experience with kids, but she was also bunking with a possible juvenile delinquent. Spence studied the shadows on the step. Maybe Alyssa should change cabins. "So if your niece released the frogs, what are you going to do about it?"

Deena shrugged. "Don't know. Guess I'll talk to her. Tell her that pranks can have pretty serious consequences."

"That's a good start," Spence agreed. "If you'd like, we could both talk to her."

"Thanks, but I think it's better if I sit down one-on-one with her."

Somewhere in the dark an owl hooted; then the night went still once more. Spence looked up at the stars. "Maybe she's the kind of kid who needs clear limits. State the rules, and if she breaks them, give her a consequence."

"So what kind of consequence should I give for putting frogs in the beds?" Spence looked at her. "Push-ups."

"Push-ups?" Deena laughed in surprise. "What's that got to do with frogs?"

"Nothing." It did seem kind of absurd, and Spence found himself grinning sheepishly. "It's what my father gave out as punishment. I'd say ten should do the trick."

"You're serious? Is that how you punish Alyssa?"

"We haven't crossed that bridge yet. You can't punish a kid for not smiling, for not wanting to talk to you." He shrugged. "Sometimes I wish I could, especially if it'd make her open up to me."

"She will, Spence. She's got a good heart. You should see her with Mr. Crackers."

"Mr. Crackers?"

"My parrot."

He frowned and tried to remember whether Alyssa was allergic to birds. "Why would you bring a parrot to camp?" How crazy was that?

"He has abandonment issues," Deena said, "complicated by low self-esteem. Alyssa helps me clean his cage and feed him every morning."

Spence pushed his hands through his hair. He didn't know what kind of abandonment issues a parrot might have and didn't care if the parrot had low self-esteem. He cared about Alyssa. "Parrots can scratch and bite."

"Mr. Crackers wouldn't hurt a flea. He and Alyssa seem to like each other. They're becoming friends."

Spence frowned. A parrot wasn't the kind of friend he had in mind for Alyssa. He'd been hoping she and Lourdes would become friends. Lourdes seemed as though she'd be a good influence on her. "What about the other girls? Is she making friends with any of them?"

"I think so," Deena replied. "Some things take time."

Sometimes people needed help to get where they needed to be. A gentle push. "But you're encouraging her to do things with them, right?"

"Oh yeah," Deena agreed. "This afternoon we all played shuffleboard. Alyssa and I discovered we both stink at it. We kept sliding our pucks into the grass."

"I didn't see her in the breakout groups after the evening devotional," Spence commented. "She was avoiding me, wasn't she?"

"I don't know." Deena sighed. "We both went for a walk. We bought some ice cream and watched the fireflies. I haven't seen them since I was a really little girl, and guess what? Alyssa has never seen them."

It was a nice picture, but he pushed it firmly out of his mind. He would have much rather heard that Deena had attended the devotional with Alyssa. Counselors weren't required to attend these sessions—the church had pastors who led them—but he thought she should set a good example. "I would appreciate it," he said stiffly, "if you would encourage her to participate in the camp activities. She needs to be learning about the Lord. The only way she's ever going to get through this time in her life is if she turns to God."

"Spence, I don't think you can force that kind of thing on someone."

It was said gently, but it irked him all the same. This sort of answer wasn't acceptable, especially not from the woman who was supposed to exert a strong Christian influence on his niece. "I would think that someone in your position would welcome an opportunity to guide someone who obviously needs it."

She stiffened. "Guide, Spence, or drag them by force to God?"

"Of course not drag her, but don't be so quick to let her skip out." He paused. "This afternoon, for instance, when I was trying to get Alyssa to do the Leap of Faith, you didn't back me up."

"Spence, she started having an anxiety attack."

"Because she was afraid. She wouldn't have been afraid if you had agreed with me. If you had assured her that she could do it."

"Oh, that's a lot of rubbish," Deena stated firmly. "She started having an anxiety attack when you began pushing her. Before you came she said she was looking forward to doing it."

They were almost nose to nose, and the expression in her eyes told Spence she wasn't backing down. "Look, I just saw her with an emergency inhaler in her hand a little bit ago. Was that my fault, too?" He felt righteous anger creep into his voice. "I don't want to argue with you. I'm just asking you to do your job."

The frog thing hadn't been her fault, and he knew it. Before he could apologize, before he was sure he even wanted to apologize, she stood. The screen door screeched open. "Asking, Spence? Or telling?"

The screen door banged lightly shut, and the wooden one after it. He heard the latch click into place and then silence.

"Sometimes you have to push a little," he explained to the empty space beside him. He wasn't forcing anything on Alyssa. You didn't wait for a drowning person to call for help. You simply jumped in and pulled her out of the water. That's all he was saying. The trick to saving someone was to get there in time. You couldn't hesitate.

He'd tried that once, and he had failed miserably.

Chapter 8

After the morning devotion and quiet time, Deena and the girls returned to the cabin to change into bathing suits. Deena slathered everyone with sunscreen, treated five cases of poison ivy, then escorted them to their kayak lesson.

Morning sunlight filtered through the trees as they walked down the path to the lake. These pines were much bigger than the ones at home. Her condo had two carefully pruned blue spruces in the front yard. The association always decorated them at Christmas. They were pretty, but nothing, really, compared to the towering trees around her.

"Hey, Aunt Deena," Evie said, falling into step beside her. "Can we look for the eagle's nest today?"

The girl's energy was contagious. She looked adorable, still young enough to have a step that bounced, yet old enough you could almost see the woman she would become someday.

"What's this about you and that eagle's nest? You've been dying to see it ever since we got here."

Evie shrugged. "Well, it's how the camp got its name, after all. My mom told me about it when we signed up. And I dreamed that I was an eagle. I had these huge wings, and I could fly."

Deena tuned out the rest of a rather colorful dream that included Stacy sitting on eggs that hatched into birds with human faces. One of those, of course, was Evie, who was placed in a cage while the other hatchling got to stay in the nest.

She suspected her niece was embellishing as she went along. Instead of paying attention, Deena wondered how to broach the subject of the frog incident. She didn't have actual proof, and she doubted Evie would simply confess. As a result, Deena couldn't just punish the girl. At the same time, the very last thing she needed was to have the prank repeated.

"Look, Evie, I'm not accusing you, but if you had something to do with those frogs, you should know that a prank like that could have had bad consequences. We're fortunate Alyssa's panic attack wasn't worse than it was."

"If I did release those frogs, and I'm not saying I did, what would happen?"

Deena studied the pine needles on the path. "I would ask you not to do it again."

"But would I get grounded? Have to scrub toilets? Or—" She paused. "Would I get sent home?"

"It was a prank. I'd let it go. This time."

"Oh," Evie said, sounding oddly disappointed.

They stepped into the clearing. A coarse sandy beach stretched along the shoreline. Reaching out, the long L-shaped dock extended into the lake. A group of campers gathered near the shore where a man stood lecturing. A man she recognized only too well.

Spencer Rossi was not only the camp nurse but also the kayak instructor? Deena stifled the urge to turn around and head for the cabin. But he'd already seen her, and she wasn't about to let him run her off. Besides, after last night she wasn't letting Evie out of her sight.

Evie whispered, "Hey, Alyssa. Your uncle looks hot in a bathing suit."

Hot? Deena considered the man in front of her. Okay. He was hot. Not that she really cared. Because she definitely wasn't interested in him. She was only doing what scientists did best—observe and analyze.

Tell that to her heart. It was beating like crazy.

"Okay," Spence said. "Looks like everyone's here now and we can get started. Today we're going to learn to paddle open-seated kayaks. They're lighter and easier to maneuver than canoes."

He held up a green-bladed paddle. "This," he said, holding the paddle chest-high, "is your friend. You don't want to fight the paddle in the water, so you move your wrists like this." He made a paddling motion. "Your wrists should only bend side to side, not rotate up and down." Deena tried not to notice the way the motions made the muscles in his chest flex. "You use your legs, too, and slightly rotate your body."

As Deena struggled to process this information, he added, "Keep your distance from other kayaks. Do not stand up. Do not jump in the water. No playing bumper boats." She tried to tune out the rumble of his voice. It wasn't as if she were in the market for a man. Especially not someone like Spence. If she were going to go for a guy, she'd pick a nerd.

A nerd would be perfect because they would have intellectual conversations about medical ethics and technology breakthroughs. They wouldn't be distracted by rogue hormones racing through their bloodstream and wreaking havoc with their nervous systems, giving them sleepless nights and sweaty palms. She wiped her hands on her shorts. Just how tall was the man anyway?

"Okay, everyone," Spence said. "Get going." He clapped his hands. Everyone charged for a kayak. Everyone except herself and Alyssa.

"We could sit on the shore and watch," Alyssa suggested.

Although she and Spence had exchanged strong words the night before, Deena agreed that Alyssa needed to get involved in the camp activities. "Or we could be partners."

"Do you know how to paddle a kayak?"

"No, and once I got seasick on the kiddie boats at Lake Compounce."

Alyssa pressed her lips together. "Why would you want to go out in the kayak if you think it might make you seasick?"

"Good question," Deena said. "But you know what? Sometimes you'll miss all the fun if you just sit on the sidelines." Goodness, that was something Stacy might say. "Besides," Deena added, "you're about to get a huge lecture from your uncle if you don't get in the kayak."

It was true. Already Spence was giving them a funny look, as if he was wondering what was going on.

"I guess we could try," Alyssa said. "You've got my rescue inhaler?"

Deena patted her fanny pack. "Yeah."

They walked over to the one kayak that no one else had picked. Built almost like a canoe, the kayak was long and thin with small plastic seats in the front and back. Unlike the kayaks Deena had ever seen, this one was totally open. No skirt covered the lower portion of the paddler. She could see the entire interior of the kayak, including a big puddle in the bottom. Deena lifted one of the life jackets and studied the brown stains along the edges. She was supposed to wear this? She'd rather culture it in the lab.

But Spence was watching, so she wouldn't let herself flinch as she eased the clammy fabric around herself. It was hard to buckle—obviously no one with a bust had ever attempted to wear it—but Deena let out the straps and cinched herself in.

Vest on, Alyssa climbed into the front of the kayak. Deena grabbed the tail, or whatever it was called, and pushed it into the water. The lake, leg-numbing cold, made her feel as though she'd dunked half her body in a vat of rubbing alcohol. When they were knee-deep, she climbed inside and settled herself in the hard plastic seat.

Sunlight warmed Deena's face and the cool pool of water she sat in. She paddled a little faster, enjoying the way the small vessel cut through the water. She could practically feel all the endorphins released by the brisk exercise shooting through her body.

She and Alyssa paddled past the long arm of the dock and toward the middle of the lake.

Ahead she saw Evie and Lourdes. The two girls were working well together, and their kayak moved smoothly through the water. Paddling a bit faster, Deena managed to catch up to them. "Hey," she called. "Isn't this great?"

Evie grinned back at her. "I didn't know you could kayak, Aunt Deena."

"I didn't either." Deena felt tremendously pleased to see the admiration in Evie's eyes.

"Hey, Aunt Deena! Race you to the buoys!"

In the distance, Deena spotted the two floating orange cones. She vaguely remembered Spence saying something about staying within the barriers. He hadn't said anything about racing, though.

"How about it, Alyssa? You up for it?"

The girl turned around. "If you want to."

Deena wanted Evie to think she was a cool aunt. She also wanted to make the activity fun for Alyssa. "I think we can take them."

The two kayaks drew alongside each other, and Evie counted down. The minute she said, "Go!" Deena paddled as fast and as hard as she could.

So did Evie and Lourdes. At first, more water was moving than kayaks as four double-bladed paddles thrashed. Screaming as the icy water sprayed over her, Deena dug her paddle into the water. The kayak responded sluggishly at first but then shot forward.

Another paddle full of water slapped her face. Deena laughed and leaned forward. Their kayak gained speed, but so did Evie's. The two boats stayed neck and neck as they raced toward the twin buoys.

Evie was screaming encouragement to Lourdes, who, with arms flailing, looked as if someone had pressed a button and sent her into fast-forward.

In the excitement Alyssa somehow was flicking more water back into the kayak and into Deena's face than she was helping move the boat forward. Doing her best to ignore the cold shower, Deena plowed forward.

The two kayaks drew even closer. They were so close Deena could have reached out and touched her niece's arm if she'd wanted to. Spence's warning— *"Keep your distance from other kayaks"*—rang in her ear, but she ignored it. They were having fun. Evie's paddle dumped even more water into her lap. That combined with the spray from Alyssa's furious paddling made Deena feel as if she were taking in as much water as the *Titanic*. She wanted to laugh so badly it took everything she had in her to keep paddling.

They were almost at the buoys, and the race was close. Then Deena felt something like a big fish smack her in the face. It stunned her for a second and hurt like crazy. She wanted to keep on paddling, but suddenly Evie was shouting, "Stop! Stop the race!" The girls slowed. "Aunt Deena, I am so sorry. Are you okay? It was an accident. I am so sorry."

"I'm fine." She still wasn't quite sure what had happened. Her face throbbed, and she tasted lake water. When she touched her check, however, her fingers came away sticky. Blood?

It dawned on her that it wasn't blood from a flying fish. It was her blood. Evie had clocked her with the paddle.

"You're not fine," Evie cried. "You're bleeding."

"Help!" Lourdes began to scream. "We need help!"

⁓

It could have been worse, Deena reflected a short time later as she lay on the narrow examination table in Spence's clinic. She could have been knocked out of the kayak, and Spence might have had to jump in the water and rescue her. Put his arms around her. Perform CPR, even.

She would have hated that. Hugging and kissing people always made her uncomfortable. Yet when Spence bent over her, Deena's stomach gave a little flip-flop, and her heart felt like it shriveled to the size of a raisin. She should have insisted that he let Miss Miriam treat her. Instead, she hadn't even protested when Spence had told the gray-haired nurse that he would take care of her. Miss Miriam's gaze had gone from Deena's face to Spence's and then back to Deena's. She had then announced she was going on a coffee break and would be gone for thirty minutes.

Now she had to deal with her riotously pounding heart as Spence bent over her. This close she could see the pores in his skin. With his gaze locked on her cheek, she could study his eyes without his looking back into her own. They were forest green, the same rich color of pine needles.

Maybe CPR from this guy wouldn't be so bad.

Deena squashed that thought as quickly as it came.

"It's not deep, and you won't need stitches," Spence concluded, still nearly nose to nose. "The important thing is to keep it clean." He dabbed her cut with a sterile gauze pad. "You're going to have a bruise, though."

"I'm sure it's fine. Can I go now?"

"Not yet. We're dealing with lake water, you know."

Deena shuddered to think of all the bacteria, parasites, and other kinds of infections that might be lurking in the waters of Lake Waramaug. "It was worth it," she joked. "We almost won the race, you know."

"I saw." Spence dabbed antiseptic cream on her cheek. "And you were losing. If Evie hadn't clocked you with the paddle, you would have crashed into the buoy. I probably would have had to fish you both out of the water."

"I beg your pardon. Coming close to that buoy was the fastest way to the finish line."

The antiseptic cream burned against her skin. "Ouch!" She felt Spence's fingers hesitate before smoothing more of it into the cut.

"Thanks for the rescue, though. I have to hand it to you. I've never seen anyone paddle so fast in my life."

"I was motivated." He taped a bandage into place. "I thought something had happened to Alyssa." He met her gaze and grinned.

Sitting up, she swung her legs over the side of the table. "Thanks, Spence."

He shrugged. "You're welcome. I hope you're not planning on trying water-skiing, or the obstacle course, or horseback riding."

"You may think I'm not athletic," Deena said, "but yesterday I actually played two games of Ping-Pong and nobody got hurt."

Spence laughed. "I'm not sure Ping-Pong qualifies as an athletic event."

"That's because you haven't seen me play it." Deena stood. She was a tall woman, but even so, she had to look up to meet his gaze. "Well, I guess I'd better get ready for rock climbing this afternoon." It was a joke, but he didn't laugh.

She started to leave, and then Spence said, "Deena?"

She turned around. "Yeah?"

"I'm sorry about last night. I didn't mean to imply that you weren't doing a good job."

"I'm sorry, too. You made some good points."

He hesitated, and she could see him thinking hard about whether he should say something or not. She found herself leaning slightly forward. "I saw it happen," he admitted. "I knew it was you." He shifted, but his gaze stayed steady on her face. "The one who was hurt. Not Alyssa. I just wanted you to know that."

Her fingers touched the small bandage he had placed on her cheek. "That's what I thought," she said and then added softly, "but it's good to know. For sure, I mean."

They stood like that for a few seconds; then they both smiled at exactly the same time. And it felt foolish and silly and completely right to be looking at him the way she was.

"See you tonight at the campfire."

Deena's heart skipped into another gear. "Yeah, Spence," she said. "See you tonight."

Chapter 9

When Deena returned to the cabin, she found the girls sitting on the floor in a circle. Holding hands and with their heads bent, they obviously were praying. The back of her throat went tight. "Hey," she said softly.

As soon as Evie saw her, she jumped up and nearly knocked her over with a massive hug. The other girls quickly joined her. Straining for room, they wiggled closer and struggled to get their arms around her.

"Aunt Deena," Evie cried. "Are you okay? I've been so worried."

"I was, like, so worried, too," Britty said. Her eyes were large within their frame of glitter shadow and purple liner. "You were bleeding pretty badly."

"I screamed so loud for help," Lourdes informed her, "that I broke one of the rubber bands on my braces and swallowed it."

Before Deena could take this in, Taylor began talking about the blood on Deena's shirt.

"I guess I'd better change," Deena said.

The five sets of arms around her lessened their pressure immediately.

"I'm so, so sorry, Aunt Deena. I almost killed you."

"It would take more than a kayak paddle to kill me," Deena said cheerfully. "Besides, it was my own fault letting my kayak get so close to yours." She looked down at that copper-colored head bowed in shame. It was so beautiful, so precious, those corkscrew curls falling midway down Evie's back.

She remembered when Evie was a baby. The first time Stacy let her hold Evie, she was so small, so perfect. Deena had been astonished by the depth of love she felt for her niece. When she bent to kiss the top of Evie's silken head, Evie had howled like a banshee, and Deena immediately handed her back. She realized now that she had been handing her back to Stacy in one way or another all Evie's life.

"So you're not mad at me?" Evie stepped back to look at Deena's face.

"Not a bit," Deena said. "I love you, honey." When was the last time she had said those words to her niece? Or to Stacy? A long time, she realized. As a scientist, she had to be analytical, observant, detached. She supposed those qualities had slipped into her personal life.

Seemingly reassured, Evie stepped back. "We cleaned while you were at the clinic."

Deena looked around. The cabin's plank floors gleamed a soft honey color, the beds had been made, and the clutter of clothes lying on the floor had disappeared.

44

"It looks great," Deena said. "You even cleaned Mr. Crackers's cage."

"Alyssa did," Evie said. "I wanted to help, but Mr. Crackers tried to bite me. And he said a bad word, too."

"Several bad words," Britty confirmed. "We lost track of how many when he started speaking foreign languages."

"He wasn't being mean," Alyssa said. "He was speaking his fear language."

"Fear language?" Taylor stared at Alyssa. "What are you talking about?"

"When Mr. Crackers gets afraid, he shows it by biting and cursing," Alyssa explained. "But all you have to do to get him to stop is talk to him."

"He's a nasty bird," Britty said. "When I tried to talk to him, I think he pooped on purpose to gross me out."

Deena laughed. "He is a character. I'll give him that."

"I'd better give this back to you." Alyssa handed Deena her rescue inhaler. "I took two puffs."

"That's okay," Deena said. "You're feeling better now, right?"

"I guess."

"This place sure is clean. As clean as my lab. And that, by the way, is always spotless. It has to be. Especially my cell culture room. We have a UV light that helps keep the area sterile."

"Cell culture room?" Lourdes asked. "What's a cell culture room?"

"It's a place where I examine tissue from people who have cancer. After a doctor does a biopsy on the patient, some of the tissue comes to us for research." Deena struggled to think in simple terms. "I isolate the cancer cells and try to figure out how to kill them in a way that they never come back."

"Are you really curing cancer like Evie said?" Taylor asked.

"I'm trying," Deena said, glad the conversation had shifted from her injury to her work. "So are a lot of really smart, dedicated people. We're making progress every day."

"Do you have test tubes of blood everywhere?" This came from Britty, who had equal parts fascination and horror on her face.

"How close are you to finding a cure?" Lourdes added.

Deena smiled. "We're a lot closer than we used to be. And no, I don't have test tubes with blood in them everywhere. All our samples are kept in the incubator— it looks kind of like a refrigerator or freezer, and it maintains a very specific set of conditions."

Deena checked her watch. "Hey, you guys are going to be late for your volleyball match. How about you head over there, and I'll take a shower and catch up with you."

The girls didn't need much convincing. The volleyball match was one of the coed activities scheduled, and the girls had been looking forward to it.

Deena took a quick shower and dressed in a pair of white shorts and a green sleeveless top. When she stepped back into the room, she saw Alyssa sitting cross-legged in front of Mr. Crackers's cage. "I hope you're not having a staring contest," Deena said. "Because Mr. Crackers always wins. He's pretty good at blinking games, too."

Alyssa looked up. Her eyes looked very green behind her glasses. "Do you ever feel sorry for him? In that cage all the time? I mean, what does he do all day but sit on that perch and watch everyone? You ever wonder what he's thinking?"

Deena tossed her towel on the chair and crouched next to the girl. "It's all he's ever known, I guess. He'd die if he were released into the wild." She paused. "You don't miss what you've never known."

Alyssa's golden head shook in disagreement. "I don't think so, Miss Deena. He can look through those bars and see a whole other world out there—he can see it through the bars and hear it and smell it, but he can't be part of it."

What should she say? The bird had been raised in captivity. "He doesn't think like that," Deena said at last. "He's in a safe place, in his home."

"You think he ever misses his old life? The one he had with the guy who had him before you?"

Just where was all this going? What was it that Alyssa needed to hear? "No," Deena said. "Well, maybe at first he did, but then he discovered rock-and-roll music." She studied Alyssa's face, unsmiling and fixed on the bird, as if she expected at any moment Mr. Crackers would open his mouth and join the conversation. "He adjusted, Alyssa. It took time, but he's happy now."

Alyssa turned to her. "What if you don't want to be happy? What if you don't want to forget?"

Deena suddenly understood the reasons for Alyssa's questions—and some of her fears, too. It had nothing to do with Mr. Crackers and everything to do with the loss of her parents.

"You won't forget them," she said gently. "The being happy part—that one is harder. But one of these days, Alyssa, you're going to wake up and stop seeing the bars. You're just going to see the world."

"How do you know?"

"Because," Deena said slowly, "that's the way it happened for me."

Chapter 10

The marshmallow made a whooshing noise and then burst into flames. Deena pulled the stick from the fire and blew out the small inferno. The smoking remains looked like they'd disintegrate if she touched them. "Spence," she said, holding the marshmallow up for his inspection. "I incinerated it."

Packed around the blazing campfire set in an open field, a group of campers stuck long skewers into the flames. Their faces glowed with excitement in the light of the fire as they laughed and held up their marshmallows, making designs with the smoke as if the skewers were Fourth of July sparklers.

"You didn't incinerate it," Spence said. "It's perfect."

"Perfect? Spence, it isn't even edible."

Spencer blew out his own blackened marshmallow. "You want it burned on the outside but soft and gooey on the inside. I'll show you."

He led her through the mass of kids waiting for a chance to toast their marshmallows to a table loaded with stacks of chocolate bars and graham crackers.

Deena copied what Spence chose and then followed him to the edge of the field where tall pines marked the beginning of the woods. They found a private spot beneath the base of one of the trees. They could still watch and hear the kids, but it was quieter. Deena began assembling her s'more. The marshmallow nearly burned her fingers as she pulled the charred remains off the stick. "It looks carcinogenic."

"Charcoal is good for digestion. Don't judge before you try it."

Deena doubted his statement greatly but smeared the marshmallow on top of the graham cracker and then added a square of chocolate. She added another graham cracker and squished the concoction together.

"Go ahead," Spence urged, already crunching happily.

As a rule Deena stayed away from sweets. She tried to eat lots of fruits and vegetables and exercise regularly. She avoided red meat entirely and made sure she ate fish at least twice a week. However, since she'd arrived at camp, she'd blown her diet completely. One small cookie wouldn't make much difference.

She nibbled an edge. Not bad. She took a slightly larger bite and tasted the mix of sweet chocolate and gooey, sticky marshmallow.

"Like it?"

"Mmm. Love it." Deena polished off the rest of the cookie in three bites. Afterward she licked her fingers. "That is the most delicious thing I've ever eaten."

"You've never had one of these before?"

Deena shook her head. "My family was never into camping. My dad was more into intellectual outings like going to museums. And my mom, well, she was sick a lot."

She wanted another s'more but didn't want to move. "When I get back to my lab, I'll have to find a way to make these with a Bunsen burner. Or maybe the microwave."

In front of them the kids laughed, shouted, and teased each other playfully. The bonfire, smelling pleasantly of smoke and woods, sent up colorful flames that danced in the darkness.

"You can't make these in a lab and have them taste the same." Spence swatted a bug. "You have to be miles from civilization, looking up at the stars and listening to the night."

Deena heard the crackle of the fire, the laughter of the kids, the deep-pitched croak of the bullfrogs, and the plaintive *wra–a–a–ah* sound of the toads. She had to admit, he might be right. Not that she'd tell him that.

"I don't know, Spence, a burned marshmallow is a burned marshmallow."

"Not burned, toasted. Think of it as Cajun, but without the spices."

"It was burned, but that's actually good news for me because I burn everything. Well, unless I can microwave it. I can't wait to tell Stacy I've actually found something that tastes great burned."

"Who's Stacy?"

"My younger sister. Evie's mother. She was supposed to be the cabin counselor, but she's in a high-risk pregnancy. That's how I ended up here."

"Oh, right—you told me about her the other night. How she's doing?"

"Talked to her yesterday. She and the baby are doing fine. She's decided that being at this camp is really good for me as well as Evie. She thinks I spend way too much time in my lab." Deena poked her empty skewer into a clump of pine needles and stirred them around.

"My brother, Evan, used to tell me I worked too hard," Spence said. "He thought I needed more fun in my life. He never understood why I would choose a job that didn't have regular hours."

"I do," Deena said in heartfelt understanding. "When people are depending on you, you owe it to them to work as hard as you can."

"You can't tell a person lost in the middle of a snowstorm to wait for Thanksgiving dinner to finish."

"Absolutely not," Deena agreed. "Am I supposed to say to some woman fighting for her life, 'Sorry, I may have found a new therapy for you, but I can't work overtime'?"

Deena jumped when Spence reached over and lightly slapped her arm. "Mosquito," he said in apology.

Someone started playing a guitar. She closed her eyes as the kids began singing "Lean on Me." It felt so right. Being there. She let herself shift slightly toward Spence. The kids' voices were so pure and beautiful. She had the strongest urge to lay her head on Spence's shoulder and for him to slip his arm around her. To let herself lean on him, just like the song said. Of course she wouldn't. "We're fortunate to have work we love to do," she said.

"Tell me about the lifesaving therapy."

She opened her eyes. "You want the whole story or the press release version?"

"The whole story, of course."

She settled more deeply into the tree trunk. "I want the same, then, about you." He nodded. "I'm into translational biology. That means instead of studying fruit flies or yeast, we study actual cancer cells. I'm studying all the pathways that cause cancer to grow."

As she spoke, she thought of Andres, Quing, Nrushingh, working even now while she was here. She wondered about the data they would have gathered by now and felt guilty because they were doing her work for her.

Spence listened and asked a lot of good questions, which drew Deena even more deeply into the discussion. It felt good to talk about her work with him. Stacy always enjoyed hearing about her work, but invariably something interrupted them. Jack wanted help with his homework, Evie had to be picked up or driven somewhere, or Jeff needed her.

"I'm sorry, Spence," she apologized, realizing they'd spent far too much time talking about her work. "I sort of got carried away."

"Don't think that," he said. "I liked hearing about it. My dad was a cardiac surgeon, and my brother was an optometrist."

She glanced at the dark outline of his profile. "And you became an EMT."

He snorted in amusement. "Much to my father's disappointment. He kept saying the pay was poor, the opportunity for advancement minimal, and the working conditions dangerous. In short, he thought I'd lost my mind."

Deena made a sympathetic noise. Her father had thought she was crazy to immerse herself in the disease that had killed her mother. "But you like it, right? Being an EMT?"

"Loved it. I quit about six months ago when my brother and sister-in-law died and I became Alyssa's legal guardian. Fortunately, I've had enough savings to be a stay-at-home dad. I can't do that forever, though."

"Well, it's good that you're doing it now."

It was hard to picture a big guy like him doing ordinary things like laundry and cooking, but she decided she liked learning about this homey side of him.

"It's been a real education," he said. "I took her shopping at the mall and discovered that buying a twelve-year-old clothing is next to impossible. Either the shirts have puppies on them, or they're way too clingy."

"Oh, Spence, couldn't you have asked your mom or a female friend to help?"

"I thought about asking one of Alyssa's friend's moms but figured the more time we spent doing stuff together, the better we'd get to know each other. But it didn't quite work out that way. We went to this one store that had lots of girlie clothes I thought Alyssa would like. I kept holding up shirts, asking if she liked them, and she kept saying no. Finally, she tried on this one shirt, and it was way too clingy. I had to shout to be heard above this awful rock music, and just as I opened my mouth, the music stopped and everybody in the store heard me. Alyssa turned red as a tomato and then insisted we leave."

When Deena stopped laughing, she turned to study his profile. "You were there with her," she said. "That's what's most important. She may not seem like she appreciates what you're doing for her, but deep inside she does."

Spence shrugged, and his mood turned more serious. "I know she's got a lot of stuff going on in her head and things won't get better overnight. But sometimes I wonder if she's ever going to be happy again."

"She will be," Deena promised. "She's lucky to have you, Spence. Not a lot of guys would give up a life they loved and relocate like you did."

"Not many people would step in at the last minute and take their pregnant sister's place as a camp counselor, especially when that person wasn't exactly the outdoors type."

"I know a lot about the outdoors. In ninth grade I got an A on my 'biology in a box' project. I identified all sorts of leaves and bugs."

"But not poison ivy," Spence teased.

"And now that I'm more familiar with it, I see it everywhere." Deena smiled wickedly. "I could be wrong, but just before you sat down, I thought I saw a very suspicious-looking patch of red-stemmed leaves. Of course, I'm sure that an outdoors person like yourself would have recognized if it was poison ivy."

Although she'd been teasing, she enjoyed the way Spence jumped from his spot. Unfortunately, it placed him even closer to her. They were practically shoulder to shoulder. Worse, she couldn't move an inch without making it obvious that his proximity made her uncomfortable.

Worse still, he put his big, warm palm right on top of her hand. It covered hers completely. She stared at their hands, felt her heart start to beat so hard it seemed as if it would pound its way right out of her chest. It was ridiculous to feel this way about a total stranger. The problem was, he didn't feel like a total stranger.

She had that urge again to lay her head on his shoulder and just sit like that for a long time—just listening to the night and watching the kids playing around the campfire. She wanted to let down her guard and fully open her heart, something she'd never done with a man before.

At the same time, she knew the situation was impossible. She and Spence were completely wrong for each other. He had Alyssa, who needed everything he had to give. Deena, well, she had her work. She might have explained what she did, but it wasn't the whole story. She hadn't told him enough—not about her mother, her aunt, and her grandmother—and most important, not about herself.

The weight of his hand on hers began to feel more like a burden than a connection. She should tell him, right now, before this went any further.

Deena searched for the stars, barely visible in the vast pool of darkness. This was exactly why she didn't like to get to know anyone too deeply. Once you got past the casual what-do-you-do-for-a-living stage, the questions got harder. It was like one of those game shows on TV where the payoff grew with each question, as did the risk of losing it all.

She was not a gambler, and she had trained herself, so she thought, not to want things she couldn't have.

Sometimes a person had to carry around things that were hard to live with, but you did the best you could because you knew sharing them would only increase their weight. It wouldn't change things. It would only give someone else another burden to carry. And Deena had no intention of doing that.

Chapter 11

Spence spent the morning stitching up a girl who had cut her leg on a rock in the tug-of-war pit, fishing a pretzel stick from the nasal passage of a boy who had placed it there on a dare, and cleaning the injury of a boy who had hooked himself in the shoulder while practicing casting.

By ten o'clock, he was ready for a break. He asked Miss Miriam to cover for him. She grinned and winked. "Heard your girl is on the archery field."

Spence grinned. "Figure I'll see if she can hit the target."

"Take your time, honey."

"Thanks." Spence pulled a brown lunch sack from the small refrigerator. "I'll be back in an hour."

On his way to the archery field, he passed the blackened remains of the campfire and smiled. He'd enjoyed seeing Deena eat her first s'more. Even more than that, he'd liked sitting beneath the tree and talking to her. He admired the work she was doing. She was a good listener, and he'd opened up to her more than was customary.

In the field he saw a line of archery targets and a group of girls standing in rows. Careful to approach from the side, Spence paused as arrows flew. Some actually hit the targets, but most sailed through the air and disappeared in the grass.

A moment later, a new row of girls stepped forward. He recognized Alyssa's small frame and honey-colored hair. He held his breath as she loaded the bow and pulled the string back. Sunlight reflected off her glasses, and the bow looked enormous in her small hands.

He laughed when her arrow landed about a foot from her. At least she'd tried.

Okay. Archery obviously wasn't her thing. A lot of things, it seemed, weren't her thing. Even before the accident, she'd been kind of a quiet kid. Not a girlie girl and certainly not an athlete.

He remembered last Christmas when the family had gathered at Evan's house as they always did. Beneath an evergreen so high it touched the ceiling in the great room, there'd been a mountain of presents—skis, clothing, an enormous stuffed polar bear, and a girl's ten-speed mountain bike.

Alyssa, however, had been curled up in the window seat with *The Lion, the Witch, and the Wardrobe*. He had a feeling those ice skates he'd given her weren't going to get a lot of use. His niece was a bookworm.

Proposing a toast, Evan had proudly told him that Alyssa had tested into the district's gifted and talented program, which would allow her to learn with, as he put it, "nerds just like her."

Spence remembered his brother's flushed cheeks and too-bright eyes. He'd looked at the nearly empty glass in Evan's hand and remembered another Christmas and another glass in his brother's hand. Something in his brain had flashed a warning signal. He decided to discuss it with him later in private.

But the conversation had never happened. His brother and sister-in-law had died less than two weeks later. The crash had been ruled an accident, but alcohol had been involved.

Spence pushed the memory aside. Regrets were useless. What mattered now was Alyssa—that he was there for her in the way he hadn't been for his brother.

Maybe he couldn't give her back her father, but he could teach her how to shoot an arrow. When everyone paused to collect arrows, Spence stepped forward. As he did, he saw Deena.

She wore denim shorts and a camp T-shirt, yet even that simple outfit looked beautiful on her. The sight of those long legs and that ridiculously small waist made his mouth go dry.

He brought his gaze to her face but found no comfort there. A small, colorful bruise stained her left cheek. It was slightly swollen and tender looking, but no sign of infection. "Hey," he said. "How're you doing?"

"So far so good," Deena replied. "This is a nice surprise."

"Yeah, well, I was just looking for a spot to eat my lunch." He held up the bag as if his words weren't proof enough—as if it wasn't obvious what he was doing there. "Hi, Alyssa." Spence tried to meet his niece's gaze. "I saw you trying. Good job."

"I stink at this."

"You're trying. That's all I care about." *And I want you to have fun, make friends, feel the sunshine on your face, and know that God has a plan for you.*

"Do I have to keep practicing? I've come closer to hitting my foot than I have the target."

Spence put his hand on Alyssa's shoulder. Although she flinched at his touch, he didn't remove it. "I'm sure you can learn. Let me show you."

"You'd better help my aunt Deena, too," Evie informed him, joining them from her place in the line next to them. Her copper eyebrows lifted. "She needs it even more than Alyssa."

"Evie," Deena said in a tone of warning. "You know I've been hitting the target consistently."

"Yeah," Evie agreed, grinning. "But not *your* target."

Deena smiled sheepishly at him. "I pull a little to the left." Her face had more color in it today—not counting the bruised area—and those light blue eyes twinkled.

"A *lot* to the left," Evie said. "People are jumping out of the way when they see you taking aim."

"Evie, that is such an exaggeration." But she was grinning, and so was Evie.

Spence wished he and Alyssa could joke like that with each other. He'd even be happy with a simple conversation as long as it was the real Alyssa talking, saying what she really thought instead of being so polite all the time.

"I'll help you both," he promised.

When it was Alyssa's turn, he stood behind her. Reaching around her, he positioned her arms correctly on the bow. As usual, the size of her arms humbled him. He could have spanned the widest part with his thumb and index finger.

"Like this," he said, and, keeping his fingers over Alyssa's, he drew the string even tighter and then released the arrow. It flew through the air and speared the target. Not a perfect bull's-eye, but Alyssa almost looked him in the eye and said, "Good job, Uncle Spence."

"Thank you." And just that quickly the moment ended. Alyssa scooted off to stand beside Evie. He glanced at Deena, saw her nodding in approval. "Okay, Deena. How about you give it a try by yourself?"

Deena shook her head. "You don't have to teach me, Spence. I came here to watch. The girls talked me into trying."

"I've got the time." Spence handed her the bow. "Besides, you never know when your archery skills might come in handy."

Deena's arched eyebrows suggested that was about as probable as donkeys flying. "I don't anticipate needing to shoot a bow and arrow in my laboratory."

"The girls are watching us," Spence said softly. "If you don't let me teach you how to shoot an arrow, they're going to wonder why I'm standing here so close to you."

Those words got her moving. It wasn't flattering, but Spence had only been teasing. They both knew their time at the camp was limited. Soon she'd be returning to her research job, and he, well, he would return to Evan's house and continue to piece together his and Alyssa's lives.

He folded his arms as she drew back the bow. For a researcher who spent most of her days in the lab, she had nice biceps, and her triceps weren't half bad either. "Tighter. Pull back tighter," he coached.

The bow strained tighter, and Deena released the arrow. It hooked left and landed dead center in the target next to theirs. Alyssa and Evie hooted with laughter. Spence felt his jaw drop.

"The same thing happened to me when we played shuffleboard," Deena admitted. "Everything went left."

"At least you didn't hit anybody," Spence said, deciding right then and there that he wasn't leaving until he was sure she could shoot an arrow straight.

As he had with Alyssa, he came up behind her to show her the proper way to hold the bow. The moment his arms went around her, he realized just how perfectly she fit into them. Those soft little spikes of hair just touched his chin, and the slightest trace of something fruity tantalized his nostrils.

"Now draw the string back," he said, wanting to draw her into his arms. It was all he could do not to nuzzle her ear.

The movement brought them even closer, aligning their bodies arm for arm, leg for leg, breath for breath. "And close one eye," he whispered because his voice had gone hoarse. Now the bow was definitely trembling. "Aim for the bull's-eye and. . .release."

Spence released his grip on the arrow and watched from above Deena's shoulders as the arrow sailed at least a foot over the top of the target. "At least it went straight," he said. His feet seemed to have grown roots.

"Yeah," Deena agreed, and her breathing sounded strained. "It went straight. Very straight."

"I think the problem was your elbow." He pushed the limb lightly against her hip. "You need to keep it lined up with your body."

The problem wasn't her alignment, though, and he knew it. No, the problem had nothing to do with archery either. It was this attraction between them. He stepped away from her to get another arrow.

He'd come to the camp to bond with Alyssa, help bring her to God, not fall for Deena, no matter how attractive or smart she was, no matter how long it had been since he'd felt this way about a woman.

He'd been in relationships before. Not many, but enough to know the odds were slim that he and Deena would end up in a forever kind of relationship. There was Alyssa to consider as well. What would happen if he got involved with Deena and it didn't work out?

Spence wasn't about to let that happen. Alyssa had to come first. He owed that much to Evan.

God, please give me the strength to resist this woman. Spence stretched his arm to give Deena an arrow. "Give it another try."

It hurt to watch her draw that arrow back and not be standing behind her. But he made himself stand to the side and keep his arms folded as she shot arrow after arrow.

All of them hooked left.

Chapter 12

After archery Deena and the girls headed to the commissary for lunch. As they neared the large log cabin, she spotted Pastor Rich sitting on one of the benches beneath the trees. His bald head slumped forward on his chest, and a low whistling noise originated from him.

"Quiet," Deena whispered as they drew closer to Pastor Rich. "The poor man needs some rest."

She was beginning to wonder how anyone made it through camp without collapsing from exhaustion. The campfire had lasted until past midnight, and then the girls had stayed up talking and laughing after everyone had gotten into bed.

"Aunt Deena, I just remembered. I left my water bottle back in the archery field. I'm going to need it this afternoon. Can I run back and get it?"

"Yes, but take a friend with you."

"I'll take Alyssa, if that's all right."

Deena smiled at the two girls. They seemed like unlikely friends—one tall and outgoing, the other small and quiet. She was pleased a bond seemed to be forming between them. "Okay," she said. "Meet us in the cafeteria. We'll be at our usual table."

It took Evie longer than it should have to return from the archery fields. Deena checked her watch and glanced across the crowded room to the door. No sign of Evie and Alyssa. She looked down at her half-eaten turkey sandwich and tried to reassure herself that nothing bad had happened. This was a church camp, and the girls knew where they were going. They were probably just enjoying a little independence. Still, when she checked her watch a few minutes later, she decided enough was enough. She headed for the door.

She didn't have to go very far before she saw them. The two girls were crouching beside the bench where Pastor Rich was napping. Deena headed toward them, wondering what they were doing bent over like that right next to Pastor Rich's feet.

Breaking into a jog, Deena closed the distance between herself and the girls. Glancing down, she felt her jaw drop in disbelief. Peeking out of the senior pastor's leather sandals were ten painted toenails. Evie held a bottle of hot pink polish in her hand, and Alyssa had neon blue.

Deena nudged Evie's shoulder. Her niece glanced up with an expression of pure mischief on her face. The little imp. Deena wanted to laugh but made herself frown instead.

Evie's lips folded in on themselves in an effort to bite back her laughter.

Her shoulders shook so hard she could barely steady her hand enough to add a final dab of hot pink to Pastor Rich's pinkie toe. Nudging Alyssa, Evie capped her polish. As the two girls exchanged glances, a small note of laughter escaped Evie's mouth. Pastor Rich stirred on the bench.

The coconspirators raced back to the building. Deena stared down at the pastor's colorful toes. She wondered for one wild moment if she had time to find nail polish remover and return Pastor Rich's toenails to their natural state before he awakened. Of course she couldn't.

She squared her shoulders and touched Pastor Rich's shoulder. "I'm sorry," she blurted out the moment he opened his eyes. "Your toenails." She pointed at his feet.

Pastor Rich studied his brightly painted toes. He looked up a moment later, smiling. "Tell the girls I like the color. They did a good job."

"Aren't you upset?"

Pastor Rich shook his head. "I've been having a hard time pretending to be asleep for the past ten minutes. I could have stopped them, but they were having too much fun."

"Don't you want to talk to them? Give them a lecture about playing pranks?"

"No. They're not in trouble. Everything is fine, Deena. When I was a kid one summer at camp, I put shaving cream on all the windows of the senior pastor's cabin so he would wake up and think we had a freak snowstorm. What I really wanted, though, was his attention."

Deena frowned. Evie got lots of attention. It couldn't be that. But if Evie didn't want attention, just what did she want? She stared down at Pastor Rich's face. She thought she had never seen anyone so much at peace.

"How do you do it? Stay so calm?"

Pastor Rich chuckled. "I just remind myself that God is the One in control. He's the One who has the power and the purpose." He patted a space on the bench beside him. "Come sit with me for a moment."

Deena shook her head. "I'd like to, but the girls are inside. I'd better get back to them. You don't know whose toenails are in danger."

He studied her face a moment then smiled. "You're doing a good job, Deena, but don't forget you're not in this alone. If you need help, just ask for it."

"Thank you, Pastor Rich. I appreciate that."

Chapter 13

The call came in around one o'clock. The cabin counselor from the boys' blue cabin had scraped up his hand in a tug-of-war match in the mud pits. Would Spence mind coming over and taping it up?

It wasn't far to the big field. Spence cut through the archery fields, empty of campers now, skirted around the soccer fields and horseshoe pits, and then headed to the roped-off area that contained a huge mud pit. A group of boys and girls huddled beneath a makeshift shade structure. Spence headed toward them and felt his breath catch as he sighted the back of Deena's head. There was no mistaking the black, choppy layers of her hair and the square of her shoulders.

"Someone needed medical help?" Spence looked around the group.

A short man with a large bald spot and thick, black-rimmed glasses held his arm out. Even covered with mud, Spence recognized Mitt Collins. Yesterday morning Mitt had gotten a blister on his palm during his cabin's kayak lesson. As Spence treated it, Mitt had given him free tax advice.

"The tape you put on yesterday came off during the tug-of-war match," Mitt said with a note of apology in his voice. "I had to ask the referee to suspend the match until you could tape me up again."

Spence washed the wound and patted it dry with a gauze pad. It wasn't a deep blister, but it was in a painful place, located in the folds of his palm near the base of his thumb. "I can tape it up for you," he offered, "but I don't think you're going to be able to grip the tug-of-war rope very easily. And you really shouldn't let it get dirty."

The boys from Mitt's cabin groaned even as the girls in Deena's cabin cheered.

"I don't want my boys to have to forfeit," Mitt said. "Is there anything you can do?"

Spence took some Coban and more gauze out of his bag. "Not really. You're probably going to make the blister worse if you try to grip the rope."

The boys groaned even louder. "We don't want to forfeit," one of them said. "We want to play."

A boy said, "Come on, Dad, please?"

Mitt looked at Spence. "Tell you what, Spence. You take my place in the match, and I'll do your taxes for free."

Spence squared his shoulders. He looked at the muddy field and the flag hanging from a line that marked the center of the pit. He glanced at Deena again and saw the challenge in her eyes. "You don't have to offer to do my taxes, Mitt," he said slowly, but loudly so everyone could hear him. "I'll do it for free."

The boys released a roar as if Spence had just announced they had qualified to play in the Super Bowl. They immediately began jumping up and down and bumping chests. Spence shot Deena a cocky grin. "If the blue girls' team finds no objection, that is."

"What do you say, girls?" Deena said. "Do you want to show these guys how to play tug-of-war?"

The girls responded with higher-pitched but no less enthusiastic shouts. Evie flexed her muscles, Lourdes grinned widely, Britty and Taylor gave each other high fives, and Alyssa gave Deena a big thumbs-up.

"Okay," Spence said. "It's settled."

"Thanks, Spence," Mitt said. "I owe you big-time. Lewis would have killed me if we'd had to forfeit."

"No problem," Spence said. "We're here to serve."

"One thing I ought to tell you. Be careful. Those girls. They're stronger than they look. The tall, black-haired gal, she could pull a stump out of the ground."

Spence laughed. "Thanks for the warning, Mitt, but we'll be fine."

The referee, a teenage boy wearing a mud-plastered T-shirt and shorts, gave a short blast on his whistle. "Everyone, take your positions on the field."

Deena walked with a very straight back into the mud. However, as she sank to her ankles, her shoulders came up and her elbows went out like wings. Her hips made an adorable little wiggle, and Spence thought he'd never seen anyone girlier in his entire life.

Releasing the grin he'd been holding back, Spence stepped into the mud after her. He had to admit, the muck had the consistency of quicksand. It sucked loudly at his feet as he picked his way to the starting point.

A dividing line hung across the middle of the field, and each team took one side. A red pennant hanging from the dividing line marked the middle of a fat, mud-stained rope.

The referee explained the rules and ordered them to take their places.

Spence organized his team by weight. He took the end position and put the heaviest kid, Zach, in front of him. He was just beginning to notice that all the kids on his team were pretty skinny. No problem. They could handle the girls.

On the other side of the centerline, the girl's team also arranged themselves by weight. He nearly laughed at Deena's expression of disgust as she gingerly picked up the mud-stained rope.

"Everyone ready?" the referee asked.

"Ready," Spence yelled, planting his feet in the slime.

"Ready," Deena echoed, hooking the rope behind her hips. She looked straight at him. "Bring it on."

The whistle blew, and the rope immediately went taut. Spence's strategy had been to hold back, letting Deena's team develop false confidence, and then drag them across the dividing line. However, as his team lost about six feet within seconds, Spence rapidly changed plans.

He leaned back and used every one of his 220 pounds to stop Deena's team from pulling them across the line. The maneuver halted their forward progress but didn't turn the tide in his favor.

To his surprise, the other team also increased their effort. Spence grunted and dug his heels into the slippery mud.

He glanced at Deena, red-faced, muscles straining, shouting encouragement to her team members. The woman might have the face of an angel, but Mitt had been right. She was as strong as an ox.

Inches in front of him, Zach leaned backward, nearly into his lap. "Pull!" Spence yelled.

His team was pulling for all they were worth, but they weren't moving. "Keep pulling," Spence roared, shifting as his feet slid forward an inch. His new strategy was simply to try to hold their position until Deena's team got tired. Then he'd reel them in like a fish on a line.

Suddenly Walter's feet flew out from under him. He fell backward into Lewis, who toppled backward into Brian, who knocked down Zach, and the next thing Spence knew, he was flat on his back. Cold mud rapidly worked its way up the legs of his shorts, and the finish line was only a few feet away.

Spence rolled onto his belly and struggled to get his legs in front of him. Unfortunately, his legs tangled up with Zach's. Before he knew it, the whistle blew.

"We have a winner!" the referee shouted. Deena's team cheered wildly. "But remember, it's a best of three match," the muddy teenager continued. "Contestants, switch sides and get ready for the next round."

Spence picked some mud from his ear. His clothing had collected about five pounds of wet mud. The rest of his team looked even worse. The girls were laughing at them and pumping their fists in the air in victory. Evie and Alyssa were bumping their hips together in a happy dance that stopped the second Alyssa saw him.

Spence felt more than the defeat of the tug-of-war match. Obviously bringing her to this camp had changed nothing. Maybe it was time he accepted she didn't want to live with him. Spence retreated. Six months ago his world had tilted, and since then it seemed everything he did was wrong.

The referee blew the whistle, signaling the start of the next round. Spence took his position at the end of the rope, and the irony was not lost on him. He was at the end of his rope. Clasping the thick, mud-coated rope, he welcomed the opportunity to vent a little frustration.

After the third game ended, Spence and his team slopped their way across the pit to shake hands with the members of Deena's team. In his entire life, he couldn't ever remember seeing a group of people so filthy looking.

There wasn't a patch of clean skin visible on anyone, but Spence had never seen any group of kids look so happy. He himself felt considerably better after thoroughly trouncing Deena's team.

He grinned as he came to a stop in front of Deena, whose red T-shirt was no longer recognizable as a shirt at all. It was a second skin of thick brown mud. The only spots of color on her were those blue eyes and red bow-shaped lips. His mood improved another notch.

"Congratulations," Deena said, offering her hand.

He grinned. "We got lucky. It was fun, wasn't it?"

She grinned back at him. "Yeah, but I think I have mud in my teeth."

"Me, too," Spence said, and it didn't bother him one bit. "You're pretty muddy." The words slipped out not the way he meant them at all. What he meant was she looked cute when she was muddy.

"You are, too," Deena said and flicked a bit of mud off her shoulder. It landed on Spence's shirt.

"Hey," he said and flicked some mud right back at her.

The next thing he knew, she shook her head, spraying him with hundreds of mud pellets. She was in trouble now. She knew it, too. Laughing, she turned and ran.

Only she couldn't quite run in the mud. Not very fast, anyway. He'd have her in two strides. Just what he intended to do with her when he caught her, he wasn't sure, but he was going to have fun finding out. He launched himself after her and quickly caught up. His arms had just barely managed to encircle her waist when his feet slipped out from under him.

They both went down, landing with a splash and the sound of cheers. He still had his arms around her, and she was shaking with laughter. He couldn't stop the idiotic grin that plastered itself across his face. Not when she smiled up at him like that.

The world had tilted again, but this time everything felt like it had fallen right into place.

Chapter 14

The beach ball smacked the concrete right next to her lounge chair. Deena reached out and swatted it back into the pool. A boy shouted his thanks, and the game of water polo continued.

Deena already had lost her iced tea to a shot that had gone wild, and twice the ball had whizzed just millimeters past her head. She was doing okay, though. Better than okay. She was actually having a lot of fun. She smiled. Spence tackling her in the mud had been really fun. In fact, she enjoyed just about anything they did together.

Darkness had not fully fallen yet, but the pool lights had come on, turning the water a fluorescent blue. A gentle breeze ruffled Deena's hair as she pondered a deep scientific question. What was Spence's best feature? He had great eyes, but that smile. . .it was killer.

She couldn't rule out his voice either. It had that rumbly, deep pitch that made everything he said sound important. Well, almost everything. He had that sneaky sense of humor, too.

Deena flinched as another shot sailed over her head. A boy, dripping wet, vaulted out of the pool after it. She had to stop thinking so much about Spence, letting her imagination go wild. What if he was serious about her, and they ended up getting married? If she had a family, then she would have to be more like Stacy, making cookies and driving everyone to activities.

She'd have to worry about harsh teachers and inappropriate friends, body piercings, driver's ed, drugs, sex education, and. . .the list was endless.

Deena didn't see how she could be the kind of scientist she wanted to be and have a family, too. That meant there could be no more scientific thoughts about Spence.

An even louder roar arose from the pool, and then youthful bodies began clambering out of the water. Game over. Pizza and a movie came next. She'd better get moving if she wanted a slice of pepperoni.

She set her striped canvas tote on her seat and headed for the tables under the trees. Hurrying because a couple of days at camp had taught her there'd be no leftovers, she found her feet leading her in a different direction when she spied Evie by the drink cooler. She'd been wanting to speak to her niece privately, but up until now there just hadn't been an opportunity.

"Hi, Aunt Deena." Her niece wore a green one-piece Speedo with a towel wrapped around her waist. She had the beginnings of a suntan and looked quite lovely.

"I need to talk to you. About what you did to Pastor Rich's toenails." Deena pulled her off to the side.

Evie grinned. "I think he likes it. I saw him walking around, and the polish is still there."

"Evie, you can't go around playing pranks on people. Even though Pastor Rich wasn't mad, it's still not right."

Evie dropped her gaze to the ground. "Are you going to make me apologize to him?"

"Absolutely, and you and Alyssa both are going to offer to remove it for him. I sincerely doubt Pastor Rich brought nail polish remover to camp."

Evie shrugged. "Okay, Aunt Deena, but I have to tell you, I'm really disappointed. I thought you were a cool aunt."

Deena held Evie's gaze even though she couldn't help but feel slightly wounded. "I am a cool aunt," she said with more confidence than she felt. "Evie, these pranks, they aren't you. Don't get labeled a prankster. You're so much more than that."

Evie tugged her towel more tightly around herself. "Maybe you're wrong about who I am."

"I'm not wrong," Deena said. "You're a great kid."

Evie made a face as if being a great kid was a terrible thing.

"You are," Deena continued. "A great kid. Now how about we get some pizza before it's all gone?"

They balanced plates with slices of pepperoni pizza and cans of soda and picked their way back to the pool area. The kids had spread out beach towels across the concrete deck and sat in small groups eating. Two counselors set up a large movie screen at the diving end of the pool. Evie spotted Alyssa sitting with Britty, Taylor, and Lourdes and stepped carefully around the bodies to join them.

Deena looked around for a spot to eat. She wanted to stay close to the pool so she could supervise the campers. She'd saved a spot with her beach bag, but the chair had been moved to make more space for the campers and their towels.

A nearby rock retaining wall seemed a good option. She wouldn't be able to see the movie very well, but it would be a nice place to eat. She had just taken her first bite of pizza when Spence walked up to her. "Want some company?"

"Sure." Her heart jumped a bit at the sight of him. She patted the top of the rock. "Just watch out. There are a few hungry ants crawling around."

Spence took his seat. "I can handle it." He bit into his pizza. "I take it you've recovered from the afternoon's activities."

"We clogged the drain in our shower getting all that mud off," Deena admitted. "I used the plunger, though, and everything went right down."

"I could look at it," Spence offered.

"Thanks, but it's under control." Which was more than could be said about her misbehaving heart thumping about in her chest like a wild thing in a cage. Her face burned, too, and she was pretty sure it had nothing to do with being in the sun. With effort, she took her gaze off his face. "You ever look at these kids and wonder what they'll do when they grow up?"

Spence laughed. "I'm still wondering what I'm going to do next." He finished his first slice of pizza and started on the second.

Deena remembered the study guide for the MCAT test on his desk. "You think you might want to be a doctor?"

Spence took his time answering. "I love being an EMT, but what I did isn't something that lends itself well to being a single dad. Not the kind of rescue I want to do."

"You mean you can't pull someone off a cliff and be home for dinner."

"More than that, I don't want Alyssa worrying all the time that something is going to happen to me."

The lights flickered on the movie screen, indicating the movie was about to begin. Neither Deena nor Spence made any move to sit where they could see the screen better.

"Well, you'll make a great doctor, if that's what you decide to do. Would you head into cardiology?"

"Maybe," Spence said, frowning, clearly unhappy with the question. "When you were a little girl, did you know you wanted to be a scientist?"

"I was never little," Deena said. "I was always tall. Every class picture, I'm in the back row." She hadn't liked being tall and would have much preferred to be average sized like Stacy. "I wasn't fat, but this girl in second grade just hated me. She always called me Diana the Giant."

"Your real name is Diana? How did you become Deena?"

Deena wiped her mouth with a napkin. "When I was sixteen I did this science fair project about DNA extraction from soil. I won first place, and afterward everyone starting calling me DNA—you know—deoxyribonucleic acid. Deena kind of stuck."

Spence set his empty plate aside. "Deena's a good name."

"Thanks. Spencer's a good name, too. Were you popular in high school?"

"That was my brother's gift. Wherever Evan went, the party started. I just tagged along."

"You're very likable, Spence." Quickly, before he took her words the wrong way, she added, "I mean, the kids in my cabin think you're really cool."

He looked away and stared into the shadows of the woods around them. "Tell that to Alyssa. Every time I get near her, she looks like she wishes the earth would open up and swallow her." He crumpled his can. "I don't know what I'm doing wrong."

"Maybe you're not doing anything wrong," Deena said gently. She thought about the fear Alyssa had expressed. The fear that she would forget her parents if she stopped grieving for them. "Give her more time."

"I don't have a lot of time," Spence snapped and then immediately apologized. "I'm sorry. You touched a sore spot. The only way I could get her to come to this camp was to promise her after the week ended she could choose between living with me and living with her grandparents in Texas."

Deena shifted on the rough surface of the wall. "She'll pick you. I'm sure of it."

"Then you haven't seen the way she looks at me. Our conversations aren't exactly deep and meaningful either. The harder I try to show I care about her, the more it seems she hates me."

In the distance Deena could see the flickering images on the screen. The shapes of the kids were nothing more than dark lumps. She wondered which lump belonged to Alyssa.

"She doesn't hate you," Deena assured him. "She's a little confused about how she feels." Just like Deena had been—only instead of being angry at her father, she'd been furious with God for taking away her mother.

She remembered Rev. Moleman's long, sad face at her front door, valiantly explaining through the six-inch crack that God hadn't caused her mother's cancer. "If God doesn't change a circumstance, He will use it to His glory. He never wastes a tear, Diana."

She had practically slammed the door shut on him. But the irony of Spence's situation wasn't lost on her now. She could almost hear the old reverend whispering that the time had come when Deena's pain could be used as a blessing to others.

"My mom died, Spence, when I was sixteen. My sister, Stacy, was fourteen. My dad avoided me like the plague and couldn't get enough of Stacy. The only thing that seemed to please him about me was my report card. Otherwise, it seemed like he couldn't stand to be in the same room with me."

She didn't look at him. "I thought I'd done something wrong to make him dislike me so much. But one day when I walked into the room, he called me Evelyn by accident. I realized then why he couldn't bear to be with me. I look just like my mother. Before she got sick, that is."

"So what did you do?"

"I cut my hair." Deena looked past Spence at the still surface of the pool water. She remembered standing in front of the mirror in the upstairs bathroom and staring at herself. The scissors had felt so cold and heavy in her hands as she lifted them. Something in her had wanted to cry when the first hunk of long, wavy hair fell to the floor.

He was silent for a long moment. "Did it help?"

"Yeah," Deena said. "It did."

Spence touched her arm. "Deena, how did your mother die?"

Her mother's gaunt face, pale and exhausted, flashed through Deena's mind. She remembered the tears and the promises and the last time she'd kissed the warm curve of her mother's forehead.

"She had breast cancer," Deena said slowly. "She found a lump and had it biopsied. That led to her first mastectomy. Then they found another spot in her left breast, and she had another mastectomy. It didn't help, though. It kept coming back and coming back and coming back."

65

Chapter 15

Spence slid closer to Deena. He wanted to comfort her, put his arms around her, but was reluctant to do something others might misinterpret. He put his hand on her arm instead. "She'd be pretty proud of you, Deena. What you're doing with your life."

"I'm just telling you this because I think Alyssa isn't trying to push you away as much as she is trying to be loyal to her parents. When you showed up at the tug-of-war game this afternoon, I think she was pleased to see you. The rest was a big act."

As Spence struggled to process this information, Alyssa, Evie, Lourdes, Britty, and Taylor walked up to them.

"Movie is over," Evie informed him.

And it was. For the first time he realized the sound coming from the speakers had stopped and no images flickered on the large screen by the pool.

"We're tired," Evie said.

"And hungry," another girl said. He thought it might be Taylor, but in the moonlight he couldn't tell if her hair was red. He always got her mixed up with Britty.

"I'm a little cold," Lourdes said.

Deena responded immediately. "Oh, honey, let's get you my towel. It's in my bag. If I can find it."

"I think it's by the picnic tables," Spence said.

It didn't take much time to locate Deena's beach bag, but then Deena wanted to stay a little longer and help the other counselors put away the movie screen and stack deck chairs in the utility room. By the time they'd finished, it had grown dark. Spence borrowed a flashlight and volunteered to walk Deena and the girls back to their cabin.

He'd never minded being in the woods at night. Just the opposite. Sometimes when he couldn't quiet his mind, he liked to walk in the darkness. Or just sit outside and look up at the stars. He and God had had more than one conversation this way.

From the giggles and the way the girls had packed into tight clusters behind him, Spence realized they saw the darkness a totally different way.

"Did you hear that?" Evie asked.

"Hear what?" Lourdes said.

"That noise," Evie answered.

"Maybe it was my chewing gum," Taylor said. "I just popped a bubble."

Spence slowed, and Deena nearly walked right into his back. He shined the light at the girls' feet. "We're fine. Don't be scared."

One of the girls giggled. "Every time someone says that in a movie, someone ends up getting chased by another person carrying a very big knife."

"Britty," Deena said. "This isn't a movie. No one is going to come chasing us with a big knife."

Something rustled in the underbrush. Spence tried to listen, but the girls were making too much noise for him to tell. It was probably only an opossum, possibly a raccoon. He began walking again.

"It feels like we're in a cave," one of the girls said.

"Taylor, we're, like, climbing up a hill. How can it feel like we're in a tunnel?" Britty said.

"Because it's really dark," Lourdes replied.

"What if we got lost?" Taylor asked. "What would we do?"

"We're on the path," Spence assured her. "We're not going to get lost. But if you did get lost, the best thing to do is stay right where you are. I'll come find you. I promise."

"What about bears?" Taylor pressed. "Should we stay where we are if we get lost and a bear comes along?"

"Don't worry about bears," Spence said. "It's far more likely we'll run into a skunk. And even then, it wouldn't be a big deal. If you guys got sprayed, we'd mix up some hydrogen peroxide, baking soda, and dish soap, and it'd take the smell right out."

"I'd rather use my cucumber melon body spray," Britty said in a slightly smug tone. "It's got, like, neutralizing odor powers. That's what it says on the label."

"But if a bear jumped out from the woods, what should we do, Mr. Spence?" Taylor asked.

Deena half expected Britty would suggest spraying it with her Freeze and Shine hairspray, but nobody said anything, which told her the girls weren't entirely convinced they were safe.

"Just stand very still and let me handle it," Spence said. "I wouldn't let any of you get hurt."

They were silent for a moment, and then Britty stopped walking. "Did you hear that? I heard something. Branches cracking. Growling. I think something is stalking us!"

"You heard my stomach digesting," Deena said very firmly. "And we're almost at the cabin, right, Spence?"

"Very close," Spence agreed. "Sometimes noises can be misleading. Remember the night I slept on your porch? It was pretty late, and I was just about to go to sleep when I heard an animal growling. I thought it was a bear, but when I listened a little longer, I realized the noise was coming from *inside* the cabin." He paused. "And it wasn't an animal growling. It was someone snoring." He paused as the girls laughed. "One of you really knows how to saw wood."

CONNECTICUT WEDDINGS

There was silence; then Evie said soberly, "It was you, Aunt Deena."

Deena laughed. "Oh, Evie, I don't snore."

"You were snoring so loudly it sounded like airplanes taking off and landing," Spence said, thoroughly enjoying himself.

The girls giggled. "I'm sure you were dreaming about a wild animal growling," Deena replied.

He denied it, of course, and they bantered back and forth until they reached the cabin steps. He paused as the girls said good night and ran inside. Of course Alyssa didn't pause to say anything to him, nothing at all, and the weight of disappointment settled over him.

Deena paused beneath the porch lights. Her dark hair gleamed, and he tried to imagine it long. Would it be straight or wavy? He wasn't sure. She would look beautiful either way. She also looked beautiful with short hair. It showed off the strength of her character, the bone structure that needed no enhancement.

"Thanks for walking us back," Deena said. "I hope you have good dreams. With no bears growling—or, rather, snoring."

"If I were dreaming," he said for her ears only as he stared straight at her, "I could think of a lot better things than a bear snoring." He locked gazes with her so she'd know exactly what he meant. "Night, Diana. Sleep well."

She stiffened. "Please, Spence, call me Deena. It's who I am now."

"Okay, Dee," he teased. "See you in the morning."

She made an exasperated noise, shook her head, and smiled as if she couldn't help herself. "Good night, funny guy. Try to take the night off from rescuing someone, okay?" The screen door creaked as she pulled it open and then lightly banged it shut behind her.

68

Chapter 16

Her alarm clock went off. Deena stirred. It felt like she'd just gone to bed. It couldn't be time to get up already. She opened her eyes and tried to focus. Everything looked a bit blurry. The ceiling looked different. Lower. A lot lower. Like inches above her face. And made out of a white, gauzy material.

She blinked and lifted her fingers to explore. Something as soft as Kleenex was wrapped all around her. Then it hit her what had happened. Someone had rolled her bed in toilet paper.

"Evie!"

A chorus of giggles split the silence.

Deena ripped a hole in the covering and sat up. Her entire bunk had been rolled, and streamers of loose toilet paper hung over the edges. From below five girls laughed up at her.

"This isn't funny," Deena said. She pulled a length of tissue from her hair. "Evie?"

"I'm sorry," Evie said, sounding anything but. "But last night you were snoring, just like Mr. Spence said, and none of us could sleep. So we decided to play a joke on you."

"What if I'd suffocated?"

"We left you air holes. Did you know, Aunt Deena, that you're a really sound sleeper? One of the rolls got dropped on your head, and you didn't even wake up."

Deena shook her head. How many times did she have to make excuses for Evie? Why couldn't a girl as intelligent as her niece understand that pranks weren't funny?

"Are you mad at us?" This came from Britty, who was twisting a length of her blond hair around her finger. Taylor, chewing her usual wad of gum, looked a little worried, too.

Deena climbed down from the bunk. "No. Not mad. But I am disappointed. Please clean this mess up while I figure out what I'm going to do about this." She marched off in the direction of the bathroom.

"Aunt Deena?"

"Yes, Evie?"

"Are you going to tell my mother about this?"

It was the last thing Deena wanted to do. Stacy needed to rest. She studied the girl's face as another thought suddenly occurred to her. "Do you want me to tell her? Is that why you keep doing things like this?"

69

Evie laughed. "Of course not. I absolutely do not want you to tell my mother."

"You sure?" What, then? What was reinforcing Evie's behavior? Deena took another step toward the bathroom.

"You might not want to go in there," Evie warned.

"Why?" The hair on the back of Deena's neck stood up. "Why wouldn't I want to go in there?"

"Because," Evie said, trying unsuccessfully not to giggle, "we're out of toilet paper."

~

They very nearly missed breakfast. By the time they'd gone through the cafeteria lines, the room was nearly empty. All except for Pastor Rich, who was just finishing a cup of coffee. He waved at her, and Deena wondered why he wasn't already at the amphitheater, preparing for the morning service.

Only on closer inspection, she realized it wasn't Pastor Rich at all.

Deena slid into a seat across from Spence. "You shaved your head." She set her tray down on a cafeteria table. "For a moment I thought you were Pastor Rich."

"I didn't shave my head," Spence protested. "I cut it short. Only it came out slightly shorter than I thought it would."

Deena tried not to stare. He'd pretty much scalped himself. She had to admit, though, that he looked almost as good in the buzz cut as he did with longer hair. "I like it."

Spence looked unsure. "You sure?"

Deena grinned. "Yeah, I do."

"The main thing is, do I look different?"

"You look very different," Deena assured him. "I hardly recognized you at first."

"Good."

"Hey, Mr. Spence," Evie said, joining them at the table. "You look like a soldier. One of those special agent guys." She and the rest of the girls from their cabin took seats around them.

"I'm still just a camp nurse," Spence replied, but his gaze traveled to his niece and stayed there. "What do you think, Alyssa?"

The girl took her time pouring maple syrup on her french toast and didn't look up. "I think you look like Pastor Rich."

Deena very nearly laughed and managed only by extreme effort to shoot Spence a sympathetic look. "She means you look very pastorish, very spiritual."

"My head is not shaved." Spence bent his head so they could examine it. "It must be the lighting in here."

"Must be the lighting," Deena agreed, and the girls laughed—all but Alyssa.

Unfortunately, Spence noticed this as well. It nearly broke Deena's heart to see the disappointment in his eyes. Obviously he'd taken the story she'd told him last night to heart. He had changed his appearance so there was no chance Alyssa would think Spence looked like his brother. However, while cutting her hair had helped her father to see Deena in a new way, it obviously wasn't working for Spence.

"What do you think, Alyssa?" Deena tried. "Do you think he'd look better with a Mohawk?"

"No. Uncle Spence looked better before." She turned to Evie. "You want my bacon?"

Spence looked at Deena, who shrugged. *Keep trying,* she wanted to whisper. Even if Alyssa didn't understand, she did.

"Be careful," Deena warned as Evie popped the entire strip into her mouth. "I nearly broke a tooth trying to chew that bacon."

"Oh, Aunt Deena," Evie said, speaking through a full mouth. "Didn't anyone tell you that you have to let it soak in your mouth for a little bit?"

Deena laughed. "No, they didn't, but I learned the trick to eating the cold eggs." She grinned. "You hold your nose when you eat them." She glanced around. No one was laughing.

"TMI." Britty shook her blond head.

"Too much information," Taylor translated.

"Your eggs wouldn't have been cold if you hadn't been so late to breakfast," Spence pointed out.

"We would have been here earlier if we hadn't had to hike to the pool cabana for extra supplies." She stared pointedly at Evie.

"We wrapped Aunt Deena in toilet paper," Evie reported happily. "I mean her bunk. When she was in it."

Spence set down his coffee cup. "You what?"

Deena nodded. "It was like waking up in a Kleenex box."

The girls exchanged looks and giggled. All but Alyssa, who pushed her french toast around her plate.

"I've never woken up in a Kleenex box," Spence said. "But one Halloween I had my brother, Evan, wrap me in toilet paper. I was supposed to be a mummy. Evan wound me so tight I couldn't bend my legs, and I couldn't climb the front steps to any of the houses when we trick-or-treated. Terrible idea. He didn't share his candy."

Alyssa stood abruptly. "Excuse me, but I need to use the bathroom."

Deena frowned and rose to her feet, only to find Evie already in motion. "I'll go," she said.

The other girls rose as well. They disappeared en masse in the direction Alyssa had gone, leaving Deena alone with Spence.

"Girls like to go in groups to the restroom," Deena said, but she hated to see Spence look so discouraged.

"The restrooms are in the other direction," Spence said. "I shouldn't have mentioned Evan."

He looked so upset that Deena wanted to wipe away the lines of worry etched across his face. "You didn't say anything wrong. Someday she's going to cherish hearing about your memories of her father."

"Not all of them." Spence crumpled his empty paper cup. "Not all of them."

~

Deena slipped into the back of the amphitheater just as the morning service began.

Several rows down, she spotted Evie's copper hair. She and Lourdes had sandwiched Alyssa, with Britty and Taylor making bookends.

The worship music began. She was getting used to the volume of it, and although her teeth began to vibrate, she couldn't help tapping her foot to the beat of the music.

Her mother would have loved this camp. She would have volunteered, too, if her health had permitted. It was easy to imagine her now, singing along in that off-key voice that Deena would give anything to hear again.

Other memories stirred. Her mother bragging to other people that Deena had read the warning label on the Pampers box before she'd been old enough to be out of diapers. Her mother telling Deena that her intelligence was a gift from God and someday she would have an opportunity to use her gift for His glory.

Deena looked across the lake. She had tried so hard to keep her promise to her mother, to help others with breast cancer. Yet sometimes she felt so empty and lonely on the inside that she wasn't sure she could even make it through another day.

The music ended, and Pastor Rich spoke into the microphone. "Good morning, Camp Bald Eagle!"

"Good morning, Pastor Rich!" the campers roared.

"I can't hear you!" Pastor Rich teased, his bald head glistening in the sunlight.

"*Good morning, Pastor Rich!*"

Not only could Pastor Rich hear that, but so could anyone within ten miles.

"What day is this?"

The kids yelled, "It's Luau Day!"

Deena groaned. She'd been dreading this part of the camp ever since she'd read about it in the cabin counselor's training guide. Everyone was supposed to dress in grass skirts and wear leis. And if that weren't ridiculous enough, that evening every cabin would put on a skit in front of the entire camp.

"It's Luau Day," Pastor Rich confirmed. "And we're going to have some fun!"

The kids cheered wildly.

"We're going to have a pig roast and a talent show tonight," Pastor Rich said. "Each cabin will provide us with a skit. It can be musical, or lyrical, or anything you choose, but it must have a Hawaiian theme. We'll have some materials available in the commissary that you can use. All of you"—here he paused to open his arms to indicate everyone in the audience—"will be voting on the skits, and the winners will get to ride on the lake on a banana boat during the last day of camp."

A banana boat? Deena didn't even know what a banana boat was. As far as she was concerned, someone else could enjoy an afternoon on the lake riding a piece of fruit. She wasn't dressing up like an island girl or as anything else. She hadn't worn a costume in twenty-five years, and even then it had been Halloween.

"You will be judged on creativity, props, and story line," Pastor Rich continued. "Good luck, and aloha!"

Aloha? Everyone else could prance around in a grass skirt, but Deena definitely was sitting this one out.

Chapter 17

Deena smoothed the strands of her crinkly grass skirt. If any of her fellow researchers saw her now, they would never let her live it down. She still couldn't believe the girls had talked her into performing with them. She wasn't a hula dancer. She was a scientist. Scientists wore lab coats, not grass skirts, plastic leis, and ridiculous pink plastic hibiscus flowers in their hair.

"Girls' blue cabin, you're on deck. Are you ready?"

Deena stared at the perky young counselor holding the clipboard. Yes, she was ready. Ready to check herself into the nearest psychiatric facility. "Yes, we're all here."

In just a few moments, she and the girls would step out onto the amphitheater stage.

Mr. Crackers shifted on her shoulder, and she winced at the feel of his claws on her skin. *It's all your fault,* she wanted to tell the bird. If only Evie hadn't thought including the parrot in their skit would add authenticity, Deena would be in the audience, maybe even enjoying the show.

Behind her Britty asked, "Does anyone have a safety pin? My skirt is, like, a little big."

And Deena's was a little small. That was the problem with one-size-fits-all grass skirts. "I thought we pinned your skirt, Britty, honey."

"We did, but the safety pin, like, must have fallen off when we walked over here."

"Tuck it into the waistband of your shorts," Deena advised.

Polite applause greeted the team currently performing onstage. Deena shifted her weight.

From the stage, two boys began talking. Their dialogue seemed to consist of two words and two words only: "Unga munga." However, each used different inflections and emphasis. It was silly, but kind of funny, too. Judging by the laughter coming from the spectators, they thought so, too.

"I feel sick," Taylor announced. "I may throw up."

"It's just stage nerves," Deena assured her. "Did you finish that peppermint Life Saver I gave you?"

"Yes," Taylor said sadly. "You don't have another, do you?"

"No."

"Unga munga!"

"Oh. Unga munga munga!"

"What are they saying?" Lourdes asked. "I don't understand a word."

"They aren't speaking English." Deena added, "You really look lovely, Lourdes, with your hair all loose like that."

" 'Lyssa," Evie said. "Take off your glasses."

"But I can't see without them."

"You don't need to see," Evie pointed out. "You just need to do everything we've been practicing all day. Besides, hula dancers don't wear glasses."

"Where will I put them?"

"Stick them in your coconuts," Britty advised, adjusting her own set.

Despite the coolness of the evening, Deena's forehead broke out in sweat.

"Are you ready?" Pastor Rich asked then swung back the sheet.

Deena drew a shaky breath and walked onto the stage. The spotlight nearly blinded her. The audience looked like one big blur of darkness. Around her the girls scurried about, setting out the cardboard palm trees that listed just as badly as Jeff's tree house.

"Ladies and gentlemen," the announcer boomed. "I now have the pleasure of introducing our next performers. Please join me in welcoming the girls' blue cabin!"

Polite applause greeted them. Deena took her place and arranged her arms in the same position she'd seen in the Internet photo of a hula dancer.

Their music, also downloaded from the Internet, started. On the fifth note, just as they'd practiced, they all started to hula.

Deena tried not to wiggle around too much. If Mr. Crackers gripped her shoulder any more tightly, it was going to take a surgical procedure to get him off.

Lourdes, who had been miked, began to narrate their skit. Her sweet voice easily carried up the hill. "We are all hunters looking for that next big trophy to hang on the wall of our lives."

This was the cue for the girls to move around the stage fluttering their arms and hunting each other among the cardboard palms.

"Every waking moment of every day we think about that next trophy, imagining it will bring us happiness."

Alyssa walked into one of the cardboard palm trees, which immediately fell over.

"We hunt popularity," Lourdes said. "But that isn't enough. We hunt good grades, but still it doesn't fill the void inside. We hunt the mall for the right clothes, for iPods, MP3 players, cell phones, and computers. And still we're restless, hunting, thinking about what we want. What we need. The next thing that will make us happy."

Britty's skirt was hanging precariously low, and Deena reached out and hiked it back up as the blond danced past.

"But what we're looking for, what we really want, isn't something you buy. You can't find it at the mall, or save up for it with your allowance, or get it from your friends. We're looking for a relationship with the God who made us. He is the only One who can fill us with His everlasting love."

All the girls lifted their arms, and Taylor and Britty, who had taken tumbling classes together in fourth grade, did simultaneous backflips then went straight into splits.

Deena beamed as the audience enthusiastically clapped and whistled. Their show wasn't over; there still was one more part of their skit. The audience needed to be quiet before they could do it, so they all had to stand there for a while. It was hard to maintain a big smile for such a long period of time, but finally all the cheers subsided and the applauding become more sporadic and then stopped entirely. Finally, the amphitheater fell quiet.

It was time for the grand finale. Deena stepped forward into the spotlight. She looked at Evie to cue the parrot to say, "Aloha!"

Her niece coughed.

The bird stretched his wings and squawked loudly, "P-U. Who cut the cheese?"

Deena felt her jaw drop. *Please tell me Mr. Crackers didn't just say that. Not here. Not now.*

Evie coughed again.

"P-U," Mr. Crackers shouted happily. "Who cut the cheese?"

The audience started to laugh. Deena glanced around. Evie was holding her nose and trying not to laugh.

Evie.

Deena felt her blood start to boil. How could she? She must have been planning this for some time. Deena turned toward her, more upset than she had been in a long time. Maybe even in her entire life. So what if the audience was laughing and applauding like crazy. Her niece had done it again, played a prank when Deena had specifically asked her to stop. And this time she'd used poor Mr. Crackers.

The poor bird, however, seemed to be enjoying his moment in the spotlight. "P-U," he squawked as the audience whistled and shouted. "Who—"

"Aloha!" Deena shouted over the bird's voice. She marched toward the side exit with Mr. Crackers clinging to her shoulder like a bird caught in a strong gale wind. She stepped behind the sheet separating the backstage area and realized the rest of the girls weren't following. She pulled the sheet back.

The girls were still onstage. Evie, the little monkey, was waving her hand around as if she were trying to clear the air. Lourdes had doubled over, and Britty and Taylor clung to each other, laughing so hard they no longer could produce any sound.

And Alyssa. Deena blinked. The girl's head was thrown back and her ponytail bounced with the force of her laughter. She was transformed—so beautiful it almost took her breath away.

This was the Alyssa Spence had known existed deep inside but could not reach. Deena couldn't breathe. She just stared at the girl who had once been Allergy Girl and saw the transforming delight on her face.

"Girls!" Deena whispered loudly. "Come here!"

With final bows to the audience, the girls moved in Deena's direction. As they slipped through the gap in the sheet, they hugged each other, limp from laughter but sparkly-eyed with success.

Deena stared at their flushed faces, wondering if she should be strict or soft and feeling incredibly stupid because she was thirty-five years old and had no idea whether she should punish Evie or thank her.

"Come on, ladies," she said, stalling and also trying to find a more private area to talk to them. The sandy part of the beach provided her solution. "That was an awesome performance," she said as they gathered around her. "Now drop down and give me twenty."

Evie stared at her with eyes as bright as stars. "Twenty what?"

"Push-ups," Deena stated firmly. "You crossed the line by teaching Mr. Crackers an inappropriate phrase. Do you know how hard it's going to be to train him not to say that whenever someone coughs?"

"I'm sorry," Evie said. "I take total responsibility. It was my idea. The punishment should be mine and mine alone." Her chin, small and slightly pointed, tilted skyward.

"No," Alyssa said firmly. "It wasn't just you. I helped." She dropped to the sand.

"So did I." Britty joined Alyssa on the sand.

A moment later all the girls were lying facedown struggling with the push-ups. None of them could actually do a push-up, but they were trying, giggling and gasping encouragement to each other.

Somehow, somewhere along the way, they'd bonded—become more than five girls who shared the blue cabin.

They'd become friends.

Chapter 18

Spence pushed his way through the laughing crowd. He glimpsed Deena heading toward the water. He picked up the pace, nearly colliding with a boy holding a huge cardboard sailfish.

"Sorry," he mumbled, steadying the boy.

Stepping beyond the perimeter of the amphitheater, he scanned the semi-darkness. What had just happened? The dance had been cute and Lourdes's narration moving. Just seeing Deena in that grass skirt had been hugely entertaining. And then the grand finale.

Who had taught that bird that phrase? Not Deena—he'd seen the shock on her face. But it really didn't matter who. He'd seen Alyssa's face. It was the face of a girl having the time of her life.

He scanned the beach area for a group. The area seemed deserted; then he spotted a tall shape near the water. He moved closer.

He saw Deena illuminated in the moonlight. She had her hands on her hips and was studying five dark shapes in the sand. He paused. The kids were doing. . . push-ups?

"Deena!"

She looked up. "Hey, Spence."

"What's going on?"

"Push-ups."

"I can see that." He reached her side. "Why?"

"Because of the prank," Deena said matter-of-factly as if he should know. "You think Mr. Crackers was supposed to ask who cut the cheese?"

"Ten," Evie shouted breathlessly. "That's ten."

"It was funny," Spence said.

"It was inappropriate. I just hope none of us gets kicked out of camp."

Spence touched her arm. The feel of her skin did things to him on the inside that he prayed didn't show on the outside. "I've never heard of anyone getting kicked out of church camp."

"We could be the first," Deena said. "Stacy warned me. She said to always be prepared for the worst. 'Stay on your toes, Deena; you can't control teenagers like you can your lab experiments. Think chaos theory.' She was right."

"Fifteen," Evie groaned. "Can we stop now?"

"No," Deena said.

"It's okay, Deena. Even Pastor Rich was laughing. Don't make more of this than it is."

"I'm not, but if I don't do something, Spence, the next time it might be something even worse. I've been much too lackadaisical about this whole pseudoparenting thing."

More groans emanated from the girls. One of them collapsed on her belly and just lay there. His gaze traveled to Alyssa illuminated in the moonlight. For a moment, he imagined it was Evan lying there struggling to meet their dad's punishment.

How many times had he and Evan lain in that same position doing push-ups until it felt like their arms were on fire and their bodies weighed a million pounds? It'd been torture then, but looking back he realized he had never felt closer to his older brother than when they were both grunting in pain and exhaustion.

He missed Evan.

He dug the tip of his sneaker into the sand. He'd let his brother down so badly. He should have seen beneath the happy-go-lucky smile and slap on the shoulder. But no, Spence had been so busy saving total strangers that he'd failed to see his brother needed him even more.

Worse than failed to see. If he was brutally honest, he'd admit he'd known something was wrong with Evan. Maybe not 100 percent certain, but he'd silenced the voice that said the drink in his brother's hand was there far too often. He hadn't wanted to know. That was the truth that kept him up at night.

He would not make that mistake again. God came first, of course, but family came second. And the best way to make up for his failure to his brother was to care for Alyssa. Best he could, he'd raise her right.

"Twenty!" Evie shouted.

Twenty had come pretty fast on the heels of fifteen, but Spence kept that thought to himself. The girls scrambled to their feet, laughing and shaking sand from their clothing and limbs.

"Can we go back to the amphitheater and watch the rest of the performances now?" Evie asked.

"Sure," Deena replied. "Save me a seat. I'll be with you in a minute." Her gaze traveled to his face, and the look said she wanted to be alone with him. Despite the orders of his brain, his heart picked up its beat.

As soon as the girls were out of earshot, Deena turned to him, grinning. "Did you see Alyssa's face when Mr. Crackers spoke? It was like looking at another girl. I didn't know she could be like that."

"She hasn't been like that for a long time," Spence said. "Thank you, Deena. I had my doubts, but you're reaching her in a way I never could have."

Deena waved off his praise. "If you're going to give anyone credit, you probably need to give it to my wild niece." She shook her head, loosening the pink hibiscus pinned just above her ear. "Every time she opens her mouth, I'm terrified what's going to come out of it."

"She's good hearted, like her aunt." Spence's fingers itched to straighten that hibiscus, and not because he cared it was drooping. He simply wanted to touch her. "By the way, where'd you learn to hula like that?"

"Oh, the Internet. You should have seen the girls practicing, Spence. Every one of us heard a different beat. And the hip movements. The instructions said to move from our knees, but none of us could get it until Britty told us to pretend we were putting on the world's tightest jeans."

He would have paid money to see that. He realized then that he didn't want to miss anything else. Not this week, and not beyond that. Here in the moonlight, his heart couldn't make it any clearer that this woman belonged with him. With him and Alyssa.

"Let's take a walk," he said.

"I probably should get back," Deena said, glancing back at the brightly lit amphitheater.

"The girls will be fine for a few minutes." He reached for her hand. "Please. It's such a nice night."

Deena hesitated. "What about Mr. Crackers?"

"He can come, too. We're not going far. There's just something I want to show you."

She hesitated a second time and again glanced at the amphitheater. "Maybe just a short one, but then I have to get back."

The shoreline quickly changed from sandy to rocky. Spence moved slowly, giving Deena time to pick her way over the uneven surface. The water lapped softly, a gentle, soothing noise that came out of the darkness, almost lost in the night. They followed the shoreline, and it wasn't long before they reached the boathouse and the long arm of the dock reaching out into the lake.

"This is where I wanted to bring you," Spence said, stepping up onto the wooden platform. "It's really beautiful out here at night."

Their footsteps sounded hollow as they walked out on the dock. It was a clear night, and the stars shone down on them. "This is beautiful," Deena whispered. "It's almost like we're standing on moonlight."

You're beautiful, he thought. *Inside and out.* He had always calculated the risk in getting involved in a relationship, but standing next to her, he felt like throwing caution to the wind. He had to clench his hands into fists to keep from reaching for her. This wasn't just a summer camp fling, he realized. His feelings went deeper, well beyond that. Spence closed his eyes.

He saw the irony of the whole situation. He had built a career based on rescuing people. Finding them when they were lost and patching them up when they hurt themselves. He'd come to this camp, in fact, with the hope that it would allow him to rescue his niece emotionally and spiritually. He had been so sure her healing would begin here.

It had never occurred to him, though, that the person who needed rescuing most just might be himself.

And Deena might very well be the only woman who could do it.

Chapter 19

I still can't believe we won the skit competition," Lourdes remarked as they headed for the stable area the next morning.

"It's going to be so cool going out on that banana boat," Evie exclaimed. "I can't wait!"

Deena had nearly been struck dumb when Pastor Rich had announced their cabin as the winner, but it had been a crazy night. Seeing Alyssa come out of herself. Taking that walk with Spence. There was something special about this camp. Stacy had been right. It was life changing.

Taylor popped a bubble. "You were right, Evie. Mr. Crackers was our secret weapon."

Deena frowned. "We were fortunate that no one was offended by what Mr. Crackers said. Absolutely no more pranks. Got it, girls?" She gave Evie a sideways glance.

"No more pranks, Aunt Deena." Evie's voice was pure innocence.

"No more pranks," Taylor, Britty, Lourdes, and Alyssa chimed in, but they giggled.

Now that she had been in charge of the girls for almost a week, Deena had a whole new respect for Stacy. Parenting required all sorts of skills—medical, psychological, athletic, even creative ones like dancing and acting. It was all very exhausting. But fun, too.

They reached the big red barn. The horses were already saddled and tied to a hitching post outside the stable. Deena's steps slowed. The only animal she was used to being around was Mr. Crackers, and he was a lot smaller than these horses. She swallowed. Why couldn't the girls simply play horseshoes this morning? Did they absolutely have to go riding?

A teenage girl stepped out of the barn. She had on jeans and a pair of chocolate-colored chaps. "Good morning," she said. "Let's get you all some safety helmets to wear; then I'll assign you each a horse to ride."

A few minutes later, Deena tugged the strap of her helmet unhappily. "Are you sure this one is gentle?" she asked. The equine giant in front of her kept tossing its huge head up and down. The horse's feet were enormous, too—like dinner plates.

"Petunia is very gentle," Kendra, the riding instructor, assured her. Of course Kendra, like most of the counselors in the camp, looked about fifteen years old. Kids that age didn't understand that when you were older than thirty, you started thinking about things like breaking your neck.

"It's chewing that bit like it wishes it were my arm," Deena pointed out.

"Don't worry," Kendra said.

Deena hesitated. The last horse she'd ridden had been on the carousel at the mall. She'd gotten kind of woozy after the second time it went around. "Isn't there a smaller horse?"

Kendra, who barely reached Deena's shoulder, was putting all her ninety or so pounds into tightening the girth. Even Deena, who knew absolutely nothing about horses, could tell the beast was holding its breath. They hadn't given her a dumb one, and this realization wasn't helping with her anxiety.

She wondered if horses, like dogs, could smell fear. She patted its hairy neck tentatively, and the horse twitched as if she'd tickled it with a feather. It rolled one huge brown eye back at her and chomped enthusiastically on the metal bit.

Kendra kneed the horse in its stomach and jerked the girth tight. Sweating, she wiped her forehead and motioned for Deena to climb aboard.

Get on now? The horse was probably angry about just having been kneed in the stomach.

There it went again, chewing on the bit and shivering as if it had something crawling beneath its skin. "Why's he doing that? I mean she."

"Petunia is just shooing flies." The teenager moved to the opposite side of the horse and leaned against the other stirrup. "You can get on now."

Yeah, right. The horse seemed tall as a mountain. Deena drew a deep breath then tried to put her foot in the stirrup. It was a bit of a stretch, so she dropped the reins and wrapped her hand around the pommel of the saddle. She leaned back a little and managed to hook the stirrup.

This accomplished, she paused to rest for a minute, and as she did, two horses walked past in single file. Without any warning, Deena's horse fell into step behind them. Deena, attached by the stirrup, had to hop alongside. She sailed right past Britty, who was in the process of adjusting her stirrups.

"Miss Deena, what are you doing?" Britty's voice rang with horror.

Deena didn't have the breath to reply. Petunia seemed to be picking up speed, and she had to use all her energy to hop along beside her. Deena had no idea how long she could keep this up, but then, fortunately, the horse in front of them stopped. Petunia, either dumber than Deena had thought or exceptionally nearsighted, bumped into the other horse's rear and stopped.

Panting, Deena tried to pull her foot free of the stirrup. No success—her left foot remained firmly wedged in the wooden triangle.

"I thought you had her," Kendra, seconds behind, snapped. "You were supposed to hold the reins."

With her legs still locked in a near split stretch, Deena did not feel in the position to argue. "Sorry."

She waited until Kendra had a grip on both the horse and the saddle, then muscled her way into the saddle. Once aboard, she realized the world had taken on a new splendor.

"Hold your reins like this," Kendra instructed. Deena barely heard her. She kept looking around, awed by how different everything looked from the back of a horse.

The transformation was amazing. Thrilling, even. Like the first time she'd peered through a microscope and watched a whole new world come into focus.

If someone had told her a week ago she would be horseback riding in the foothills of the Berkshires, she would have laughed them out of her laboratory.

But now she could see Stacy had been right—there was a whole world beyond her laboratory that she knew nothing about. She took a deep breath. Well, she was discovering it now. And she liked it.

She wished Spence was there to see her being adventurous. Successfully adventurous. Not falling into a patch of poison ivy, getting clunked on the head with a kayak paddle, or hitting other people's targets on the archery field.

The line moved forward, each horse following the one in front through a wooden gate and into a grassy field. A thin brown line marked the path, and on each side lush green grass grew as high as the horses' knees. A cool, gentle breeze riffled the strands of Deena's hair, and the sunshine felt strong and warm on her face.

The rocking motion of the horse lulled her. She allowed herself to relive last night's moonlit walk with Spence. Standing on the dock with him had been the most romantic moment she'd ever experienced.

The reins slipped through her fingers as Petunia put her head down to graze. The mare's strong jaws ripped off a good-sized chunk of grass. Deena tried to pull the horse's head up, but it would have been easier to lift a block of concrete.

"Give her a kick," Kendra yelled from atop the lead horse.

Deena tapped the horse's sides tentatively with her heels. The horse didn't move.

"Harder," Kendra yelled.

Deena nudged Petunia's sides a bit harder. She didn't want to hurt her. She strained to pull up the horse's head, which now seemed firmly bolted to the ground. Nobody else's horse seemed so hungry. Petunia tore at that grass like a power mower.

Deena peered down the long slide of the mare's neck. She didn't see how the horse could chew with that metal bit in its mouth. What if Petunia started choking? Did you give a horse the Heimlich?

Petunia now had a substantial wad of grass sticking out of her mouth. Deena was about to point this out to Kendra, but then the horse went into a convulsion. Every inch shivered violently.

Deena's feet flew out of the stirrups. She had a last, awful thought that they'd given her a horse with mad cow disease; then the world turned upside down. The next thing she knew, she was lying flat on her back in the grass.

Chapter 20

Spence was getting ice for a boy who had bitten his lip on the Leap of Faith when Deena limped into his clinic. She waved feebly and sank into one of the waiting chairs.

He instructed the boy to ice his lip for fifteen minutes, patted his bony shoulder, and told him to be more careful next time. The boy had hardly made it through the door, when Spence hurried over to Deena.

She seemed okay—there was grass in her hair and a small dirt stain on her jeans. "Deena, what happened?"

She smiled. "I hurt my toe. It's nothing, really. I wouldn't have bothered you, but the girls insisted."

"Let's take a look." He put his arm around her. Leaning most of her weight against him, he walked her to the examination table.

"Spence, I can walk. You really don't have to—"

"Shh. Just tell me what happened." He helped her onto the exam table and reached for her sneaker.

"I fell off a horse," Deena admitted.

He checked her eyes for signs of a concussion. Thankfully her pupils looked fine, and Spence relaxed a little. "You fell off a horse and landed on your toe?"

"No. That happened afterward."

Spence pulled off her white cotton sock and saw the problem immediately. Her big toe was swollen and an angry red color.

"Can you move it?" He tested the joint, and when he was satisfied it wasn't broken, he set her foot down and retrieved an ice pack from the mini refrigerator.

"Yeah, but it hurts. Spence, the horse had an agenda."

Horses didn't have agendas, and he had to hide a smile at the notion. "And you think this because. . . ?"

"It pretended to be dumb, but it wasn't." Deena stiffened as he placed the ice pack on her injured toe. "It pulled the reins out of my hands and started eating grass. When I peeked to see if it was choking, it started shaking wildly, throwing me off. And then when I got to my feet, it stepped on my toe and wouldn't get off. I pushed and pushed. This was not a thin horse, Spence."

He was going to laugh. If he as much looked at her face, it was all over. He bit his lip. "I don't think your toe is broken," he managed. "You just need some ice and some ibuprofen."

"You think it's funny." She looked wounded.

84

He swallowed. "No, I don't. It had to be very frightening. And painful." And funny. He wanted to laugh so badly it hurt.

"I'm not much of a nature girl, huh?"

No, she wasn't. She looked so cute sitting there, all blue eyed and rumple haired. It was all he could do not to pull her into his arms. Instead, he pulled a blade of grass from her hair. "You don't have to be an outdoors girl. I like you just the way you are."

She looked away. "Maybe you just don't know me." It was almost a mumble and the last thing he would expect her to say. The small showing of insecurity gave him the impetus to plunge forward.

"Listen, I've been thinking. What do you say I take you out when this camp ends?"

"Out?" She paused. "Out where?"

"Anywhere you want."

"You mean go out on a date?" Her light blue eyes found his. The fear in them wasn't flattering. Still, he'd come this far, and there was no retreating.

"Yeah. Dinner and a movie."

Silence.

"You can pick the movie." He heard the tension in his voice but couldn't seem to do anything about it. "I prefer an action type, but I'm open to one of those chick flicks, too."

Deena studied the speckled tile floor. A very bad feeling took root in his stomach. "You're involved with someone, aren't you?" Idiot. He should have guessed.

"No, it's not that."

"Then what?"

"It's my job, Spence. I practically live in my lab. I don't have time for a personal life." She shifted higher on the exam table. "But thanks for asking."

He should let it go. Question asked and answered. Anything further bordered on harassment. Yet as he looked at her, she seemed more in pain than when she'd limped into his clinic. He leaned forward. "We can forget the movie, then, but how about the dinner? Even cancer researchers have to eat."

She shifted on the table. "Spence, I'm sorry, but I can't." She looked at the open door. "How much longer do I have to keep the ice on my foot?"

"Ten more minutes." Ten more minutes to try to convince her to go out with him. It might be the last opportunity he had. "Deena, I really like you, and I think you like me, too. Will you at least tell me the truth about why you won't go out with me?"

She continued to study the floor. "I am telling you the truth," she said at last. "I can't have a relationship with you because of my work."

"Deena, I didn't come here to find a relationship. It was the last thing on my mind, but the more I get to know you, the more I believe God has brought us together for a reason. Don't you?"

Deena considered his question for so long he thought she wouldn't answer.

But then she lifted her head and pushed her hair behind her ears. "Spence, I'm here because I chose to come, and so are you. I used to think everything happened for a reason, but then my mom got sick. I believed God could do anything. All you had to do was believe hard enough and ask Him. Well, I asked Him to heal my mother. My whole family, my church, my school, and my town asked Him to spare her, and He didn't. Where was He when my mother was lying in bed in so much pain that you couldn't touch her without making her cry?"

"He was with her, Deena."

"She suffered a lot, Spence."

"He didn't cause the pain."

"But He allowed it. She suffered, Spence, just like thousands of women are suffering every day. I promised my mom I would find a way to help other women with breast cancer."

"I understand you're doing important work, but that doesn't mean you have to sacrifice everything else."

"Sometimes at night I dream about my mother. I wake up at three in the morning. I see her tortured, exhausted eyes. I wasn't in time to help her, but I might be able to help other women."

Spence's heart ached at the sight of Deena's beautiful blue eyes swimming with tears. "I admire what you're doing and your passion for helping others, but, Deena, you don't have to do this alone."

"I have Mr. Crackers."

"He's a nice bird, but he's a bird all the same."

She shifted, and the ice pack fell from her foot. He replaced it and held it there. He had the feeling she'd jump right off the table and run out the door if he didn't hold on to some part of her.

"I'm not as selfless as you think," Deena said flatly. "I told you about my mother, but not about Aunt Betsy or Grandma Dee. They both died of breast cancer, too. Have you ever heard of BRCA1 or BRCA2?"

Spence felt a chill even greater than the one seeping through the ice pack into his hand. "They're genetic tests for breast cancer."

"Yes." Deena swallowed. "Spence, I have BRCA1. My sister and my dad know, but Evie doesn't. Please don't tell her."

Spence released the ice bag, and it fell to the side of her foot. He racked his brain for everything he'd ever read about breast cancer and for something encouraging to say. "That means you have a higher risk of getting cancer than other women, but it doesn't mean you will absolutely get it."

"It means I have a 70 percent chance of developing breast cancer sometime in my life."

"What about surgery? Or drugs like tamoxifen? Isn't that supposed to be a preventive medication?"

She shook her head. "Prophylactic surgery won't guarantee I won't get cancer. And tamoxifen hasn't been proven to help women with BRCA1. BRCA2, yes." She shrugged. "Do you still want to take me to dinner?"

Spence ignored the warning flash in his brain that told him he should think about his answer, take his time and pray about it. "Yeah, I do."

"Well, you shouldn't. What if we got involved, and I got sick? Do you really think you and Alyssa could handle another loss?"

He swallowed. She had a point—one he couldn't simply dismiss. Yet what kind of man would he be to walk away from someone purely because someday she might get sick? "Every relationship is about taking risks, Deena. You don't know what's going to happen. But that's what faith is all about—trusting that God is the One in control and that He has a plan for all of us. A good plan. He doesn't want us to live in fear. Deena, one of the reasons the Lord came was so we could have life—life to its fullest."

"I can live with BRCA1, Spence, but I couldn't bear it if I had a family and they had to watch me go through breast cancer. Trust me, I know what I'm talking about."

Spence sat up straighter. He thought of Evan. "No matter how you lose someone, it hurts. That's just the way it works."

Deena swung her legs over the edge of the table. "I am thirty-five years old. The same age as my mom when she got sick. My sock, please."

He didn't want to give it to her, but she snatched it from his hands. "You can't look me in the eye and tell me you don't have any feelings for me, can you, Deena?"

"It isn't about feelings." Deena stuffed her foot into her sneaker. "It's about doing the right thing. People are counting on me, Spence. You'd just be a distraction."

He jerked as if she'd hit him. A distraction? That was how she saw him? He set his jaw. "I happen to be pretty good at helping people."

"I don't need your help." She limped to the doorway.

"Deena, you're the most accident-prone woman I've ever met in my life." He smiled to let her know he found this aspect of her appealing. "You've hardly gone a day here without needing to be rescued."

Her face darkened like a thundercloud. "You're a nice guy, Spence. When you think about this more, you'll see that I'm right."

"What if I were the one who told you I have a history of heart disease in my family and every male member died before he was fifty years old? Would you turn your back on me?"

Deena frowned. "That's different. And it's not true, is it?"

"No. I'm just trying to make a point. You wouldn't walk away from me. I know you wouldn't. If I had a heart attack, you'd be the first person to give me CPR. You'd be pounding on my chest with your fists and screaming for me to stay away from the light."

He wanted to make her laugh, but she frowned harder. "Spence, there's a child involved. It isn't funny."

"I know, but I'm not scared off either."

Deena shook her head. "It wouldn't be right."

He clenched his fists. Of course it would be right. He'd make it right; she just had to trust him and have a little faith that God would keep her healthy. He opened his mouth to tell her so then hesitated.

What if she was right? What if he distracted her from her work and therefore delayed or prevented her from developing a treatment?

He wasn't sure what to say, and before he could decide, it was too late. Deena was gone. Spence stared at the empty doorway. He could run after her, but it wouldn't change anything. It wasn't as if he could take away her chances of getting cancer. Just like he couldn't turn back the clock and rescue Evan. He absolutely hated the feeling of helplessness rapidly settling over him, a fog that enveloped him, formless and unfightable. He hated it with a passion.

Looking around his desk, he picked up the first thing he saw—a round pencil holder. He drew his arm back and threw the container against the wall. Pencils flew like small missiles across the room and scattered across the tile floor.

Chapter 21

Deena heard the clatter of something falling, but she kept walking. She swiped at the salty tears stinging her eyes. *Fool,* she told herself, *silly fool. What good is crying over something you can't change? I thought you learned that lesson a long time ago.*

Her throat ached with the effort of holding back the emotions. Work. She'd think about work. About her laboratory. About Quing, Andres, and her other students. She'd think about the most recent group of inhibitors she was studying and. . .anything but Spence. She turned down the hallway and caught a glimpse of bright copper hair just before the door closed.

Evie.

Deena's heart began to thunder in her chest. The girl must have come back from the stable to check on her. Had Evie been eavesdropping? Of course she had, but just how much had she heard? With a sick feeling, she replayed the conversation. She limped faster, ignoring the pain in her bruised toe.

She pushed open the door and squinted into the bright sunlight for a glimpse of her niece. She saw a couple of kids sitting on the grass and two others throwing a football around, and there, at the trailhead, was her niece, her shoulders hunched, her head bent. "Evie! Wait!"

Her niece turned at the sound of her name, but when she recognized Deena, she took off. Deena ran after her, wishing with all her heart that Evie hadn't overheard her conversation with Spence and wondering what she'd say to her when she caught up with her.

Evie had youth and ten good toes, but Deena had longer legs and strength born of desperation. She caught up with Evie, when her niece, proving that she was related to Deena, stumbled over a root on the trail. Evie didn't fall, but in the time it took to regain her balance, Deena caught up with her. "Evie, please, let me explain."

Panting, she faced the girl who stared back at her, red faced and defiant. Evie's light blue eyes locked on Deena's. For a moment the two of them just looked at each other, panting hard. Deena had grown up with everyone telling her she was the spitting image of her mother. She also remembered the feeling when she'd learned she'd inherited more than her mother's black hair and blue eyes. Evie was tall with the same wide jaw and light blue eyes as Deena. She wondered if Evie was seeing their physical similarities and wondering if she, too, had inherited the cancer gene.

"Genetics are complicated," Deena began, struggling to sound professorial and calm and not winded and afraid. "We're just beginning to understand what causes some genes to mutate and what it all means." She stepped closer to Evie, but the girl backed up an equal distance. "I inherited a mutated gene, but like I told Spence, it doesn't mean I'm going to get cancer."

Evie studied the ground. Deena tried again. "Look at me. I'm as strong as an ox." She studied the girl's bent head. "Your mother doesn't have the mutation, so you probably don't either. We didn't tell you because we didn't want you to worry."

More dead silence. Deena clenched her fists. What else could she say? The truth was what it was. How much more could she sugarcoat it? Couldn't Evie see Deena hated talking about this?

"There are so many more treatments available now than when your grand-mother was diagnosed. And detection is so much earlier now, too. That's a really big key in fighting cancer, Evie, catching it early."

Evie looked up. Her blue eyes seemed to have grown two sizes larger. There was an adult expression in them now. "If you're not worried about getting cancer and there's so many good treatments now if you do get it, how come you wouldn't go out with Mr. Spence?" Her chin came up a notch, just like Stacy's. "I know you like him."

It was Deena's turn to study the ground and feel the burn on her cheeks. She couldn't deny the truth of Evie's words. She lifted her gaze. "It's complicated."

Evie grunted in disgust. "Complicated? I think it's very simple. You're just like my mother. There's the truth, and then there's what she tells me."

"What are you talking about, Evie?"

The girl didn't answer. She backed away from Deena and shook her head, and as if she couldn't bear whatever thoughts were spinning in her mind, she turned and ran.

～

As Spence considered breaking something else, he realized two things. First, Deena had left her black fanny pack—the one that held Alyssa's rescue inhaler—on the chair. And second, Alyssa hadn't dropped by the clinic that morning for her allergy medications.

She'd gone horseback riding. He couldn't imagine a place more full of aller-gens. Mold, dust, grasses, animal dander—just to name a few. And she was there, right now, with no rescue inhaler in case she had an asthma attack.

He poked his head into the office next to his and asked Miriam to cover for him. With the medical fanny pack clutched in his hand, he jogged off to the stables.

Less than ten minutes later, he stood in front of the barn. Panting, he wiped the sweat from his forehead and looked around for Alyssa. The setting looked picturesque, a scene from a New England painting. Only there were no signs of either horses or riders. The paddocks were empty and so was the hitching post. Only a few annoying flies buzzed around his head.

His gaze traveled to the thin line trampled in the grass that disappeared into the woods. Were they still on the ride?

For the first time he hesitated. About a month ago Alyssa had forgotten her lunch, so he'd brought it to school. Not trusting the women in the front office, he'd insisted on delivering it himself during her lunch break. The minute she saw him striding toward her table, sack in hand, she'd turned a shade of scarlet and scooted low in her seat as if she were about to slide right under the table.

He didn't look forward to repeating the experience. Well, too bad. Alyssa shouldn't be without her medication.

He opened the Dutch doors to the barn and stepped into the semidarkness. A radio playing Willie Nelson and the sound of voices filled the aisles. Moving deeper inside, he walked past horses standing in cross ties as their riders scurried about, putting away tack or rubbing their saddle areas dry.

Other horses wearing nothing but halters and lead ropes stood lined up by the wash stall.

He touched the flank of a bay mare and slipped underneath the cross tie. Where was Alyssa? Despite himself, he was starting to get worried. Maybe something had already happened. Then he heard voices coming from inside one of the stalls.

"You're a really good rider, Alyssa," a girl said. "That was so cool when you jumped Jericho over that fallen log."

Alyssa had jumped her horse over a log? He didn't know she could do that. He wasn't sure he would allow her to do it again. Evan used to jump his bike over things, too. Once, he tried to jump it over a garbage can and ended up breaking his collarbone. Spence had needed to run for help.

He started to pull the stall door open but hesitated as he heard Alyssa say, "I used to take lessons. There was this pony, Peanuts, and I was going to lease him. But that was before."

Spence's heart began to hammer. *Before* meant before the car accident. He felt that strange sensation of the strength being drained from his body.

"Did you ask your uncle? He might still let you do it."

"My granny in Texas says if I come live with her I can have my own horse. To own. Not even lease."

"Seriously?"

"Seriously. She lives on this big piece of property with this cool pond you can swim in. And she knows how to drive a four-wheeler."

Spence's heart sank into his shoes. Was bribing Alyssa the only way to keep her? He hated to think of competing with Dixie Everett for Alyssa. There was Evan's life insurance money—he could use that to buy Alyssa a horse, but he didn't want to resort to that.

Maybe he should let her go.

Spence pushed the stall door open. Alyssa and Lourdes sat shoulder to shoulder in a pile of hay. The black-and-white pony lifted its neck and seemed mildly surprised but not displeased to see him. He wished Alyssa's expression were as friendly.

Spence's feet sank into the clean, sweet-scented pine shavings. " 'Lyssa, you forgot to take your allergy medicine this morning. You get a special delivery."

"I don't need it."

"Is Miss Deena okay?" Lourdes asked.

The pony stepped toward him, sniffing his hand for treats. Its breath was warm, the hair soft on its muzzle. "Miss Deena is fine. Her toe is bruised, not broken." He looked at Alyssa, who concentrated fiercely on braiding together three strands of hay. "Come on, 'Lyssa, it'll just take a second."

Without argument, she dropped the braided hay onto the ground. Spence struggled to hide his frustration. She had the look of someone who had just agreed to undergo a root canal. He'd rather have her defy him than give him this blank, almost zombielike acquiescence.

"You want something to wash it down with?" He led her into the office area of the barn and to an ancient-looking soda machine.

"Water's fine."

He fished in his pockets for some change and fed the slot. "So you had fun riding this morning?"

"Yes."

A bottle of water tumbled to the bottom. He twisted the cap off and handed the bottle to her.

"I didn't know you could ride."

"Well, I can."

"Well, so can I. Maybe we could do it together sometime."

"Our cabin already had its turn." Alyssa took the small white pill and washed it down with a drink. She used the nasal spray but refused the inhaler.

"I mean at home. There's a stable nearby, right?" When she nodded, he added, "So we could go there sometime."

She shrugged. "Sure." She handed him the water.

The way she said it, it wasn't going to happen. Spence wanted to bend down, look her in the eye, and tell her he was hurting, too. That he missed Evan and Mattie all the time. That he wished he could turn back the clock and do things differently. He even would gladly take Evan's place in that car. He feared, though, that sharing his pain would only fuel her own unhappiness. So he pushed back his feelings. Reaching over, he mussed her hair. "Now go have some fun."

It took her half a second to tear out of there, leaving him with the fanny pack of allergy medicine and the knowledge that if God wanted Alyssa to stay with him, He was going to have to step in. Because Spence had no clue what he was doing wrong or how to make things right.

Chapter 22

Deena wiggled her big toe, although the movement made it hurt even worse. Part of her welcomed the pain, even foolishly hoped it would wipe out her inner misery. Evie probably hated her. And Spence. She couldn't bear to think how she'd left him. The look of frustration and pain on his face haunted her.

She checked her watch for the millionth time and sighed as Pastor Rich marched back and forth across the amphitheater stage. Only one o'clock, and the rest of the day seemed like forever. She tried to cheer herself up by reminding herself that tomorrow afternoon she and Mr. Crackers would be on their way home.

She tried not to think of what Stacy would say when she brought Evie home. Evie, who now knew all about the gene for breast cancer that ran in their family.

Pastor Rich paced the stage enthusiastically describing the afternoon's event—a camp-wide scavenger hunt—with words such as "awesome" and "amazing." All he needed was to insert "like" every other word and he'd be speaking teen perfectly.

Deena's gaze shifted to the ripples on the lake. Even more than the slight chill on her arms and the grayness of the sky above, the movement of the water announced the coming change in the weather.

A cold front combined with rain was due by evening. She couldn't watch the ripples without thinking the ground beneath her life was just as unsteady, pushed by a wind she couldn't see, leaving her shaken, feeling off balance.

She glanced down the row. Evie, her hair loose and thick as if to look as different from Deena as possible, sat at the very end of their group. Alyssa sat next to her, almost shoulder to shoulder, in a way that spoke as loudly as words that the two of them were friends.

Deena remembered sitting with Stacy like that. She and her sister had been so close they could practically read each other's minds. It wasn't like that now. They loved each other, but each led a very different life. She feared the distance between them would grow even wider when Deena returned with Evie tomorrow afternoon.

"Safety comes first," Pastor Rich said loudly. "Everyone stays together. If I see a camper by himself or herself, he or she becomes my buddy for the rest of the day." He grinned. "As entertaining as I am, I don't think you want to hang out with a middle-aged guy."

She spotted Spence seated a few rows ahead of her. Her gaze rested on the close-cropped hair on the back of his head. For the first time, she thought she understood how frustrating it had to be for him to watch Alyssa shut down every time he came near.

"Secondly," Pastor Rich continued, "each item on the scavenger list has been given a point value. The winning team will be the one that earns the most points."

Like her team was likely to win. Deena nearly snorted. She'd never seen a group so disorganized in her life. Every morning somebody was missing something—a hairbrush, a tube of mascara, a ponytail holder. Taylor and Britty had even mixed up their matching toothbrushes.

"Thirdly, all items must be brought back to the commissary to be counted and recorded by 5:00 p.m. No items will be accepted after the 5:00 p.m. deadline. Okay, cabins, please send your representative to pick up the clues."

Deena glanced at Evie's profile, willing the girl to meet her gaze. She wanted to choose Evie, to give Evie something, to acknowledge that she was special to her, but the girl pretended not to see her. So Deena asked Britty, who was seated next to her.

The girl nodded and along with about fifteen other kids hurried down the log steps to the front of the stage.

When all the representatives from the cabins had their envelopes, Pastor Rich asked for the Lord's blessing on the hunt and that He would hold off the rain. Then he raised his hand theatrically in the air. "On your mark," he said. "Get set.... Go!" Waving his arm as if it were a checkered flag, he started the hunt.

The kids thundered back to their seats. Despite her misgivings about the activity, Deena found herself leaning forward, shouting encouragement to Britty, who was racing a much bigger boy up the steps.

"Hurry, Brit!" Taylor shouted. Even Evie seemed to come to life, rising to her feet and cheering as Britty passed a girl who had tripped over her shoelaces.

Maybe this scavenger hunt would not be a pointless exercise in futility. Deena closed her eyes. *If You're up there, God, if You can hear me, please let this race bring Evie and me together. Please help us end this camp experience on a good note.*

Breathless, Britty joined them in the seats. She handed Deena the long white envelope. Ripping it open, Deena read aloud:

Dear Campers,
    " 'Seek and you will find' " (Luke 11:9).
    We have spent the week learning more about the Lord and about the Bible. Below is a list of Bible-related objects. Good luck on your journey, and may you find that the answers you seek can sometimes be found in the most unusual places.

                        God bless each of you,
                        Pastor Rich

Scavenger List

- *A handmade cross—created without use of tape, string, or nails (10 points)*
- *A crown of thorns (10 points)*
- *Something rare and precious (25 points)*
- *A slice of bread (5 points)*
- *A fish (dead 5 points, alive 10 points)*
- *A seed of faith (5 points)*
- *A Christmas tree (3 points, decorated 10 points)*
- *Four nails (2 points each)*
- *A symbol of hope (5 points)*
- *Something eternal (10 points)*
- *A prayer written by a stranger (15 points)*
- *Living water (10 points)*
- *Body of Christ (5 points)*
- *Blood of Christ (5 points)*
- *Not a her, but a homonym for him + al (5 points)*
- *A bit of truth (5 points)*
- *Life's guidebook (5 points)*
- *Eve's temptation (5 points)*
- *A pillar of salt (5 points)*
- *A praying mantis (15 points)*
- *Ashes (5 points)*
- *An eagle's feather (25 points)*
- *Armor of God (10 points)*
- *Pastor Rich's sunglasses (lost near the amphitheater two days ago, 25 points)*
- *This list, intact, no stains (1 point)*
- *A doughnut (10 points, chocolate 15 points)*

Deena looked up. The girls had pressed around her so tightly that she almost bumped her forehead on Lourdes's chin.

"This is, like, seriously impossible." Britty's eyes, framed in heavy black eyeliner, blinked furiously. "I mean, how are we going to hold a cross together?"

"Easy." Taylor pulled her wad of bubble gum out of her mouth. "We find two sticks and glue them together with my Dubble Bubble."

A cheer went up from the group. "Next?" Lourdes prompted excitedly. "What's next?"

"If we go in order," Britty said, "it's find a crown of thorns. Where are we going to find that?"

"Ha," Taylor said. "We don't find it—we make it. My gum and your headband. Britt, let's find a rosebush, and we're all set."

"Bubble gum on my headband?" Britty shook her head. "No way."

"We can use one of mine," Alyssa offered, removing a white plastic band from her head.

"And I know where to find a rosebush," Evie shouted. "The baptismal pool!"

"Shh," Lourdes said, holding her finger to her lips. "You want the other teams to hear? Hey, if we get some water from the baptismal pool, that would take care of another clue, too." She grinned, showing a multitude of silver bands. "The living water one."

"You're, like, a genius, Lourdes," Britty said. "Keep going. What's next?"

Around them, kids spoke in excited, overlapping voices, and small groups split off from the bench seats, running in every direction.

"Come on, Miss Deena," Lourdes said, rising to her feet. "We've got a lot of ground to cover."

Two hours later excellent progress had been made. Their team had created a very respectable cross out of twigs and bubble gum. They'd fashioned the crown out of Alyssa's head-band and thorns from the rosebushes.

To decorate a Christmas tree, they'd found an evergreen branch and decorated it with Britty's earrings and a chain of Taylor's bubble gum wrappers.

A trip to the commissary had netted several items from the scavenger hunt list: a saltshaker for a pillar of salt, crackers (body of Christ), a can of grape juice (blood of Christ), an apple (Eve's temptation), a can of tuna (fish), a slice of bread, and a package of pumpkin seeds (for a seed of faith).

At the stable they'd retrieved a horse's bit for "a bit of truth" and found four horseshoe nails. They'd figured out that "life's instruction book" was the Bible (which they retrieved from Lourdes's suitcase) and "not a her, but a homonym for him + al" was a hymnal.

Deciding that the "armor of God" was a life jacket, they raced to the boathouse.

The air had grown even heavier with the coming rain. Deena's lungs labored, and her big toe burned as if it were on fire. She could hardly keep up with the kids, who bounded like deer down the trail. Even Evie seemed to have gotten into the spirit of the competition. Watching her bright copper head lead the way gave Deena a small hopeful feeling. This was like the old Evie, charging ahead, full of enthusiasm.

She gratefully slowed to a walk as they reached the beach area. The girls ran ahead, and she followed slowly, favoring her hurt toe. The huge lake spread in front of her, nearly spanning the parameters of her vision. A line of orange buoys bobbed amid the choppy waves, and the water matched the same dark color as the sky. Leaning her hands on her knees, she managed an out-of-breath greeting as a teenaged boy with a sunburn lifted an empty kayak and hauled it toward the boathouse. He'd almost reached the open door, when a group of boys rushed past him, nearly knocking the kayak from his arms.

"Hey, dudes, careful there."

"Sorry," one of the boys said. Deena recognized him from their tug-of-war match, although she couldn't quite remember his name. The boy didn't sound overly sorry, though, and a moment later he whooped and bumped chests with another boy. The two boys danced in place like football players who had scored the winning touchdown.

A tall boy with long blond hair raised his arm into the air. He had something clutched in his fist. Deena felt her heart sink. She walked over to her group of girls. "Do you see what I see?"

"Yeah." Evie dug the toe of her sneaker into the sand. "Pastor Rich's sunglasses."

"Twenty-five points," Alyssa pointed out. The unofficial accountant, she'd been tallying the score as they went along.

The glasses were worth a lot of points in the scavenger hunt, and no one had to tell the team what this meant. Deena pushed her hair behind her ears. "We can still win, girls. We've found a lot of things on the list."

Britty, who was holding their bag of items, shook her head. "Everything we've found has probably been found by, like, everyone else, too. We really needed to find those sunglasses."

Deena watched the boys continue to dance around the beach. "Give me the list. Let's see if there's another big-ticket item."

She studied the list. "Okay. We've still got a praying mantis, a live fish, a prayer written by a stranger, a chocolate doughnut, something rare and precious, and an eagle's feather." She looked up. "Any ideas?"

"Yeah," Britty said. "We just give up and go back to the cabin and take a nap."

"And eat candy," Taylor added. "Or ice cream. Like we did when we lost the tug-of-war challenge."

"No way are we giving up," Lourdes said. "We can catch a fish, for starters. The prayer of a stranger—I've been thinking, maybe we could use one of David's psalms in the Bible. I mean, no one has actually met David, have they?"

"Well, we know who he is, so he isn't exactly a stranger, is he?" Taylor snapped her bubble.

The girls fell silent. Then Evie said, "We should go after the eagle's feather."

"Where are we going to find an eagle's feather?" Taylor asked.

"Near the eagle's nest," Evie replied. "Across the lake. There's supposed to be a nesting pair near the watchtower. Pastor Rich told us about it, remember?"

Deena looked across the water. Barely visible, but rising from the tree line, she could just make out the brown tower. She frowned. It wasn't a good idea, not with bad weather coming.

"How would we get there?" Lourdes asked.

Evie pointed to the kayaks lying on the sandy beach. "We'll take one of those."

"I'll go with you," Alyssa said.

"It's settled, then," Evie said. "Alyssa and I go after the eagle's feather, and the rest of you should continue looking for the rest of the items on the list."

"I'm sorry, Evie, but no one is going on that lake," Deena said. "The water is a lot rougher than the last time we were out, and it might rain."

Evie lifted her gaze. Her eyes were filled with a yearning and a need that seemed to reach all the way to her soul. "Remember my dream, Aunt Deena? About the eagle? I think we're meant to go."

Deena looked at the rows of waves marching across the water and then up at the gray sky hanging low and heavy with the promise of rain. "No way," she said firmly. "Besides," she added, wanting to soften the look of disappointment on her niece's face, "we can't just take one of these kayaks without asking."

"Then let's ask." Evie's voice had a stubborn note that was pure Stacy. "I saw a staff counselor a moment ago."

As if on cue, the sunburned teenager returned from the boathouse and walked right past them.

"Excuse me," Deena said, hoping to put an end to this conversation. "We can't take out one of the kayaks, can we? The weather and all. . ."

"Have you had safety training?" the boy asked.

"Yes," Evie said eagerly. "And we'll only be gone for a short while."

The boy looked at Deena. "As long as a counselor is in the boat and everyone has had safety training, its okay." He glanced at a fat silver watch on his wrist. "You'd have to be back in an hour, though. That's when I take my break."

"We'd be back in, like, half that time," Evie said confidently.

"But the weather," Deena hinted broadly. "Isn't it a bad idea to take a kayak out when it might rain?" She ignored the death look Evie shot her.

"Oh, it isn't supposed to rain until tonight."

Deena glanced up at the sky. It really didn't look that bad. She probably was being overprotective. After all, from the looks of things, kayaks had been going out all morning. Would taking one out for another hour make much difference? Besides, she didn't want to disappoint the girls, particularly Evie. Deep in her heart Deena believed if she and Evie could just spend more time together, they could get past what had happened this morning.

There would be a headwind, but she was strong. She liked the idea of Evie seeing her physical strength. It would wipe out any notion that Deena might implode at any moment, like a building being demolished. Only in her case, it would be the work of an abnormally dividing cell instead of dynamite.

"Okay," Deena decided. "We'll do it!"

～

"There's a three-person kayak, Aunt Deena," Evie offered. "Three people can cross that lake more quickly than two."

"I'll go," Alyssa offered. "Evie and I were partners last time." She exchanged nods with Evie. "We make a good team."

Evie was right; they could go faster with three people. If they were really going to do this, it would be better not to waste time arguing. Besides, none of the other girls seemed to want to come. "Could you bring us the three-person kayak?" she asked the teenager.

The sunburned boy grinned and pointed to an orange kayak on the beach. "Make sure you wear your life jackets," he said.

"Okay, then," Deena said after the boy left. "Evie, Alyssa, and I will go after the eagle feather. The rest of you stay here and try to catch a fish. There are fishing poles and nets in the boathouse. And for goodness' sake, don't fall in the water."

"We won't," Britty promised. "But I'm not putting a worm on the hook."

Taylor grinned. "You won't have to. I've got Gummi Worms!"

Chapter 23

Deena and the two girls paddled into a fairly steady headwind. There was more of a chop in the water than the last time Deena had been on the lake, but still nothing to worry about. She kept her eyes on the green hills ahead and focused on timing her paddle strokes with Evie's and Alyssa's.

In just minutes her arms began to ache. The wind and current kept trying to push them back to the shore. She had to brace herself with her legs and pull and push with each stroke. In front the girls paddled with determination, ignoring the dull *thunk* of ripples, solid as logs, hitting rhythmically against the bow.

The kayak picked up enough water to soak the bottom of her jeans. She kept paddling, trying not to think about how far away the other side of the lake looked or wonder how deep the water went beneath them.

Deena's grip tightened on her paddle as a gust of wind pushed against the kayak. Something in her welcomed the opportunity to fight against something tangible like the wind. For so many years, she had fought against cancer, a silent enemy that was as stealthy as it was deadly. This wind, though, could be fought against with a stroke of her paddle, and the battle would be won when she reached the shoreline.

They reached halfway, then three-quarters—then the shoreline neared. Deena slowed her paddling as she looked for a safe spot to land the kayak. The tops of slick, black rocks stood between the kayak and a rocky beach. There might be underwater rocks as well. To avoid the rocks, she'd have to land the kayak in a different part of the shoreline. From what she could see, this meant trying to muscle it through the arms of trees growing out from the bank of the water's edge.

Evie looked back, her face flushed and her hair plastered back from the wind. "Where?" she yelled.

"To the left. Over there."

"But the trees. . ."

"We'll go between them."

Deena picked a spot between two trees and turned the boat. The wind pushed her too far, though, and Deena found herself pointed between the branches of a leafy tree overhanging the water. Too late to adjust, she yelled for the girls to duck and hoped they could go beneath it.

The idea might have worked, but Deena felt the kayak scrape bottom. A moment later it came to a complete standstill. Caught in the leafy arms of a tree, the kayak rocked in the small waves.

Deena pushed aside a leafy branch. She peered around another. "You okay, girls?"

More branches were pushed aside, and then two heads popped up. "Yeah, we're fine," Evie replied. "Now what?"

"Well, tie the kayak to the tree and let's get going," Deena said. "The watch-tower is just above us. We can take a quick look, but we've got to be out of here in ten minutes."

They hopped out of the kayak, gasping and laughing as the knee-high water lapped their legs. Evie sloshed to the front of the kayak and tied its rope around a branch. "To the eagle's nest!"

They dropped their life vests on higher ground. From where they stood, the land rose at a steep pitch from the shore. The pines grew thick and wild, littering the ground with needles, their roots sticking up like knobby knees.

Using small trees and branches for balance, she and the girls started up the hill. The going was slippery. Deena led the way, keeping a sharp lookout for snakes. Several times she had to grab a branch for balance as the needles gave way beneath her feet.

Behind her she heard the labored sound of Evie, or maybe Alyssa, huffing and puffing after her. The cracking of deadwood beneath their feet resonated in the forest. It gave Deena a very bad feeling, as if they were the only living creatures moving about in the woods. It was like everything else knew something they didn't and had taken shelter.

She climbed another fifty yards and reached the lip of the hill, panting hard. There it was. The watchtower, a three-story brown structure, rose high, over-looking the lake and valley behind them.

Moving closer, Deena studied the blistered brown paint on the side rails that looked as though they'd break if even a squirrel leaned against them. The steps sagged, and a lone strand of pine peeked through a tiny gap. No way was she letting either of the girls up that structure.

"Where's the nest?" Alyssa asked, tilting her head to look up at the watchtower.

"It's supposed to be at the top," Evie said. "We just can't see it from the ground."

"Well, you're not going up in the tower," Deena announced. "It's not safe."

"I'm the lightest," Alyssa said. "I could go up there."

"Absolutely not." Deena put her hands on her hips and drew herself up to her full five feet ten inches. When she saw the tilt of Alyssa's chin, she added, "I weigh a hundred forty-five pounds, Alyssa. You do not want me to sit on you, but I will if that's what it takes."

"Well, you're not going then either," Alyssa said, mirroring Deena's stance right down to the hands on the hips. "I'm only seventy-five pounds, but I can bite like a shark."

Deena hadn't planned to go up herself and blinked in surprise. Just who was protecting whom? She held up her hands in mock surrender. "Okay. None of us are going up there. Let's just look around and see if maybe a feather or two blew out of the nest."

Just in case one of the girls tried to slip into the tower, Deena planted herself at the base of the steps, alternating between checking her watch and staring up at the sky, which seemed to be darkening by the minute. "Hurry up, girls."

The wind had picked up, too. It came in gusts that tore at her hair and plastered her T-shirt to her body. The little swells in the lake below seemed to be moving more quickly as well. She still thought they could make it back before the storm hit.

"Come on," she yelled. "We have to go. Now!"

Evie yelled, "We haven't found it yet. Just give us a few more minutes."

"There is no more time," Deena said, feeling the wind pushing her words back at her. She waited for it to pass, and her gaze fell on something racing across the grass. It was dark, sort of brownish gray. For a moment she thought it might be a rodent, but when it caught beneath a bush, she recognized it for what it was.

"Girls! Come here!"

Evie and Alyssa charged around the side of the tower just as Deena picked up the slim feather. "The wind blew, and suddenly there it was!"

Evie started jumping up and down. "I knew we'd find it!" Taking the object from Deena, she waved it in the air. "Twenty-five points! We're gonna win, win, win!" The two girls grabbed hands and bounced in place.

"You two are going to make it rain," Deena teased. "Come on, guys, let's get out of here."

Slipping and sliding and leaving long trails of black earth exposed where their heels dug into the ground for balance, they raced back to the shoreline. Descending the hill took far less time than climbing it had, and soon they found themselves at the base of the tree growing out over the water.

"Where's the kayak?" Alyssa looked at Deena, who suddenly had a very sick feeling in her stomach. "Is this the right spot?"

"Yeah." Nature girl she wasn't, but Deena was positive this was where they'd left the kayak. Her gaze moved to Evie. She didn't like her train of thought, but Evie had been the one to tie up the kayak. Had she deliberately not tied it tightly enough?

"Look!" Alyssa cried, pointing.

Across the water, the empty kayak rocked in the waves. It had turned sideways and was moving steadily away from them. Silhouetted against the gray water, it had a lost, abandoned look to it, like a ghost ship about to disappear into the mist.

"This is all my fault," Evie cried. "I didn't tie it tight enough. I'm so sorry, Aunt Deena. It was an accident. I swear it was an accident."

Deena remained silent. She couldn't help but think of all the pranks Evie had played, and she knew the girl was still angry with her.

Evie tugged at her hair. "You have to believe me!"

Deena studied her niece's face. The fear and dismay in her eyes seemed real. If the child was faking, she deserved an Academy Award. She sighed. "I believe you, Evie. I know it was an accident."

"Now everyone is going to hate me!" Evie put her face in her hands. "We're losing the scavenger hunt because of me!"

"Evie, that isn't true. No one is going to blame or hate you." Deena stepped closer to her niece. She wanted to hug Evie, yet she held back. She hated this inner reserve in herself, but it was ingrained and impossible to dismiss. She patted the girl's shoulder. "Don't worry."

"No wonder Mom wanted to send me away," Evie said bitterly. "I'm a horrible person. I don't blame her a bit."

Deena's hand froze on her niece's shoulder. What was Evie saying? Stacy adored this child. "Your mother didn't send you away because she doesn't love you. My goodness, Evie, just the opposite. She was more than willing to put her health and the baby's health at risk to come with you to camp."

Evie looked at her, near tears. "I heard you and Mom talking about me, how Mom couldn't have me home anymore because I was too much for her." Her lip trembled, and her gaze dropped. "She wants another boy. I heard her say that to my dad. It's true!"

Alyssa stepped closer and put her hand on Evie's other shoulder in a show of silent but heartfelt support. Deena studied the top of her niece's head. Stacy did hope for another boy, but not for the reasons Evie believed. It was the genetics Stacy feared. How did she tell Evie the truth without scaring her, though?

"Your mother loves you more than she loves her own life," Deena said. "And that's the truth you need to hold on to."

"How can I trust you?" Evie stepped away from Deena. A branch popped beneath her foot, and the sound of it breaking was cruel and final. "You lied to me about yourself. You didn't tell me about the cancer stuff."

"I never lied," Deena corrected. "We were just waiting for you to get older. You're so young, Evie. We didn't want you to worry, to have to carry this burden. When we get home, you, your mom, and I will talk everything over. I promise."

Even with the breeze now steadily rolling off the water, Deena felt herself sweat. The expression on her niece's face nearly broke her heart. All the boldness, the cockiness that was Evie had drained right out of her. She looked so young, so unsure, so afraid.

Deena remembered staring up at her father like that, wanting comfort and watching him back away from her. She didn't want to be like him, to hold people at arm's distance.

She opened her arms and pulled Evie next to her. When this didn't seem enough, she reached out with her right arm and drew Alyssa into their embrace.

"It's going to be okay," Deena said.

"Yeah," Alyssa agreed. "We're having an adventure. This is much more fun."

Evie wiped her eyes and squirmed out of the group hug. She squared her shoulders. "I'm going to swim out to the kayak and tow it back."

"Over my dead body." Deena lifted her chin. "We're hiking back to camp."

"Uncle Spence says if you're lost in the woods, you should stay right where you are and someone will come find you."

Deena smiled reassuringly. "We aren't lost, Alyssa. All we have to do is follow the shoreline, and it'll bring us right to camp. Hopefully we'll be back before anyone starts to worry about us."

Chapter 24

A trail led from the watchtower to the campground. Deena remembered seeing the thin white line on a map. They'd hiked partially there on the first day they had come to the camp—the day they'd wandered into the patch of poison ivy.

The best plan seemed to be to find that trail. As they began the hard work of climbing the hill, she heard drops of rain splattering on the leaves. A fat bead plopped onto her nose.

She climbed faster.

The drops fell more frequently, and then there was a rush as if someone had turned the handle of a faucet to full volume.

Deena looked around for shelter. Blinking as a steady stream of rain pounded over her head, she spotted an overhanging rock half buried in the hill and herded them beneath it. It wasn't much, but it was better than nothing.

Deena pressed both girls into the small crevice and shielded them with her body. The rain battered the earth, bringing with it a darkness that virtually eliminated the last bits of daylight. She shut her eyes, held the girls, and felt the rain pound her back. Deena wished with all her heart that she'd never allowed the girls to talk her into searching for the eagle's feather. She wished she'd never volunteered to take Stacy's place. Ever since she'd arrived, things had gone wrong. She'd come to this camp thinking herself a fairly strong person. Now, huddled beneath this rock, she felt small and helpless. She pressed deeper into the crevice and hugged the girls more tightly. If anything happened to Alyssa or Evie, she'd never forgive herself.

She couldn't tell how much time had passed before the rain eased and the woods quieted. The sky cleared, and a glimmer of sunshine appeared behind a layer of clouds. Deena straightened and pushed her wet hair back. Her shorts were soaked, and she could have wrung out her shirt. The world also had changed. The trunks of trees were stained almost black, and the leaves gleamed a glossy green color.

"Wow. That was so cool!" Evie emerged next, also soaked, but grinning. "Kind of scary, too. Were you scared, 'Lyssa?"

Alyssa's honey-colored hair lay plastered to her skull. Her face had a white, pinched look that Deena didn't like. Worst of all, when she opened her mouth, no sound came out. She flapped her arms and looked at Deena with clear panic in her eyes.

The girl was having an asthma attack.

Deena reached for her fanny pack and realized she wasn't wearing it. In a flash of horror, she remembered taking it off in Spence's clinic earlier that morning. In her mind's eye, she saw it sitting on the black vinyl chair.

Alyssa's rescue inhaler was in that fanny pack. Now here she was, in the middle of nowhere, with no inhaler and a girl in trouble. A fear like none Deena had ever felt in her life shot through her veins.

Please, God. Help her breathe.

Deena bent low and grabbed Alyssa's small hands. "Honey, you've got to listen to me." Her voice sounded steady, but on the inside it was screaming, *Oh God, oh God, oh God,* like a distress signal from a sinking ship.

Alyssa made a long, whistling noise. Her eyes had the sick look of an animal caught in a trap. Deena gripped the girl's hands more tightly. *Please, God. I can't do this alone.* "Try to calm down. Slow and easy breaths."

"What should I do?" Evie shouted. "What should I do?"

"Pray." Deena struggled to keep her voice calm. "Alyssa, you're going to be fine. Close your eyes and listen to my voice."

"Heavenly Father," Evie began, "You are a great God. You can do anything. Please help Alyssa breathe. Help her, God. She needs You. Please, God, help Aunt Deena save Alyssa. Please, God, please. I'm so sorry for all the things I've done wrong. We need You so much. . . ."

Deena continued gripping Alyssa's hands. She'd never been responsible for someone else's life. Nothing in her training had prepared her for the terror or the helplessness she felt as she watched Alyssa struggling for breath. She was all alone. There was no one to turn to. No one to help her. And then something inside her told her she was wrong.

A feeling of quiet peace settled over her, and energy seemed to flow into Deena's ice-cold hands. She heard herself say, "Breathe in through your nose, Alyssa, and out through your mouth. Slowly. Like I'm doing."

Alyssa's chest heaved with the effort. She produced a thin, wheezing noise.

"That's it. Another one."

Alyssa managed another breath.

"You're doing good, honey." A bead of water from Deena's hair plopped onto Alyssa's face. She wiped it off. "Breathe in. . .one, two, three. Now breathe out. . . one, two, three."

Some of the panic receded from Alyssa's face as she followed Deena's order. "Breathe in. One, two, three, four. . ."

Evie finished praying and began reciting Bible verses. Deena continued to coach Alyssa's breathing, taking heart as the color slowly returned to the girl's lips. When she was finally satisfied that Alyssa was truly past the attack and breathing normally, she sat back.

She looked at Alyssa for a long time and then at Evie. She studied the shadows deepening in the woods. She thought about how she had turned away from God after her mother died. How she'd believed once the door was closed between herself and God, it could not be fully opened again. And yet that wasn't true at all. He had been close, just waiting for her to call out to Him. She might have given up on Him, but He hadn't given up on her—not at all.

She reached for Alyssa's hand and then one of Evie's. She bowed her head, and the three of them prayed.

Chapter 25

A glance at her watch told Deena they had about four hours to make it back to camp before total darkness. It would be plenty of time, she told herself, as long as the path they were following was the right one. The storm seemed to have passed, but the sky was overcast, the forest draped in shadow. There was enough light to follow the twisting path through the woods, but at the same time Deena felt the darkness coming.

Behind her, the girls trudged along single file. They walked in silence broken only by the sound of their feet crunching over the underbrush and the occasional slap as a mosquito landed on them.

Furtive scurrying noises came from the underbrush, and louder cracking sounds suggested larger, heavier animals roaming. Deer probably, Deena told herself, but she couldn't help imagining a huge black bear silently tracking them, or maybe a hungry bobcat.

If an animal jumped out at them, how would she defend the girls? She thought longingly of Spence, who would know what to do. But that gave no comfort because Spence wouldn't have gotten himself into this position in the first place. She, with all her years of education, with all her awards and degrees and training, had proven to be stupid beyond words.

And yet, a small contrary voice insisted, hadn't something truly amazing happened because they had come? Hadn't she felt some kind of presence, some kind of power flow into her as she'd helped Alyssa? That couldn't have been an adrenaline rush. It couldn't have been.

It was growing darker. How long had it been since their shadows had disappeared? She paused to check on the girls, and a flicker of light in the distance caught her eye. At first she thought it was a big firefly, but then she saw the light was constant, only giving the illusion of turning on and off as it passed through the woods.

Her heart leaped in her chest. "Girls, look." She pointed behind them.

"What?" Evie asked.

"It's a flashlight." She cupped her hands around her mouth. "Over here!" She paused. "Over here!"

A muffled shout drifted back.

Evie and Alyssa added their voices to Deena's.

The light moved closer. They continued to shout back and forth. The voice that replied grew more distinct and definitely familiar.

"Uncle Spence," Alyssa announced, joy evident in her voice.

The light moved faster. They tracked the figure jogging through the woods. The light grew larger as it drew closer, and they glimpsed Spence, a large, dark figure in a rain poncho. He closed the last stretch of trail between them and stood breathing hard, shining the light on each of them. He didn't speak for a moment, but Deena felt the fear and relief rolling almost tangibly off him. Deena blinked back tears. She had never been so grateful to see someone in her entire life.

"Everybody okay?" Spence hardly had the breath to get the words out.

Alyssa flung herself into his arms and hugged him hard. "You came. You found us. Oh, Uncle Spence. . ."

The light dipped and fell to the ground as Spence bent and hugged Alyssa. He enveloped her in his arms, obscuring her completely. He kept his arms around the girl even as he asked Evie and Deena if they were okay. Finally, he released Alyssa and retrieved the light from the ground.

"You sure you two are okay?"

"Yeah," Deena replied.

He swept the light over Deena. She folded her arms, embarrassed by what he must see—her soaked hair and torn clothing and the scratches on her arms.

"Hold on," he said, lifting the poncho out of the way and pulling out his cell phone. "I have to call off the search party."

He spoke a few curt words into the cell phone, assuring whoever was on the other end, probably Pastor Rich, that everybody was okay. Everyone must have been frantic looking for them. She'd probably ruined the scavenger hunt for everyone, not to mention how scared Britty, Taylor, and Lourdes must have been.

Spence clicked the phone shut and replaced it in his pocket. "What happened? Just before the awards ceremony, the camp staff notified us three people had not returned from taking a kayak on the lake, and Britty told me you guys had taken the kayak to the watchtower."

"We went looking for an eagle feather," Alyssa informed him. A small note of pride entered her voice. "We found one, too."

His gaze shot back to Deena, who felt disapproval slicing through the distance between them. "What in the world were you doing looking for an eagle's feather?"

"It was an item on the scavenger hunt list," Deena explained, realizing how lame that sounded. "Look, maybe we should get back to camp before we talk any more about this."

"In a minute." He stepped closer to Deena. "You took the girls out in the kayak when you knew a storm was expected? And then led them on a wild-goose chase in the woods? All for an eagle's feather?" His voice rose on the last part of the sentence.

"It wasn't a wild-goose chase," Alyssa said. "We found the feather. And we would have made it back before the storm, but our kayak came untied."

"It was half sunk by the time I reached it." There was no disguising the anger in Spence's voice. "Do you know what I thought?"

"I'm so sorry we scared you," Deena said.

"I thought you had all drowned," Spence continued, his voice rising. "If I hadn't seen the life jackets on the shore, I'd have been dredging the lake."

"I'm sorry," Deena repeated.

"And not just me," Spence continued, "but just about every cabin counselor is out looking for you all."

"It was an accident," Deena tried again.

"It was sheer irresponsibility." Spence's voice rose, and he punctuated the sentence with a sound of disgust. "That no one got hurt is a miracle."

"It *was* a miracle, Uncle Spence," Alyssa said eagerly. "I had an asthma attack, and we realized my inhaler was left in your office. But Miss Deena helped me, and we all prayed. God helped us."

Spence's gaze swung to Alyssa as if to make sure she was really okay. He gripped the girl's slim shoulders. "You had an attack? And you didn't have an inhaler?" Above the girl's head, he gave Deena a look of disgust.

Deena swallowed the lump in her throat. "I'm sorry. I'm so sorry."

"You never should have gone out on that kayak in the first place. And then not bringing along the inhaler?" He tore at his hair. "How could you have let that happen?"

"Because I left my fanny pack in your clinic, Spence?"

He glared at her. "Are you trying to tell me this is my fault?"

"Of course not. I'm just trying to explain."

"Uncle Spence, it wasn't Miss Deena's fault."

"We'll talk about this later, Alyssa."

Releasing his niece, Spence pushed past Deena and began to lead them down the trail. "Stay close behind," he said to Alyssa in a gentle voice. It changed completely as he addressed Deena. "You go last."

She winced at the coldness in his voice but made no move to defend herself. He was right. She had acted irresponsibly. Alyssa could have died. And it would have been all her fault. She pressed her lips together to keep them from trembling. The glow of her newfound faith began to fade. Her feet hurt, and Spence hated her. What had seemed like an act of God now seemed exactly what Spence had said, an act of irresponsibility.

She never should have come to this camp. She should have stayed in the safety of her lab. She had tumor specimens to study, cells to stain, promising combinations of powerful cancer cell inhibitors to test and study.

She wanted to go back to her old life where work was all that mattered. The trouble was, she didn't think she was that same person anymore.

Chapter 26

They arrived back at camp shortly after eight o'clock. The first thing Deena saw was the tall poles of the Leap of Faith apparatus. It was empty of campers now. She heard the music coming from the amphitheater, suggesting the campers were having their evening devotional. She was glad there were no campers to see them. No one to witness her shameful return. She would not have to see her failure reflected in their eyes.

They passed the commissary, and Spence led them to the single-story building that housed the administrative offices. Every light was burning as Spence marched straight to Pastor Rich's office.

Britty, Taylor, and Lourdes were seated on the senior pastor's ancient leather couch. When they saw them, the girls shouted with joy and leaped up to greet them with fierce hugs and cries of how worried they had been.

Pastor Rich hung up the telephone. A broad grin spread over his round face. "Thank God," he said. "Are you all okay?"

"Yes, Pastor Rich." Deena explained what had happened and took full responsibility for the accident. When the girls tried to intercede on her behalf, she just talked louder and faster.

When she finished, Pastor Rich sat back and steepled his fingers. "Well, that was some adventure. You had us all worried. I was just calling your sister, Deena, when you walked in. We've never lost anyone before at Camp Bald Eagle, and I'm glad you all weren't the first."

"I apologize," Deena said. "And of course, you'll want me to step down as cabin counselor."

"Deena, even if camp wasn't ending tomorrow, I still wouldn't want you to quit. It's not the way we do things here." His gaze turned to Spence. "I'm glad you found them, Spence. Your search-and-rescue skills were a real blessing to us today." He looked at Deena. "He had us all organized in search parties and out looking for you within thirty minutes."

Spence nodded. "I'm just glad it all worked out."

"I am, too," Pastor Rich said. "Now you all are probably tired and hungry. My wife is heating a pot of stew for you in the kitchen. The biscuits are a bit tough, though. Just a friendly warning."

They could have been serving prime rib for all Deena cared. Alyssa and Evie probably were starving, though. She turned to leave. "Hold on a second, Deena," Pastor Rich said. "There's one more thing."

She paused.

"We all make mistakes," the pastor said gently. "We forgive others as we want God to forgive us." He looked at her as if he understood that most of all Deena would have a hard time forgiving herself. "Talk to God about this, Deena. You'll see that He loves you no less. And neither do I."

She drew her trembling fingers through her hair, still cold and damp from the rain. Would Spence forgive her as well? Her heart began to pound. She turned slowly, afraid to look but unable to stop herself.

Both Spence and Alyssa were gone.

Chapter 27

As if to make up for the day before, the Connecticut morning was picture perfect. The sky wrapped the earth in a shade of light blue, the temperature was in the seventies, and the air smelled clean and fresh.

The powerboat rocked gently in the small swells of the lake as Spence climbed inside. Stationing himself in the back, he watched the girls wade into the lake.

As its name suggested, the long, yellow inflatable looked exactly like a big banana. A long cable connected it to the powerboat.

The girls gasped at the temperature of the water and climbed aboard the raft as fast as they could.

Alyssa mounted the yellow tube with a boost from Evie, who then settled herself in front of his niece. "Let's make like a banana and split!" Evie yelled.

Spence's grin faded as Deena stepped out of the boathouse and headed straight for them. She wore a sleeveless white shirt, a pair of red shorts, and a red baseball cap.

He felt disgusted with himself, yet he couldn't make himself look away as she walked onto the pier.

The bruise on her cheek had faded, but she had numerous cuts and scratches on her arms. Spence wanted to both heal them and use them to remind himself of Deena's irresponsibility. She had endangered Alyssa. He forgave her as his faith required, but that didn't mean he'd be quick to forget.

"I know you think I don't deserve to be here," Deena said, joining him in the back of the boat. "Believe me, I wouldn't have come if the girls hadn't insisted."

"You won the skit challenge. You deserve this as much as anyone." He pretended to take great interest in the way the girls had arranged themselves on the banana boat and firmly ignored the part of him that wanted to watch Deena strap on the life vest.

"Britty," Deena shouted. "Did you remember to take out your earrings?"

"Yes, Miss Deena."

"Taylor? No bubble gum, right?"

Spence's gaze swung to Taylor. He hadn't thought of stuff like that. "No bubble gum," the girl confirmed.

"Everybody ready?" Pastor Rich called from the wheel of the boat.

"Yes," Spence said. As soon as this was over, he'd go back to the clinic and finish packing.

The engine coughed to life and the floorboards began to rumble. A moment

113

later they began pulling away from the pier, dragging the banana boat along behind.

The girls screamed as cold water rose over their knees. The boat picked up speed as they left the dock. Alyssa's long, honey-colored hair streamed behind her, and her mouth opened in joy. She had her arms wrapped around Evie, who had her head thrown back laughing.

Spence wished Evan could see Alyssa. His heart ached for all the moments of this girl's life his brother would miss. He vowed not to miss a single thing himself if he could help it.

The boat accelerated, sending cool air rushing past his ears. Trees and boulders along the shoreline passed in a blur of greens and the flash of silver rock.

Behind them the big yellow inflatable bounced in the wake. The girls clung to the small handles. The boat leaned into a wide U-turn. It wasn't a steep pitch, but Deena, who had been holding on to her hat, lost her balance and bumped into Spence. Instinctively his arm shot out to steady her. As the boat continued to turn, she pressed against his side, leaning the full length of herself against him. For a few seconds they were agonizingly close, and Spence thought he'd have to either kiss her or jump overboard. Then Deena's hat flew off.

"Hat overboard," Spence shouted, not caring a bit about the baseball cap but welcoming the excuse to focus on something besides the feel of Deena against him.

Pastor Rich cut the engine, and the boat came to a slow idle. "Do you see it?"

"Over there." Deena pointed.

Spence caught a glimpse of red among the ripples in the water.

"Want me to swim over and get it?" Evie yelled.

"No," Deena and Spence shouted at the same time. "Pastor Rich will bring the boat around, and I'll fish it out," Spence yelled.

"It's just a hat," Deena protested. "You don't have to get it back."

Spence looked at all the colors in her face. Blue eyes, red lips, white teeth, and tanned skin. She dazzled him, thoroughly and completely. Yet he couldn't pursue a relationship with her. After yesterday he'd understood this. Understood that being a father would mean making personal sacrifices. As the pastor slowly brought the boat into position, Spence pulled out the fishnet.

"I'm sorry."

"No big deal," Spence replied.

"Not just about the cap. I'm sorry about yesterday. I tried to explain last night, but I couldn't find you."

"There's no need," Spence said, his own voice sounding as if someone had shoved a cheerful note into it by force. "I accepted your apology yesterday."

"I want to tell you," Deena said in a low, serious tone, "that what I did, taking the kayak out and all, was wrong. But, Spence, something really amazing happened last night. I don't think any of us will be the same."

Spence already knew this. He'd known it since the night before when he'd stood at the door to Alyssa's cabin and she had looked up at him. Really looked at him in a way she hadn't since that first day he'd shown up. To his amazement, she'd asked him to pray with her before she went inside.

"Look. You don't need to go into this any further," Spence said. They'd neared Deena's cap, bobbing about like a red turtle. He fished it out and handed it to her, dripping wet.

Deena took it gingerly, wrinkling her nose. "It smells like a dead fish."

The girls in the banana boat laughed. Spence's gaze stayed on Alyssa the longest. She looked tiny tucked between Evie and Lourdes.

"You all ready?" Spence yelled.

"Ready," the girls shouted.

The line between the powerboat and inflatable tightened, and the banana boat jerked forward. Spence kept his gaze peeled on the cluster of girls and appreciated the rush of wind and the roar of the motor that prevented him from further discussion with Deena.

Alyssa gave him a thumbs-up sign. He gave her the same, although it took quite a bit not to yell that she should keep holding on to the handle and not be waving at him.

Yet he'd been given very specific instructions that morning. "Uncle Spence," she'd said when she came to his clinic for her morning medications, "if you come with us on our reward trip this morning, please don't ask me if I'm feeling okay, or wearing enough sunscreen, or drinking water regularly. I'm not a little kid."

From his perspective, she was a little kid. "Okay," he'd agreed. "I'll just bring my stethoscope and blood pressure cuff."

"This isn't funny," Alyssa said and gave him a piercing look that reminded him so much of Evan that he couldn't breathe for a moment. "And in the future when I'm around my friends, please don't make a big deal about my health. Don't fuss over me. It's embarrassing. And unnecessary." She'd given him a calculating look. "Miss Deena doesn't do it."

"In the future," Spence had repeated casually as if his mind had not already leaped to its own conclusion about what those three words meant. "As in the rest of the week, or as in. . .something more permanent?"

"More permanent." Her gaze dropped to the floor.

With those two simple words, Spence felt his life change forever. A change that both thrilled him and scared him to death. He was pretty good at rescuing people, but sticking around them afterward, that was new territory.

Pastor Rich began a series of turns. Spence's jaw tightened as the banana boat jumped the wake and caught a good two feet of air. The girls screamed bloody murder as the boat slapped down.

"Are we supposed to be going this fast?" Deena shouted, her hair wild and her eyes bright.

"Yeah," Spence shouted back, although he'd been thinking the same thing.

If any one of those girls fell off that banana, he'd be in the water immediately. In that moment, he realized he would not be going to medical school. God had called him to be a paramedic, and that was what he would continue to do. He'd find work that wouldn't take away from his time with Alyssa, but he'd stay an EMT. When the camp finished, he'd start looking for another paramedic job in Winsted.

He pushed his sunglasses more firmly onto his face. They would begin building the life he and Alyssa had discussed that morning.

"You sure you want to stay with me?" he'd asked.

"Yes."

Spence had bent to look her in the eye. Eyes that were the same color and shape of Evan's. And his, too.

"What about Texas?"

She shrugged. "What about it?"

Spence ignored the voice telling him not to push. "What's changed?"

Silence. He didn't think he could bear it if she put up that wall between them again.

"Me," she said. "That's what's changed. When I had that asthma attack, I realized I didn't want to die."

Spence had felt the hair on the back of his neck stand bolt upright. A panic like he'd never encountered on any rescue mission shot through him. "Alyssa," he said gently, "you weren't thinking of killing yourself, were you?"

"No," she'd said. "Not physically. But if I went to Texas, I think part of me would have died, too." She looked up at him, her eyes looking far older than her twelve years. "I really wanted to live with you, Uncle Spence, but I felt like I didn't deserve it."

"What?" Spence had heard her clearly, but her words made no sense to him. "Why would you think that?"

Alyssa's gaze dropped to the tile floor. Spence gently placed his finger under her chin and lifted her face.

"Because it was all my fault." Her mouth trembled. "The accident."

"Alyssa," Spence said, "none of that was your fault."

She shook her head. "I should have been with them. In that car. Only I was reading this book I wanted to finish. I argued and argued and finally they let me stay home." She looked up at him. "If I'd been with them, it would have changed the timing. They wouldn't have been in that exact place at that exact time. They'd still be alive."

If, if, if. How many times had Spence said the same thing to himself? If only he had been more direct with Evan, shared his concerns instead of fearing he would hurt his brother's feelings. If only he had insisted that Evan get help for his drinking. If only he'd called for a family intervention.

"One more loop," Pastor Rich shouted, bringing Spence back to reality.

He glanced at Deena, wild haired and flushed from the wind and speed of the ride. He wondered if he'd done the right thing, telling Alyssa that Evan had been drinking and this had been a contributing factor in the accident. He had not told Alyssa that her father had been intoxicated or that he had a drinking problem. His goal had been to free Alyssa from her guilt. She'd cried, and so had he. The first tears since Evan had passed away.

He wanted to tell Deena, but this new bond with Alyssa seemed much too new and fragile. Plus he felt compelled to protect his brother in death, even as he had not in life.

The boat completed its final loop and slowly glided toward the shore. As the sandy beach neared, Spence turned to Deena. "In case things get crazy and I don't see you before we leave this afternoon, I just want to thank you for all you've done for Alyssa. She's not the same girl as the one who arrived."

"I know." Deena looked into his eyes. "And she's got the poison ivy spots and bug bites to prove it."

"And she's got a good friend in Evie," Spence said. "I think they're going to stay in touch."

The boat came to a gentle stop, and Pastor Rich cut the engine. The sudden quiet seemed loud in Spence's ear. What about them? Did he want to stay in touch with Deena? He read the question in Deena's eyes and let his silence be the answer.

He busied himself with reeling in the banana boat, glad for the feel of the thick cable in his hands. The inflatable drifted closer, and when the water became shallow enough, the girls hopped off.

The next time he looked at Deena, she was halfway out of the boat. Their eyes met, and his heart hammered in his chest. It would take so little to open that door between them.

He glimpsed her straight back and glossy, wind-blown hair. Then she walked down the long arm of the pier and out of his life.

Chapter 28

Only a few hours remained before the buses left camp and took her back to her old life. Deena gathered her beach bag from the boathouse. Most of her packing had been completed early this morning, but she had no desire to go back to the cabin and pretend everything was okay.

Because it wasn't. She wasn't. She wasn't sure who she was anymore or what she wanted in life. Yesterday she'd felt the door reopening on her faith, and with it she had let herself start to believe God had a plan for her—a plan that actually included a family.

She walked more briskly down the needle-laden path. All these years she'd been telling herself relationships were distractions and the responsibilities that came along with them would keep her from giving the best of herself to her work. It had all been lies, though, lies that protected her from being vulnerable to someone, from letting people get too close.

Yet despite these very strong walls she'd built around herself, Spence had gotten close to her.

She passed the archery field with the targets neatly lined up, waiting for the next group of campers. The pool was empty, as were the volleyball courts and the horseshoe pits.

Just what was she supposed to do now? If God had a plan for her life, why was He so mysterious about it? Couldn't He just come right out and tell her what to do?

Deena found herself at the base of the Leap of Faith. She stared up at the telephone pole and thought about the time when Spence had soared through the air like Superman. Evie, too, had successfully completed the jump.

"Hey. Can I help you?"

Deena jumped at the sound of a man's voice. Turning, she saw a teenager wearing a nylon vest with a coil of rope slung over his shoulder. "Oh no. I was just looking."

"Because if you wanted to, you could try it. I haven't started taking everything apart yet."

"Oh no. No thank you." She started to walk away and then hesitated. This exercise—it was all about learning to deal with fear. Deena touched the hard surface of the wooden pole. Suddenly she was tired—so tired of living with all the fears she kept bottled up inside her.

"You have to put a harness on if you're going to climb," the boy said. He had one in his hands as if he'd known all along she'd try it.

Deena stepped into the nylon straps and held her breath as the young man pulled the straps tight around her. She didn't flinch as he clipped the safety rope to her back. "Okay, you're all set."

The first rung felt warm and reassuringly solid. It felt right to be doing this, as if she was meant to do it.

Halfway up it felt less right. In fact, she felt awfully woozy. Looking up at how high she still had to climb made her stomach shrivel to the size of a raisin. She didn't dare look down. The rungs slipped in her sweaty palms, yet she was afraid to let go and wipe her hands on her shorts.

The higher she went, the more wobbly the pole became. No one had prepared her for this. No one had warned her that the pole would shake as if moved by a small earthquake. It made her angry. She used the anger to keep moving.

Finally, her hands found the top of the pole. She traced the pole's flat surface, no bigger than a dinner plate. The anger disappeared, and in its place the fear returned, roaring in her ears like a jet engine.

Replacing fear with faith was the point of this exercise. She had to find her faith. There was a harness on her back. Even if she lost her balance, the safety line would keep her from falling to the ground.

Gathering her courage, Deena pulled herself onto the top of the pole. There wasn't much space, but she managed to get both her hands and her feet onto the circle of wood. For an agonizing few seconds she posed with her rear end skyward, the pole swaying slightly and her own fear bringing bile to the back of her throat.

She had to look ridiculous from the ground, perched like this. Yet Deena didn't think she could let go. She'd stay in this yogalike position until one of her muscles cramped or they sent the helicopter to come and get her. *Faith, Deena. Find your faith.*

She stood up.

The world swayed. She glimpsed the ground a million miles away. Moving her eyes increased the feeling of vertigo. She reached her arms out, but there was nothing to help steady her.

The trapeze hung just a few feet away. She should jump for it before she lost her balance completely. Before she lost her nerve. *Dear God*, Deena prayed. *I'm letting go.*

The world dropped away from her. She stretched out her arms like Wonder Woman and with a rush of adrenaline flew through the air. The trapeze bar rushed closer and closer. A second later, her hands smacked painfully onto the hard, round pole. Her fingers frantically scrambled, but she had too much momentum. The pole slid out of her grasp.

In the blink of an eye, Deena felt herself falling. A second later, she felt the jerk of the safety line and found herself hanging like a giant fish suspended just above the safety net.

"You did great," the boy said, managing somehow to sound sincere, excited even, as he lowered her slowly. "You almost made it. Want to try again?"

Deena shook her head. She hadn't done great. She'd failed. All those fears she wanted to replace with faith were still firmly attached to her. Just look at her, trembling like a leaf. It would be a miracle if her legs would even hold her upright.

Earlier she'd asked for answers, and she'd gotten them.

Deena was going home.

Chapter 29

Deena keyed in the code to the cell culture lab and pushed open the door. She'd only been gone eight days, but it seemed much longer. She felt as though she were stepping into the room for the first time, looking around and taking in all the sights.

She pulled her lab coat from its peg on the back of the door and slipped it on, then donned a pair of latex gloves. The room seemed quieter than she'd remembered. It was a good quiet, though, a good thinking kind of quiet. Problem solving. Troubleshooting. Figuring out which tumors would react to what treatments. This was what she had always loved about her work.

She flicked on the UV light to prepare a sterile area behind the glass hood and removed a subculture plate from the incubator. She gathered a few more supplies—her pipettes and the nutrients she would insert into the cancer samples that would keep the cells alive—and sat down to get to work.

The next time she looked up, it was six o'clock. Driving home, she almost stopped at a pizza parlor for a pepperoni pie, but she wouldn't let herself. It would only remind her of eating pizza with Spence. She needed to put him and everything associated with him behind her.

In her condo, Deena popped a frozen dish of macaroni and cheese into the microwave. Maybe not the best nutritional choice, but she really needed comfort food.

As the dish heated, she wondered how Stacy was doing, if the heart-to-heart talk had worked and if her sister's relationship with Evie had improved. The night camp had ended, she and her sister had sat down and talked. Deena had shared Evie's fears of not being loved as much as the new baby. Stacy had been shocked, then hurt, then resolved to make things better between herself and Evie.

Deena turned on the television for background noise. When the microwave pinged, she removed the dish and poured herself a glass of filtered water from the refrigerator. She wondered how Spence and Alyssa were doing, if they were eating dinner right at this very moment.

From the living room, she heard a man's voice on the television inviting watchers to call an 800 number if they had been involved in a car accident and were seeking compensation.

From his perch, Mr. Crackers squawked, "Call 203-555-3393."

Deena threw away the plastic covering the macaroni. "That's not even the right number," she said.

She carried her dinner back into the living room and plopped down on the couch. She stirred the gummy pasta with her fork. The news returned, bringing with it disasters happening around the world. Deena barely listened.

Everything was exactly as she'd left it before camp, and yet nothing seemed the same. The macaroni was tasteless. She set it down on the coffee table.

"Call 203-555-3393," Mr. Crackers said.

"Quiet," Deena snapped.

"Call 203-555-3393," Mr. Crackers said, and there was something familiar about the way he said it that drew Deena's attention.

Deena frowned. She must be imagining things, but for a moment there Mr. Crackers had sounded a little like Alyssa. She walked over to his perch by the sofa. "Did you get that number from the television, or did someone teach you that?"

The bird regarded her solemnly. Smart as he was, he didn't speak English. Deena would have to try something else to get the answer. She coughed.

"P-U. Who cut the cheese?"

Okay. Not that prompt. She'd try another. "Call. . ."

"Call 203-555-3393." Mr. Crackers cocked his head just like he did when he expected a reward.

Again, she wasn't totally sure, but he sounded a lot like Alyssa. Deena gave the bird a bit of dried pineapple.

If Alyssa had taught the bird that number, it probably meant the number belonged to Spence. Should she call him?

Deena didn't think she had much to offer Spence. She couldn't cook, sew, iron, or do anything a good wife and mother should be able to do. And he might want more children. Did she really want to risk passing along any of her cancer genes? And yet hadn't she secretly always longed for children?

She closed her eyes. It was all too much to contemplate. Like standing atop that telephone pole and trying to take the Leap of Faith. She'd learned that wanting to put aside fears and actually being able to do it were two different things.

Yet looking back she wondered if she had missed the whole point of the exercise. Maybe it wasn't catching that trapeze bar that mattered. Maybe all God cared about was that she had taken a step in faith.

She thought about what had happened the night of the scavenger hunt. She could choose to believe Alyssa's asthma attack had been nothing more than an anxiety attack, or she could choose to believe something else had been at work—that God's voice had been whispering in her ear and telling her what to do.

If she believed this, then it was not too big a stretch to believe other things. That her mother's death had a purpose. It had served to direct her into research and had prompted her to reach out to women battling this disease as if they were her sisters.

It felt awkward, but thankfully no one saw her drop down on her knees and clasp her hands together.

I've been so angry at You for letting my mother get sick and die. Please forgive me for not trusting You, for turning away and thinking I could run my life better than You. Thank You for showing me the truth—for hearing me when I called out to You. I know I need to change. I want Your will for me.

The same commercial came on with the lawyer telling viewers to call a toll-free number.

"Call 203-555-3393," Mr. Crackers said.

Deena closed her eyes tightly. She wanted a voice to assure her that she, Spence, and Alyssa could lead a long and happy life together. That she would stay cancer free and be able to balance a personal and professional life.

It didn't happen. There wasn't any lightning flash of insight into her life. But she became aware, gradually, of a peaceful feeling. As if just by bringing the problem to God, she'd found the answer.

She wasn't sure, but she thought it meant He was giving her a choice. She could call Spence or not—God would love her either way. If she chose to focus on her work, He would help her deal with the loneliness. If she called Spence, He would be there to rejoice or to console her if things didn't work out.

She could mess up or succeed, and God would love her just as much. No problem was bigger than Him, and there was nothing He could not overcome.

She rose. The phone sat on the kitchen counter. She stared at the black receiver. All she had to do was punch in the numbers Mr. Crackers had recited and she'd be talking to Spence. She picked up the receiver and set it down again.

She couldn't do it. She couldn't stand it if he was polite but distant, and she didn't know what she'd say if he seemed happy to hear from her.

It was the Leap of Faith all over again. She was too scared to take the jump. *Small steps,* Deena reminded herself. Small steps made in the faith that God would direct them.

One little phone call. She'd simply ask Spence how he and Alyssa were doing. She'd read some promising articles about new treatments in asthma. They could discuss that.

Before she changed her mind, she punched in the numbers.

A man answered on the first ring. "Joe's Pizza."

Deena very nearly dropped the phone. "I'm sorry. I must have the wrong number."

All this agony of wondering whether or not to call and what to say. Stupid. Stupid. Stupid. Mr. Crackers had memorized a pizza parlor's phone number.

"Deena, please don't hang up."

It was Spence's voice, but what was he doing working in a pizza parlor? Deena discovered she didn't care. "Spence?"

"Yeah."

She gripped the phone harder. "How are you?"

"I'm fine," he said. "But your pizza is getting cold."

"I didn't order a pizza."

"And I don't work at Joe's," Spence said. "But I am standing downstairs, and I do have a pizza. Can I come up?"

She buzzed him up, and a moment later, there he was, all six feet four inches of him, standing at her front door with a pizza box. She pulled the door open wider, and he stepped inside.

"How did you know I was going to call you?" Deena asked.

"Call 203-555-3393," Mr. Crackers said.

Spence's gaze jerked to the bird, who watched them from his perch near the sofa. "What?"

"Every time someone says 'call,' he says your number."

"He sounds like Alyssa."

"I think she helped teach him your number." She gestured helplessly.

"I'm really glad she did, but I was coming here anyway to talk to you."

She stared at him, looking oddly just right in her condo. Pottery Barn meets mountain man. Would they both live happily ever after?

She folded her arms. "What did you want to talk about?"

He looked around for a place to set down the pizza box. Deena motioned him to the galley-style kitchen. He set the box on the counter. "I just didn't like the way we left things."

He looked so handsome and serious. That short, pale hair. His tan, rugged face. Those forest green eyes watching her so carefully. "I've been thinking a lot. And praying about this." He took a step toward her. "I don't know what the future holds for us, but I know the present isn't quite right without you."

Deena leaned against the refrigerator. The world was tilting just the way she'd wanted it, but it scared her so badly she didn't know what to do. "I...I could get cancer."

"And so could I. We're all in God's hands."

"Well, I can't cook."

"I don't want a cook. I want you. I want to get to know you better."

She shifted, and a magnet holding a takeout menu crashed to the ground. She couldn't take her gaze off him. "I don't know."

"That's okay. I do." He touched her cheek gently. His fingers were warm and wonderfully rough against her skin. "Deena, I love you. Will you give us a chance?"

The old fears were there pumping away beneath her skin with every beat of her heart. But there was faith as well, urging her to step forward, to love and let herself be loved.

God, I'm letting go.

"I say yes—a thousand times, yes." Deena placed her arms around his neck and lifted her face to his. He laughed and locked his arms around her. For a person who didn't like being hugged or hugging, she had to admit it felt pretty good.

He said her name softly, lovingly.

Deena tilted her head back to see his eyes. "Whoever thought I'd fall for the pizza delivery man?"

"The same person who knew I'd end up with Wonder Woman."

"I guess God is smiling pretty big right now," Deena said.

"Yeah. I think He is."

They looked at each other for a long moment, knowing what was to come and not wanting to hurry it. Finally, he tilted his head toward her.

Deena closed her eyes and fell into his kiss.

Epilogue

Six years later

C an you believe it? We're going to be counselors this year!" Evie's voice, high and excited, overflowed into the hallway.

"You think one of us will get our old cabin?"

The stack of clothing nearly overflowed the plastic laundry basket as Deena stepped into Alyssa's bedroom. She set the basket on the bed and regarded both girls.

"Maybe," Deena said. "But whatever cabin you end up in, it'll be the right one. You'll see."

Alyssa, who had long given up her thick, black-rimmed glasses in favor of contact lenses, smiled up at her. "Did I tell you that Lourdes is going to be a counselor, too?"

"Only like a million times." Deena perched on the edge of the bed. During the past six years, both girls had changed so much.

Evie had grown to her full height—six feet—a full two inches taller than Deena herself. She would attend UConn in the fall and study child psychology. Alyssa, also bound for UConn, intended to go premed. Not into research, she'd explained almost apologetically, but into cardiology like her grandfather.

"So what are you going to do, Mom, with an empty house for a week?" Alyssa asked.

No matter how many times Deena heard that word, it still had the power to take her breath away. She'd never thought she'd marry, much less be a mother, yet she had been both these things for the past four years.

"The house won't be so empty," Deena teased. "Not with Spence and all the animals."

During the years, stray animals had a way of finding their way to the Rossi home. There was Mr. Crackers, a middle-aged bird now, close to thirty. Spence's German shepherd, Tyler, had passed away, but Spence had been unable to resist the pleading looks on the faces of two shaggy dogs he'd found by the side of the road one night. Several years ago Grandma Dixie had sent Alyssa a four-legged birthday present for her fourteenth birthday—a quirky but sweet thoroughbred named Willis who had been named after the Texas town where Grandma lived.

"I remember all the pranks I pulled that year you were our cabin counselor." Evie plucked at the bedspread. "I don't know how you put up with me."

126

"Oh, honey, that was the best week of my life. I wouldn't change one thing about it." Deena thought about the night Evie had unleashed the frogs and the morning she'd awakened to find herself wrapped in toilet paper.

"Remember how you couldn't hit our target in archery until we had you aim at the target to the right of ours?" Evie laughed. "Spence looked so surprised."

"And how you taught us to hula by downloading the instructions off the Internet?" Alyssa shook her head, sending her long blond ponytail flying. "That was so funny."

The three of them sat there together remembering. Of course for Deena, finding her faith and making a commitment to the Lord had been the pivotal moment of her life. Everything good that had happened to her could be traced back to the moment when she got down on her knees and gave her life to God.

So much had happened since then. She and Spence had started dating. The following summer when they'd returned to Camp Bald Eagle, he'd proposed to her during a moonlit walk on the dock. He'd gotten down on one knee and looked up at her with his heart in his eyes. "I love you," he'd said, "and I want to spend the rest of my life with you. Will you marry me?"

They'd gotten married on that dock, too. A summer wedding, of course, held right after the first camp session.

She'd worn her mother's wedding dress, and Stacy had cried when she'd seen Deena in it. "You look so beautiful," she'd said. "Mom and Dad would have been so happy."

"You look gorgeous, too," Deena said, handing her sister a tissue. Stacy wore a lilac-colored dress. She'd lost all her pregnancy weight and once again hardly weighed more than a hundred pounds.

"The music is about to start," Jeff said. "We should line up." He fingered the paper in his hands—a poem he had written just for this day. Deena hadn't heard it yet, but Stacy said it was beautiful.

Deena gripped her bouquet of flowers more tightly. A small crowd of well-wishers stood near the dock. She recognized Lourdes, Taylor, and Britty, who had come with family members. There were Quing and Andres and two more of her friends from the lab. Even Alyssa's grandparents had flown up from Texas to be there.

Deena's heart began to pound, and despite herself a flood of old doubts rushed through her mind. Could she really do this? *Absolutely,* her heart said. She wanted to do this.

Guitar music started, and Jeff walked Stacy down the pier. Alyssa, escorted by Deena's nephew Jack, went next. Evie followed, holding on to two-year-old Thomas's hand. The little boy scattered rose petals over the wooden planks. It was Deena's turn. The hem of her dress brushed the surface as she moved, every step bringing her closer to Spence and to a future she had never expected she would have. The light sparkling off the water was brighter than diamonds, and the blue sky was a joyous color. Her heart beat much too fast, not out of fear, but out of love for the man waiting for her at the end of the pier. Spence, tall and handsome in the navy suit. Spence, looking at her with so much love. Spence, the man with whom she would spend the rest of her life.

"Aunt Deena?"

Deena jerked back to the present. She had so much to be thankful for. She looked from Alyssa's face to Evie's. "Yes?"

"You okay?"

"Oh yeah, I'm just going to miss you all."

So soon they would be going off to college, leaving to begin their lives as adults. But what a blessing they had been to her. Sometimes she almost couldn't believe she was forty-one and cancer free.

She'd had some scares, but every six months she continued to get good reports. Each time it surprised her to hear someone actually say she was fine. Spence, however, firmly felt it was just not her time yet. Daily he encouraged and supported her research.

Sometimes Deena felt like pinching herself. She looked at Spence and couldn't believe that any two people could be so happy together. Oh, they had their fights—she still didn't like that motorcycle he'd bought—but mostly they were happy.

Maybe it was because they knew life could be fragile and had to be appreciated each and every day. But mostly, Deena thought, it was because of God's goodness. By His grace, she lived a life fuller than she ever could have imagined.

Sometimes she still dreamed of her mother. Not as she was, but how she could have been. In her dreams, her mother's face was unlined, smiling, and pain free. Her long black hair tumbled in a thick, wavy mass to her shoulders, just as Deena's did now. The face was her mother's, and it was also her own. It didn't matter that this was impossible. All Deena knew was they both were happy.

A WHOLE NEW LIGHT

Dedication

Many thanks to Kathleen Y'Barbo and Kelly Hake. Without the help of these two awesome Christian women and amazing writers, this book would never have happened.

Chapter 1

"Y ou working late again, Celie?"

Celie Donovan lowered the nozzle of the portable steam presser and smiled at James Terelli who had escaped his office in accounting and was now standing behind her, clutching what was probably his sixth cup of coffee. "Libby wants all the outfits ready to ship Wednesday morning. You know she's going to go over everything with a magnifying glass."

At George Marcus Designs, perfect was the name of the game. A loose thread, a minuscule sag in the drapery, a hemline a fraction too long or short, elicited an immediate and scathing dressing-down from head designer Libby Ellman.

Celie didn't like the woman's managerial style but respected her flair for design. With Libby's help, George Marcus was one of the top design houses in New York City and arguably the world. "What are you still doing here, James?"

"Ah, show stuff, lots of invoices." James took a long swallow of coffee. "Besides, Frieda's cousin is visiting from Atlanta. Last night it was *Steel Magnolias*. Tonight it's *Beaches*. Why anyone wants to see a movie that makes them cry is beyond me."

Celie laughed and checked the hemline for the third time. "It's a girl thing, James. You need to embrace your feminine side." Judging from the way his hand shook, James also needed to embrace the idea of caffeine-free coffee. She'd been trying for more than a year to get James to cut back.

"I have enough exposure to my feminine side in this business." He gestured around the room. "I'm surrounded by dresses all day long."

"And you love it."

"Who wouldn't love the long hours, high stress, and low pay?" James pushed aside a bolt of chartreuse satin and perched on the edge of the worktable. "A bit of fatherly advice. Go home, Celie. Don't let Libby work you so hard that you don't have time to get your own outfits ready." He pointed the coffee cup at her. "This is your big chance, and you only get one in this business."

He didn't have to tell her this. Ever since she had been a little girl using a box of crayons to sketch, Celie had dreamed about being a designer. Growing up, she'd practically learned to read by poring over magazines like *Harper's Bazaar*, *Elle*, and *Glamour*.

"I know. Every time I think about it, I feel as green as"—she pointed to the bolt of fabric near James—"that satin."

It was true. Even now as she slipped a protective plastic covering over the tangerine silk, her stomach rolled as if she were on the Staten Island Ferry. The

Fashion Walk of Fame was Saturday. What if she stunk? What if everyone hated her dresses?

Although Libby had approved her sketches and George Marcus had selected Celie out of everyone else at the store, she couldn't quiet her preshow nerves.

"Don't worry. You're going to be a hit." James nodded knowingly. "I may work in accounting, but I have spies everywhere."

"Just promise me you and Frieda will be there." She'd feel much better if James and his wife were at the show.

"You know we'll be there," James said. "So will the other design assistants, the administrative staff, and as many of the cleaning crew as we can slip in. We're all pulling for you, Celie."

"Thanks, James." Her throat went tight. "You know that means everything to me. I can't wait for you and Frieda to meet my parents. They're flying in the day after tomorrow."

The thought of her parents coming sent a pleasant shiver of expectation through her. They'd never been to Manhattan before, and she couldn't wait for them to see the Empire State Building, Broadway, Rockefeller Center, and of course, the Garment District.

"They've got to be proud of you, Celie. Having your dresses modeled in the Fashion Walk of Fame is a huge accomplishment for any designer, much less one as young as you are."

Celie felt herself blush. Her parents *were* proud of her. Her mother had mailed her a photo of the banner her parents had placed on the window of their dry cleaning business. It read: HOME OF FASHION WALK OF FAME DESIGNER CELIE DONOVAN. There had even been an article in the town paper.

"Thirty isn't that young," Celie joked.

"It is to me," James said. "You're barely out of diapers."

"Like you're so ancient. You're not even old enough to be vintage." Celie scanned the contents of a plastic bag to make sure all the accessories that went with the gown were there—the Jimmy Choo stilettos, the David Yurman gold spiral earrings and sterling-silver bracelet.

"Just don't go and forget the little people when you're rich and famous."

"I don't think that's going to be a problem." Celie smiled at the man who had been her friend ever since she'd found him frantically searching the showroom for a clean shirt and tie. He'd accidentally spilled coffee all over himself and had been just about to step into a meeting with George Marcus and the board of directors. There were no men's shirts in the store—all the company's designs were for women. Within minutes, Celie had transformed a woman's silk scarf into a stylish tie that coordinated perfectly with James's suit and completely covered the stain. He earned high praise not only for his professional presentation but also for his personal sense of style.

James crumpled the Styrofoam cup and tossed it in the trash can. "You ready to go? I don't like you taking such a late train."

"Just a few more minutes, James."

It took more than a few minutes. Celie ended up taking the 10:40 p.m. out of Grand Central Station. The train was nearly empty, and she had no trouble finding a seat. She closed her eyes as the train slid forward through the long black tunnel. Best to nap while she could. It might be her only sleep that night. She wanted to add a few beads to her strapless evening dress, and she still had more work to do on the hand-painted floral gown. James would kill her if he knew she'd taken that dress home, but what else was she supposed to do? Milah, a single mom and the new assistant designer, had accidentally damaged the dress when she'd tried to press it. Since Celie had been the one to paint the fabric in the first place, she had offered to fix it. Milah, fearing she'd be fired if anyone found out, had begged Celie to fix it secretly. It went against store policy to bring a dress home without permission, but Milah's tears had been impossible to ignore. Celie felt confident she could slip the dress back on the rack just in time for Libby's inspection in the morning.

It was raining lightly a little more than an hour later when she stepped off the train at the Stamford station. She pulled the thin trench coat around her a little more tightly. The flirty little skirt and cotton top had been optimistic choices, but she hadn't been able to resist the lightweight fabrics. Spring might have officially arrived, but the temperature refused to recognize it. She'd be surprised if it were even fifty degrees.

She walked briskly off the platform, her Jimmy Choo heels clicking on the concrete, and retrieved her Honda from the outdoor parking lot. Stamford was pretty much empty as she drove through the business district. People went home after work, unlike Manhattan.

She turned onto Hickory Hill Road. Halfway up she smelled smoke. Her heart began to thump, and she drove a little faster. She knew it wasn't someone barbecuing. The smell of smoke grew stronger as she reached the top of the hill. Three yellow road barriers blocked her from driving any farther down the street. She pulled the Honda to the side of the road and stepped into the cold, rainy night. Clutching her purse, she began to run. In the distance, she saw the flickering blue lights of a parked police car and beyond that three fire trucks. The smell of smoke was so strong now that she could taste its acrid bitterness.

A stab of fear propelled her forward. She pushed her way through the crowd that had gathered behind a line of yellow tape and police barriers. *Oh God, no!* She stifled a cry at the sight of flames pouring out of the shattered windows of her apartment building. This couldn't be happening. She could feel the urge to scream rising up in her. Her fist clenched, and a low moan escaped her.

Firemen in bulky tan coats were everywhere—on the ground and in baskets at the top of ladders. They pointed gushing hoses at the building, drenching it in water that seemed powerless to extinguish a fire that sparked and crackled as if it enjoyed devouring the building. *Dear Lord, what happened? Had everyone gotten out all right?*

She scanned the faces in the crowd around her. "What happened? What's going on?" She spoke to anyone and everyone, but no one answered. Their shell-shocked, haggard faces seemed to look right through her. Behind the police barricade, she spotted a man wearing a dark jacket with FIRE MARSHAL written across the front. She was about to try to climb over the wooden barrier when the man lifted a megaphone.

"Good evening, folks. My name is Edward Townser, and I'm the fire marshal. First of all, I'd like to say how sorry I am that this happened. If you have any information about how the fire may have started, I'd appreciate it if you would give me your statement." He paused as the crowd shuffled, but no one stepped forward. "Secondly, I am declaring this building a total loss. This means you will not be allowed inside the building for any reason. The Red Cross is getting set up at the other end of the parking lot. They will help you with food and clothing as well as provide shelter for those who need it."

"Did everyone get out okay?" Celie shouted. She felt sick at the thought of Mrs. Jacobs, who had recently had a hip replacement, stuck inside the burning building. The Krenzincos had young children. Were they okay?

"We're in the process of determining that right now," the fire marshal replied. "We'll let you know as soon as we hear anything."

Someone patted her shoulder. She turned. It was old Mr. Arnold from 304-B. She gave him a hug, and they clasped hands and prayed.

Her hair was soaked, and the night's chill seemed to have worked its way right into her bones before the fire marshal made the next announcement that there had been no fatalities. Celie whispered a prayer of thanks and walked over to the Red Cross station. She stopped when she saw the long line of people waiting for help.

The enormity of what had happened began to hit her. Her legs started to shake, and she leaned heavily against the side of a car for support. *The dresses! The hand-painted silk. The layered peach chiffon. The beaded black and gold gown!* She bit her lip hard. *All gone—and so is my career. I am so dead when Libby finds out what happened.*

Lord, she prayed, *what am I going to do?*

Her mind immediately began to spin. She could call James and get his advice. No. He would try to intervene on her behalf and get in trouble by association. She could drive back to Manhattan and start sewing. But even if she worked all night, she wouldn't be able to replace the ruined gowns.

It began to rain harder. Celie felt cold wetness trickle down the back of her bowed neck. *Call Kiera,* a voice inside seemed to say. *She'll know what to do.* Yes. She'd call Kiera, and together they'd figure a way out of this mess. Celie nearly dumped the contents of her handbag searching for her cell phone.

She finally found it and punched the speed dial. *Come on, Kiera, pick up.* The call rang into voice mail. Celie wanted to cry with disappointment. "Kiera," Celie said, "I really need you. Please call me. There was a fire." Celie's throat tightened, and she pressed her hand to her eyes to push back the tears. "I'm not injured. But I'm in trouble. Just call me as soon as you can. Okay?" She flipped the phone shut and swiped her eyes again. Surely the fire was more important than their recent disagreement. Maybe Kiera had gone to bed early to get ready for an early morning fashion shoot. Yes, that had to be it.

I'll drive to her apartment. Her apartment buzzer is loud enough to wake the dead. And when she finds out what happened, she'll help me figure out what to do.

Her hands shook as she searched her purse for her keys. She'd almost reached her car when she remembered Kiera would be in Connecticut this week. She bit her lip, thinking hard. Kiera had said something about doing some catalog modeling. Celie couldn't remember the name of the company, but she did recall Kiera joking about having to stay at her family's apple orchard. "The house where time stands still," she'd said.

Celie stepped into the car just to get out of the rain. She could feel the panic creeping back, blocking her ability to think logically. What was the name of the town? *Something biblical,* she thought. *Bethlehem. That's right. Kiera mailed both our Christmas cards from the post office there so the stamp would say Bethlehem.* She searched her day timer and found an address but no phone number. It didn't matter. She'd find the orchard.

Celie started the Honda's engine, made a U-turn, and headed for I-95 North.

Chapter 2

Toaster's barking awakened him. Swinging his legs over the side of the bed, Matthew Patrick reached for a pair of jeans and a sweatshirt. For the past several nights, there'd been a fox stalking the barn. It was after the pygmy goats.

He pulled back the curtain and strained to look through the rain-streaked glass. Nothing but darkness and the fog of his own breath. Good. The motion detectors hadn't triggered the lights at the barn. No fox.

Toaster continued to make urgent, high-pitched noises. The dog might bark soprano, but he had the heart of a lion. Something was wrong.

"Mom, you all right?" he called into the dark house.

"Yeah, but Toaster won't quiet. You think it's the fox again?"

"No." Matthew padded downstairs in his bare feet. Toaster charged ahead and began urgently barking at the front door. Matthew pulled back the edge of the curtain in the living room. Through the falling rain, he spotted a small four-door sedan of a dark color—maybe blue or gray—parked in their driveway. Just sitting there. No headlights. He couldn't tell if it was empty or not. He thought about retrieving his rifle and then stared some more at the unfamiliar car.

It was three o'clock in the morning. Whoever was sitting there and whatever he wanted, it wasn't good news. Good news did not arrive in the middle of the night and sit in the driveway on a rainy night that couldn't be warmer than forty degrees. He'd get the gun.

"What is it?" his mom called from her bedroom. Her voice rang with worry. "What's going on?"

"There's a car in the driveway, Mom," Matthew said. "Stay in your room and let me handle this."

"You think it's Kiera?"

"No. Please stay in your room."

Before he could get the gun, though, the car door opened and a small figure stepped into the rain. Hunched over, a small woman in a trench coat and a pair of high-heeled boots raced across his driveway. A moment later, she knocked at the front door.

Matthew flipped on the porch lights and cracked open the front door. She was young—Kiera's age—but far shorter than his sister. This woman barely reached his shoulder. She had pale skin, and her dark-colored hair hung shoulder-length in wet strands around her face.

"I'm sorry to bother you," the woman said. "I was going to wait until morning,

136

but then the dog started barking. I saw the lights go on in the house." She peeked around him. "Is Kiera home? I'm one of her friends."

Matthew relaxed slightly. Now he understood the late arrival. She must have just heard. "I'm sorry, but Kiera's already gone. She left two days ago."

His mother's voice was sharp with fear. "Who's there? What's going on, Matthew?"

"A friend of Kiera's."

The next thing he knew, Toaster shot past his legs and ran onto the front porch, barking at the woman as if he might attack then messing up his tough-guy act by wagging his skinny little tail. "Get in here, Toaster."

As usual the dog paid no attention whatsoever to him. Toaster kept barking and circling. His mom'd kill him if the dog caught a cold. He opened the door wider and asked the woman to come inside. As he'd hoped, the dog followed. As the woman stood in the foyer, Toaster dropped the guard-dog act and began sniffing the woman's high-heeled boots with great interest.

The woman crouched and began petting Toaster. "Look how pretty you are," she said. "But what happened to your hair?"

Matthew almost laughed. Toaster did resemble the survivor of some scientific experiment that had gone terribly wrong. "He's a Mexican Hairless. He's supposed to look all bald like that."

The woman smiled. "Well, he's cute. And he's got really sweet bangs."

Matthew found himself smiling back. "His name is Toaster, and I'm Matthew Patrick. Kiera's brother." He extended his hand. The woman's fingers were cold. Their slender bones felt incredibly delicate in his hands. He smelled a very faint trace of smoke on her.

"I'm Celie Donovan. Nice to meet you."

The name hit him as sharp as a slap. He released her hand abruptly. This was Celie Donovan?

"Sorry you've come all this way for nothing," Matthew said, making little effort to conceal his disgust, "but Kiera isn't here. She's on her way to Mexico."

"Mexico? What's she doing in Mexico?"

As if you don't know, Matthew wanted to say. *As if you aren't Miss New York City's number one party girl, smelling like cigarette smoke and showing up on my doorstep in spike heels in the middle of the night.*

"On a cruise," his mom answered. "Kiera is taking a vacation cruise to Cozumel."

He turned, and there his mother was, on the second floor landing, looming over the top of the staircase with only her walker standing between them and disaster. "Go back to bed, Mom. Kiera's *friend*"—he paused significantly so his mother would know this woman was the exact opposite—"was just leaving."

"Leaving?" His mother's voice rose. "Matthew Joseph Patrick, you are not letting one of Kiera's friends go out in weather like this. Have you lost your senses?"

"It's all right," Celie said. "I'm so sorry to have bothered you. Please ask Kiera to call me the next time you talk to her."

"You shouldn't be going anywhere tonight," his mom stated. "Matthew, please bring in this girl's luggage and show her to Kiera's room."

The last place Matthew wanted Celie to stay was in his sister's room. He didn't want this woman touching Kiera's things, sleeping in her bed. Not after what she'd done.

"Really, Mrs. Patrick," Celie protested. "It's okay. I love driving at night. There's less traffic, and the moon and stars are so pretty."

"There are no moon and stars out tonight. It's raining." His mother's voice brooked no argument. "The road's probably flooding. We'll talk more in the morning, but for now, you stay with us." She nodded at him as if he agreed with her, which he clearly didn't. "Matthew, take Celie's coat and go get her luggage."

He wanted to argue but not with his mother perched precariously at the top of the stairs. As Celie protested about not wanting to impose, etc., etc., he reached his arms out for the trench coat.

She untied the sash, unbuttoned the coat, and then it was in his hands. Matthew blinked.

That purple skirt hugged her shapely hips then ended with little flippy pleats just above her knees. And if that wasn't enough, there were the textured stockings for his eyes to contend with. Her black leather high-heeled boots rose to just above her ankles. The shirt, some sort of frothy white concoction, had more froufrou than he'd ever seen in his life. She was lovely, which at the moment wasn't something in her favor.

"I'll get your luggage."

"I don't have any," Celie admitted. She pushed a strand of chin-length hair behind her ear.

What in the world had happened to have her show up in the middle of a rainy night with no luggage? Matthew bit his tongue. Whatever it was, he didn't care. "I'll just show you to your room, then." With her coat still clutched in his hands, he led her up the stairs.

His mother stepped back to give them room, and as they passed, she had the nerve to wink at him. Even worse, she said to Celie, "What a lovely outfit."

"Thank you, Mrs. Patrick," Celie said. "And thank you so much for letting me stay the night. There was a fire, you see, at my apartment building, and. . ." Celie felt her throat get tight. "I. . ."

"Shhh, child," June said. "You tell us all about it in the morning. There's extra blankets in the closet. You show her those, Matthew."

Matthew made a noise of agreement, but mostly he was assuring himself that it was only a few hours until daylight. After breakfast—an early breakfast—he'd send this woman packing.

Chapter 3

Y ou sleep okay, honey?" Mrs. Patrick had the same wide, generous smile as Kiera. Tall and slender, she also had the same strong facial bone structure and blue eyes. Only Mrs. Patrick's looked at her from behind a pair of oversized wire-framed glasses.

"Yes, thank you." Celie stepped into the large farm-style kitchen. She had slept well—sort of, when she wasn't lying in the big four-poster bed listening to the sound of the rain and trying not to worry about things. God had always provided for her, but she knew she was in big trouble with George Marcus Designs. When Libby Ellman discovered Celie had ignored company policy and taken home a gown, the head designer would be furious.

"Come have a seat." Mrs. Patrick patted the wooden chair next to her at the big, rectangular table. "Hope you like oatmeal." She gestured to Matthew, standing in front of a white range, stirring the contents of a large pot.

"I love it," Celie said, studying the straight line of Matthew's back. He was a tall man, muscular but not heavyset. He had thick, chestnut-colored hair more wavy than straight. His green flannel shirt and jeans looked comfortably worn, but there was nothing warm about the look he shot over his shoulder at her.

"It'll be ready in a minute," he said.

The room was clean and spacious—at least four times the size of Celie's galley-style kitchen in Stamford. The appliances looked old but fit well with the pine cabinets and butcher-block counters. A cheerful array of herbs sat in a bay window above the kitchen sink. Everything looked right, but something didn't feel right. Celie crossed her arms. Maybe it was just her, but the room felt a little cold.

The hairless dog, Toaster, leaped from Mrs. Patrick's lap and rushed over to greet her. She bent to pet him, glad for the warmth of his skin against her hands.

"Come sit, Celie." Mrs. Patrick patted the space next to her.

Celie moved aside Mrs. Patrick's metal walker and took a seat at the table.

"Oatmeal's ready." Matthew pulled three bowls from a cabinet. The clattering china sounded angry. He didn't look at her as he set a bowl in front of her. Well, showing up in the middle of the night probably hadn't earned her any popularity points.

"The rain's stopped," June commented. "You're lucky you got through last night, Celie. Doesn't take much to make the McGillis pond overflow."

"There was a lot of water on the road," Celie agreed, "but I just kept driving." She'd been terrified, gripping the wheel and leaning forward, struggling to see more clearly. A couple of times she'd heard water scraping the bottom of the car, but she'd just kept going, praying she wouldn't miss one of the signs pointing to the Patrick Orchards.

She hadn't seen the orchard last night, but she could see the trees now, acres and acres of them, visible through a large bay window. The sun had just come up enough for her to see trees filling the landscape, their gnarled and bare limbs gracefully posed as far as her eyes could see.

"Coffee, dear?"

"No thank you, Mrs. Patrick."

"Tea, then? That's what I'm drinking."

Celie's gaze swung to Matthew, who glared back at her.

"I'd love some tea, if it's not too much trouble."

"We don't have any of those fancy tea blends," Matthew said, ladling oatmeal into their bowls. "All we've got is plain old Lipton."

Even across the room, she could see the deep blue of his irises. Kiera's were the same color, but unlike his sister, there was no friendly twinkle in them. "I love Lipton."

Matthew's mouth twisted as if he doubted this very much, but he put the kettle on the cooktop. Returning to the table, he blessed the meal and picked up his spoon.

"So tell us, dear, about the fire."

Celie's mind jumped to the crackling flames, the foul black smoke, and the horror of watching her home burn. She couldn't begin to describe it. "It was awful. Nobody knew what to do, where to go. . . ." She twisted her fingers together as she described the burly firemen in oxygen masks, the charred face of the ruined apartment building, the blank and lost expressions of her former neighbors, the terrible smell of acrid smoke.

June stroked her dog. "Oh, Celie, I'm so sorry."

She stirred her oatmeal. "At least no one was killed," she said. "Everyone got out."

"Thank God," June declared.

"Yes," Celie echoed. "He kept everyone safe."

June squeezed Celie's arm with a thin but surprisingly strong grasp. "Whatever we can do to help, we will. Please feel free to borrow Kiera's clothing or mine. Anything you need."

"I appreciate that, Mrs. Patrick. That's really nice of you. Just letting me stay last night was a blessing." Celie nibbled at her oatmeal then set the spoon in the bowl.

"Please call me June. Kiera has told us so much about you that I feel like I know you already. She loves your designs. Half her closet is filled with your clothing."

"Or used to be," Matthew said pointedly. "I think she took most of *those outfits* with her to Mexico."

The way he said "those outfits" made Celie's chin lift. She wanted to ask him just what was wrong with her outfits but then held her tongue. Now wasn't the time to start an argument. She focused on the last part of his statement. "You said Kiera was in Mexico?"

"Well, on her way," June said firmly. A look that Celie didn't understand passed between the two Patricks. "She's taking a cruise ship out of Florida."

"I'm surprised she didn't mention the cruise to me." Kiera tended to be impulsive. "Let's be spontaneous" was her battle cry. But usually Kiera told her everything—then again, Kiera had been pretty upset with her the last time they'd spoken.

"Wallace Blake dumped her," Matthew stated bluntly. "Left her a text message. Didn't even have the decency to tell her face-to-face."

"What?" Celie set her mug down. "He did what?"

"He also gave the modeling job she wanted to another girl—one he's now dating. I'm surprised she didn't tell you," Matthew said. "You being her best friend and all."

Celie dropped her gaze. Matthew was right. Kiera should have called her—and would have if Celie hadn't called Wallace Blake a player and warned her that he wasn't the kind of guy to stick around. Kiera's response had been to slam down the phone. That had been about two weeks ago. It was longer than they'd ever gone without speaking, but Celie had been so wrapped up in work she hadn't had time to fix things between them.

"When is she coming back?"

"We're not really sure," June said. "A couple of weeks, we think. I know she would want you to stay with us, Celie, until things get settled with your apartment."

Matthew set his spoon down. "I'm sure Celie has to get back to the city."

Kiera on a cruise, brokenhearted. The fire. The burned hand-painted silk and her own lost designs. Her future at George Marcus. Celie put her hands flat on the table as if that would keep her mind from spinning. She'd yet to call her parents or work. She didn't know which was worse—telling her parents or Libby Ellman about the fire. Her mother had been packing and repacking her suitcase for a straight month and would be tremendously disappointed. Crushed, really. And Libby Ellman. Celie shuddered. Libby was going to kill her. *Please God, help me handle both of them.*

"Thank you for the offer, June, but I can't stay. I really need to get back to the city. May I use your phone before I leave?"

Matthew smiled for the first time since she'd walked into the room. He gestured toward a hallway off the kitchen. "Absolutely. You can use the one in my office."

❧

As soon as Celie left the room to make the necessary calls, Matthew said, "Don't you know who that is?"

His mother moved the half-eaten bowl of oatmeal closer so Toaster could lick its contents. "Of course I know who she is."

Matthew frowned as the small dog lapped up the contents. "You need to be eating more, Mom. If you want your hip to heal, you need the calcium in that oatmeal."

"My hip will heal, or it won't," she replied as if she didn't care one way or another. Matthew's stomach tightened the way it always did when she got like this, embracing the idea that this injury was the beginning of a slow downhill slide.

"If it weren't for her, Kiera would be here, with us. She never would have met that Wallace guy, and she'd never have gotten her heart broken."

"You don't know that, Matthew."

"She introduced them at a business party. Don't you remember Kiera telling us?"

"Maybe. It doesn't really matter."

"A girl like Celie is trouble."

"I like her."

Matthew pulled the oatmeal bowl right out from under Toaster's nose. He ignored the wistful look the dog gave him.

"You ought to help me convince Celie to stay," his mom added, giving him a look as unbending as steel. "If Kiera hears that her friend is staying with us, maybe she'll come home earlier."

Matthew set the dishes in the sink and turned on the faucet. When he'd driven Kiera to the airport, she'd given him a long hug, probably the longest she'd ever given him, and a look that said she wasn't coming back soon.

He'd always been able to fix things for Kiera—the china shepherdess that had fallen from her dresser, the frayed rope on the tire swing that she'd worn out, the first dent she'd put in their mom's old, blue Buick.

Matthew set a dish in the drying rack. "Let it go."

"Excuse me," Celie said quietly. He turned. She stood framed in the arched entranceway; her face was as white as her frilly blouse. "I was wondering if your offer was still open." She paused and swallowed. A bit dramatically, he thought. "I'd love to stay a few days with you all."

"Of course," his mother said, shooting him a triumphant look. "We'd love it."

"Thank you," Celie said, and her eyes shimmered with tears.

If she cried, he'd throw water on her. The water pressure in the sink was pretty good, and the spray from the hose might well cross the room. She was acting. Taking advantage of his mother's hospitality. Just like she'd taken advantage of Kiera's tendency to see the good in people. Celie was a good actress but an actress all the same. He wasn't buying it.

"Will you tell us what happened, honey?"

"Yes," Matthew echoed but made little effort to conceal the skepticism in his voice. "What happened?"

"She fired me," Celie said, and her lips quivered. She covered her mouth with her hand and looked embarrassed.

"She fired you," Matthew prompted.

"I took a dress home from the store, and I wasn't supposed to." Celie's breath hitched, and her cheeks flushed. "I was trying to fix it in time for the fashion show, but. . ." She sighed—again a bit too dramatically, he thought. "It got burned up. And so did three other dresses that were supposed to be in the show—my designs." She blinked hard. "Libby said I would be lucky if they didn't press charges against me."

"Oh, honey," his mother said in her most sympathetic voice. "She sounds like a horrible person. It wasn't your fault a fire burned down the building."

"Yes, but I shouldn't have taken a dress home without clearing it with Libby. George Marcus—he's the owner of the business—is really strict about us doing that. It's a security thing. He doesn't want anyone seeing his designs until he's ready."

"Well, he sounds like a horrible person, too," his mother said.

Matthew turned on the faucet. His mother hadn't seemed to grasp the concept that Celie had done something wrong—practically stealing from the company—and had gotten fired for it. Clearly they were getting stuck with Celie, at least for a few days. He refused to be part of this new drama. As far as he was concerned, the sooner Celie left, the better.

Chapter 4

Celie set the grocery bags on the kitchen table. She found June in the living room, gently snoring in a reclining chair of blue velvet fabric. The hairless dog, Toaster, sprawled across her lap, and the television droned on in the background.

Celie tiptoed away. Good. June probably needed to rest after last night. Returning to the kitchen, Celie began dinner. As well as a few clothing and personal essentials, she'd picked up some chicken breasts at a cute little general store in town.

She found a glass baking dish in one of the lower cabinets and pulled a frying pan with a shiny copper bottom from a hook on the wall. She seared the meat in the frying pan and made a glaze out of some peach jam.

Toaster came in to watch. When he began whining at the back door, she figured he needed to go out. She reached for her trench coat and opened the door.

The bald little dog dashed ahead of her, happily watering a bush, then refused to come back when she called.

Celie grabbed her coat and ran out the door. She chased Toaster through a grove of medium-sized trees—apple trees, no doubt—and ground her teeth in frustration when the dog refused to let her catch him.

What's going on, God? I've lost my house, my job, and now I can't even catch a dog?

Toaster led her to a big red barn. From the Dutch door of a front-facing stall, a horse greeted her with a low-pitched rumble. She was just about to pat its head when Toaster began yipping. Celie hurried to investigate.

Behind the barn, three small goats stood in the middle of a grassy pasture area. They were facing off with Toaster. Celie shouted for the dog to come, but, of course, he ignored her.

She didn't like the way the biggest goat was pawing the ground. Its horns looked capable of turning Toaster into doggy shish kebab. She shouted at Toaster, but the dog didn't seem to realize the goat meant business.

Celie's heart thumped as she swung her legs over the fence and dropped lightly into the paddock. The enclosed area had not seemed so big from the fence, but now it seemed like miles. She was almost to the little dog now; all she had to do was reach down and grab his bouncy little body. She reached for him, and then, as if by some unknown signal, the horned goat charged.

Celie screamed, turned tail, and ran for her life. Toaster shot past her. Her Jimmy Choos weren't designed for running across a pasture, but Celie had no choice. Her trench coat tore as she reached the fence line and jumped. Safe on the other side of the fence, Toaster trotted up to her, panting as if he were about to hyperventilate. Celie scooped him up. "Troublemaker," she whispered. Toaster licked her face enthusiastically.

"You're faster than I thought."

Celie spun around. Matthew stood behind her, and judging from his broad smile, he'd seen the whole thing. "Which is fortunate for me," Celie snapped. She shifted the dog in her arms. "You should post a sign warning people the goats are dangerous."

"Your life was never in danger," Matthew said. A very slight breeze lifted his wavy, chestnut hair. "Happy isn't an attack goat. The only thing that was ever in danger was the buttons on your coat."

"You obviously didn't see *Happy* charging me. He would have *horned* me if he'd caught me."

"You mean, butted you." There was the smallest twitch at the corner of his mouth that could have been a smile. "And you were moving much too fast. Never knew anyone could run in fancy shoes like those."

"It's not like I had a lot of choice," Celie snapped. "Besides, it just proves that you can wear Jimmy Choos anywhere."

Celie glanced down at her boots, stained with mud but still lovely. Even on sale they'd cost her a week's paycheck. But they were worth every penny. A less-quality heel would have snapped under that kind of stress.

"Next time you take Toaster for a walk, you need to put him on a leash." Matthew's voice had taken on a definitely stern quality.

Celie nodded.

"And he needs to wear a coat," Matthew continued. "There's a dog coat in the mudroom. A dog that has no hair is very sensitive to cold weather."

Celie held the dog a fraction closer. She could feel the dog's heart beating rapidly. "You think he'll be okay?"

"Yeah, but you'd better take him back to the house. I'll be down after I finish closing up the barn."

Celie hurried back to the house, hoping that Toaster hadn't gotten chilled. They hadn't been at the barn long, but the sun had started to set. The air felt much colder than when she'd left the house earlier. She walked quickly through the trees. In the distance, she heard the wind moving through the valley, and seconds later it sliced through her coat. Toaster shivered, so she opened her coat and slipped him inside. He snuggled against her like a baby.

Another gust of wind moved through the orchards, a dull, strong roar that burned her ears and carried with it, she thought, the ever-so-faint smell of something sweet, like roses.

Chapter 5

After dinner Matthew washed the dishes and Celie dried them. As he handed Celie a dish, he thought of Kiera and the countless times they'd stood at the porcelain sink doing dishes. It'd only been two days since she left, but he couldn't stop worrying about her. He still couldn't believe she'd tossed her cell phone out the window of her car as she'd driven away. That hadn't seemed like a very rational thing to do, but then again none of her recent decisions had been rational.

Kiera'd always been a bit impulsive, but a cruise to Cozumel seemed over the top, even for her. If his father had been alive, Matthew wondered what he would have done.

One of Matthew's strongest memories of his father was when Matthew was six years old. They had been taking down a tree with blight—it had unexpectedly split in half, trapping one of the workers beneath. Matthew's father had single-handedly lifted the trunk off Eustis Jones—a feat that Matthew later heard should have taken at least two men. When he'd asked his father about it, Dermott Patrick had simply said, "You take care of your own. You find a way to do what you have to do."

He'd tried. He'd been doing pretty well until Wallace Blake came along and lured Kiera away. Before Wallace, Kiera had been dating Aaron Buckman, his best friend since kindergarten. Aaron was quiet and steady, a strong Christian who ran the True Value hardware store. Matthew had foreseen many enjoyable family dinners with them.

A gust of wind rattled the windows. The last breath of winter. He passed the dripping plate to Celie. If the *Farmer's Almanac* was correct, and it usually was, the trees would be budding soon. He'd call Sue Enderman and set a date for the bees.

"You sure Toaster's okay?" Celie asked, casting an anxious glance at the dog in his mother's lap.

His mom stroked the little dog. "Toastie's fine. It's not the first time he's chased those goats. Right, Matthew?"

He nodded. "You can stand two feet away, bellow that dog's name at the top of your lungs, and he pretends he doesn't hear you."

Celie shot Matthew a sympathetic glance, which he pretended not to notice.

"You have to be nicer to him, Matthew. He likes cheeseburgers. If you started giving him cheeseburgers when you called him, he'd come running." She scratched behind the dog's upright ears. "Wouldn't you, little Toastie?"

"If I started making him cheeseburgers, his belly would be scraping the floor, which it nearly is already. You have to stop feeding him so much, Mom."

"But that chicken was simply delicious," June said. "Celie will have to tell you how to make it."

As he rinsed the plate, Celie babbled enthusiastically about herbs and searing a crust. It sounded a lot more complicated than the store-bought barbecue sauce he usually used. Celie happily finished the recipe, concluding that she and June would have to shop together at Tom's Market.

His mother's smile vanished abruptly. "I really don't get out of the house much anymore." She gestured to the walker. "Lugging that ugly thing around is a real pain in the neck."

The china plate clacked gently as Celie set it in the cupboard. "You know, we could decorate it. Put some cheerful ribbons on it or spray paint it hot pink."

Matthew finished the last dish and turned off the faucet. "Or Mom could do the exercises the doctor gave her and get stronger."

"As far as I am concerned, the Radio City Music Hall Rockettes would find those stretches challenging."

"The point, Mom, is to work at them. You'll get more flexible the more you do them."

His mother snorted.

"I could help," Celie volunteered. "We'll put on some good music, and it'll be fun."

Although his mom agreed, Matthew doubted it'd ever happen. He'd tried countless times, even gotten down on the floor, demonstrating how easy they were to do. His mother had nearly split her sides laughing as Toaster had licked his face and then sat on his chest.

He set the sponge in its holder and retreated to his office.

～

"Paperwork," June sighed as she settled herself into the velvet fabric of the reclining chair. "The computer is supposed to make it easier, but all it does is complicate things."

June patted her lap, and Toaster jumped onto her. Reaching for the television remote, she punched a button.

"We use computers all the time for designing," Celie said, "but you're right. I much prefer to draw by hand." She sat back on a rather formal sofa with a lovely blue and white chintz fabric. She'd asked June if she could borrow a sewing basket, and now Celie searched for a needle and thread to repair her torn coat.

Just the act of holding the needle in her fingers soothed her, as if she were repairing not just the fabric but also something deep within herself. She kept the tension even, and soon a neat line of tiny stitches formed. Looking up, she found June watching her. "Do you sew?"

The old woman nodded. "Oh, I used to. There's a fabulous fabric store in town called Fabric Attic." She pointed to a set of plain white curtains flanking the windows. "I made those, too." She smiled wryly. "About a hundred years ago."

"They're pretty."

"Oh, they're pretty plain. Every once in a while, I think about redecorating, but then it seems too much work."

"Your home is beautiful. That wing chair in the corner and that secretary on the wall—they're antiques, aren't they?"

"Yes, from Ireland. Matthew's grandfather Thomas brought them over when he immigrated in 1922. He built this house—no plumbing or electricity back then—but lots of land to farm. They started with vegetables." June paused and took a breath. "Don't get me started. I could talk for hours about the orchards."

"I'd love to hear more."

June was only too willing to oblige. Before Celie knew it, the trench coat was mended and June was deep into a story about the depression and how relatives from Danbury, Connecticut, had come to the farm because it was their only source of food. "There was always enough here," June concluded proudly. "Thank the Lord."

"Mom?"

Celie jumped at the sound of Matthew's deep voice. She hadn't realized he was there, standing with his arms folded beneath the arch of the entrance, and she had no idea how long he'd been there.

"Getting late," he said. "We get up early here."

Celie bristled. Just because she was a city girl didn't mean she didn't get up early. Plus, he'd practically come in and flipped off the light switch. The decision about when to go to bed should have been up to June.

"Okay, dear," June said. "Go on, Toastie. Go to Matthew."

The little dog jumped to the ground with a light *thump*. Matthew slipped a worn quilted jacket over the dog's body and clipped on Toaster's leash. "Be right back."

"He's a good man," June said, staring at the place her son had been. "Don't know what I'd do without him."

He might be a good man, but he wasn't a particularly friendly one. "Kiera said he was a big teddy bear."

June chuckled. "That sounds like her." A wistful expression passed over her features. "Maybe she'll call tomorrow."

"Maybe," Celie echoed, wishing that she had not mentioned her friend's name at all. As June continued to perch on the edge of the chair, Celie added, "Is there something I can do to help you?"

June shook her head. "No, honey, I'm fine."

A moment later Matthew and Toaster returned, the chill of the night still clinging to Matthew's thick wool sweater. "Celie," Matthew said as Toaster dashed between her and June, greeting them as if he'd been away for hours and not minutes, "can you bring the walker?"

She wasn't sure what he meant, but then it became clear as Matthew scooped June into his arms and carried her to the staircase. *Oh.* With her bad hip, she probably couldn't manage the stairs by herself.

The wooden steps rose in a straight, steep climb, but Matthew climbed them all without pausing. His breathing didn't change either. If it hadn't been for the way his muscles strained beneath the tight stretch of his sweater, Celie might have thought it required no effort on his part at all.

On the landing, Matthew gently set his mother down and kept a steadying hand on her elbow as Celie placed the walker in front of her. June thanked them both. "Good night, then," she said and started down the hallway.

"Good night," Celie echoed. "Sleep well."

Matthew watched June make her way down the hallway, but Celie watched him. The overhead light illuminated the grooves forming along the straight line of his mouth, the way his chestnut hair waved where it touched the top of his ear, the faintest trace of a tan line just visible beneath the collar of his shirt.

He turned suddenly, and she dropped her gaze, embarrassed to have been caught staring at him. She studied his stocking-clad feet, the fabric all but worn away at his big toe. He obviously cared more about taking care of June, the house, and the orchards than he did himself.

"Good night, Celie," Matthew said formally. "See you at breakfast." The corners of his mouth tugged ever so slightly. "Six a.m."

Was he mocking her? His eyes sparkled with unspoken challenge. It had to be the whole city-girl thing. As if she somehow wasn't tough enough to get up early in the morning. She felt the tender feelings she'd started to have toward him drain away. He had no idea how hard it was to ride a packed subway in high heels or deal with a boss who could skewer you verbally just for saying good morning if the caffeine in her morning cappuccino hadn't kicked in yet.

Matthew had no idea how tough a city girl had to be. Not yet. But she'd show him.

Chapter 6

The next morning, Celie slipped into the jeans she'd bought in town and a turtleneck sweater. She accessorized the outfit with a colorful silk scarf she found in Kiera's closet and, of course, her trusty Jimmy Choo ankle boots. The wooden stairs creaked under her weight as she tiptoed through the dark, silent house. A single light burned in the kitchen. No sign of Matthew. Good.

She put a filter in the coffee pot and filled the tank with several cups of water. A large pot hung from a hook on the wall, and she set it on the counter.

As a child, Celie had spent two weeks every summer with her maternal grandmother, Rosemary McMullin, in Dennis, Massachusetts, a small town just south of Cape Cod Bay. Nanna had loved cooking and spent hours teaching her all the family recipes.

It didn't take long to find the right ingredients, and soon the hot cereal bubbled away on the range. She turned to the table next, scrubbed clean from last night and completely bare of anything but the shine of its wood. It needed a tablecloth or a runner—something to give the room a little more color.

An old maple dresser with pretty lines and tarnished brass knobs sat against the sidewall. When she opened one of the drawers, she found a stack of neatly folded linens. She selected the one on top—a spring green cloth with lace edging.

The material was creased, as if it hadn't been used for a long time, but its dimensions fit the table exactly. As she smoothed it flat, she noticed a dark stain in one corner and a hole in another. After breakfast she'd clean and mend it.

She found a pair of silver candlesticks in the dining room and placed them on the kitchen table. Standing back, she smiled at the effect. Stunning, really. Warm and inviting, too. She'd light the candles when Matthew came downstairs.

She was just finishing cutting up some apples and oranges when the door of the mudroom opened and Matthew came in, along with a rush of cold air. He took off his boots and walked into the room. His gaze went from the table to Celie's face. "What in the world is going on?"

"I'm making breakfast for you and June," Celie said. "It's my way of thanking you for letting me stay here." She gestured toward the blue ceramic coffee mug. "You like your coffee with milk, no sugar, right?"

He just stared, and she wondered what was wrong, then June's voice called softly from the top of the stairs. As Matthew hurried to bring her downstairs, Celie poured June's tea.

When June saw the table, she covered her mouth with her hands, and her blue eyes grew large behind her bifocal lenses. "It's so beautiful." She turned to Matthew in excitement. "It's like a banquet for a queen."

Celie beamed. "Sit down, Your Highness, and I'll serve you breakfast. If you're ready, that is."

Matthew folded his arms. "I'm ready for you to put it all back. Right now."

"Put back what?" Celie read anger in the tight set of his jaw. His response made no sense, no sense at all.

"The linen tablecloth. That is a family heirloom. It isn't something you use."

Heirloom? Celie looked from Matthew's angry face to June's smiling one. "I didn't know. I'm sorry. It was in the dresser with a lot of other tablecloths. I just assumed..."

"You assumed wrong." Matthew narrowed his gaze.

"I'm sorry. I'll put it right back."

"And those candlesticks," he added, managing, without raising his voice, to sound tremendously intimidating. "They belong in the dining room."

"Okay, okay. I get the picture." She stepped toward the table, intending to get right to work putting things back, then tripped over Toaster. She saw the kitchen table flying toward her and put her hands out to break her fall. Then somehow Matthew was in front of her, catching her right before she crashed into the table.

He staggered as she fell against him. The juice glass sloshed but didn't fall over, and then all she could see was the hard wall of his chest. He straightened but continued to hold her. "And that's exactly why we don't use that tablecloth," Matthew said as she stepped back from him. "If you'd knocked into the table, you'd have spilled everything everywhere."

Celie stepped away. As Matthew started to follow, something in his back pocket caught on the lace edging. Before he realized what had happened, he jerked the tablecloth. The juice pitcher crashed over, dumping its orange river across the table. Matthew's coffee cup sailed off the table edge, along with a bowl of fruit and a pitcher of cream. The mug shattered as it hit the ground.

Worst of all—the old linen tablecloth lay in a bath of coffee, milk, and juice.

Celie knew she should run for a towel or unhook the tablecloth from Matthew's pocket or upright the fallen dishes. However, the horror of it all had her feet rooted to the ground.

June started applauding then, and when Celie's disbelieving gaze turned to her, she began laughing. June pointed to the tablecloth still attached to Matthew's back pocket, tried to say something, then lost it to another round of laughter. "Wha–wha–what do you do for your next trick, Matthew?" she managed finally. "Pull a ra–ha–ha–ha–rabbit out of your hat?"

Matthew shot her a dark look. "This isn't funny." He unhooked the tablecloth and righted the fallen juice pitcher.

"It's very funny," June corrected, pausing as another round of laughter shook her. "You're just being stodgy."

She hooted with laughter. Toaster began licking the puddle forming beneath the kitchen table. Celie came to life and gathered up the soaked tablecloth and brought it to the sink. She held the fabric beneath the cold water. Her knees felt weak. "Do you have any baking soda? Sometimes it lifts the stains out."

"In the pantry," June said, wiping her eyes. "Oh golly. If I'd only had a camera. The look on your face, Matthew. It was something to behold."

"You should see your face right now," Matthew countered. "Like a beefsteak tomato."

June let out her breath along with another hearty chuckle. With effort, she gathered herself and stood very stiff and straight. "This is why we don't use that tablecloth," she said in an impressive imitation of her son. She lapsed into another series of whooping noises.

"It's coming out," Celie announced with relief as she rinsed the cloth.

"Oh who cares?" June wiped her streaming eyes. "I haven't laughed like that in a coon's age."

"I know," Matthew replied. His gaze shifted from June to Celie, and something flickered in his eyes. The anger was gone, and he was smiling a bit sheepishly.

Celie helped pick up the rest of the mess, working silently with him, but every now and then, she'd look up and find he was looking at her. Each time their gazes met, something stirred inside her, a little shivery feeling. When Matthew wasn't glaring at her, he sure was handsome.

Yesterday the kitchen had seemed cold and a little lacking in something, although she hadn't known just what. She remembered her mother saying cheerfully how sometimes it took a good mess to get things cleaned up.

"Is the oatmeal ready?" June commented from her supervisory seat at the table. "Hope you made a lot. Toastie and I are hungry."

Chapter 7

I t's here!" June cried.

Celie didn't have to ask what "it" was. Around two o'clock every day, June took up a post at the window and didn't move until the mail arrived.

June let the living room drapery fall back, and the room dimmed slightly with the loss of light. She turned to Celie. "I have a good feeling about today."

June had been saying the same thing ever since Celie had arrived at the orchards, and every day she slumped with disappointment when the mail failed to bring news of Kiera. Clipping a leash to Toaster's collar, Celie headed for the front door. *One small postcard, a note, anything from Kiera. Please, God.*

The sun warmed Celie's cheeks as she hurried down the Patricks' long, tree-lined driveway. In the twelve days since she'd arrived, the trees had formed small green buds, tightly wrapped along the wiry ends of their branches. The angle of the sun seemed higher, the light flowing through the trees stronger.

Please, God, let a note from Kiera arrive today, she repeated as Toaster play fully jumped up and took the blue nylon leash in his teeth.

She grabbed the contents of the box and rushed back to the house. June searched the pile eagerly, making no effort to hide her sigh of disappointment when she failed to find any communication from Kiera. "Oh well," she said. "Maybe tomorrow." She handed Celie a long, cream-colored envelope. "But there's something for you."

The return address said HECKMAN AND ERLIS and bore a Hartford, Connecticut, address. Celie ripped the edges and pulled out two slim sheets of paper. She skimmed the contents of the letter and looked at the check.

From her seat across the kitchen table, June said, "Everything all right, dear?"

"Yes." Celie folded up the papers and stuck them back in the envelope. "It's the check from the insurance company."

"That came very fast, didn't it?" June flipped indifferently through an L. L. Bean catalog. "We had a terrible time getting the insurance company to pay when one of the cold barns—that's where we store the apples after we pick them—got hit by lightning. Matthew had to call several times to straighten everything out."

Celie fingered the slender envelope. It seemed strange to think she held the sum of her life in her hands, that everything she'd owned could be reduced to numbers on a thin, unsubstantial piece of paper. She could rip the check into tiny pieces and watch the wind carry it off, and then she would be left with nothing.

"You look a little sad, honey." June lowered the catalog and studied Celie's face. "If that check isn't the right amount, we'll get Matthew to call. They'll listen to him."

Celie shook her head. "It isn't that." She forced herself to smile reassuringly at June. "I guess it's finally sinking in—the fire and everything being gone." She sighed. "I guess I'm a little sad about leaving, too. You've been so good to me, June. I really appreciate it."

June leaned forward, her blue eyes troubled. "Leaving? Who said anything about leaving?"

"I can't impose on you forever." Celie'd been praying for a miracle, a divine intervention—something that involved Libby Ellman calling on the telephone, her voice oozing apology. "Milah told us everything. There's been a terrible misunderstanding," she'd say. "We need you back here." However, according to James—who didn't know the full story either—Celie had a better chance of getting hit by lightning than she did of getting her job back at George Marcus.

"But where will you go, Celie?"

Restless, Celie stood. "Centerville, a little south of Dayton, Ohio. My parents have a dry cleaning business there. You want some tea?"

"Yes, thank you. But, Celie, dry cleaning? Why not get another job as a designer? There's got to be plenty of companies that would hire you."

Celie filled the kettle with tap water. "When I went to work for George Marcus, I signed a nondisclosure agreement. It said if I were dismissed that I couldn't work for a competitor for one year." She shrugged. "It was supposed to protect the company against corporate espionage. I never dreamed I'd be fired."

"If you ask me, you're better off without them. I've seen your fashions, and you have a real gift for design."

"I messed up. I shouldn't have taken that dress home without permission."

"I'm sure you had a good reason."

Celie thought about Milah. "It really doesn't matter now."

June clucked sympathetically. "You really want to go back there, don't you?"

"It was my dream job."

"Then you've got to get it back."

The teakettle whistled. Celie pulled two ceramic mugs from the cabinet. "I think that door has closed."

June seemed to consider this for a moment. "God could open it."

"What if God wants me in Ohio?"

"Then you'll end up in Ohio, Celie," June said firmly. "God puts us right where He wants us. And there's a reason you're here and not in Ohio. If He's given you a dream to be a fashion designer—and I think He has—then maybe you need to stay right where you are. Why don't you use that insurance money to sew a dress so amazing your boss will have no choice but to hire you back?"

Celie let the tea steep. She thought about her mother seated at her sewing machine in the small nook just off the cash register. Day after day, year after year, her mom worked on altering and repairing garments that came into the dry cleaners. She never complained, but Celie knew she'd once dreamed of being a designer herself. An early marriage and Celie's birth had put those dreams on hold. The day before Celie had left for New York, her mother had thrown a party, and later that night, she'd pressed a check for a thousand dollars into her hands. "I'm so proud of you," she whispered.

Celie heard the thump of the metal walker on the hardwood floor and the softer, scuttling noise of Toaster, then she felt a warm hand touch her shoulder. "You're welcome to stay here, Celie, as long as you like. I'm not saying you'll have enough money to recreate all the dresses you lost in the fire, but you'll have enough to do what you need. God will see to that."

Celie didn't want to go back to Ohio a failure, but she didn't want to impose herself on the Patricks either. Plus she had bills to pay—those would eat up a lot of the insurance money—and if she sewed anything, it was going to be another hand-painted silk dress like the one that had gotten her into this trouble in the first place. "I appreciate your offer, but I don't want to impose on you all."

June laughed. "You aren't imposing at all. I'd welcome your company."

"It would take me at least a month to sew those dresses."

"All the better," June said. "You'll be here when Kiera comes home. She should be back by then, don't you think?"

"I hope so. But what about Matthew? I don't think he'd be too happy if I stayed."

"You just concentrate on the designing. I'll handle Matthew. Do you know how to make chicken dumplings? No?" Her silver eyebrows lifted. Behind her lenses, her eyes sparkled. "Well don't worry, I'll show you."

Chapter 8

Matthew heard the music before he even stepped into the house. Someone was playing his stereo full volume, and it wasn't hard to guess just who either. He hung his coat on a peg in the mudroom and unlaced the damp laces of his work boots.

The smell of something delicious assaulted his senses, distracting him momentarily from the loud music. He took another deep breath and felt his stomach practically flip with hunger.

His mood improved a notch. He'd spent the day working on the malfunctioning air-conditioning unit in the south barn and still couldn't get the storage area below thirty-four degrees. It wasn't an issue right now, but leaving a job unfinished always bothered him.

He lifted the lid on a black, cast-iron pot on the gas range. Chicken and dumplings. His mouth watered.

"In the Blink of an Eye" started to play. He followed the notes into the living room and paused beneath the arched entranceway. The coffee table had been pushed back, and all the cushions from the couch were on the floor. His mother lay flat on her back on top of the cushions with Toaster draped over her hips like a doggy heating pad.

His mother was doing leg lifts—the very exercises the doctor had been telling her to do for months. Celie, kneeling by his mom's side, helped raise his mother's leg a few inches above the ground. "That's it!" Celie said, sounding as excited as if they'd just discovered the cure for cancer. "That's it! One more and then we'll rest."

"One more," his mother said dryly, "and I'll be dead."

But she made that last lift and with Celie's help sat up. Each woman positively beamed with pride.

He looked at Celie. How had she done it? He retreated before she saw him. Then, and only then, did he let himself grin. The music continued—and so did their voices, singing along. Both of them about as off-key as he'd ever heard. His mother's alto was as flat as the tire on the wheelbarrow, and Celie missed a high note by about a mile.

Peals of laughter—Celie's and then his mom's—floated in from the living room. He sat down at the old wooden table. How long since the house had been filled with that sound? He couldn't remember. *Maybe never*, he thought.

～

His mom ate every bite of dinner. She said the exercises had given her an appetite.

Matthew took shameless advantage of her high spirits and kept adding dumplings to her plate. She'd always been slender but never as thin as now. She seemed so fragile to him lately, like a twig that'd snap under the least bit of pressure. He thought if he could fatten her up that she'd be stronger.

He glanced at Celie, who'd also put a good dent in the dumplings. She liked to eat. She was curvy but not heavy, and he wondered just where she was putting it. He realized then that both Celie and June were staring at him, and the room had gone silent. "What?"

"I just asked you twice, Matthew," his mother said, "about your day."

"Not much," he said. "Usual stuff. Your goat"—he paused to give June a significant look—"jumped in the wheelbarrow this morning when I was cleaning the stall. Wouldn't get out either." He forked a dumpling in half and anticipated June's reaction.

"Happy used to do that all the time with me," his mother agreed. "Stand there like he was king of the world. You should see him, Celie."

"Only from behind the fence," Celie said. "I have no desire to be shish kebab for a goat."

Matthew chuckled. "Those horns aren't meant for impaling. They're used for flipping."

"That makes me feel so much better." Celie rolled her eyes dramatically. "I'd so much rather somersault over Happy's back and have him trample on top of me."

She winked at him, and Matthew winked back before he could stop himself. He chewed another bite of dumpling and ordered himself to stop looking at her.

Yesterday he'd tried to get his mother out of the house. He'd asked her to go to church with him and ended up with Celie instead. They'd arrived a little late and had squeezed into one of the back pews. He'd endured an hour and a half of sitting pressed tightly against her. She'd smelled very faintly of honey, and he'd been fascinated by the way one strand of her dark hair escaped the messy bun and curved around her pale cheek. Afterward, he realized, he could barely recall one word of the sermon.

Matthew set down his glass of milk and wiped his mouth with a napkin. "I'm going to True Value tomorrow. I need a part for the air conditioner in the south barn."

"Wonderful!" His mother beamed as if he'd just announced he held the winning lottery ticket. "Celie needs to go to town, too. I'm sure you won't mind taking her."

"It's okay," Celie said quickly. "I can drive myself. I don't know how long I'll be, and—"

"That's ridiculous," his mom interrupted, ignoring the frantic appeal that had to be clear in his eyes. "It'll give you both a chance to visit on the way. Celie came up with the most interesting plan this afternoon. Another dumpling, dear?"

Matthew had a bad feeling. His gaze swung to Celie who seemed to be exceptionally thirsty all of a sudden. "Plan? What plan? Maybe you'd better tell me now."

"Celie is going to be staying with us for a little while longer." His mom stabbed another dumpling. "She's going to use the insurance money to buy sewing supplies."

Celie set her glass down and gave him a tentative smile. "If it's okay with you, that is."

"Of course it's all right with Matthew," his mom said before he could disagree. She gave him a calculating look. "I don't think I could do my leg exercises without her."

Matthew recognized blackmail when he heard it. He also knew when his mother was bluffing and when she was serious. And she was serious. He put another dumpling on her plate. He knew a little bit about blackmail, too.

∽

The Fabric Attic was located on South Main Street, just past the Old Bethlehem Historical Society. He watched Celie's reaction as they pulled up to the old Victorian building.

"It's purple," she said. "How cute!"

"It is purple," he agreed.

Since childhood, the tall skinny house with yellow curlicue trim and long, narrow windows had always reminded Matthew of a Halloween house. He supposed it had something to do with the orange cat that was always curled in the window box and the bowl of candy that always sat next to the cash register.

The yellow door stuck and then creaked open as if he'd caused the house physical pain. "Welcome to the Fabric Attic," he said.

She stepped past him into the dim interior. "Oh Matthew, this place is so cool!"

He couldn't help but smile as she rushed past him to explore. *Like a kid at a candy store,* he thought as he followed her down aisle after aisle of floor-to-ceiling shelves containing fabrics of every color, texture, and pattern.

"Look at this," Celie declared, tugging at a bolt of gauzy blue fabric covered with tiny pearls. "This would make the coolest hat—all I'd need is a little velvet of the same color."

He lifted the fabric from the stack and watched her unwind a length and hold it against her head, grinning from ear to ear. The strong color set off her fair skin, and the sparkle in her eyes looked like light off water. He looked away, commenting on the first fabric that caught his eyes. "I like that blue plaid."

Celie grinned. "It just happens to be the exact plaid of the shirt you're wearing. Pick another fabric you like, and I'll make you a shirt."

Matthew glanced down. Sure enough, his flannel shirt matched the colors in the bolt just above his head. He grinned a bit sheepishly. "Thanks but no thanks." He pretended interest in a blue pattern with white palm trees. "Stick with the plan."

What there is of a plan, Matthew amended. Other than buying materials to replace the dresses that'd burned up in Celie's apartment, the plan was to walk around until one of the materials "spoke" to Celie. That was it. Depending on the fabric, she'd sew something and get her old job back. The whole way in the car, he'd tried to talk to her about studying the market, talking to potential buyers, or targeting a particular audience. All his ideas had been met with a polite, "No thank you."

"Is anything speaking to you yet?" He followed her down a long aisle filled with bolts of white and pale yellow fabrics. Who could have imagined, though, there would be so many shades? How could anyone make a choice?

"They're all talking to me." Celie shot him an amused glance. "Could you please reach that bolt of cream silk for me?"

She unwrapped a small portion, fingered the texture, then held it to the light. Shaking her head, she had him replace the fabric and then had him pull down another bolt, which looked exactly like the first one.

Her lips pursed, and her head cocked thoughtfully. "It doesn't have the embroidery on it, but it's a douppioni, and the shade of ivory is exactly right. It just might work. Now we need to find the right trim—and fabric paint."

Matthew blinked when he saw the cost per yard of the fabric—nearly fifty dollars a yard. He followed her into another department and watched as she filled a basket with additional supplies. Just how much was this dress going to cost?

She paused in another aisle in front of a bolt of frothy pink fabric. Pulling it off the shelf, she sighed in pleasure and draped a length of it over her arm. She also bought a chocolate-colored shiny fabric with a tiny white floral print. A bolt of yellow silk joined the other fabrics on the worktable. As more bolts of fabric were added to the table, Matthew began to understand why his mother had wanted him to go along in the first place. Celie was going to need help carrying everything.

"That ought to do it," Celie announced, but she had her gaze on a bolt of green fabric.

The material was the color of moss. Just looking at it made him think of cool, silky things like river water flowing over stones. They both reached for the fabric at the same time, and their hands touched. He jerked back as if she'd stung him. But it hadn't hurt. Quite the opposite. He looked at her carefully. How had she done that? Had she felt it, too?

With pink cheeks, Celie looked at the price of the fabric and winced. She started to put the cloth back, but he stopped her.

"Hold on. I like that one," he said.

"Me, too." Celie replaced the fabric. "But it's too expensive."

"Put something else back, then. The pink one."

Celie shook her head. "That one doesn't cost very much, and I need the others." She looked once more at the green fabric. "Let's get going."

He hesitated. "Why don't you bring it over to the register? Maybe it's on sale or something."

It wasn't, though, and Celie went pale as the salesperson finished ringing up all her purchases. "Don't cut the green silk," she said. "I'll have to come back for it."

Don't do it, Matthew told himself. *Don't you get involved in this.* And then he heard himself say very clearly, "Well, how much extra would you need for that green silk?"

The salesperson named a sum. It was more cash than he had in his wallet. He really didn't have that kind of money to throw around on fabric, but something inside him was telling him to purchase it anyway. It made no sense, but the little voice in his head kept saying, *Go ahead, Matthew. You need to do this.* He needed to do this? Matthew didn't think so. He didn't even want to like Celie, much less help her. But the feeling in his gut was so strong that he found himself reaching for his wallet and pulling out the debit card.

He was an idiot. Just as bad as his sister and mother. He waved off her expressions of thanks and promises of paying him back. Yet looking at her face, he found himself unable to regret what he'd just done. He started to whistle as they carried the bags of sewing supplies back to the truck.

Chapter 9

"Come on, Toaster," Celie urged as the small dog paused for about the twentieth time to sniff a bush. "We've got work to do. The light is perfect."

The May sun bloomed high above her as she walked deeper into the grove of apple trees, her impatience with the dog replaced with a sense of wonder as she gazed at row upon row of apple trees. After spending the morning painting flowers on the ivory silk, it felt great to be outdoors. The branches had filled in with leaves now, and as Matthew had pointed out yesterday when they'd driven past the orchards on their way to the Fabric Attic, there were tiny, white blooms nestled in the arms of the trees.

Toaster stopped to sniff. With a resigned sigh, Celie opened her new sketchbook. She needed both hands to draw, so she dropped the dog's leash and stepped on it with the toe of her Jimmy Choo boot.

Better. She knew how to recreate the fashions lost in the apartment fire, but she still hadn't completely decided what to do with the green silk. Opening her sketchbook, she flipped past the drawings she'd made last night preliminary sketches of possible dress designs—and moved to a fresh page. The tree in front of her had a nice triangular shape. She began to draw it, striving not so much for detail as to capture its raw bones, the patterns the leaves made against the branches.

She shifted her weight, leaning closer to study an oval-shaped leaf. The way it absorbed the light fascinated her, and she wanted to draw the light and dark tones as well as the veins.

Toaster must have sensed her distraction because the next thing she knew, she was watching his brown body tear down the grass path between the rows of trees. The blue leash followed behind him like an afterthought.

Celie shouted the dog's name but wasn't surprised when Toaster didn't come or sit or stay or anything else she ordered. They ran deeper into the grove. The trees seemed to grow larger and thicker, the distances between them becoming greater. She spotted Toaster just ahead and slowed her steps so she wouldn't frighten him. "Toastie," she called, trying to make her voice sound as much like June's as possible. "You want a cheeseburger, little Toastie?"

The small dog looked suspicious but interested. Celie kept promising cheeseburgers, and the dog seemed to understand that word very well. "And you'll get one just as soon as we get home," she said, grabbing the end of the leash and sighing with relief.

She was just about to turn around when a tall, bushy apple tree caught her eye. Its leaves shone a brilliant silver yellow, reminding her of the color of the silk fabric she'd bought yesterday. Opening up her sketchbook, she began to draw. Her fingers tingled as she sketched, the way they always did when a good design started to take shape.

Excited, she studied the shadows in the trees and thought of how they might translate to draping the fabric. A slight breeze moved through the trees, and the entire tree seemed to shimmer before resettling. Celie's pencil paused as she wondered how to translate the movement.

Toaster growled. Celie looked down at him. His gaze seemed fixed on something just ahead of him. She felt a slight nudge of misgiving but ignored it. The little dog jumped up on her knee and gave a short, urgent bark. Celie hushed him. Toaster ignored her and barked again. A small bee buzzed past her ear.

Celie froze. For the first time, she saw a medium-sized brown box sitting on the ground just a few trees away from them. Her heart began to thump as she realized it was a beehive. Matthew had said to stay out of the west orchards today because they were pollinating the trees. She took a cautious step backward. Toaster started barking, so she picked him up. Another bee rumbled past.

Toaster squirmed so hard she almost dropped him. And then, suddenly, there were a lot of bees. She tried to wave them away and felt one sting her arm.

The sketchbook fell from her hand as she gripped Toaster, who was barking and snapping ferociously. She slapped the air, trying to protect them both. She spun around when a bee stung the back of her neck. She screamed. More bees were all around her now, blocking every direction.

"Celie," Matthew shouted. "Run!"

She glimpsed Matthew running toward her. Relief flooded her veins and gave strength to her legs. She ran toward him, clutching Toaster. The bees pursued, their awful droning filling her head.

She grabbed Matthew's hand, and together they raced through the grove of trees. The heel of her Jimmy Choo boot caught on a soft piece of earth. She almost fell, but Matthew steadied her just in time. Celie felt a pinch on her neck and another on her ear. Her lungs began to burn. Toaster felt as if he weighed a hundred pounds in her arms. When she tried to slow down, Matthew pulled her arm. The strength of his grip suggested her arm was coming out of the socket before the two of them stopped running.

It seemed like miles before the bees dropped back. And even then, Matthew barely let her slow down. They must have run another half mile before he allowed them to stop.

Celie set down Toaster and doubled over, breathing hard, dizzy, and slightly nauseous.

"Celie!" Matthew bent near her, grabbing her upper arms and peering anxiously into her face. "Celie! Are you allergic to bee stings? I need to know right now!"

Her brain wanted to answer, but her body couldn't seem to draw enough breath to form the words. He shook her urgently. "Are you allergic?" He was nearly shouting now, as if he thought the problem was her hearing. His face, mere inches from her own, was contorted with emotion.

"No." She gulped air and felt her stomach roll as if she had the flu. She concentrated on not throwing up on Matthew's brown work boots. He had huge feet, twice as big as hers. There was no way she could miss those feet if she got sick. She would have backed away, but he had a tight grip on her shoulders. "I'm fine," she panted. "Just give me a second."

He couldn't seem to do that, though. "Let me see the stings."

The stings didn't hurt as much as the stitch in her side, and she would assure him of this the minute she stopped gasping for breath. She lifted her face to let him see the damage was minor.

He snorted as if he were angry as he studied a sting just below her cheek. "Hold still," he ordered. "I'm going to get the stingers out before your skin starts to swell."

She braced herself as his fingers neared her. Like everything else about him, his hands were large. Her cheek tingled when he gently positioned his fingers around the stinger. Yesterday at the fabric store, his touch had been electric. She wasn't sure she could handle electricity right now.

"Hold still," he ordered gruffly. There was a small pinch on her cheek, then he said, "Got it." A small hesitation. "Did it hurt?"

"No," Celie said. "I hardly felt it."

"Good." His voice was gruff.

She watched his eyes as he took out the next one. Blue and serious, intent on their mission, the skin around them creased with concentration.

It felt strange to be eye level with him, nose to nose, their mouths level, eyes able to look straight into each other's. She'd never noticed how perfectly formed his lips were, softer, more full than she had thought. Another small pinch and a stinger seemed to pop miraculously into his hands. There were five of them all together. "Any more?" His gaze searched her face.

She shook her head. "No." His eyebrows still had that pushed-together worried expression. "Matthew, I'm fine. Seriously, I've had worse accidents with sewing machines. When I was eleven, I actually sewed right through my thumbnail."

He made a face that suggested he'd rather not have known that, but he seemed to relax slightly. "In that case, would you mind telling me exactly what you were doing in the orchards when you knew I was pollinating the trees?"

"I heard you," Celie admitted softly. "But I wasn't going to go far—just sketch the apple trees near the house—and then Toaster got loose. When I finally caught up with him, there was this really great tree I wanted to draw." She watched his lips tighten and spoke a bit more rapidly. "The light on the leaves matched the colors of the fabrics we bought yesterday, and. . ."

"You risked getting hurt to sketch a tree?"

She looked away from the disbelief on his face. He thought she was an idiot.

"Well, I didn't realize we'd gone so far." Celie decided she liked Matthew's worried face a lot more than this one. "And I didn't think we'd run into a swarm of bees either. I figured there'd be some kind of warning sign. I'd hear them or see one or two, and I could turn around."

"It's not like New York City," Matthew said, frowning. "We don't have signs. You wandered too close to the hive. Toaster's barking probably made them feel threatened. That's why they attacked you."

"I'm sorry," she said, hoping to interrupt the safety lecture. She looked away from his eyes and focused on Toaster, who was in the process of eating grass. Poor thing was probably as unnerved about the whole bee thing as she was.

"This is the country."

"I know." Celie braced herself for some warning about getting eaten by wolves or getting lost and wandering for days in the orchards. He didn't say anything, though, and she turned back to him, confused.

"I heard you scream," he said gruffly. "And I knew right away it was you." He had a funny look in his eyes, and his mouth had a hard, set look. "You scared me."

Her hands shook as she brushed her bangs behind her ear. The way he was looking at her—it was like he really cared about her. "I'm sorry. Thank you, Matthew, for coming to my rescue."

"It's okay." His voice was matter-of-fact, the expression in his eyes frank. She wondered if she'd imagined there had been anything in his eyes moments before. He rose from the ground and did not offer to help her up. "Now let's go home."

Chapter 10

Why don't we open up the windows, June? It's a beautiful morning." Celie crossed the living room to draw back the curtain and peer into the orchards. She had just finished helping June do her leg exercises, and the rest of the day stretched out in front of them.

"We don't have any screens in the windows," June replied and sighed with relief as she dropped into the velvet recliner. "Matthew took them out last fall when he winterized the house."

Through the glass, the May breeze moved through the vast orchards, bringing tree after tree to life. The wind chimes clanged lightly from the hook on the front porch. "We could put the screens back in the windows."

"Oh, but Matthew always does that."

"We could do it for him." Celie released the curtain and turned to face June.

"You'd have to take out the storm windows before you can put the screens in."

"I could do that," Celie said.

A slight flush remained high on June's cheeks, and a few wisps of silver hair floated free of her usual, neat bun—silent reminders of her morning exertion. "You're allowed as far as the mailbox, Celie, if you feel the need for fresh air, but remember, Matthew doesn't want you farther than that while they're pollinating the trees." She smiled. "How's the sewing coming on your dresses?"

"It's coming along fine—thanks to your Singer—but what about some fresh air? It smells so good outside, June. Like flowers."

"You can smell the buds, Celie? Everyone sees them, but not everyone smells them." Her eyes held a trace of interest. "Kiera thought Matthew and I made that up, that we could smell the trees long before they produced any fruit."

Celie smiled. "You could be smelling those trees before the morning is over if you'll let me install the screens. We could make the whole house smell like roses."

June's mouth puckered as she considered Celie's words. She glanced at the windows and twisted her hands in her lap. "They're in the basement," she said at last, sounding as if she didn't care but sitting up a bit straighter. "Leaning up against the boxes with the Christmas decorations."

Celie retrieved the screens from a basement so crowded it was impossible to walk a straight line. She inched between stacked boxes, climbed over several old wooden sleds, and squeezed past an old Ping-Pong table holding a collection of pots, dishware, and an old pet carrier. There had to be at least twenty boxes of

Christmas decorations, then she spotted the screens leaning against the sidewall, exactly where June said they would be.

"What's with all the boxes in the basement?" Celie asked as she walked into the living room and set the screens on the floor. She tied back the curtains and flung open the window. "I've never seen so many in my life."

"Oh, I never throw anything out," June said firmly. "It all comes in handy sooner or later."

The gutters in the windowsills needed cleaning, as did the metal tracks that held the screens. The windows themselves were dirty. June didn't have any Windex or Glass Plus, but she told Celie how to make a homemade cleaning solution out of ammonia, soapy water, and vinegar.

June supervised from her recliner at first but, seemingly unable to resist seeing Celie work, had begun following her from room to room, holding back the curtains as she lifted out the storm windows and installed the screens.

"Those storm windows are tricky things to install. Dermott, Matthew's father, always pinched his fingers on the levers. If that wasn't enough, I used to have a heart attack watching him leaning way out of the upstairs windows. He was such a big man, Celie. Hard for a man that size to have much grace, but he did." She paused. "He was a good man. Loved this family with every breath he had. One winter he duct-taped his boots together because we couldn't afford new ones. He bought the kids Flexible Flyer sleds for Christmas, though." She pointed with her finger. "You missed a spot there, honey."

Celie rubbed at the smudge on the glass. "I saw his picture on the wall. He and Matthew have the same eyes and jaw line."

"Yes," June agreed. "They do look alike. Matthew was only ten when he died." She paused. "Overnight he had to grow up. I would have had to sell this place if it weren't for him. Still would. Sometimes I wonder if it would have been better for him if I had."

Celie turned to meet June's gaze. "Matthew loves this farm. I can't imagine him being happy anywhere else."

"That's what I tell myself," June agreed. "But it's a lonely life here. For a while he was seeing Emily Taylor. Lovely girl. Her family has a horse farm a couple of miles from here. Raises Morgans. Most beautiful animals God ever created. Your eyes, Celie, are almost that same velvet brown as their coats." She paused as if to give Celie a moment to appreciate this compliment. "Emily used to pony a horse over here, and she and Matthew would ride for hours together in the orchards."

Celie fiercely scrubbed a minuscule smudge on the glass. "So what happened? Why didn't they get married?"

"Oh, she went to college and then graduate school and then got a writing job with the *Hartford Courant*. Life in the country wasn't her cup of tea."

Celie gazed out into the orchards. She imagined a teenage Matthew—all blue eyes and big-jointed bones—riding beside a beautiful blond girl named

Emily. She pictured Emily saying something to Matthew, who would turn to her, laughing, his face open and beautiful.

The smudge was gone, but Celie kept rubbing. She wondered if Matthew still cared for this woman—if Emily Taylor was the reason he hadn't married or, for that matter, was not even dating.

A cool breeze moved through the installed screen, cooling cheeks Celie hadn't realized had grown so hot. Behind her, June inhaled deeply and sighed in pleasure. "Smell that, Celie? Only God's breath could be sweeter."

She smiled. "It's amazing. We should bottle it up and sell it." She moved to the next windowpane and swiped it with the ammonia mixture. The glass immediately went gray with the dissolving dirt and began to clear. Celie was less successful in eliminating the image of Emily Taylor from her mind.

~

By lunchtime they'd finished installing all the screens in the downstairs windows. Celie heated a can of tomato soup and made grilled cheese sandwiches. As the food heated on the stove, she wondered about Matthew—silly things, like his favorite flavor of ice cream and what color he liked best. What had his childhood been like? And of course, she was consumed with curiosity about anything and everything involving Emily Taylor.

She set a plate down in front of June. "Here you go. I made an extra in case Matthew decided to join us."

June tore off the corner and slipped it to Toaster. "Oh, I doubt we'll see him for lunch until after the bees finish pollinating the orchards." She gave Celie a sly look. "Of course, he may come home early and check on you. He asked me three times when you were out of earshot to keep an eye on you."

"I don't need anyone keeping an eye on me."

June's voice was gentle. "Everyone needs someone looking out for them."

After lunch Celie suggested the windows would look even better if they washed the curtains. June resisted. "Those old drapes are so old they'll fall apart."

"If they do," Celie assured her, "I know someone who can fix them."

Standing on a kitchen chair and reaching up with every inch of her five-foot-one frame, Celie unhooked the cotton panels and took them down to the basement to wash. While the curtains dried, Celie vacuumed. After that was finished, June glanced around. "Feels so much fresher in here. Now if we could only make the furniture look less tired."

Celie liked the sparkle in June's eye. "The mirror in the dining room would look great on the mantel, and the portrait of Great-Grandma Caroline could hang in the dining room."

June cocked her head uncertainly. "The mirror's heavy, Celie. I'm not sure a regular picture hook will hold it."

"We aren't going to hang it, exactly. I'll show you."

~

Celie was upstairs, getting changed, when she heard Matthew come through the back door. There was no mistaking the thump of the door or Toaster's howl of pleasure. She checked the back of her earrings. The house looked beautiful, and she wanted to look her best as well. She'd decided her pencil skirt and ruffled blouse would be festive choices.

She hurried down the stairs and into the living room. Matthew stood with his back to her, hands on his hips, staring at the mirror on the mantelpiece. She couldn't wait to see his reaction. "You like it?"

Matthew spun around. "What did you do?"

Celie drew back at the coldness in his voice. "We cleaned the curtains and moved a few things around."

"I can see that."

If Matthew's jaw got any tighter, it was going to take surgery to loosen it. She couldn't understand. The room looked great, and the air smelled fresh and clean.

"You don't like it." Behind her bafflement, Celie felt the sharp edges of disappointment.

"It was fine the way it was," Matthew said. "What did you do with Great-Grandmother Caroline's portrait?"

"In the dining room." Where it belonged. If he would only look, he would see that.

"I don't think it's safe for a heavy mirror like that just to be leaning against a mantel." Matthew crossed the room in three strides and tested the mirror's stability. He looked even less pleased when it didn't budge. "Where's the Log Cabin quilt?" he said abruptly. "The one that hangs on the back of the sofa?"

"Upstairs," Celie replied. "I'm going to sew a backing and get a wooden hanger. It'll look great on that big wall over there."

She gestured to the wall flanking the steep staircase, but Matthew's gaze didn't falter from her face. "The quilt belongs on the back of the sofa."

"Matthew Patrick." June thumped into the room behind her walker. "I heard you clearly from the kitchen. That is no way to talk to a guest in our home. You will apologize to Celie immediately. She's worked hard all day to bring a little beauty into our home and doesn't deserve to bear the brunt of your foul humor."

Matthew's eyebrows pushed together. "Our house was beautiful enough."

"I wasn't saying your house wasn't beautiful," Celie said, trying hard to keep her temper. How could this be the same man who had so gently removed her bee stings? "All I was trying to do was bring more light into the room."

"We don't need any more light in here. Put everything back. In fact, I'll help you right now."

As he reached for the mirror on the mantelpiece, however, the front doorbell rang. Matthew froze, a quizzical expression replacing the look of annoyance. He turned to June, who looked equally surprised. Then a hopeful smile appeared on her face. "You think it's Kiera?"

Chapter 11

Toaster beat him to the door, barking and showing every sign of making a run for it the minute an opening appeared. Matthew scooped the excited dog into his arms. "Stop yapping," he told the squirming Toaster.

He pulled open the door. His neighbor, Jeremy Taylor, stood on the porch. Jeremy was a tall, thin man with white hair as thick as a lion's mane. He was in his seventies, and yet the handshake he gave Matthew was firmer and stronger than men half his age.

"Jeremy," Matthew said, smiling. "Come inside. It's good to see you."

"You, too, Matthew," Jeremy said, following him into the foyer. "Sorry to stop by without calling."

"You don't have to call," Matthew assured him.

"You never need to call," June echoed as Matthew led Jeremy into the living room. "You're always welcome here. Can I get you something to drink? Coffee?"

Jeremy smiled but shook his head. "I won't stay but a moment." His gaze moved from June to Celie, who stood wearing that frothy-looking shirt, the slender skirt, and those high-heeled boots. Matthew frowned, but mainly at himself. He didn't want to feel attracted to her, but he did.

"You remember Celie Donovan," Matthew said, remembering his manners. "Kiera's friend?"

Jeremy smiled. "Of course. We spoke at church last week. It's nice to see you again."

"You, too," Celie said, smiling her usual, warm smile. Matthew could see Jeremy visibly brightening in response.

"How's Emily?" his mother asked. "We were just talking about her this afternoon, Celie and I. We were doing some spring-cleaning."

"Oh, she's doing fine," Jeremy said. "Working too many hours, as usual. We keep up, though. On the computer. Never imagined that instant messaging would replace a phone call, but that's the way it is with young people these days."

"Maybe for you," June replied, "but I will never use the computer for anything. I leave all that technical mumbo-jumbo stuff to Matthew."

The gazes turned to him. "Well, tell Emily I said hi and not to neglect the country," Matthew said, smiling, although it had not always been easy to hear Emily's name and smile.

"The reason I'm here," Jeremy said, fishing in the pocket of his coat, "is to bring you this. It came to my mailbox by mistake. Got caught in a magazine."

Jeremy handed his mother a colorful postcard. Matthew glimpsed the flash of a beach scene. His mother's face went white, and she all but snatched it from the older man's hands. She turned over the back and eagerly scanned the contents.

Matthew lifted the card from his mother's shaking hands. It was from his sister.

"*Hola, Mom and Matthew,*" he read. "*The cruise was amazing! Now I'm in Mexico. It's beautiful! I miss you all but am having fun. More later, and love, Kiera.*"

Noticeably absent were Kiera's plans to return to Connecticut. Matthew returned the card to his mother and hid his disgust in what he hoped was a neutral expression.

"Well, at least we know she's alive and kicking," his mother said calmly, passing the card to Celie who read it and glanced at him as if he could explain what in the world was going on with his sister.

"Thank you so much for bringing this over, Jeremy," his mom continued. "We've been worried. Kiera's in Mexico—on an extended vacation—and this is the first word from her."

Jeremy studied his mother's face. "Is everything okay, June?"

She sighed. "Yeah, I think so. Kiera needed a little time to herself. That awful man from the city dumped her, and she needed to get away for a while." She gave him a small smile. "Kids. They never grow so old that you stop worrying about them. You'll stay for supper, won't you? Celie made a roast, and there's plenty of it."

"It smells delicious," Jeremy said. "Nothing an old widower likes more than a home-cooked meal. But I don't want to impose. June, while I'm here, I wanted to talk to you about this year's rummage sale at the church. I raised my hand at the wrong time and ended up being the chairperson of the event."

"Oh Jeremy, why didn't you simply unvolunteer yourself?" his mother asked.

"I tried, but all the ladies in the room thought it would be great to have a man's perspective." He shrugged unhappily. "I told them I don't know a thing about clothing, but they said it was more a matter of organizing things than anything else. By the time they'd finished, Rev. Westover said he'd take it as a personal favor if I would lead this event."

"You're too nice for your own good." June stroked Toaster, who had jumped into her lap.

"Well, like it or not, I'm the chairperson." He paused. "I was hoping you'd be my cochair." He paused again. "I'm already getting boxes of donations, and I don't know what to do with them."

"Me?" His mother's silver eyebrows lifted. "I'm flattered you would think of me. But Jeremy, my hip really slows me down these days. I rarely leave the house."

"I'm slowing down, too. However, the Lord made rabbits and He made turtles and He uses them both." Jeremy laughed. He had an easy way about him that Matthew had always admired. After his dad passed away, Jeremy had put his hand on Matthew's shoulder, looked deeply into his eyes, and promised to be there if Matthew ever needed him. "I won't try to take your dad's place," he'd explained, "but I'm here for you as a friend." Matthew had never taken him up on it, but there had been times in his life when he thought long and hard about doing it. It'd always seemed a bit disloyal to his dad.

"I don't know, Jeremy," June said doubtfully. "It's a lot of work."

That was the understatement of the century. Matthew ran his hand through his hair. The rummage sale traditionally was a disaster. People enthusiastically emptied their closets, but nobody really bought much. Last year he'd transported an entire truckload of unwanted clothing to the Salvation Army.

"I'll bring everything to you. You wouldn't even have to leave the house."

"I could help, too," Celie commented. "We could get some garment racks, June. You and I could sort and tag the clothes, and then Matthew could return the racks to the church. It'd be fun."

Matthew's gaze shot to Celie's face. He mouthed *no* and shook his head. Celie had no idea. This wasn't just a few boxes of donations. It was mountains of clothing. He wasn't sure June could handle the amount of work required. His gaze narrowed. Was Celie volunteering his mother just to extend her stay?

"Why don't you ask Susan Grojack?" June suggested. "Didn't she lead this last year?"

"She's taken a secretarial job with the town."

"Oh," his mother said, her lips puckering. "I didn't know."

"We could do this," Celie said. "It'd be fun, June."

"You have your own sewing to do." His mother looked at Jeremy. "Celie's a marvelous designer."

"Aspiring designer," Celie corrected. "Currently unemployed and available. This rummage sale sounds like a good cause." She shot Matthew a significant look. "I'm sure June's friends at the church would be glad to come over and help, too."

"Of course they would," Jeremy said.

His mother rubbed her left hip as if it had suddenly started to ache and shot Matthew a mute appeal for help.

He frowned. His mom had been on one church committee or another practically her whole life. Declining this opportunity seemed to be one more example of his mother's giving up, reducing her world to nothing more than the four walls around her.

He glanced back at Celie and suddenly understood. Her intention wasn't to prolong her stay but to bring more action and a purpose into his mother's life. He felt stupid for not seeing this earlier. "You should do it," Matthew urged. "Celie's right. It's a good cause."

June's mouth opened. She looked from his face to Celie's and then back to his again as if searching for an excuse and not finding one.

"If it gets to be too much work for you, I promise to get someone else," Jeremy offered.

171

His mom wrung her hands and glanced once more at Matthew, who smiled encouragement. "I guess I could give it a try."

"We'll have fun," Celie promised.

"The last time she said that," his mother said in a deadpan, "I ended up flat on my back doing leg lifts."

"This will be easier than leg lifts," Jeremy said, laughing. "I'll start dropping boxes off tomorrow, whenever it's convenient."

"Anytime's good, Jeremy." His mom's cheeks pinked up a bit. "Why don't you come for lunch?"

"I'd love to." Standing, he thanked everyone and said it was time for him to go. Pausing beneath the archway, he looked back, his eyebrows bunched together. "Did you change something in here?" He glanced around. "The room looks bigger than I remember. Brighter, too. I like it."

The two women exchanged smiles. With a sinking feeling, Matthew realized the furniture arrangement was going to stay.

Chapter 12

The next morning, Celie found her sketchbook lying on the braided rug outside her bedroom door. With a small exclamation of surprised joy, she flipped it open. The pages were slightly curled, the cardboard backing damp, but her sketches were completely intact.

The last time she'd seen this book was when she'd been swatting bees and trying to hold on to Toaster. Matthew had gone back for it. There was no other explanation. She clutched the book to her chest and hurried down the stairs.

June sat at the kitchen table sipping a cup of tea, Toaster firmly ensconced in her lap. Instead of the sweat suits Celie had grown used to seeing her wear, she'd dressed in jeans and a green wool cardigan. "Morning, Celie."

"You look nice, June." She gazed from June to the empty place setting at the head of the table.

"You just missed him," June commented, following her glance. "He went up to the barn."

"Oh." It was barely six thirty in the morning. Matthew usually didn't leave until seven. She glanced at the half-empty pot of coffee and the bacon drying on its bed of paper towels. Her gaze lingered on a ceramic mug with a tea bag hanging over the side. He'd made her tea.

"Is there anything I can do, dear?"

Celie shook her head. "He found my sketchbook." She held out the wire-bound spiral as if in explanation. "I wanted to thank him."

"Why don't you run up to the barn? I'm sure you can catch him before he heads into the orchards." June smiled. "Take Toastie with you. He loves going up to the barn, don't you, little Toastie?" She patted the dog's tufted head. "Go on now."

Toaster bounced about her, pulling at the boundaries imposed by his leash as they stepped into the cold May morning. Celie pulled the belt of her trench tighter.

She found Matthew outside the barn's oversized front door. He was emptying plastic water buckets into the grass. Picking up the pace, she pulled Toaster away from an interesting scent and reached Matthew just as he was emptying the last bucket. "Missed you at breakfast."

Matthew straightened. "Is everything okay?" He looked back at the house.

"Everything is fine." Even in her heels, she hardly reached Matthew's shoulder. "I just wanted to thank you for finding my sketchbook."

He shrugged, picked up a spray hose lying nearby, and began to rinse out

173

the buckets. "You're welcome. Thanks for encouraging my mom to take on the rummage sale."

"Oh yeah, well, I figured she could use a project. You didn't get stung or anything, did you?" She scanned him for injury. It was hard to tell with his head bent and a thick chamois shirt covering his upper body, but he seemed okay.

He looked up then, and she read something in his eyes. "You got stung, didn't you? Oh, Matthew. I would never have let you go back for the sketchbook."

"Let's just leave it at thank-you," Matthew said, carrying the buckets back into the barn. "It wasn't a big deal."

"It was a big deal. It has some sketches I need." She followed him into the dimly lit barn, stopping short as he entered the stall of the enormous brown horse. Tall as Matthew was, his head just barely came up to the horse's shoulder. He clipped the water buckets back in place.

"You'd better step back," Matthew warned. "I'm going to take Bonnie out of her stall."

Celie retreated to the other side of the barn as Bonnie slowly clomped into the aisle. Outside her stall, she seemed even bigger, with huge hindquarters and rippling muscles. The shaggy hair on the bottom of Bonnie's legs reminded Celie of a dress she'd once designed out of feathers.

She twisted her fingers together, reminding herself that Matthew had risked injury to get her sketchbook and she ought to do something to thank him. "You want some help?"

Pitchfork in hand, he looked at her over the top of the waist-high stall door. "What?"

"You want some help?" Celie repeated, this time a bit more loudly. She tightened her grip on Toaster's leash, who was trying to lick something awful off the concrete floor.

"No," he said.

"You sure?" The goats bleated from their stall, and Celie nearly jumped a foot. "I could help you clean."

His dark eyebrows lifted. "You? Clean a stall?"

Celie squared her shoulders. "Yes, me."

He laughed. "No thanks."

"Oh. Well. I could sweep the aisle or dust or. . ." She looked around trying to come up with another chore a person might do at a barn. "Matthew, those sketches meant a lot to me. I'd really like to help you."

He seemed to think about this a bit. "Bonnie could use some grooming."

Celie gazed at the horse standing placidly in the aisle. She looked harmless. But she was awfully big. Celie wasn't sure what he meant by groom her.

"The brushes are right in that tack trunk over there."

Celie brightened. Brushes. He meant make the horse look pretty. Bonnie's mane did look a bit tangled, and there were bits of white shavings clinging to her coat. She tied Toaster's leash to a ring on the wall and went to work.

∽

"So how, exactly, are you going to get your old boss to look at your green dress when it's finished?" Matthew turned over a pitchfork of bedding and separated the clean from the soiled. "Since they fired you, I doubt you're going to be allowed back in the building."

"Good point," Celie replied. "I'll have to talk to James about that. He's really smart. And he got really mad when they fired me. He'll help."

Matthew stopped with the pitchfork in midair. Just who was James? Her boyfriend? He digested the possibility slowly and didn't like the way it sat with him. It was none of his business, but he heard himself ask, "James is another designer?"

"No." She laughed. "James is in accounting. He works in the executive suites, but he spends a lot of time talking to us in the workroom. We kept having to hide him from Libby Ellman—she's the head designer. Libby's always checking up on everybody."

One of the things Matthew liked best about working on the orchards was the freedom to control his day. He couldn't imagine working in an environment where someone was constantly looking over his shoulder.

"This one time, Libby went on the warpath looking for James because he signed off on too much overtime for the hourly employees. He ran into the workroom with Libby hard on his heels, and we disguised him as a mannequin." Celie giggled happily. "A girl mannequin! We padded him up, strategically draped fabric around him, and put a hat on him. Libby walked right past him! We laughed so hard we almost cried."

She laughed, and the sound filled the barn. Matthew found himself laughing, too. She told him other funny stories, and all too soon Matthew finished cleaning the stall. He pushed the wheelbarrow into the aisle, stopping short when he saw Bonnie. "What in the world did you do to her?"

Celie beamed down at him from atop a bale of hay. "I groomed her."

He pointed to the mare's head. "She's wearing a hat and sunglasses."

"I know. Doesn't she look nice?"

Bonnie's ears stuck through the top of a floppy straw hat that had once graced the head of a homemade scarecrow. For years the straw man had guarded June's vegetable garden. But then the garden had become too much work, and they'd stored the scarecrow in the corner of the barn. Unfortunately, the goats had gotten loose a couple of times and eaten most of the scarecrow, including part of the hat. He wasn't sure where she'd found the sunglasses.

"I thought you were going to groom her, not deck her out like she's going to a garden party."

"You said groom her, and that's exactly what I'm doing." Celie smiled down at him from her perch. Her fingers twisted Bonnie's mane into small braids.

"I meant get the dirt off her."

"She likes the hat, Matthew. It makes her feel pretty."

"Horses don't feel pretty—or ugly or fat or skinny either."

"That's nonsense," Celie said. "Everyone feels better about themselves if they feel attractive. The minute Bonnie saw that hat, she put her head right down so I could put it over her ears."

"If she lowered her head," Matthew argued, enjoying himself tremendously, "it was because she thought it was something to eat." He had to bite the inside of his cheek to keep from laughing.

He moved closer to Celie. On the bale of hay, she stood just a little taller than him. Matthew had to look up to meet her gaze. He found this new perspective very intriguing. He could lift her right off that bale with one arm if he wanted to. To his dismay, he discovered he very much wanted to.

He reached for the mare's hat instead. Celie's cry stopped him. "I think June should see Bonnie before you undress her."

"She won't come up," he said gruffly. "Not anymore."

"Why not?" The words were said gently, but they still stung. "Why won't she come up to the barn anymore, Matthew?"

He shook his head, the last bit of Celie's laughter fading from his mind. "I don't know. For a while I thought she was scared of falling again, but now I don't think that's it at all."

"What happened?" Her voice was velvety soft. "How did she break her hip?"

The familiar guilt rose like a wave over him. For a moment he couldn't speak, could only remember walking through the house, taking his time to eat a peach over the sink, and having no idea that his mother was flat at the bottom of the hayloft steps, unable to even crawl for help.

"She slipped on those steps and fell," he said, pointing to the open staircase leading to the loft. "It was two hours before I found her. I should never have allowed her to throw down bales of hay. What was I thinking, allowing a seventy-year-old woman to do something like that?"

It didn't matter that right until that point his mother had been striding around the farm, ordering people around, and hefting fifty-pound sacks of feed over her shoulder. He should have seen her growing more fragile. He should have seen some sign of her aging.

He felt a light touch on his arm. Celie was looking down at him with an expression of deep sympathy in her velvet brown eyes. "It wasn't your fault."

"Of course it's my fault. I should have looked after her better." His gaze hardened. "I should have looked after Kiera better, too." Why was he confiding things to Celie he had never admitted to anyone else before?

He wanted to reach for her. He knew if he let himself, he'd kiss her. And that wasn't a very good idea at all. *Why her, God? Why do I have to like this woman? Why couldn't I feel this way about Bekka Johnson?* Bekka was pretty, loved children, and sang in the church choir. She would never put a straw hat on a horse if he'd asked her to groom it. And she never would have moved all the furniture around or nearly wandered into a beehive.

And maybe that's why he'd felt nothing for Bekka. He couldn't remember her making him laugh either.

He set his jaw, more aware than ever of Celie so close.

Please Lord, not her.

Matthew pulled the straw hat from the mare's head and tossed it into a corner. Bonnie lifted her massive head, startled by the abruptness of his gesture. He felt Celie's gaze on his back but did not let himself look at her face as he led the big horse back to her stall.

Chapter 13

Celie helped June make a salad and spinach quiche for lunch. As she whisked the eggs and cheese together, she kept thinking about Matthew—the frustration on his face, the pain in his voice. It wasn't his fault June had fallen, and it wasn't his fault Kiera had run off to Mexico either. Sometimes bad things happened. You simply had to live with them and trust God to use them for His purpose. It pained her to think of Matthew living with guilt.

June sat at the kitchen table, tearing lettuce into a pretty glass bowl with hand-painted flowers. "You think spinach quiche is too feminine a meal for Jeremy? You think we should have made cheeseburgers?"

"He'll love the quiche," Celie assured her. "And if he doesn't, he can always fill up on the blueberry pie and ice cream."

"That's true," June agreed. "You think we have time to bake some rolls?"

Celie hid a smile. She had a feeling June would keep adding to the menu until Jeremy walked through the door. She just hoped Jeremy came hungry.

Soon the house was filled with the delicious aroma of baking quiche. Celie was testing the quiche for doneness—it needed a few more minutes—when she heard the front door open. She was just in time to watch Matthew and Jeremy walk through the hallway, their arms full of large cardboard boxes.

"Where do you want them?" Jeremy asked.

June looked at Celie. "I don't know."

"How many are there?" Celie asked.

"Ten," Matthew said.

"Oh my," June said. "That many already?"

"The ladies dropped off a few more at the church today," Jeremy admitted, shifting his weight, "and there are more coming in every day."

"Why don't we put them in the dining room?" Celie suggested.

June brightened. "Perfect."

As Matthew and Jeremy brought in more boxes, Celie and June opened the first two. June pulled out a pair of light blue jeans. The denim had worn through at the knees, and it looked as if someone had taken a pair of pinking shears to the ends of both legs. "We should just throw those away," June said, casting them aside to search the rest of the box.

Celie took the jeans. The material above the knee wasn't bad. The rise was a little high, but with a little alteration, she could turn the jeans into Bermuda shorts. She laid the denim aside and pulled out a crumpled yellow dress.

June made a face at the garment in Celie's hands. "That's just plain ugly. The only use for that would be if someone wanted material for a tent."

Matthew and Jeremy returned with another stack of boxes. They stopped dead in their tracks when they saw Celie holding up the yellow dress.

"Why did someone donate a yellow tablecloth?" Matthew asked.

"It's a dress," Celie said. "And with a little work, it could be pretty. You just add some ruching here and add a waistband—an empire waist would work well, I think, and some trim."

"What's ruche?" Jeremy continued to study the dress with an expression of horrified fascination.

"It's a term for gathering."

"You could gather that dress from one end to another, and it'd still be a sow's ear." June cast aside a patchwork skirt. "It's like the rest of what's in this box. All the sewing in the world can't turn these garments into silk purses."

"Maybe we should have lunch," Matthew suggested. "Something smells good."

Celie pulled a pair of black wool slacks out of another box. "The cut of the leg is wrong, but they have a beautiful lining." She turned the fabric inside out to demonstrate. "I could turn these pants into a pencil skirt. I'd put a slit in the back, so the lining could peek through. We could pair it with this blouse." Celie held up a black-and-white patterned shirt.

"It's very nice," Jeremy said, but he sounded unsure.

June laughed. "What woman wants to dress up in zebra stripes?"

"Lots of women," Celie promised. "Animal prints are fashionable right now. Besides, this shirt has great seaming. We might add a pop of color somewhere— a red purse maybe—or red high heels. But an outfit like this one would sell for a lot of money in New York City."

"Well, I guess so. If anyone knows fashion, it's you." June turned to Jeremy and said, "If her designs hadn't gotten burned up, they would have been show-cased in a very important fashion show in New York City."

Celie already had her hands around a velvet jacket. She liked the poufed shoulders—but the mutton-shaped arms had to go. She'd turn the jacket into a vest. *Hold on a second,* a small voice inside her said. *Do you really want to get so heavily involved with this project? The more time you spend on these clothes, the less time you'll have for sewing your own dress—and the longer you'll be staying on this farm.* She thought of all the sacrifices her parents had made so she could attend the Rhode Island School of Design, of all the hours she and her mother had spent dreaming about the day when Celie's dresses would hang in the windows of stores like Saks Fifth Avenue and appear in the pages of magazines like *Harper's Bazaar.*

She fingered the velvet. Maybe, like June had said, she was exactly where God wanted her to be. *Do You want me to do this?* She wasn't completely sure, but it felt right. "It wouldn't take me long to put together some outfits you could showcase at the sale. It might inspire people to look at the rest of the clothing a little differently."

"And maybe buy things," Jeremy stroked his chin. "You know what would be even better?"

"Lunch?" Matthew suggested hopefully.

"If we could get some volunteers from the church to wear the clothes Celie alters." Jeremy ran his hands through his thick cloud of white hair.

"You mean model them?" June looked excited.

"Exactly," Jeremy said. "When we want to sell a horse, we take it out of the stall and put it through its paces. My guess is that if you want to sell clothing, you have to show how great someone can look wearing it."

Celie put the velvet down and stared at Jeremy. "You're talking a fashion show, aren't you?"

Jeremy nodded.

"We could call it 'Castoffs to Couture,'" Celie suggested, already picturing the event. "That way it'd suggest original designs but also let people know the clothing isn't new."

"Every woman in town would want to come. It could be a huge fund-raiser for the church." June turned eagerly to Celie. "You could invite your boss and then dazzle him with your designs."

Hmmm. She hadn't considered that aspect. Would Mr. Marcus laugh at a small-town church fashion show—or would he see that he'd made a huge mistake letting her go?

"Hold on, Mom," Matthew said. "I think we're getting a little ahead of ourselves here. A fashion show is a lot of work. And besides, aren't you forgetting something?"

June's lips puckered. "Like what?"

"Like you should talk to Rev. Westover and the rest of the church elders before you completely reinvent the rummage sale."

"I don't think that would be a problem," Jeremy said slowly. "The numbers from last year's rummage sale really weren't that good. I think that's why everyone was so quick to draft me into the chairperson role in the first place. I'll talk to the reverend in the morning, but I don't see anyone objecting to this change." His gaze softened as he looked at June. "And I'll make sure we get extra help."

"That'd be great, Jeremy," Celie said. "I could really use some dress dummies—as many different sizes as possible. And I'll need a worktable, sewing machines, lots of sewing notions, ironing board, and iron. And racks for hanging the clothing." She wrinkled her brow. "If anyone can sew, that'd be a help, too. Oh, and a mirror. As big as possible."

"I've got an old dress dummy and a standing mirror, too." June turned to Matthew. "Could you please bring them down?"

～

Matthew started up the old, wooden stairs. A fashion show? A burst of laughter followed him up. He reached the second-floor landing and started up the third flight of stairs. He didn't want to picture half the ladies in town trying to wear the same kind of formfitting skirts and frothy white shirts as Celie wore. The town had absolutely no idea what it might be getting into, not one small bit.

The attic boards creaked under his feet. The wind stirred the cold air in the rafters. This high up, he could see for miles out the dusty window—cold storage barns, the rows of trees budding, ready for the seedlings that would form and grow. Change was coming to the orchard, as it did every season. This was a good thing, a God thing. He understood this. Gave thanks for this.

The changes in the house, the stirrings in his own heart—these things felt uncomfortable to him, unsettling and vaguely threatening. He'd started having trouble sleeping, too, catching only a few hours at a time. When he woke, he couldn't remember his dreams, only that they had been vivid and sweet and that Celie's name was on his lips.

Matthew tucked the sewing dummy under his arm and headed down the steps. He prayed that God would give him guidance.

Chapter 14

Is this too tight?" June pulled the back seams of the muslin fabric tightly together.

"As long as I don't breathe," Celie said, feeling as if her ribs were touching. The pressure on her rib cage eased a bit. "Thank you." She gave a sigh of relief.

"I think it should be tight," June said unapologetically. "You need to show off that tiny waist."

"It's not that tiny," Celie stated. "And the way I'm eating, it's getting less tiny every day."

They stood in the dining room, curtains drawn for privacy, and gazed at each other from the image within the frame of an antique standing mirror.

"You think it looks right?" With all the sewing work she had, it had taken Celie more than a week to translate the drawings from her sketchbook into a pattern and then several more evenings to cut the pieces and baste them together.

"Yes. And it'll look even better," June observed dryly from behind her, "without Kiera's old ballet leotard and tights on underneath."

Celie laughed. She shifted to catch another angle. The bodice fit well—she didn't see any major changes she needed to make. But this was just a test garment, sewn from inexpensive muslin.

She tugged the bodice a fraction higher, imagining the way she'd weave together strips of green and yellow silk for the bodice and the way the silk would spill to the floor. It would look completely natural but would take hours of carefully placing darts. Lifting herself onto her toes, she pictured someone tall and elegant-looking wearing the finished dress. Someone taller, less curvy than herself. Someone like Kiera.

She felt a quick pang of anxiety and a longing to talk to her best friend, gone now almost a month and not a word since that postcard two weeks ago.

June met her gaze in the mirror's reflection. "Poor Matthew. When this dress is finished and he sees you in it, he isn't going to have a chance." She tsked happily. "Poor, poor Matthew."

Celie rolled her eyes. "It isn't like that with us, June." She turned away from the mirror, unable to define just what her relationship was with Matthew. They weren't friends, and they weren't enemies. They were sort of like oil and water. Two liquids that wouldn't blend together unless forced to.

"It's exactly like that," June said but more gently this time.

Celie pretended to study the side seam very closely. Matthew had seemed to be in a better mood these past couple of days, but she felt sure the change had everything to do with the progress June's hip continued to make. She'd stopped using the walker and now relied on a glossy black cane. And occasionally she didn't even need that.

The telephone rang. Ever since Jeremy had gotten the church to agree to the fashion show, the phone had been ringing off the hook. "Shoot me dead the next time I volunteer for something," June said, but Celie noticed a certain eagerness in her step as she headed for the kitchen.

Celie could hear June's voice as she changed into a pair of jeans, layered a couple of T-shirts, and slipped on her battle-scarred, but still lovely, Jimmy Choo boots.

"Claire is either giving me measurements prior to child-birth or else she's had one too many cups of herbal tea," June commented, returning to the room. "She wants to model swimwear. I told her we wanted to sell clothing, not make people cover their eyes."

Laughing, Celie picked up a brown blazer and began opening up the seams. "I heard you clearly, June. You told her you'd put her down for swimwear, if there were any."

June walked slowly over to Celie, the glossy black cane thumping on the hardwood floor. "I know. I couldn't think of anything else to say. I guess you'd better be generous in your sizing, Celie. Half the women who've volunteered to model are subtracting inches off their hips."

The two women exchanged smiles. "We'll have a fitting prior to the show. Everything will be fine."

"If anyone should be modeling swimwear, it's Kiera," June mused. "She was always beautiful from the day she was born. Difficult, though. Screamed her head off as a baby and had that awful reflux—threw up over *everything*. Not like Matthew. He was always smiling, always content in himself."

Matthew—a happy baby? It was hard to reconcile this image with the strong, serious man he had become.

"Dermott loved both his kids," June continued, pulling up a chair next to Celie. "But Matthew was his favorite. Dermott used to sit him on top of his shoulders and take him out into the orchards. Before he could walk, Dermott had introduced him to every tree on the farm. 'I want him to love three things,' Dermott always said. 'The Lord first and foremost, then his family, and of course, the land.'"

She picked up a pincushion from the table and absently began rearranging the pins. "I wish Dermott had been able to instill the same love of the land in Kiera. Maybe he would have, if he'd had more time. Maybe I should have done things differently. God knows I did the best I could."

Celie touched June's arm. "She loves you. She'll be back. You just have to hang in a little longer."

June nodded. "I know it, but some days I feel about as strong as a limp noodle."

"I understand," Celie said. "I've felt like that, too. You just have to trust that God will work things out. Like you told me, you have to keep trying, keep believing, no matter what." She slipped her arm around the older woman and pulled her against her side.

"What if something bad has happened to her?" June's voice was hardly a whisper. "I couldn't stand it."

Celie's arm tightened. How thin June's bones felt, how very breakable. Celie wanted to take her in her arms and hold her, love her as if she were her own mother. At the same time, June sat with her back ramrod straight, as if some small part of her refused to succumb to the weight of the fears inside her.

"I'm sorry," June said at last. "Usually I try not to burden anyone with my own fears." She shook her head. "I know Kiera is a grown woman, but in some ways, she's so fragile. Losing her father so young. . ." She paused. "In some ways, I think she's still missing him, looking to fill that void he left."

"She may have lost her father," Celie said gently, "but she knows she has a heavenly Father who will never leave her. Did she ever tell you that she and I used to meet for services at Saint Patrick's Cathedral?"

June glanced up, relief in her large blue eyes. "It helps to hear that, Celie. It helps to see you living your faith. I know you lost everything in that fire. Yet I've never heard you complain."

Celie smiled. "Trust me. God and I have had a lot of talks."

In the distance, the sound of a car drifted into the room. "Is that Jeremy already?" June asked.

Celie rose to her feet to peer out the window. Light flooded the room as she pulled back the curtain, and she saw the familiar colors of the U.S. Postal truck. "Not Jeremy, but the mail's here. I'll take Toaster and go bring it in."

Chapter 15

Jeremy's car wasn't parked in the driveway, and when Matthew opened the back door, the house seemed much quieter than usual. He found Celie in the kitchen, stirring something in a big pot on the cooktop. "Hey," he said in greeting. "I didn't see Jeremy's car. He leave already?"

She turned around, her expression tense. "He didn't come today. June asked him not to."

He frowned. "Why? Where is she, anyway?"

"In her chair. Resting." Celie crossed the room and picked a card off the kitchen table. "This came today."

The postcard showed a picture of a red-hued sunset over the water and a man and a woman taking a romantic walk on the beach. His pulse picked up. Kiera. He flipped the card over.

> *Hola, Mom and Matthew!*
> *The best news ever. I met a nice guy. His name is Benji Bateman, and he's the ship's photographer. We're staying in Cozumel at this beautiful old villa. My room has a beautiful view of the water, but poor Benji has to sleep in the basement. The señora here is very strict—but that's okay. Both Benji and I want to get things exactly right this time. I really think he's special. Please don't worry about me.*
>
> > *I love you both,*
> > *Kiera*

He clenched his jaw and resisted the urge to rip the postcard into a thousand pieces. What was she thinking? Running straight from one man into the arms of another? And a ship's photographer? *The ship's* unemployed *photographer,* he corrected himself.

"I'm going down there and bringing her back," Matthew said. "She's obviously lost her mind."

"You can't do that," his mother said from the doorway. She looked awful, her face devoid of color and the lines deeper than he had ever seen them. "You make her come back here, and she'll just run away again. She's a grown woman, able to make her own choices."

"She can make her own choices when she starts making good ones," Matthew stated, wondering what papers he needed for a passport and how much time it would take.

"Maybe you should just give her a little more time," Celie suggested. "If we don't hear from her in a week or so, then look into going down there."

"Wait? When she's obviously in a fragile emotional state?" Matthew glared at Celie—the woman who'd tripped the first domino in this mess that had become his sister's life. "I'm supposed to sit around and let some guy who probably sees that she's vulnerable take advantage of her? Isn't Bateman the name of the guy in *Psycho*?"

"That was Bates. And I don't think you have a choice," Celie said. "Even if you had a passport, it's not like you have an address or a phone number. How are you going to find them?"

"Celie's right," his mom said. "You have to let this be, Matthew. At least for now. She's in God's hands now." She exchanged glances with Celie.

Although part of Matthew registered that this might be true, he also couldn't help but feel that he was responsible for his sister's welfare. You didn't promise your dying father that you'd look after everyone and then forget about it just because you didn't have a passport.

His mind raced. There had to be a multitude of villas, but maybe the ship's captain would have an idea where his ship's photographer might have gone. But he could do all these things, he realized, and Celie and his mother could be right. Kiera could flatly refuse to come home.

"I'm going out." He grabbed his Windbreaker from a peg in the mudroom. The door shut with a satisfyingly loud *bang* behind him. He walked quickly, taking deep breaths of cold air and trying to calm down. He glanced up at the silver stars.

Heavenly Father, why is she doing this? How can she possibly think some womanizer from the ship is special? How can she be so naive? Please open her eyes to the truth.

His thoughts led him to the wooden shed discreetly tucked to the side of the house. The small building housed his four-wheeler, tools, and worktable. Growing up, he'd spent hours in this place, lifting the tools from their hooks, imagining them in his father's calloused hands, hoping to feel some small part of his father as the cold tool warmed in his hands.

The interior smelled of pine and fertilizer. He crossed the room to the slab of wood that served as a worktable and slapped his hand on the cool, hard surface. His skin stung, and the silence of the empty room rang in his ears. Matthew oiled the belt on the chain saw and added new plastic string to the weed whacker. He stacked old paint cans and added compressed air to the four-wheeler's tires. All these things he could fix, and it only made him even more aware of the things he couldn't.

Restlessly, Mathew walked out of the shed and headed into the grove of trees separating the house and the barn. The trees were Early Macs but had been called the grandfather trees for as long as he could remember. They seemed to hunch sympathetically over him as he walked among them.

God, do I hire an investigator and try to find her? Should I do what Celie suggested and simply wait? If my mom goes into a depression over this, how do I help her?

He stopped near the base of one of the trees and laid his hand on the scabby bark and closed his eyes. Listening as hard as he could, Matthew waited for some sort of answer. He tried to empty his mind of his own thoughts, his desires, his fears, anything that kept him from understanding God's will. He closed his eyes and concentrated on breathing the cool air. It was harder than usual. He kept hearing the rustle of leaves as a breeze moved through them, the chirping of crickets, and then the soft thud of approaching footsteps.

He opened his eyes. Celie and Toaster were moving toward him. "What are you doing out here?" He was no longer angry. Just tired.

"June fell asleep in the recliner. Toaster and I came looking for you to see if you wanted any dinner." She gave him a small smile. "Toaster tracked you down just like I asked him."

Great. Sold out by his own dog.

In the moonlight, her hair was as dark as the night and her skin was pale and smooth. He set his jaw at the flicker of attraction that shot through him. She was a fashion designer, and he'd never been comfortable in anything but blue jeans. She was ambitious; he wanted only to provide for the family and ensure the financial stability of the orchards for future generations. She was wrong, wrong, wrong for him. He hated the part of himself that knew this and didn't care.

"I'm not hungry."

She shifted her weight. "I'm sorry about Kiera. I know you're worried—I am, too—but she's stronger than you think. I've seen her handle some pretty tough situations. She's got some street smarts, and her faith is strong."

He was about to argue that jumping ship with a man she'd only known for a short time didn't sound like an act of faith or intelligence. However, the retort never left his mouth as the motion detector lights snapped on at the barn. At the same time, Toaster, growling low in his throat, began tugging at his leash.

Matthew's gaze swept the area. The crickets had stopped chirping, and the sudden stillness in the air made the back of his neck tingle. Toaster let loose a series of urgent barks and lunged at the end of his leash.

The motion detector light winked off, but Toaster continued to fuss, ignoring Celie's efforts to calm him. "Take him back to the house," he ordered. The goats started to bleat up at the barn, sending Toaster into another frenzy of barking.

"What's going on?"

"I've got to check something at the barn. Go back to the house." He couldn't waste any more time arguing. He started to run.

"I'm coming, too!"

"No you're not."

But she was. He heard her running closely behind him, then Toaster got under his feet and almost tripped him. They zigzagged among the trees, dodging branches and running half blind through the dark grove. All the goats were bleating like crazy now.

The motion sensors illuminated the area as they stepped within range. He saw the open side door, and his stomach dropped to his shoes. He must not have shut it all the way after he'd fed the animals. He charged into the barn and grabbed the first thing his hands found—a metal shovel off the wall. Gripping it tightly, he crossed the aisle to the oversized stall that housed the goats.

Flinging back the stall door, he took in the cowering goats at the back of the stall and the dark shape of something much larger than a fox. He raised the shovel shoulder high and stepped toward the crouching dark shape. Yelling "Get out!" at the top of his lungs, he swung at the creature's head. It moved like a shadow, though, crossed the stall in a single stride, jumped out the open half of the Dutch door, and disappeared into the night.

For a half second, he saw a coyote, then it disappeared into the night. Its movements scattered the goats who charged out of the open stall door behind him and clattered into the center aisle. Celie screamed. Toaster barked. The goats bleated. Matthew raced out of the stall. "Celie?" He fumbled for the light switch.

Celie stood on top of the old blue tack trunk, holding on to Toaster. The goats had jumped onto the top of two bags of shavings Matthew had stacked. Both girl and goats wore similar expressions of fear.

"Oh Matthew, look," Celie said sadly.

Pressed together as they were, he hadn't noticed until now the blood dripping down the side of the bedding bags. Speaking gently to the animals, he walked over to them. Behind Joy, the female goat, and Lucky, the baby, he saw Happy, bleeding from a gash in his shoulder. Matthew's stomach tightened. Even with just a glance, he knew this wound needed stitches.

He called Doc Bradley's number and left a message with the service. While they waited, he herded the goats back into their stall and fed them additional hay and grain. Happy wouldn't touch a bite, and when Matthew stared into the goat's amber eyes, he saw pain and confusion. His spirits sank even lower when the service called back and informed him that Doc Bradley had been called out to treat a horse with colic.

"What are we going to do now?" Celie asked after he gave her the news.

Matthew shook his head. "I've got a suture kit. The problem is I don't have a tranquilizer or an anesthetic. I could probably stitch him up myself if I could figure out how to hold him still."

"I could hold him."

He almost smiled. "That goat is a lot stronger than you."

Her chin lifted a notch. "Then you hold him and let me stitch him up."

He blinked. "You'd do that?"

She met his gaze. "I don't think we have much of a choice."

"You won't pass out on me, will you?"

She held her hand out. It shook a little, but she said, "No way. I'm a New York City girl. I've seen a lot worse."

He doubted that. She was as white as a sheet. But he didn't see any other way. Retrieving the suture kit, he threaded the curved needle. "You sew the flaps of the skin together, side to side, just like two pieces of fabric. Only you do one stitch at a time and tie off each stitch with a double square knot. Got it?"

She swallowed. "Yeah."

"Okay."

He gathered the necessary supplies and isolated Happy from the other goats. Happy let himself be cornered without too much protest. Matthew grabbed him by both horns and sank to his knees for better balance. He used his body mass to pin the small animal against the barn wall. Celie crept forward with a bucket of water and the sewing supplies.

The goat began to squirm the moment she came near the wound. Matthew spoke reassuringly to the animal and held him pinned against the wall. Happy was anything but happy about the situation, and Matthew had to use all his strength to hold him steady. Celie cleaned the wound and cut the hair around the area as short as possible. "Good," he said and then grunted as the goat strained to free himself. Their struggle made him shift his weight and brought him even closer to Celie, bumping into her as the animal fought to free itself.

"Just like a New York City subway," she quipped, but he thought her voice sounded strained. "I'm ready to stitch him up. Are you sure I should do this, Matthew?"

"Yes. And do it fast." Matthew's arms ached with the strain of holding on to the goat.

He glimpsed Celie's face, white and set, frowning slightly in concentration as she worked.

"One down," she commented.

"Good job." He would have said more, but Happy tried to wrestle free. Matthew tightened his hold, and after a few moments the animal gave up. A bead of sweat rolled down his face. He couldn't spare a hand to wipe it.

They counted time in stitches. There were six of them all together. And when she finally tied off the last one, he felt her tremble against him. "Go on," he said gently. "Get out of the stall before I let go of him."

When she was safely out of the stall, he released Happy, who lunged away from him and tried to hide beneath the hayrack. Matthew stood and wiped his hands on his jeans. From what he could see, Celie had done a very good job. The bleeding had stopped. He'd still have Doc Bradley check out the goat tomorrow, but for now everything looked good.

Celie waited outside the stall for him. Her eyes were huge in her pale face. She had blood on her hands, on her sweater, all over her jeans. There was a piece of hair that had fallen out of her ponytail. She tried unsuccessfully to blow it out of her eyes.

"You did good in there," he said.

"Thanks." She looked at her bloodstained hands as if she didn't know what to do with them. They shook a little. "Who knew sewing skills would come in so handy?"

He handed her clean gauze. "You could have a whole new career—Celie Donovan, goat doctor."

"I don't think so." But she smiled as she wiped her hands.

He looked down at her. "You were pretty amazing, you know."

"I couldn't have done it if you hadn't kept Happy pinned against the wall."

His arms seemed to open of their own accord; then Celie was somehow inside them, and he was holding her tightly. He rested his chin against the top of her hair. If anyone had told him a month ago he'd be holding her like this—that he'd like holding her—he would have laughed. She relaxed against him. He tightened his arms, closed his eyes, and gave thanks.

Chapter 16

Celie lined up the side seam and set down the metal foot of June's old Singer. She pressed her foot to the pedal, and the old machine's electric motor revved, then the needle began its high-speed dance. She guided the fabric gently through the machine.

It had been a week since she'd stitched up that goat. Happy was doing well—the vet had praised her work—and Matthew had not only added a latch to the barn door but also covered the open half of the Dutch door in the barn with wire mesh.

She finished the seam and pushed the unwelcome thoughts about Matthew from her mind. "What year did you say this machine was, June? It sure sews well."

"Dermott bought it for me as a wedding gift," June replied. She was dismantling a linen dress that Celie planned to modify. "In its time, it was considered a very good machine."

"It still is." Celie clipped a loose thread and held up the dress. "Would you turn the iron on, June?"

"It's already hot," June replied, fanning herself. "Like today. Here we are, barely into June, and it feels more like August." She glanced at the dress Celie held in her arms. "Oh, that looks nice, Celie."

It wasn't exactly like the hand-painted floral gown destroyed in her apartment fire, but it was a close replica. The fabric had the same Chinese-inspired pattern of magnolia blossoms as the original. It also had a deep, plunging neckline, a ribbed bodice, and a romantic, full skirt. However, Celie had embellished Libby Ellman's original design with delicate green ruffles along the bodice, small pearl buttons, and a cloth flower at the base of the opening in the back.

Pressing the seam open, Celie slid the iron along the fabric. "Hope so. It's the third time I've made this."

"Third?"

"Libby sketched it the first time, and I made the pattern, but then Mi—" She caught herself just in time. "I mean, then it got damaged at the store, so I took it home and remade it, but that version got burned." Celie adjusted the setting on the iron. "And now there's this one. We'll see if three times is a charm."

"Just exactly how did the original get damaged?" June asked.

Celie avoided her gaze. "I really don't want to talk about it."

"You were covering for someone, weren't you? Does that female who fired you know?"

Celie looked up. Matthew was standing there.

"I came back to get more spacers out of the basement," Matthew explained. "I'm putting them in the Jersey Macs." He looked at Celie. "Nice dress."

She busied herself with hanging it on a garment rack, glad for the change of subject. "Thanks. What are spacers?"

"Some are like clothespins. Some are a couple of feet long. You put them in young trees to get them to grow out, not up."

"You ought to show Celie," June suggested. "She needs a break anyway. We've been working all morning."

"It's okay, June. I know Matthew is probably too busy, and I still have a lot of sewing to do."

"It's not that exciting," Matthew warned. "But if you'd like to see, I'll take you. I could bring you back for lunch."

"Go on," June urged.

Moments later they were bouncing over the uneven path between the trees in Matthew's four-wheeler. Strands of Celie's hair blew out of its bun, and she gripped Matthew's waist as they sped through the orchards. When he finally came to a stop, they were in an unfamiliar part of the property. The trees were much smaller, most about the same size as herself. "Short ones," Celie said, getting off the four-wheeler. "Like me."

"They'll grow," Matthew teased. He handed her a bag of wooden clothespins. "Come on."

They walked over to the first tree. Matthew showed her how to push back the branches growing from the trunk and insert the spacer. "Oh, it's sort of like bobby pins. Only instead of pushing back hair, we're pushing back leaves."

"Branches, Celie," Matthew corrected. "We're training the limbs, not leaves."

"You think it hurts the tree?"

He laughed. "I haven't heard any of them complain." He handed her another spacer and watched as she carefully inserted it between branch and trunk. "So what were you and Mom talking about in there, about you covering for someone else's mistake?"

Celie moved to the other side of the tree. "It was nothing, Matthew."

"It's not nothing if you got fired for someone else's mistake."

The leaves felt slightly waxy between her fingers. She imagined sewing a dress made out of them, lining row after row of them and then stitching them in an overlapping pattern. "I was the one who took that dress home—nobody forced me to do it."

"And why exactly did you take the dress home?"

"Oh Matthew, what does it matter? Done is done."

"I could talk to that woman." Matthew moved a branch that was blocking his view of her. "And explain how you were covering for someone else." He peered through the foliage at her, his eyes a vivid blue, contrasting with the green branches.

She thought of Milah, struggling to make ends meet in her loft apartment in the Bronx and her cute little girl. "That's nice of you to offer but no thanks."

He picked up another spacer and slipped it into the tree. "Why would you want to go back there if they fired you unfairly?"

"They're only one of the top design houses in the world," Celie informed him. "You can't open a copy of *Elle* or *Harper's Bazaar* without seeing our dresses. And Libby—she drives you crazy—but she's got a great eye."

"I get that George Marcus is a big deal in the fashion world, but why not go out on your own? Start your own label?"

"Lots of people are really good designers, but they can't make it because they have no contacts. And no investment capital. People don't want to take chances on someone who doesn't have a proven track record in the industry."

They finished the tree and moved to another. Celie was getting the hang of putting the spacers in the branches now and worked more quickly. "Did you always know you'd run these orchards?"

"Oh yeah," Matthew said. "My father was very clear on what he wanted. He always felt that God blessed us with this land and said that it's our family's obligation to take care of it."

"But did you ever want to do something else?" She nearly poked herself in the eye trying to look through the foliage at him.

"When I was really little, I wanted to be a baseball player. I was a New York Yankees fan and thought I'd be the next Graig Nettles."

"Who was Graig Nettles?"

"A third baseman. He was an amazing fielder and a great hitter. My dad and I used to watch him play." He pulled a branch down and anchored it with a long spacer. "How about you, Celie? Did you always want to be a designer?"

"Pretty much," Celie admitted. "My mother taught me to sew—she's really talented—and we used to take scraps of fabric and sew gowns for my Barbies. As I got older, we designed dresses for me."

"Oh, so she's a designer, too?"

"Well, she helps my dad run their dry cleaning business. She does all the alterations." Celie frowned. "You know, taking things in and letting them out. Hemming and. . ."

"Your voice changes when you talk about her," Matthew said.

"It does?"

"Yeah. Why are you frowning?"

Celie sighed. She glanced at Matthew's profile. "It's complicated," she said. "My mom is ten times more talented than I'll ever be. She could have been more famous than George Marcus, even." She paused as several low-flying birds passed overhead.

"Being famous doesn't guarantee you'll be any happier than if you aren't."

"I know that." She hesitated. The quiet, serene orchard somehow made it easier to confide in him. "It's just that sometimes I think my mom wonders what her life would have been like if she had put career over family." She had never admitted this aloud to anyone. "Every so often I'd catch her standing at the kitchen sink, looking out the window with this dreamy expression on her face."

"She made her choice, Celie. I think at some point everyone wonders what their life could have been."

"I know. But she's only told me like a million times, 'Don't settle.'"

"That sounds like good advice."

Celie stepped back from the tree and shielded her eyes with her hand. "I think it means, 'Don't end up like me.'"

He turned slowly. "And what's so bad about her life?"

"She lost her dream," Celie said sadly.

"Are you so sure?" He was looking at her with a strange expression.

"I think so. And it didn't help that I got fired. She was devastated for me." She looked long and hard at him. "Hasn't there ever been anything you really wanted but couldn't have?"

A guarded look formed in his eyes. "Of course," he said. "Lots of things. But it doesn't mean those were the right things for me." He wiped his face. "Nobody likes disappointments, but I believe God allows them into our lives for a reason." He gave her a crooked smile. "I know it's hard, but I believe God wants us to have life in its fullest. Sometimes we can take a wrong turn—make the wrong choice—but He always gives us another chance to get back on the path He means for us to take."

He was right, and it was something to think about. As they walked back to the house, she thought about the turns a life could take—about right ones and wrong ones and sometimes how hard it was to know the difference.

Chapter 17

Celie parked the Honda in the outdoor lot at the Danbury train station and took the 9:55 a.m. into Manhattan. Even traveling off-peak, the compartments were crowded. She had to take a seat that had her riding backwards, sitting next to a young man with three rings in his eyebrow and across from a woman typing furiously on her laptop.

She clutched her sketchbook and watched the buildings give way to greenery as the train sped down the New Haven line. She could feel the anticipation of being in the city warring with the unexpected longing for the orchard—and if she were honest, for Matthew.

She thought about the dresses, carefully laid out on the rack above her. They weren't exact replicas of the ones lost in the fire—she could have made them exact replicas, but she'd followed her instincts, adding embellishments, lengthening a hemline here, and tailoring the sleeves there. She was proud of them. There was a good chance Libby Ellman and George Marcus would see them and be willing to forgive her. And if this wasn't enough, she had the drawing of the green dress in her sketchbook.

When they reached Grand Central, people still moved in a slow, hot shuffle through the tunnel and into the station. Uno and Sudgi waved at her from the coffee shop, and Duncan McCloud, wearing the familiar NYPD uniform, still stood at the exact spot next to the 42nd Street exit.

Her Jimmy Choo boots—a little more battle-scarred than the last time she'd been in the city—clicked smartly as she slipped into the steady stream of people heading east on 42nd Street. She breathed in the stale, slightly smoky scent of city air and smiled at the sound of a car's horn, protesting the bumper-to-bumper traffic. All around her, buildings and skyscrapers towered, filling every bit of available real estate.

On the corner of 42nd and Fifth, she spotted James standing beside the halal cart. His light gray pinstripe suit was new, but the ubiquitous cup of coffee in his hand wasn't.

"James!"

He grinned when he spotted her. "You're a sight for sore eyes," he said, hugging her. "Let me help with those." He took the garment bags out of her hand.

She was wearing a slim pencil skirt made from some of the material she'd purchased at Fabric Attic and had paired it with a tangerine blouse she'd pulled out of the church box and remodeled. "You're not so bad yourself," she said. "Calvin Klein?"

"You like it?"

"Love it. You're sure having lunch with me won't get you into trouble?"

"Are you kidding?" James joked. "They can't tell me who I can and can't be friends with." He reached for her arm with his free hand. "Come on, I'm starving."

They bought plates of spicy dark chicken meat covered with an even spicier green sauce and walked the remaining blocks to the New York Public Library. Celie's heart swelled at the sight of the massive stone lions flanking the steps to the building's entrance. They found an empty table in the courtyard. Celie shooed away the pigeons and took a seat.

As they ate chunks of the savory chicken, James quickly brought Celie up to speed at George Marcus Designs. "Got a lot of orders from the spring show at the Javits, but now Libby is freaking out because George hates everything she's shown him for Paris. Everybody's working late and on weekends and grumbling because she keeps changing her mind about everything."

"Sorry to hear that." Celie gestured toward the garment bags. "Maybe those dresses will help."

"I hope so." James washed down his chicken with a long drink of coffee. "You're really missed."

Celie pulled out her sketchbook. "Missed so much that she might be interested in seeing this?" She slid the opened book over to James, who moved his lunch to make room.

"It's gorgeous." He angled the page into the light. His gaze lingered on the page. "Maybe the best thing you've ever done."

"Gorgeous enough to get me my job back?"

James's mouth twisted. "Celie, designing wasn't what got you fired. You broke company policy by taking a gown home without permission. You don't know how close you came to George pressing charges against you. Fortunately, Milah stayed up for two days straight and came up with a couple of substitutes."

Celie tossed a piece of pita bread to a begging pigeon. She wanted to tell James exactly why she'd taken the hand-painted gown home in the first place, but she didn't see what good it would do, other than make her feel better. "I'm sorry about what happened, James. You have to trust me—it wasn't completely my fault. All I want is my old job back. Will you please help me?"

"Sweetie, I'd swim the Hudson River in December for you. Of course I'll help. But it will take time." He ripped the page out of Celie's sketchbook then stared at the exposed page. It was a pencil drawing of Matthew with the apple orchards in the background.

"Who's this guy?" James lifted his gaze from the page to study Celie's face. She felt herself blush. "That's Matthew."

"That's Matthew?" James laughed. "The guy who doesn't like you? I thought you two were cat and dog."

"Oil and water, actually." Celie tugged the sketchbook out of her friend's hands. "But now we're friends. I think." She heard the defensive note in her voice. "It's complicated."

"Sure," James agreed. "Love is complicated."

"I don't love him."

"That's not what this drawing says. It's not what I see in his eyes."

"I don't see anything special in this drawing. And Matthew most definitely doesn't love me."

"If you believe that," James scoffed and pushed his glasses more firmly onto the bridge of his nose, "I've got a very nice bridge to sell you."

~

It was nearly eight o'clock when Celie parked her Honda in the Patricks' driveway. The wind had picked up. She heard it in the heavy rustle of leaves in the trees. A flowerpot had fallen, and she bent to straighten it as she stepped onto the porch steps. Toaster barked a welcome at the sound of her footsteps on the porch.

Matthew opened the front door before she even knocked. The sight of him holding on to the squirming dog made her heart thump in her chest. All at once it felt as if it'd been ages since she'd seen him, and it felt so good that if she hadn't had two shopping bags in her hands, she might have done something crazy—like hugged him.

"Hi," Celie said, looking up into his rugged, sun-tanned face.

"Welcome back." Matthew pulled the door wider. "Mom's in the living room," he said, although this information was redundant. The volume of the television could be heard clearly. What was less clear was whether Matthew seemed glad to see her. His mouth had that tight *Celie, why did you move that candlestick?* look to it. His blue eyes, however, seemed to say, *I'm glad you're safely back.*

From her recliner, June punched the MUTE button on the remote control and grinned up at Celie. "Did it go all right? I want to hear everything."

Celie set the shopping bags down and plopped onto the adjacent club chair. Toaster immediately launched himself into her lap and jumped up to lick her face.

"Toastie!" June ordered. "Leave the girl alone. Get down. Why aren't you minding me, Toastie?"

"It's okay, June."

June called the dog again. This time Toaster obeyed. With an audible grunt, he heaved himself into her lap. "My goodness, this dog has put on weight," June said. "How did you get to be such a plumpie, Toastie?"

"Because you give him too many cheeseburgers," Matthew observed dryly.

"You think so?" June asked very innocently.

"I don't think so. I *know* so."

Celie laughed. A bigger gust of wind rattled the windows before heaving itself silent. She automatically glanced at the darkness outside, grateful for the safety of the old house, the coziness of the living room, and the sounds of Matthew's and June's voices.

"Animals shouldn't be too thin," June argued. "People either. Did you get anything to eat for supper, Celie?"

"I grabbed a sandwich at Grand Central," Celie assured her. She bent over to retrieve the shopping bags. "I brought you both back a little something." She handed June the first bag.

"You didn't have to do that," June admonished but reached eagerly into the bag. "Oh," she exclaimed, pulling a pair of silver chandelier earrings from their tissue wrapping. "They're beautiful. Thank you, Celie."

"I thought the blue stones would match your eyes," Celie said. She handed Matthew another bag.

His dark eyebrows drew together in a puzzled look that quickly turned to pleased surprise as he pulled out a new coffee mug with a big red apple on it. "The Big Apple—New York City," he read. His gaze shifted to her. "Thank you, Celie."

Their gazes met, and her heart started to thump. "It's to replace the one I broke. Glad you like it."

He set the mug on the table but continued to trace his fingers along the smooth rim. "I'll use it tomorrow morning."

Celie thought about his lips touching that cup and felt her heartbeat kick up another notch. Lucky mug. That she could be jealous of a coffee cup was ridiculous. She wasn't a country girl. She liked short skirts, high heels, makeup, and pedicures when she could afford them.

"Now tell us about the meeting," June prompted. "You and James."

"Well," Celie began, "James liked the sketch. He said he'd show it to Libby when the time was right."

June clapped her hands. "It'll all work out. I just know it! Did you invite James and the big muckety-mucks to the Castoffs to Couture show?"

"Yes."

Another gust of wind hit the house, and the lights flickered and then died. Startled, Celie gripped the armrest of her chair, straining to see beyond the wall of darkness around her. The blackness was absolute, and the sudden silence told her the power had gone out. A few seconds later, though, the lights came back on.

"We'd better get the lanterns and some candles, Matthew, in case we lose power again." June already had gotten to her feet and was leaning on the cane. "I guess the weatherman was right for once. We're in for a doozy of a storm."

Chapter 18

Celie woke in the darkness to the sound of rain. Not a steady little beat on the roof but a full-fledged assault that pounded down on the house as if it intended to pulverize it. She pulled the warm comforter higher under her chin and listened to the wind slash sheets of water against the windows.

The clock said five thirty as she turned on the china lamp and swung her legs out of bed. Her bare feet registered the drop in temperature as she slipped on a pair of jeans and a gray NYU sweatshirt leftover from Kiera's college days. She tied her hair back and headed down the stairs.

Matthew helped June down the stairs shortly after Celie had started breakfast. "Sounds like a monsoon out there," June said, raising her voice to be heard above the drumming on the roof.

"I'm just glad it's not hail," Matthew said, pouring himself a cup of coffee. He was holding the new mug, and Celie was disproportionately pleased to see it in his hands.

June frowned. "I was going to get my hair done today." She patted her hair, pulled back in its usual, neat bun. "I am so tired of this hairstyle. I want something more contemporary. Something more youthful."

"You should reschedule, Mom." Matthew added two heaping spoonfuls of sugar to the dark brew. "We'll be lucky to keep our power."

"I don't want to reschedule," June snapped. "It took me two weeks to get this appointment with Clint. Jeremy is coming over this afternoon, and I look like the wreck of the Hesperus."

Matthew shook his head. "You look fine. It's a good day to stay inside. The McGillis pond is sure to flood. I don't want either you or Celie on the road today."

"You could take me," June argued. "The pickup has good water clearance."

"I'm going to be working on the tractor's engine," Matthew said. "And I doubt very much that Jeremy will come out in this weather anyway."

Celie watched the edges of the scrambled eggs start to solidify.

More rain slashed against the windowpanes. She understood June's desire to make herself attractive. Yesterday Celie had walked past her favorite place to get her nails done, and it had taken extreme effort on her part not to go inside. "Maybe I could take you, June, in Matthew's truck."

Matthew swallowed his coffee the wrong way. Coughing, he waved away June, who reached over to thump him on the back. "It's a stick shift," he managed at last. "I could just see the two of you ending up in the middle of the McGillis pond, sinking fast."

Celie set a platter of eggs on the kitchen table. She'd never driven a manual transmission vehicle, but Matthew shouldn't just make assumptions like that about her. "How do you know I can't drive a stick?"

The corners of his mouth lifted a fraction. "Because you're a city girl."

She waved the serving spoon at him. "Exactly. Driving in New York City is not for the fainthearted. For your information, I can be a very aggressive driver."

Matthew's lips stopped curving. "That does not make me feel better and has nothing to do with the ability to change gears."

"All I need is one gear," Celie argued.

"Let's just do it," June urged. "I can talk you through it."

"Neither of you is going anywhere," Matthew said loudly. "Do I have to take the keys, or do I have your word that you won't go anywhere?"

"Oh take the keys, then," June said irritably.

The minute Matthew left through the back door, June turned to Celie. "He's being totally unreasonable, isn't he? It's not even raining that hard."

It was pouring rain and still so dark outside that she couldn't see the orchards. Celie sensed pointing this out to June wouldn't help. "Well, it's a good day for sewing. We've got a lot of work to do."

June followed her reluctantly into the dining room. She sat on one of the mahogany chairs and stared out the window. Celie saw the unhappy pucker to her lips and remembered the pink floral fabric she'd bought a few weeks ago at the Fabric Attic. Retrieving it from her room, she went to work.

June sewed seams on the old Singer and from the sound of the engine had the pedal plastered to the floor. They worked for almost an hour, then June rose restlessly to stand at the window, peering out into the gray morning.

"Light's on in the shed," June commented. "Matthew'll probably hole himself in there for hours." She glanced at her watch. "Still time to make my appointment."

"Hmmm." Celie snapped off a bit of thread. She held up June's new skirt. It still needed a zipper and hemming, but she liked the shape and the way the fabric hung. She'd wanted something romantic, something soft and feminine for June. "What do you think, June? You like it?"

June turned at the sound of her voice, and there was a determined glint in her eyes. "I love it, Celie, and I know just what would go perfectly with it."

"A pink blouse?" Celie suggested. "Something with a V-neck?" Something fitted would work best. For being so tall, June really was tiny. Maybe a narrow belt around the waist.

June smiled. "Not a shirt or a sweater. A new haircut." The glimmer in her eyes grew stronger. "I think there's a pair of spare keys to the truck in the junk drawer in the kitchen."

～

Matthew wiped his hands on a rag. He had a carburetor problem. Even after removing the parts, cleaning them thoroughly, and replacing them, the engine continued to race, even in the lowest gear. He probably needed at least one new cylinder.

Overhead, the rain continued in a steady beat, a pleasant drumming noise. It no longer sounded as if a waterfall were pounding the roof of the building. The storm was passing, just as predicted. There'd probably be some flooding and slight wind damage to the trees, but overall they'd been fortunate. Thank God.

Matthew remembered the storms of his childhood. His mother humming a cheerful tune as she set out the candles, filled the bathtubs with water, and turned on the battery-powered radio.

He and Kiera had made tents in the living room and counted the seconds between the flashes of lightning and the crack of thunder. They'd seen some bad storms, too. Hail stones as big as a man's fist, a hurricane that had thrown a tree through the bay window, and several times June had sent them to the basement when the sky turned green and the clouds created suspicious-looking formations.

There were no funnel clouds, though, as Matthew hiked the distance from the shed to the house. He hung his dripping slicker on a peg and greeted Toaster who danced around him, wagging his tail.

The mudroom held a vague chemical odor. Frowning, he looked around for the source of the smell. Nothing seemed out of place. The washer and dryer were empty, the double sink was scrubbed clean, and the usual containers of detergents and cleansers sat with their caps securely tightened in their places. Ammonia, he decided. The ladies had been cleaning.

He stepped into the kitchen. The chemical smell disappeared, but to his disappointment, nothing delicious bubbled on the cooktop. But this didn't surprise him entirely. It was barely three o'clock in the afternoon.

"Matthew? We're in here!"

Matthew followed his mother's voice into the living room and stopped beneath the arched entrance. Company. He hadn't known they were expecting anybody. Hadn't seen any cars. A tall, ash-blond stood with her back to him. The unfamiliar woman wore a floral skirt that floated just below her knees and a pink sweater that was the same shade of flowers in the skirt. "Hello," he said politely.

The ash-blond woman turned, and Matthew's jaw dropped.

"Matthew," his mother said, striking a pose and positively beaming at him. "What do you think?"

Think? His mind went blank. He couldn't seem to wrap his brain around the image of June standing there looking nothing like herself. He'd grown used to the sight of her dressed in comfortable sweat suits, her silver hair pulled back into a tight bun. He couldn't remember the last time he'd seen her wearing a skirt. It shocked him further to realize that, even at seventy, his mother had nice legs.

If this wasn't enough for his brain to process, there was the hair. It looked different, slightly on the blond side of silver. She'd cut it, too—short layers framed her face. And she had light, wispy bangs.

"Do you like it?" June prompted, turning slowly.

Matthew crossed his arms, frowning, as it occurred to him that June had kept her hair appointment after all. After he'd specifically told her to stay home. She knew how dangerous the road became when it flooded. What had she been thinking? "I told you not to go out today."

"I didn't," she said smugly.

"Then how did you get new clothing and a new hairdo?"

Grinning from ear to ear, she pointed to Celie. "Celie did this. We had so much fun, Matthew. I had some old hair dye in my bathroom, and the rest is history. Do you like it? Every time I walk by a mirror, I surprise myself."

She surprised him, too. It made sense to him now. The chemical smell in the mudroom had been the hair color. They'd had to use the downstairs sink because June still had trouble doing stairs.

His mom touched her cheek. "She even did my makeup. I haven't worn foundation in years."

She didn't need to be wearing it now either. Matthew pinned his gaze on Celie. His blood started to boil. He remembered the weekend Kiera had come for a visit wearing a dress that was much too short and tight. She'd had on heels so high that it'd almost put her on eye level with him. "My friend Celie designed this just for me," she'd said, spinning slowly.

"Isn't she beautiful?" Celie asked, turning to him, smiling proudly.

"She was beautiful before, too," Matthew said sharply. He forced a calm note into his voice. "Can I see you in my office, Celie?"

"If you're going to offer to pay her," his mother admonished him, "I've already offered, and she's refused. I told her all this would have cost me at least a hundred dollars at Clint's."

"I'm not offering her money." Matthew marched off to his office. He closed the door behind them and only then allowed some of the fury to release itself. "How could you do that to my mother?"

Celie's cheeks paled and then turned red. "She looks great. Why are you so upset?"

Matthew paced the small, wood-paneled office that had been his father's and his father's before him. "Couldn't you see that she was beautiful before?" He came to a stop a few feet in front of her. "Why do you always have to change everything around you? People. Furniture. Clothing. Even the dog has to have a designer coat."

She planted her hands firmly on her hips. "What was I supposed to do, Matthew? She was going for the spare set of keys to the truck. You know your mother. This was the only way I could think to stop her."

"She was bluffing." Matthew's voice rose, but he couldn't seem to help it. "With her bad hip, she can't hold down the clutch. She couldn't have gone anywhere unless you drove her."

"Oh." Celie seemed momentarily taken aback. "She was going to cut and color it anyway. It's not a capital offense to change a hairstyle, Matthew. That hair dye wasn't so old."

He glared at her. He had about a foot and more than a hundred pounds on her, and yet she met his gaze unflinchingly. "I liked how she looked before better."

"Get over it." Celie's eyes flashed. "June likes it, and I do, too." Her chin lifted a notch. "Maybe what bothers you the most is you're afraid that Jeremy is going to like it as well."

"I don't care if Jeremy likes it or not." His mother and Jeremy? Not a chance. They were old friends, and Celie had no right suggesting otherwise.

"Why do you think your mother was so set on getting her hair cut today?"

"You should mind your own business." He struggled to hold back his temper and thought he might have a brain hemorrhage with the effort required.

"What's wrong with helping your mother feel more attractive?"

He took a deep breath. "You start changing the way people look, you change their lives, and maybe their lives don't need changing."

"Maybe you should let them be the judge of that."

"Maybe you should stick to sewing dresses."

The rain drummed steadily down, filling the silence in the room. The mahogany-paneled office had always seemed small, a tight fit for the built-in bookcases and the keyhole desk. It felt huge now, cavernous, and Celie seemed a mile away from him, although he could have reached out and touched her if he wanted.

Matthew pushed his hands through his hair. All he was doing was trying to protect his family. Kiera had been hurt, and he wasn't about to stand still and let the same thing happen to his mother.

"All I'm saying is no more makeovers. Not my mother, the dog, the house, the horse, or the goats." Had he left anything out? It was hard to think straight with all these emotions buzzing around his head like a swarm of angry bees.

"Fine," Celie practically spat the word. Her eyes were almost black, and her small fists were clenched.

He watched her walk away from him, her shoulders stiff and her spine as straight as if he'd jabbed her in the back with a poker. She took the steps at a slow jog and disappeared down the hallway. He heard the *click* of a shutting door. He turned to find June staring at him. Her lips twisted in concern. "What was that all about, Matthew?"

He looked at the silver chandelier earrings hanging from her lobes. She'd always worn the pearl studs his father had given her as a wedding gift. Pushing his hands in his pockets, he shook his head. "Nothing. Nothing important."

Chapter 19

Jeremy arrived the next day shortly after ten o'clock. "There's still a few inches of standing water on the road," he explained as Celie greeted him at the door. "Don't know why the town doesn't do something about the way the McGillis pond fl—"The word died on his lips as June stepped into the hallway.

"June," Jeremy began, working visibly to push that one word through his lips. "June," he repeated, his gaze locked on June's tall, thin body. "You are stunning. Simply stunning."

"You look pretty nice yourself," June said. "I like the green suspenders."

"And I like your skirt."

Celie put her hand over her mouth to keep from laughing. Thank heaven Matthew wasn't here to see the two of them gazing at each other like moonstruck teenagers.

"Celie made it for me. You really like it?" Her cheeks turned the same pink as her sweater.

Of course he liked it. Celie could hardly keep herself from prompting Jeremy, who couldn't seem to tear his gaze from June. "I love it," he said.

Celie beamed. Jeremy was reacting just the way a man should act when an attractive woman dressed up for him. Awestruck. Slightly bemused and highly appreciative.

"Shall we get started then?" June led the way to the dining room. "Celie and I made good progress yesterday. We finished off two cocktail dresses." She gestured toward two dresses—both former bridesmaid dresses—hanging at the front of a crowded garment rack.

Jeremy slung his jacket over the back of a chair and rolled his sleeves to his elbows. Celie noticed that he took a seat across from June instead of stationing himself at the ironing board as he usually did, and he couldn't seem to stop looking at June.

"The ladies on the luncheon committee are meeting today to decide the menu," Jeremy said. "We can fit about a hundred people in the church basement."

"A hundred people!" Celie had pictured maybe fifty. "You really think that many people will come?" Jeremy pushed his hands through his thick white hair, looking more than ever like a combination of Einstein and the sweetest grandfather in the world. "I think double would come to the rummage sale, and who knows how many people would buy tickets to the luncheon if we had more space."

"We ought to move it outdoors," June stated. She was cutting out the lining from a man's brown suit. "We could fit more people under a tent."

Jeremy shook his head. "I thought about that, but the road construction on South Main won't be finished by then. It'll be too hard to hear the announcer over a jackhammer. Plus, if we use the parking lot, what will people do with their cars?"

"We should have it here," June declared. "In our front yard. People could park in the field across the street, and we could have the show under the grandfather trees."

Jeremy sat up a little straighter. His bushy white eyebrows rose almost to his hairline. "You know, that might just work. We haven't started advertising yet, the clothing already is here. . ."

"And the orchards would be a perfect setting," Celie finished. She could already imagine the branches in the apple trees heavy with bright red apples, their trunks wrapped in white tulle. She saw ladies sitting among the trees at round tables with crisp white linen cloths and vases stuffed with wildflowers.

And then she imagined Matthew's face, scowling down at her. *Why'd you have to change them,* he'd say. *Weren't the trees pretty enough for you to begin with?*

"The trees would be full of apples," June agreed, her hands pausing with the scissors still buried in the fabric. "The Early Macs would be ready to harvest. We could probably sell some. That'd raise some more money for the church."

"I like this idea," Jeremy said. "Having the fashion show in the orchards has a lot more atmosphere than the church's basement. Don't you think so, Celie?"

Celie drew the thread through the needle. "Are you kidding me? It would be great. But someone besides me ought to ask Matthew."

June read Jeremy's puzzled expression. "The two of them were in Matthew's office, fighting like cats and dogs, and then neither of them would eat a bite of dinner." Her gaze turned to Celie. "What did he say to you last night?"

So Matthew had been upset enough about their argument not to eat. The knowledge made Celie feel unaccountably satisfied. "We just disagreed about things, that's all." She knotted the thread, unwilling to risk hurting June's feelings by sharing Matthew's true opinion of the older woman's makeover.

"What things?" June pushed a pair of reading glasses higher on her face. "What things, exactly."

Celie shrugged and began to tack down the lapel of the jacket in her hands. "You know. The way I always change things. Same old. Same old."

"Oh." June sighed. "She's talking about the furniture we rearranged. I should have told you to return the quilt to the back of the sofa." She shook her head. "You'd think he'd be ready to put aside those memories."

What memories? Celie's hands tightened on the jacket. She all but held her breath waiting for the older woman to continue. The only sound June made, however, was the whisper of her scissors cutting through cloth. Celie cleared her throat. "Umm, what memories?"

June put the fabric aside. "Old, old ones. Bittersweet ones."

Celie didn't want to pry, but she wanted very much to know. She pulled the needle in and out of the brown fabric, glancing up when she felt June's gaze on her.

"When Dermott started having digestive problems," June began quietly, "he went to the doctor and was diagnosed with colon cancer. Of course by then, the cancer had already spread. The doctors knew it was hopeless, but they wanted to give Dermott as much time as they could, so they did a couple rounds of chemotherapy and radiation. Took a terrible toll on him." Her gaze went to Jeremy. "You saw what it did, the weight he lost."

Jeremy nodded. His gray eyes looked sadder than Celie had ever seen them. "Dermott kept fighting, though," he said. "He went through it all with honor."

"Never complained," June agreed. "Never lost his faith. If anything, it made his relationship with the Lord even stronger. He got thinner and thinner until he was just a shadow of himself. Always cold. At night I'd light a fire and he and Matthew would wrap up in that old quilt and sit on the couch together. The two of them." She paused and smiled fondly. "Snug like two bugs in a rug."

June looked at Celie but seemed to be seeing Matthew and Dermott snuggled up together as they had been all those years ago. "Dermott would read Matthew stories from the Bible, and then they'd talk about them. About what they really meant. Dermott could explain things as well as any preacher I've ever heard." She smiled. "Matthew soaked it all up like a little sponge. Dermott held on as long as he could, but eventually the Lord took him home.

"Afterward, most nights Matthew would wrap himself and Kiera up in that quilt and read the Bible to her. She was just a toddler when he started, and they did it for years—I don't know when he stopped—but ever since then, we've kept that quilt folded on the back of the sofa."

"June, that is the most beautiful story I've ever heard." Celie had to dig her fingernails into the palm of her hand to keep from crying. "I'm so sorry I moved that quilt."

June shook her head and smiled. "Don't be sorry. This house needed a change. I just didn't realize how much we needed it. I guess you get used to living a certain way."

"I'm putting that quilt back immediately." Before June could protest, Celie leaped to her feet and hurried up the stairs to retrieve the quilt from her bedroom. She kept thinking of Matthew and Dermott together, then Matthew and Kiera, and this one quilt that had bound them together.

As she carefully folded the quilt and draped it exactly the way she'd found it over the edge of the sofa, she thought of her own parents. The traditions she'd grown up with—the week in July at Madison Lake State Park, Christmas caroling, the crazy birthday hat—the one with the singing fish—that each of them wore at his or her birthday dinner. She longed suddenly to talk to her parents, especially her mother, and resolved to call them later.

She lifted down the mirror from the mantelpiece and put back the portrait of Great-Grandmother Caroline. The candlesticks went back to the dining room. In their place she carefully put the knickknacks and hurricane lamps in their original positions.

"You don't have to do that, honey," June called out. "Come back and sit down with us."

Celie shook her head. "Not until I finish. I can't remember—where was the china shepherdess before we put her on the bookshelf?"

"In Kiera's room."

Celie hurried upstairs. When she returned, June and Jeremy had their heads bent toward each other in an easy, conversational way. "Jeremy was telling me some very good news!" June exclaimed. "Tell her."

The old ladder-back chair groaned as Jeremy shifted to see Celie more easily. "Emily would like to be in the Castoffs to Couture show."

"I wrote her measurements down for you," June added, waving a piece of paper at Celie. Celie looked at the numbers on the paper and felt a wave of envy. It didn't help that June and Jeremy were raving about how beautiful Emily was, too—all tall and blond. She fought the urge to crumple the paper. What was wrong with her? She'd never been envious of Kiera's measurements—or good looks. So what was the difference? *You're jealous,* a voice in her head said. *Emily is Matthew's former girlfriend.*

She put the piece of paper on the table. "I'd love for Emily to be in the show. I'll find her something really great to wear."

"Oh, she'll be happy with anything," Jeremy said. "She's not hard to please. Did I mention she's coming home for the Fourth of July and also taking all her vacation this summer here?"

"That's wonderful," June cried. "Sounds like she misses this old town. You think she might be ready to come home for good?"

"It's what I've been praying for," Jeremy replied.

"I'll start praying for this, too."

Celie was spared from making any comment as the doorbell rang. She jumped to her feet, glad of the excuse not to hear any more about Emily Taylor.

"Shirley Elliot's here already?" June shook her head. "The time just flies by."

~

A small group of women—and Jeremy Taylor—sat sewing in the dining room when Matthew got home. He was in no mood to socialize and headed straight for his office, barely pausing to say hello. After the fight he'd had with Celie last night, he had no desire to face her anytime soon.

To his surprise, his office door was shut and someone had taped a sign to it. MODEL'S CHANGING ROOM.

Matthew gritted his teeth. He knocked loudly, intending to tell whoever it was to find a new place to change. The words died on his lips when the door opened and Lilac Westover, the minister's wife, stood there in a black tuxedo with a frilly white shirt sticking out of the jacket.

He blinked, his feet rooted to the ground more securely than any of the grandfather apple trees in the orchard. In thirty-something years, he'd never seen Lilac Westover in anything but an ankle-length skirt and blazer. The sight of her in a tux made him want to rub his eyes. Not because she looked funny—just the opposite. She looked great. It made him realize how talented Celie actually was to turn something that had probably been a man's tux into something so feminine.

His mother tapped him on the shoulder. "Matthew. I need to talk to you." She glanced around him at Lilac. "Oh! You look amazing! Everyone, look."

Lilac moved gracefully into the foyer, and everyone peeked around the boxes and hanging clothing in the dining room to see her. The ladies in the dining room twittered approval. He recognized Jill Lane, the town's one and only policewoman, and Susan Grojack, retired now but with those hawklike eyes that missed nothing. She'd been his seventh-grade science teacher and had called on him to read the most embarrassing slides during their human reproduction unit.

Esther Polino, the town's librarian, moved past him, something slinky and purple in her petite arms. She tossed him a grin before disappearing into his office.

"I want to ask you something," his mother said, "and I want you to think about it before you answer."

In other words, she was about to ask him to do something he didn't want to do. He frowned. His gaze moved of its own will to Celie, willing her to look at him then looked away when she did.

"Matthew?" Her cane thumped on the wood floor. "Are you even listening?"

He forced his gaze back to his mother. He was getting used to the feathery bangs on her forehead, the slight wave in her hair. He couldn't deny she looked more purposeful. Happier, too, than she'd been in a long time. The harsh words he'd exchanged with Celie echoed uncomfortably in his head.

"With more space," she continued, "we could expand the show and bring in more revenue for the church. You wouldn't have to do much. We'd have the caterer bring in the tables and Shirley Elliot's pretty sure her husband can have his sound team wire some loudspeakers in the trees."

They wanted to move the show to the orchards. Matthew's gaze traveled to the racks of clothes. He wasn't much of a fashion expert, but even he could tell these remakes of other people's castoffs were good. Really good. He'd encouraged this project in the first place and was more than willing to help make it a success. Besides, he felt badly about the things he'd said to Celie. "Okay," he said.

"Okay?" his mother echoed in disbelief. "You really mean that?"

The women in the dining room stopped chatting. Even the sewing machine went still. "You can have the show in the orchards," Matthew confirmed. "Just as long as it doesn't interfere with the picking schedule."

"It won't. We'll have it early. August instead of September," June assured him, a triumphant smile stretching across her face. "You hear that, everyone? Matthew said yes!"

A loud cheer went up. Matthew shrugged off the thanks. He fervently wanted to get out of the house before Esther Polino stepped out of his office in the purple number. He didn't want to see the librarian in anything but her customary turtlenecks and slacks.

He retreated through the house, pausing in the living room. Something looked different. The mirror was gone, and the knickknacks on the mantelpiece were back. The furniture also had been returned to its old arrangement. And the blue quilt with the Log Cabin pattern hung neatly over the back of the couch as if it had never been moved.

The room looked almost exactly the way it'd been before Celie arrived. Matthew glanced at the curtains, drawn to protect the antique furniture from bleaching. Everything sat in its right place, but nothing felt right to him anymore. The room seemed almost gloomy to him. He wondered if it'd always been like this and he was just seeing it now.

Isn't this what you wanted? For her to stop changing things? He rubbed his face hard. It was exactly what he'd wanted, and yet having it brought him no pleasure. No pleasure at all.

Chapter 20

Matthew hadn't said anything about the changes to the living room, but Celie thought he approved. The next morning, he handed her a cup of tea with extra sugar in it, just the way she liked it. "You up for a surprise?" he asked.

"If it's a good surprise." Celie smiled. Now that she knew the story behind the quilt, she was as anxious as he seemed to be to put their argument behind them.

"It's a good one," Matthew assured her. "Give me about an hour and meet me on the front porch."

Celie didn't know what to expect, but it certainly wasn't the sight of him driving Bonnie hitched to a shiny black buggy down the long driveway. She shielded her face from the morning sunlight. He was smiling at her. Hmmm. He didn't do that often enough.

"Want to go for a ride?"

She was already halfway down the porch steps.

It seemed as if she'd stepped back a hundred years in time as she climbed into the shiny black buggy and settled on the smooth leather seat. "Central Park and Fifth," she quipped.

"Would you settle for a really nice ride through the orchards?"

"Are you kidding? I'd settle for down the driveway." Celie could hardly keep herself still on the seat. "I've always wanted to do this."

June waved them off from the porch. "You all be careful," she shouted. "Been a long time since Bonnie's pulled anything but grass out of the ground."

"You want to come, June?" Celie called back. "I'll squish over. There's room."

"No thanks." June pulled a weed from one of the hanging pots overflowing with bright red geraniums. "I'm going to bake some double chocolate brownies. Have fun, though."

Matthew slapped the reins lightly over Bonnie's broad haunches, and the buggy rolled forward. Celie squealed, earning her an amused glance from Matthew, who couldn't possibly know of all the times she'd sat on a bench in Central Park and watched the horse-drawn carriages roll past. She'd planned to splurge on a ride when her parents came to visit.

They crossed Route 303, passed through a long, swinging gate, and followed the bumpy dirt road into a forest of pear-shaped trees. Apple trees. Celie was beginning to recognize the oval shapes of the leaves, although she still couldn't tell a Jersey Mac from an Empress.

It'd rained the night before, and the tree limbs still hung heavy with their darkened, water-soaked leaves. Bonnie plodded along, occasionally trying to steal bites from the trees. "What kind of apple trees are these?" She didn't really care, but she didn't want to ride in silence either. What she really wanted to say was that she admired the way he'd held the family together after his father's death.

"Early Macs," Matthew gestured to the right. "The Paula Reds are a couple of rows over."

End of conversation. She was seated right next to him and yet felt like there was a big elephant on the bench between them. The elephant was their fight. She supposed she should just put what'd happened behind her. Pretend it'd never happened.

Celie sighed. "About your mother's makeover," she began. At the exact same time, Matthew said, "About yesterday."

They looked at each other and laughed. Celie took a deep breath. "I'm sorry about changing things in the house, and I promise not to cut your mother's hair again."

"I overreacted. Mom's hair doesn't look that bad."

"What?" She'd heard him clearly but couldn't believe he meant it.

The color darkened beneath his tan. "I may have gotten a bit carried away the other day. You didn't have to rearrange the furniture again. I was just getting used to it."

She'd seen his anger, his protectiveness, his family loyalty, even his sense of humor—but an apologetic Matthew? This was new. She liked it.

Bonnie continued walking down the path. The reins looped loosely over the mare's back. Matthew didn't seem to notice how the horse kept ripping leaves from the trees. He seemed more interested in looking at her. Being pressed against the hard wall of his side gave her an opportunity to study his perfectly formed lips, the straight line of his nose, the thick fringe of his black eyelashes.

Celie's heart began to beat harder. It was her turn to try to explain things. "I should have understood what I was doing before I moved things around." She pushed her bangs behind her ear. They immediately fell to her chin. "When I was about fifteen, Grandma Rosie came to live with us. She had lymphoma and needed some help. She was this great lady, Matthew, always trying to give you something every time you saw her—food, a book she liked, something sparkly she saw when she was out shopping." Celie's throat grew a bit tighter. "When she couldn't get out of bed, I used to cut her hair and sew her pretty nightgowns and bathrobes. It made her so happy, Matthew, to look pretty. She told me I had a gift for design—and with that gift came a responsibility. 'We're blessed, Celie,' she told me, 'so we can be a blessing to others.'"

Bonnie's walk slowed then stopped all together. Matthew didn't seem to notice. He was staring at her, and suddenly he was leaning toward her. And she was leaning toward him. Her heart beat even faster. *What are you doing?* a voice all but shouted in her head. *You're going to let yourself fall for a guy who lives on an apple farm in the middle of nowhere?*

It would be crazy to kiss him. She'd die if she didn't.

The buggy suddenly lurched forward, throwing them both off balance. She started to laugh and then gasped as a cold shower rained down on her. It was over as soon as it started. She looked up. There was an enormous branch above her head, and beads of water still dripped from the leaves.

She looked at Matthew. His skin gleamed from the unexpected bath, and the shoulders of his blue T-shirt clung to his body. He was grinning from ear to ear. Before either of them could say anything, the buggy lurched forward another foot. There was a tearing noise in the leaves, and then another shower of cold water rained down on their heads. Celie screamed at the shock of it hitting her skin.

If that wasn't enough, she had suddenly become eye level with a thick tree branch. Clearly Bonnie had taken advantage of their preoccupation and pulled them off the trail. Each time she took a bite, it shook the leaves and released the rainwater from the night before.

Bonnie grabbed another branch. It was a big one. Celie screamed. "Get the reins, Matthew!" A fresh shower pelted down on them. "Come on, Matthew!" He was laughing too hard to do anything about it. She looked at him, water turning his chestnut-colored hair a deep brown and his mouth wide open, showing very white, very even teeth.

She could fall for this guy, Celie realized. Fall deep and hard if she let herself. Her heart told her he was a good man as well as an attractive man. But could she really picture a city girl like herself living on the orchard forever?

Chapter 21

His mom was sitting in the porch swing sewing when Matthew dropped Celie back at the house.

"How did you all get so wet?" his mother asked, gazing at them somewhat suspiciously.

Celie looked at Matthew, and they both laughed at the same time. Matthew felt himself turn red. "Bonnie took us on a side trip under some of the trees."

"Oh," his mother said. "Is that so?"

"Yes," Matthew said, not trusting himself to look at Celie.

"Well, Matthew, maybe she wouldn't want to eat so many leaves if you fed her more."

"I guess you're right, Mom." Matthew played along. "Maybe you should come to the barn and supervise."

"I guess I should," she replied.

Matthew blinked in surprise. He'd only been joking. Yet his mom was walking down the steps and right over to the buggy. "I'll drive," she said.

Matthew had to half lift her into the leather seat, but once inside she picked up the reins. He'd barely made it back into the buggy before she slapped them across Bonnie's back. "Giddyap," she said.

He gave one last look at Celie as she disappeared into the house, then he turned his attention back to his mother, who was urging Bonnie into a trot. "Move along," she urged the heavyset horse.

"What's the rush?" Matthew wanted to say but stopped, not wanting to spoil his mother's fun.

When they reached the barn, he helped her out of the buggy. For a long moment, June gazed at the goats in the pasture. "They look good," she commented. Her hands were clenched into fists, and the lines in her face cut deeply into skin that seemed even more fragile in the morning light. "I thought I'd see more of a scar on Happy's back."

"Celie did a great job sewing him up." He saw the emotion in his mother's eyes and wanted to reassure her. "Come see the latch on the door and the wire mesh I put on the windows."

He quickly unhitched the horse and led her into her stall. His mother watched from the middle of the aisle, her eyes semiclosed. She was taking long, slow breaths with obvious pleasure. "Don't breathe like that near the goats' stall," he joked, "or you'll faint."

"I like how a barn smells," she stated.

Matthew watched her gaze go to the steps of the hayloft. He felt the familiar tinge of guilt. Two long hours. Two long painful and helpless hours, wondering if help would come. He stepped closer to her. "Anytime you want to smell the barn, I'll bring you up. We can take the four-wheeler."

"Thank you, Matthew. But I'll walk."

Matthew blinked in surprise. "What? I mean, that's great." He turned the question over in his mind before he asked it. "But why now?"

She stared at him with a glint of determination in her eyes. For a moment Matthew glimpsed the mother of his youth standing there, running the orchards with a sure hand, dealing with everything from hurricanes to helping him and Kiera with homework.

"Six months ago," his mother said slowly, "I broke my hip. I thought the best of my life was over. All I could see in the future was how I would become more and more of a burden to you and Kiera. I didn't see that the Lord was preparing me for something else entirely."

"What do you think He was preparing you for?"

His mother smiled. "The next phase of my life."

Matthew shifted uncomfortably. What exactly did that mean? "What are you talking about, Mom?"

She shook her head a little cryptically. "Things are happening here, Matthew. Good things. God things. I wasn't ready to receive those gifts before, but I think I'm ready now. It's amazing how He can take a worn-out life and make it feel like something new."

She wouldn't say more, and after a short time, he walked her back to the house. She wanted to sit on the porch swing by herself, and he went inside to get her a cup of tea. The house was quiet when he came through the mudroom door. Celie had her back to him with the black telephone receiver pressed tightly to her ear.

"I know you don't want to hear this, Kiera," Celie said, "but I think you're rushing into things. This guy may be the perfect one for you, but you've only known him a couple of weeks."

Kiera? A surge of blood rushed to Matthew's face. He clenched his fists as relief collided with worry, joy with anger.

"Kiera, how do you know this isn't a rebound thing?" Celie paused. "Jumping ship with the cruise's photographer sounds romantic, but basically, what do you know about this guy?"

Matthew knew he should make his feet move, his voice work, do something instead of just stand there.

"What about your life here?" Celie demanded. "You have a family who's worried about you. I'm worried about you. When are you coming back?" Another pause. "Please don't hang up. I'm not lecturing you. I'm trying to help you."

Matthew couldn't wait any longer. He stepped forward, but before he could reach Celie, she said, "You're what? Kiera! Please talk to your mother or to Matthew.

I'll get them. It'll take a second. No! Don't hang up." A brief pause. Celie's voice changed, pleading now. "Give me a number then where we can call you."

He knew Kiera's response by the sudden slump in Celie's shoulders. She stood, staring at the receiver and shaking her head. He cleared his throat loudly.

She whirled around, her eyes wide and startled. "How long have you been standing there?" And before he could even reply, she said, "That was Kiera. She, ah, couldn't stay on the phone long, but she wanted me to tell you and June that she's fine."

Matthew nodded.

Celie's oval face creased unhappily. "Actually, she's better than fine." She paused again and studied his face. "Maybe you'd better sit down, Matthew."

"Just tell me," he ordered gruffly.

"Well, she's in love." Celie winced as if saying the words gave her physical pain. "And she's engaged."

∼

June set the kettle on the burner and turned the gas on full blast. "Please tell me again what Kiera said."

Celie repeated the conversation for the third time. Matthew paced across the kitchen. Every so often he'd stop, start to say something, then shake his head. Celie had never seen his jaw clenched so tightly.

"We're starting a prayer chain," June announced. "I don't see any other thing we can do."

"I'll help make calls," Celie offered, jumping at the chance for action.

"Just what are we praying for, Mom? To be invited to the wedding?"

"Stop being silly, Matthew." The kettle whistled a piercing note. "We're praying for God's will." June poured the boiling water into the mugs. "For all we know, this man might be the right one for Kiera."

Matthew snorted.

"You sound exactly like Happy," June pointed out, stirring sugar into her tea. The humor fell flat, and June's hand trembled slightly as she set the spoon in the sink. "Are you sure Kiera knows about the fashion show, Celie?"

"Positive."

"We're having a big fashion show at the orchard. I have the perfect dress for you."

"Sorry, Celie, but Benji and I need to get to know each other as a couple before we let anyone else influence our relationship. We need more alone time together."

June sipped her tea. "I would have thought she'd come back for the fashion show, if nothing else. She's loved modeling since she was two years old."

"Unfortunately she's still acting like she's two years old," Matthew snapped. "Who goes on a cruise ship to Mexico and ends up engaged to the ship's photographer?"

Celie winced at the disapproval in his voice. "Maybe June's right. Maybe this guy is the right one for her."

"A ship-jumping, unemployed photographer?" Matthew snorted. "He's probably some kind of fortune hunter who preys on vulnerable women."

"I admit he sounds like a leech, but we don't know for sure." June met Celie's gaze. "We should start by calling Lilac Westover. She'll start the chain."

"I'm going out." Matthew crossed the room in three powerful strides. The door to the mudroom opened and slammed shut. Celie would have put her arm around June, but something in the older woman's eyes stopped her. She reached for the telephone instead.

Chapter 22

Kiera might think she was in love, but when it came to men, she didn't exactly have the best track record. In her bedroom, Celie pinned a waistband to the bodice of her couture dress. It was well past eleven o'clock. A gentle breeze lifted the sheer curtain, cooling the room.

She loved Kiera like a sister. At the same time, Celie wanted to stick a pin into her. Jolt some sense into her.

How many times had Kiera thought she'd been in love? At least four times. All attractive, older, charismatic men who told Kiera they loved her and then dumped her a week later. As far as Celie could tell, the only man who'd ever treated Kiera decently was Aaron Buckman—the hardware guy—and by the third date, Kiera was calling him boring and not returning his calls.

Celie pushed another pin into the fabric, taking care not to let the charmeuse slide. The weaving had come out even better than she'd imagined. Usually the feel of the silk soothed her—allowed her to dream about catwalks and fashion shows, the look on Libby Ellman's face when she offered Celie back her job. Tonight, though, the silk felt too rich, too opulent. She would have traded it in a heartbeat for a plane ticket to bring Kiera home.

She glanced at the clock, nearly midnight, almost time for her link in the prayer chain. She knelt on the braided rug by the side of the bed and closed her eyes.

Thump.

Her eyes flew open. The noise had come from downstairs, and it sounded like something, or someone, had fallen. Her heart began to pound. June had enough mobility to get herself up and down the stairs. What if she'd gone downstairs to get a snack and fallen?

She raced down the semidark hallway and down the stairs. At the foot she paused, struggling to see in the pitch-black. A small sliver of moonlight barely gave her enough light to make out the dark shapes of the furniture.

She couldn't remember where the light switch was and started toward the thin silhouette of a standing lamp when she heard a soft rustling noise coming from the kitchen. She spun around and groped her way to the back of the house. Beneath the arched entrance, she paused. A dark figure sat hunched over on the hardwood floor.

Illuminated by the stove light, Matthew crouched on the floor mopping up a dark liquid puddle in front of him. "Matthew?"

He jumped at the sound of her voice. "You startled me."

"Well, you *scared* me," Celie echoed. "I thought June fell."

Her gaze searched out his features, blurred in the dim light. His eyes, stripped of their color, were nonetheless beautiful. She felt an odd stirring in her stomach and a pleasant tingle in her veins.

"I couldn't sleep," Matthew admitted. "I thought a glass of warm milk would help, but then I tripped over Toaster's bone." His gaze swept over her, taking in her jeans and T-shirt. "What are you doing up so late?"

Celie shrugged. "It was my turn to pray for Kiera, but then something went *thump*."

"I kicked Toaster's bone by accident into the cabinets."

"Why didn't you turn on the light?"

"I thought I could see just fine."

"Let me look."

He held his foot up, showing off a very large big toe. It was a manly toe, fat but with a neatly trimmed nail. Right now it was held in such a way as to suggest it was a very painful manly toe.

"I'll get some ice." She retrieved a pack from the freezer, set it on his foot, and joined him on the floor. "Leave it on for twenty minutes."

"You don't have to hang out here," Matthew said in a low rumbly voice. "I don't think it's broken or anything."

Celie settled herself with her back to the pine cabinets. "If I don't stay here, you won't ice it."

He didn't contradict her. "Besides," Celie added, "it's cooler downstairs, and I can just as easily pray here." She paused. "You could join me if you want."

He did. Even after the ice pack had been long removed, he seemed content to sit on the wide planks of the floor. The heat coming off his body contrasted to the summer breeze blowing in through the open window, bringing with it the sweet scent of the orchards and the tinkle of porch chimes.

Somewhere in the night, an owl hooted and she jumped. "City girl," he said, but she heard the smile in his voice.

She didn't protest when he slipped his arm around her or move an inch when she saw the dark shadow of his face moving toward her. Her arms seemed to lift of their own accord and find their place behind his neck. In the moment before his lips touched hers, she felt an incredible sense of rightness, of completeness. She closed her eyes.

And he kissed her.

Chapter 23

Celie melted into his kiss. She felt his hands gently cupping her face and the warmth of his body pressed closely to her own. Everything tumbled around her. She couldn't think. Couldn't move. Couldn't do anything except hold on to Matthew.

His hair felt like silk threads in her hands. And then a voice in her head practically shouted, *Are you crazy? Do you want to end up like your mother—looking out windows and wondering what could have been?*

It took all her strength, but she managed to pull away from him.

Matthew gazed down at her. "Hey," he said, his voice full of wonder.

Her heart began to thump at the sound of that one word. Her gaze went back to his lips, but that incessant voice inside her head pointed out that Matthew lived on an apple orchard and she wasn't exactly a farmer kind of girl. She liked stores and shopping, the bustle of a city and having lots of people and action. "I'm sorry," she whispered. "I can't do this."

Matthew smiled gently. "You were doing just fine. Better than fine."

She slid a few inches away from him. "Please, Matthew. I can't." She wouldn't let herself look at him. "This never should have happened. I. . .I'm sorry." Before he said anything else or, heaven forbid, kissed her again, she got to her feet and ran out of the room. He didn't come after her.

The next morning he made bacon and eggs and teased Celie about sleeping late, although it was barely six thirty. It was like nothing had happened. Celie was relieved. She also was unaccountably disappointed.

The next two weeks passed in a blur of marathon sewing sessions, meetings with ladies from the church, and trips to the Fabric Attic for more supplies. Celie spent the mornings and afternoons altering clothing for the Castoffs to Couture show and the evenings working on her silk dress. The days grew longer, and the temperature settled in the high eighties.

The Fourth of July arrived, and Matthew took Celie and June to see the town fair and fireworks show. They all squeezed into the front seat of his truck. He drove them to the town park, the lush, green ball fields now filled with vendors selling everything from hot dogs to jewelry. Happy shouts overflowed from several huge inflatables for the kids, and a man dressed up as Uncle Sam walked around on stilts.

They walked to a temporary wooden stage first. June had brought a chocolate cream pie for the pie-eating contest and wanted to drop it off before they wandered around the fair.

Seated behind a table and writing on a clipboard, Celie recognized Susan Grojack. The tall, silver-haired woman had come to June's house several times to help with sewing and also was one of the models.

As June and Susan visited, Celie's gaze wandered around the area. The fair already had been going on for hours, and a good-sized crowd filled the park. She saw a little brown-haired boy with his family. Her heart gave a tug at the sight of the wand of cotton candy that was almost as big as the little boy.

And then her heart skipped a beat as she spotted a familiar blond head bobbing in the crowd. Kiera? Celie strained for a glimpse of the woman's face then sighed in disappointment.

It wasn't Kiera. This woman had her build and coloring, but her features were different—stronger. Plus, Kiera would never have worn Keds or gone out without makeup. The blond, however, headed straight for them, picking up speed as she went.

"Matthew!" The woman cried and launched herself into his arms.

"Emily Taylor," June cried in delight. "As I live and breathe. Come give this old woman a hug."

Either Emily was hard of hearing or just plain chose to ignore June's request. The statuesque blond remained wrapped around Matthew as if she were drowning and Matthew were her life preserver. Truth be told, Matthew didn't seem to mind. From what she could see of his face, he was smiling.

"I'm so glad to see you." Emily finally emerged from Matthew's arms, gave June a much gentler hug, and looked back at Matthew as if she'd like to jump right back into his arms. So this was Emily Taylor. The girl who had broken Matthew's heart. No wonder. What man could resist those big blue eyes and dimples?

"You, too, Em. You just get in?"

"Yes, late last night." Her voice lowered, and her gaze moved to include June. "Look, I know about Kiera. I've got an investigative reporter at the *Hartford Courant* making some phone calls." She turned to June. "Try not to worry too much. We'll find her."

"Bless you." June patted the tall blond's cheek. "Sure is good to see you, honey."

"You too, Mrs. Patrick. You look wonderful. I like your haircut."

"Celie did it." June's fingers closed around Celie's arm, gently squeezing. "Oh. You haven't met yet, have you? Emily Taylor, this is Celie Donovan—a friend of Kiera's."

"Oh I know all about you," Emily cried, turning the full wattage of her dazzling white smile on Celie. "My dad told me all about the fashion show you're putting together!"

Celie winced at the strength of Emily's grip. "Nice to meet you."

Emily brushed a long strand of hair behind her ear. "Isn't this fair great?"

Celie glanced down at Emily's blunt-tipped fingers. Not a scrap of polish on them and no rings either. She shifted on the wedged heel of her espadrilles and pondered the unpleasant possibility of Emily joining them for the day.

"Girls!" Susan Grojack's strident voice interrupted Celie's thoughts. "Girls! Could you please come over here? I need your help."

Celie hurried over to the registration table, eager to escape Emily.

"The pie-eating contest is supposed to start in ten minutes, but we don't have enough entries for the women's category," Mrs. Grojack said, holding up her clipboard as if it were evidence. "In order for this to count toward the state pie-eating competition, we need seven entries, and I've only got five. Would you girls be willing to help me out?"

Celie exchanged glances with Emily, who shrugged good-naturedly. "What kind of pie is it?" Emily asked. And then, before Mrs. Grojack could answer, said, "Oh, who cares? I'll do it."

Celie glanced up at the long narrow table on the raised platform. When she, June, and Matthew had arrived, it'd been empty, except for a checkered tablecloth. Now five women sat side by side, wearing bibs and very serious expressions.

"I'll do it, too." She didn't actually have to be competitive. She could just sit there and nibble whatever they put in front of her.

She signed the necessary forms and listened to Mrs. Grojack explain the rules. The winner would be the one to eat the entire pie the fastest. Celie thought about the mountain of whipped cream she and June had put on their chocolate cream pie. She didn't even want to think about the calories.

She took a seat at the very end of the table, and Emily sat next to her. Celie tied a tacky paper bib with lobsters on it around her neck. She weighed the fork in her hands and stared at the audience. Matthew and June waved from the front row. June scrunched up her face and gave Celie a nod. *Be tough,* the look seemed to say.

Next to her, Emily nudged her. "Use your hands instead of the fork. And look out for Grace Higgins. She was fifth in state last year. I don't think she chews the crust."

Celie laughed. "I'm not going to try to beat anyone." As the pies came out, people in the audience began talking. "Grace Higgins has it made in the shade," a man in a checkered red shirt said.

"Grace Higgins," another voice echoed. "In forty-three seconds flat."

Celie looked down the table at Grace Higgins. She was a heavyset woman with small eyes and thick, frizzy hair. Right now she was flexing her arms, stretching as if she were getting ready for a wrestling match.

"Emily Taylor can take her," Matthew yelled. "Go, Em!"

Go, Em? Celie felt a stab of disappointment. Not *Go, Celie?*

"Emily Taylor," another male voice shouted. "Three minutes, forty-two seconds."

"Who's the cute little gal sitting next to Emily?"

Celie sat up a bit straighter. Little gal? She was five foot four—in heels, that was.

221

"That's the city girl—the one who's staying with the Patricks," someone explained.

"Oh, a city girl," a voice said.

Celie bristled. Just because she was a city girl, it didn't mean she couldn't hold her own in a pie-eating contest.

"You might want to move your seat a little to the side." Emily tested the space between herself and Celie with her elbow. "This could get kind of messy."

Celie moved her chair a little farther from Emily, who was now grinning in anticipation of the event. The referee asked if all the contestants were ready. Emily said, "Ready for you to buy me dinner, Matthew Patrick—if I win this!"

Celie's eyes narrowed. She glanced sideways at Emily. The blond was bigger, but Celie thought she could take her—if she wanted to. And that's when she realized she very much wanted to.

The referee's whistle blew, and Celie dug into the pie.

Chapter 24

Anyone ready for a break? I just pulled some double fudge brownies out of the oven." June stood in the doorway of the dining room, holding a plate.

"Brownies?" Claire Innetti laughed. "Not chocolate silk pie?"

Celie groaned. It'd been two weeks, and everyone was still joking about her second-place finish in the pie-eating contest. "Please stand still, Mrs. Innetti," she requested, "so I don't catch your skin when I zip you up."

She braced herself and tried to erase the gap between the sides of the zipper. Mrs. Innetti was trying on a yellow cotton sundress with an empire waistline. June had been correct—Celie should have added a good inch to the measurements she'd been given. A fresh bead of sweat popped out on her forehead, despite the fan going full blast.

"Everybody in town is still talking about it." Mrs. Innetti, who was the senior pharmacist at CVS, met Celie's gaze in the antique standing mirror. "Word is, you're going to state next year."

"No way." Celie tugged the fabric hard, and the zipper slid up the dress. "What I'm going to do is never eat chocolate silk pie again. Now what do you think of the dress?"

She stared at Mrs. Innetti's reflection. The halter neckline drew attention away from the tall brunette's broad shoulders, and the seaming beneath her bust showed off her curves without making her look heavy.

"I think," Mrs. Innetti said, "you could've taken a couple seconds off your time if you hadn't used the fork."

"Celie definitely was the neatest eater." A note of pride entered June's voice.

Celie had a dim memory of shoveling huge mouthfuls of pie into her mouth and an even dimmer memory of chewing. She mostly remembered the startled sideways glance Emily Taylor had given her, though, when she'd realized Celie meant business.

"Most competitive match people have seen in years," Mrs. Innetti continued. "A real horse race. You and Emily Taylor neck and neck, right up to the end."

Celie smiled a little. She might not have beaten Grace Higgins, but she'd edged out Emily Taylor by 4.3 seconds. She wouldn't soon forget the look of surprise on Matthew's face.

"The dress," Celie said, firmly steering the conversation back where it belonged. "You want me to let it out a little?"

Mrs. Innetti turned sideways to see another angle. "Oh definitely not. It fits perfectly." She sighed in pleasure. "I never would have thought I could wear something like this and not look like a ripe summer squash."

"You definitely don't look like a ripe squash," Celie assured her. "Now how about shoes? A strappy sandal. The higher the heel, the better."

"I don't know." Mrs. Innetti frowned. "Haven't worn them in years. . .but I guess I could try." Her chin came up a notch. "And Celie, after the show, I'd like to buy this dress."

Celie smiled. "Great."

"I'll put you down for it." June named an amount and laughed as Mrs. Innetti eagerly nodded. "Celie, we're going to be sold out before the show even begins."

〜

A few weeks passed. The end of July came. Matthew brought home fresh corn from the farmer's market in town. He roasted it on the grill, and they ate ear after ear with sweet-cream butter. June provided a steady supply of pies, cookies, and cakes, which she gave to all the women from the church who showed up day after day helping sew and press, put together sample outfits, and organize the clothing which would be sold in the rummage part of the church event.

One afternoon after she'd just finished a fitting, Celie slipped upstairs to her room. She pinned her hair off the back of her neck and waved her hand to try to cool off a little. She had a little free time before the next model came for a fitting, so she took the green couture dress out of the closet.

She'd finished it two nights ago. Examining it on the hanger, she *knew* it was the best dress she had ever designed. The green and yellow strips of silk wove together in just the right places to enhance a woman's bustline, and the skirt was neither too full nor too clingy. It fell organically, creating a graceful silhouette. She moved the hanger and watched the fabric float. She couldn't look at it without thinking of the orchards.

Returning the dress to the closet, she decided to give James a call. He picked up on the second ring. "I've been meaning to call you," he said.

"Did you get the tickets to the fashion show? You're coming, right?" She wanted to ask if Libby or George had seen the design for the green silk but couldn't quite bring herself to ask.

"Wild horses, kid, couldn't keep me away."

Something was wrong. She could hear it in his voice. "What is it, James?"

There was a long pause. Celie felt her heart sink.

"I don't know how to tell you this, but yesterday morning I saw Milah making a dress almost exactly like the one in the sketch you gave me."

The realization sank in slowly, but when it did, Celie crumpled to the floor. "Libby stole my design?"

"She denied it, of course," James said sadly. "She's changed enough details to make it seem like a different dress, but it's your design." He paused. "I'm so sorry, Celie."

Celie hung up her cell phone and wished she'd never made the call in the first place. A curious numbness settled over her. Libby had stolen the design. Worst of all, there wasn't anything she could do about it. She wanted to scream or stomp her feet or break something. Anything but stand here and know that she'd been a fool. She ran down the stairs and out the back door. The ground passed in a green blur as she sped across the lawn and into the grove of apple trees. She wanted to outrun the knowledge of what Libby had done, outrun the pain of betrayal and the loss of a dream. She wanted to run until the world changed into a better place, and she didn't hurt anymore.

Why had God let this happen? Was she so far off the path He wanted her to choose that it had come to this?

Only when her lungs ached and her legs felt as heavy as concrete did she allow herself to slow to a jog, and then even this became harder than she could maintain. She slowed to a walk then came to a complete halt.

Celie sank to her knees in the grass. She put her face in her hands. *What do I do now, Lord?*

She heard the dull sound of feet thumping on the path, and then Matthew said, "Celie? What's the matter?"

Leaping to her feet, Celie brushed the grass from her shorts and wiped her cheeks. She tried to tell him she was fine, but her facial muscles weren't working right. Her smile kept crumpling.

"Talk to me. Whatever it is, we'll fix it." His blue eyes fixed on hers as if he were trying to pull the answer out of them.

"I called James." She heard her voice shake. She didn't want to tell him, but she couldn't not tell him either. "My couture dress. Libby stole the design."

His brow furrowed. "What do you mean she stole the design?"

"She copied it but then changed enough details so she could call it an original."

"Can't you sue her? You have the original hanging in your closet!"

Celie shook her head. "It'd be my word against theirs. And right now I don't have any clout."

"Wouldn't James stand up for you?"

"If he did, he'd lose his job. What would he do then?"

Matthew seemed to consider this for a moment. "He'd find another job. It's a matter of honor, Celie. He shouldn't let them do this to you."

"I was stupid, Matthew. I shouldn't have let James show that design to Libby and George." She blinked back tears that continued to fall anyway. "I was sure they'd want not just the dress but me."

Matthew patted her back awkwardly, as if he wasn't sure how to comfort her. "We can't let them get away with this, Celie. We've got to fight them."

"How? I can't pay for a lawyer. And even if I could, I wouldn't win. This sort of thing happens all the time in the fashion industry." She wiped her eyes with her sleeve. "I'm just an idiot. Why am I so stupid, Matthew?"

"You're not stupid. You have a trusting heart. There's a big difference between those two."

Celie laughed bitterly. "It doesn't matter. I'm finished."

"You're not done." Matthew raked his hand through his hair. "We'll figure something out."

"Like what?"

He handed her a crumpled but clean handkerchief. "You could stay here."

Celie wiped her face. "And do what?"

He shrugged. "Start your own Internet business, get a job in town, or Mom had this idea a couple years ago to start a mail-order apple butter business. We've still got the canning jars in the garage. You could help her."

He actually thought she should consider a career in apple butter? "All this time," Celie sputtered, "you've known me, and you don't see who I am? You don't understand what sewing means to me? You think I could can apples for a living?"

Matthew held up his arms in mock surrender. "I'm just giving you suggestions. You don't have to take them."

She kicked a clump of grass. "What if you couldn't grow apples? What if someone took away your orchards and told you to work in a factory?"

He frowned down at her. "But would it be so bad to stay here? Is working in Manhattan really what you want?"

Celie didn't pause to listen to the small voice in her heart that said maybe it wasn't. Maybe what she wanted was standing right in front of her. She thought only of her mother, standing at the kitchen window, looking out at lost dreams. "Yes," she replied firmly. "It's exactly what I want."

Chapter 25

If Manhattan was what Celie wanted, Manhattan was what she was getting. Matthew, however, had no idea how to give it to her. He just knew he had to find a way. When he returned to the house, he found his mother standing at the railing, tapping her cane in impatience. Her face creased in worry.

"What's going on? I saw Celie take off like a cat with its tail on fire."

She leaned on her cane, a sure sign she'd been on her feet too long. Matthew led her to the swing. "The designer in New York City stole her dress design. She's not getting her old job back."

His mom stamped the porch floor with her cane. "I knew those people couldn't be trusted." She sighed. "The poor girl. No wonder she took off like that. You didn't just leave her alone in the orchards, did you, Matthew?"

She gave him a reproachful look. So did Toaster.

"She wanted to be alone."

His mother shook her head. "When something upsetting like this happens, people say things they don't mean. Women, especially, say they want to be alone, but they actually mean the exact opposite."

Matthew stifled a groan. June was only trying to help, but right now he didn't need a lecture on understanding women. "She's fine." He kept his tone neutral to hide a pain he wasn't quite letting himself feel. Celie had been very clear on what she wanted. It wasn't this orchard. And it wasn't him. "If she isn't back in an hour, I'll go get her."

His mom nodded. The slight pucker to her mouth relaxed, and she patted the seat next to her. "I wonder what she'll do." When he didn't comment, she said, "Stop pacing, Matthew. You're making me and Toastie dizzy."

He hadn't even realized he'd been walking back and forth. When he stopped, it felt wrong. His hands and feet seemed to hang uncomfortably from his limbs. He gazed as far into the orchards as he could see for a flash of Celie's yellow shirt.

"Maybe this is a blessing in disguise." June patted the empty space on the porch swing. "Maybe God has something even better in store for her. Come sit, Matthew."

"I'm fine."

"You're like a cat on a hot tin roof."

"Please stop the cat analogies. I'm going to take the four-wheeler out." He'd check the south field, which was as far from the grandfather orchards as he could get. The wind blasting in his face would clear his head; it always did.

"Just tell her how you feel," his mother stated firmly. "Don't be like me."

He stopped cold. He understood neither statement. A ray of sunlight striped the porch step. It felt like a line he wasn't quite ready to cross. "Just what do you know about how I feel about Celie?"

"Quite a bit."

Matthew turned slowly. She was rocking the swing gently, a soft smile on her face. "I feel it," she said. "When you're around her, you come alive. I've never seen any two people as much aware of the other in my life."

"You're wrong."

"Don't be like me, Matthew. Don't deny what your heart knows."

Matthew frowned. The urge to escape faded as he studied the harsh planes of his mother's face and the proud, determined set of her shoulders. "What are you talking about?"

"Jeremy Taylor." Her chin lifted. "We've waited a long time—and I've prayed a lot about this—and we're going to dinner next week." As if this wasn't crystal clear enough, she added, "We're going on a date, Matthew." She held her hand up as he started to speak. "You probably think I'm too old. You probably think I'm dishonoring your father."

Matthew let his breath out slowly. "I don't think that. And you don't need my permission to date him, if that's what you want."

"I'm not asking for it," his mother said gently. "I just don't want to hurt you, Matthew. You've looked after me and your sister and this farm better than any-one could have asked."

"You're not hurting me."

She rose from the swing awkwardly and came to stand beside him. "No one can ever take Dermott's place, but I have feelings for Jeremy, too."

He shifted his weight. What did his mother want from him? His blessing? A tug of loyalty to his father warred with his genuine desire to see his mother happy. He sighed. "He's a good man, Mom. Just don't expect me to call him Dad." He smiled to let her know he was only joking.

"I think I always knew he was there for me, waiting." His mother's eyes half closed in remembrance. "I'd see him sometimes in church looking at me. . . ."

"I'm okay with you dating him. We don't have to go into detail."

Her eyes snapped open. "I was going to explain that I turned away, Matthew, because I knew what the look on Jeremy's face meant." She kept her gaze on his face. "Sometimes we know what's right for us. It's right under our noses, but it scares us, so we don't do anything about it."

Matthew didn't want to see any truth in her words. "Thanks for your con-cern, Mom, but let's just leave the romance stuff to you and Jeremy."

"Don't wait too long to tell Celie how you feel," she warned. "You'll lose her if you don't say anything."

Matthew gave an indifferent snort, but his gaze strayed back to the orchards. He thought about her out there, making decisions he couldn't control, wanting things he couldn't give her.

In the distance, trees swayed gently in the summer breeze. The vastness of the land, its beauty—even the great aloneness of it—stirred through him. He understood why this life might be right for some people and totally wrong for others. Like Kiera.

He'd known Kiera dreamed of far-off places, but selfishly he'd wanted her to stay tied to the family through the land. After his sister had moved to New York City, he'd encouraged her to visit then tried to make the time they all spent together a positive experience. The simple truth, however, was that he couldn't hold the family together any longer. He'd lost Kiera, was losing Celie, and even June seemed ready to embrace a new life.

What am I supposed to do, God?

When his alarm went off at four thirty in the morning, Matthew sat up, relieved he no longer had to lie in bed trying to sleep. He'd gone over and over his plan, rehearsed every detail. There was nothing left to do.

His only suit—a dark gray color—stood out in a closet filled with work shirts and jeans. It was wool and much too hot for a day sure to reach the mid-nineties, but he thought it would be better to dress up. He chose a blue and red striped tie and pulled it tight around the collar of his white shirt. He stuffed his feet into a pair of stiff leather shoes, usually worn only to weddings and funerals, and tied the laces taut.

Toaster barked once as he crept down the stairs. He heard his mother hush the dog, then the house went quiet again.

Mom and Celie, he wrote on a scrap of paper, *I'll be gone for the day. Thomas and his crew are mowing around the grandfathers today, so they'll be nearby if you need anything. Don't wait dinner for me, Matthew.*

The moon shone a beacon of light as Matthew stepped quietly out of the house. The soles of the leather shoes felt slippery on the surface of the gravel driveway. The orchards were lost in the night, but he paused to peer into the darkness. *Heavenly Father, please bless this day and grant me the words and strength to serve Your purpose.*

He got in the car and did not look back as he drove away.

Chapter 26

Several times during the next two weeks, Matthew disappeared for the entire day. June clammed up whenever Celie tried to question her. But once she'd let something slip about train schedules. Celie wondered if he was going to Hartford to see Emily Taylor. She buried herself in sewing and preparations for the rummage sale.

Celie was even more confused when Emily Taylor came back into town. True to her word, the blond reporter had taken off the two weeks prior to the fashion show as vacation. She called Celie the day she arrived and scheduled a fitting for the next morning.

When Emily arrived, Celie had a beaded black cocktail dress waiting for her. Emily grinned from ear to ear when she saw it and lost no time in putting it on. She had just stepped out of the changing room when Matthew walked into the dining room. "Emily? Thought I saw your car."

"Matthew!" Barefoot, Emily practically sprinted across the room to hug him. Although Matthew's face turned bright red, he didn't step away from her.

"Do you like the dress, Matthew?" Emily asked. She turned slowly to give him the full view.

How could he not like what he saw? Celie put her hands on her hips. Emily was drop-dead gorgeous. She watched Matthew wipe his face with his hand. He glanced briefly at Celie then back at his voluptuous former girlfriend. "Yes."

"It needs some alterations." Celie nearly dragged Emily back to the mirror and away from Matthew.

"Doesn't this dress remind you of the one I wore at the Great Gatsby party?" Emily didn't wait for Matthew to answer. "Remember? You wore your grandfather's pinstripe suit, and we won first place for the best costume?"

Matthew chuckled. "Oh yeah. We hid Dillon Mayfield's mattress in the hayloft."

"He itched for a week," Emily said, winking.

Celie gritted her teeth as Emily and Matthew continued their stroll down memory lane. The back of the dress was a little loose, so she reached for the pincushion to mark the alteration needed. Emily was still talking about the costume party as Celie pulled out a pin. The shiny metal seemed to wink in the light. It could look like an accident, a simple slip—one little poke—and Emily would be firmly detoured off memory lane.

"Are you free for dinner tonight, Matthew?" Emily asked. "A couple of things I'd like to talk to you about."

"Sure," Matthew said.

That woman was making a move on Matthew! The hand with the pin seemed to move of its own accord toward Emily. Celie jerked it back right before she poked her. What was she thinking? Her hand was shaking and had almost stabbed Emily Taylor. What did Celie care if the two of them wanted to rekindle their friendship and possibly their romance?

Evidently she cared a lot. But in a way, it helped her come to a decision.

∾

"I'm leaving tomorrow, June." Celie tied a length of white tulle ribbon around the base of the grandfather apple tree. "Right after the show."

"You're what?" June dropped the basket of scissors and ribbons but made no move to pick it up.

Around them, preparations for the next day's fashion show continued in full speed. A group of men standing on ladders hung speakers in the trees. Caterers rolled out large folding tables, and a small group of women stood at the beginning of the runway, talking and laughing.

Celie watched a range of emotions play across June's weathered face—surprise, disappointment, uncertainty, and then finally, understanding. "You sure?"

"Positive." Celie retrieved the scissors and spools of tulle. "I'm sorry just to spring this on you, June, but I didn't know if there would ever be a good time."

"Why?" June's mouth puckered. "Why don't you stay longer?"

"I just can't." Celie found her gaze drawn to Emily Taylor's bright blond head. She was standing with the other models who were waiting their turn to practice walking down the runway. More than ever, Celie suspected Emily was more interested in Matthew than she was being in the fashion show. Even as jealous as she was, Celie couldn't help but think Emily fit Matthew's world a lot better than she ever would. The best gift she could give either of them was to step out of the picture.

"Where are you going to go?"

The worry in June's voice broke Celie's revelry. "Centerville."

"You're going to work at your parents' dry cleaning business?" June clucked her tongue. "I wish you would reconsider. Stay here awhile longer."

"I appreciate the offer, June, but my mind is made up. Besides, I think it's time for me to go home. I need to figure out what God wants me to do next."

June studied her face then nodded slowly. "I'll pray for you," she said.

"Excuse us!" Two muscular men rolled a heavy folding table past them. With a loud *bang*, they set it into place. Celie tied a tulle bow and cut the extra ribbon. When she was finished, all the trees lining the runway would have bows. Tomorrow she'd place tin buckets filled with freshly harvested apples along the path the models would walk.

"Have you told Matthew?"

"No, but I will."

"Celie! Am I doing this right?" Jill Lane, who was wearing blue pants with a stripe down the side, had obviously just gotten off her shift at the police department.

"Perfect!" Celie applauded as Jill strutted past them, lifting her knees high and keeping her gaze fixed on the treetops.

"When?" June pressed.

"Today, I promise. Mr. Beecham, please move that table a little more to the left." The sudden blare of music from the loudspeakers nearly made her drop the roll of tulle. She recovered just in time to watch Mrs. Innetti walk past, beaming and waving regally to an imaginary audience.

"You're doing great." Celie smiled as the tall brunette walked past. "You're right in step with the music."

"Stop waving your hands and start moving your hips more," June ordered. "This is a fashion show, not a royal wedding."

Another table rolled into view, followed by a group of women carrying folding chairs. Celie recognized Betty Rogers, Amanda Jackson, and Leslie Yazmine from the church choir. Behind them, pulling a dolly loaded high with chairs, was Matthew.

He wore a simple blue T-shirt and a light wash pair of jeans. Just ordinary clothing but so exactly right for him; she couldn't imagine him in anything else. Her breathing grew quicker as he neared.

"The ladies are done setting up the tables in the driveway for the rummage sale," he said, wiping the sweat from his face with the shoulder of his shirt. "They want to know if they should put the signs up tonight or wait until they put the clothing out tomorrow morning."

June turned to Celie. "I think tomorrow would be fine, don't you?"

Celie nodded. She didn't really want to think about the clothing neatly folded into boxes. She had to tell him about her leaving, but she didn't want to.

"Okay, I'll tell them." He looked at Celie. She remained frozen and mute.

June said, "Excuse me, but I want to make sure the sound crew has the right music."

Alone, Celie looked up into Matthew's beautiful face. A wave of confusion passed through her. "Um," she said.

"Um?" He smiled, and for a moment everything felt like it was going to be okay. But was leaving really the right thing?

"Um." She paused, bit her lip, and steeled her resolve. "I wanted you to know I'm leaving. I'm going back to Ohio." There, she'd said it. She searched his eyes to read his reaction.

"You're leaving?" His lips tightened. "When?"

"Tomorrow. After the fashion show."

"Oh," he said. Was it her imagination, or did he relax slightly? Her shoulders slumped at the thought.

"You have my cell phone number. Will you call me when you hear from Kiera?"

"Of course."

That was it? He wasn't even going to try and stop her? "Thank you, Matthew, for letting me stay here." Her throat grew tight. "You and your mother have been so good to me."

"Look," Matthew continued, and she knew a moment's hope when he looked into her eyes. "I know we got off to a rough start—I was pretty hard on you. I. . ." For the first time, he seemed to struggle to find the right words. "I blamed you for introducing Kiera to the wrong crowd. I thought you'd supported a destructive relationship." He paused, wiped his face, and continued. "I was wrong, though. I just wanted you to know that."

Celie could only nod. Her throat was too tight to talk. The loudspeaker blared out the opening notes to "The Star Spangled Banner," and June's voice shouted, "No, no, no! That's wrong."

The music was a minor wrong compared to the greater sense of wrongness in Celie's heart as she watched Matthew tip back the dolly and walk away from her.

Chapter 27

Celie woke to a picture-perfect August day. The sun shone brightly, and the sky was a perfect shade of cerulean blue. Even the temperature cooperated, hovering in the low eighties.

She spent the morning helping the caterers place crisp white tablecloths on the tables and fill glass vases with wildflowers picked from the pastures on Jeremy's land. Lilac Westover and Esther Polino arrived and helped line the runway with tin buckets piled high with shiny Early Macs—the first of the orchard's harvest—and wind the backs of the folding chairs with yet more tulle.

Before Celie knew it, it was time to get the models ready. Within moments, Celie had her hands full. Barbara Willis zapped herself in the eye with a can of hair spray, Mrs. Innetti couldn't zip her dress, and Shirley Elliot stumbled in her stilettos, knocking off her glasses, which Jill Lane accidentally stepped on and broke. If this wasn't enough, Esther Polino had gotten a case of stage fright so bad that she had locked herself in the bathroom.

"Come on out, Esther," Celie coaxed the librarian from the other side of the door.

"I can't do it," Esther moaned. "Sorry, Celie."

"You can do it," Celie said, trying to sound calm when her own nerves jangled.

"Can't," Esther moaned. "My stomach feels awful." She paused. "I think I might throw up."

Celie remembered how she felt after eating an entire pie in less than five minutes. "Keep swallowing," she encouraged. "You have a little stage fright, that's all."

"Celie!" Shirley Elliot called. "We have a problem. I can't see without my glasses!"

Something crashed in the kitchen—it sounded like a stack of plates—and then someone yelled, "Oh my stars!"

Celie ran into the kitchen to see what was going on and stopped in her tracks when she saw Kiera crouched on the floor helping the caterer pick up pieces of broken china.

Laughing, Kiera said, "This is so totally my fault, Gina. I am such a klutz. Always have been and always will be," she added cheerfully.

"Kiera?"

Kiera's blue eyes lit up when she saw Celie standing there, and she jumped to her feet and opened her arms.

With a happy cry, Celie launched herself forward and hugged her friend as hard as she could. "I can't believe you're here!"

"Celie, I can't breathe."

"Sorry." Celie released her grip and stepped back to examine her friend. "You look great. You're so tan. I'm so happy to see you! When did you get back?"

"Last night." Kiera tucked a strand of blond hair behind her ear. Her silver hoop earrings flashed almost as brightly as the big smile she gave Celie. "Hold on. First things first. I want you to meet Benji." She motioned to a bald, middle-aged man of medium height standing just inside the back door. A Nikon with a huge lens hung from his neck. "Benji, this is Celie Donovan—one of my best friends in the world. Celie, this is my husband, Benjamin Bateman—the love of my life."

Celie blinked. Husband? Kiera was married? And to this man? In the past, Kiera had gone either for male models or rich, powerful men. In his floral shirt and Bermuda shorts, Benji radiated neither power nor wealth. He did, however, have a friendly smile and a firm handshake.

"Celie, dear," June said, walking into the kitchen. "Lilac isn't sure whether to wear hoops or pendant earrings. Could you. . ." The rest of her sentence died on her lips. She moved faster than Celie had seen her move since she'd arrived and wrapped Kiera in her arms. They were of identical height and build. Even their hair color was only shades apart.

Celie sighed with pleasure. They both looked so happy. She heard a soft click and turned to see Benji lowering his camera. He gave her an apologetic smile. "She likes my pictures."

When at last June released Kiera, the older woman's face was flushed and tears streamed down her face. She held Kiera at arm's length, studying every inch of her and visibly trembling. "Oh thank God," June said. "Thank God you're home."

"Of course I'm home," Kiera said, wiping her own flushed face. "Mom," she said shyly. "Benji and I got married. The ship's captain did the ceremony on our way home."

"Married?" June's gaze swung between her daughter and her new son-in-law. "Married?"

"I love him," Kiera said simply.

The back door creaked open. "They're almost ready for dessert," Jeremy Taylor reported, slightly out of breath, as if he'd run all the way from the grandfather orchard to tell them. "Matthew says fifteen minutes until showtime."

Celie's heart skipped a beat. Esther Polino was still bolted inside the bathroom, and Shirley Elliot needed another pair of glasses.

"What do you want me to do?" Kiera asked. "How can I help?"

Kiera was a professional model. The best way to have her help was to put her in the show.

"There's a green dress upstairs in your closet," June said, following the

235

direction of Celie's thoughts as if she had spoken them aloud, "wrapped in a plastic dry cleaning bag. Put it on, dear, and come get in line. You'll close out the show."

"We haven't done a fitting," Celie said.

June smiled at her. Her face glowed. In less than five minutes, she seemed to have taken ten years off her age. "I have a feeling it will fit Kiera perfectly."

∽

Celie heard the music as she walked out the back door. Behind her, the models, each wearing one of her redesigns, fell into step as they crossed the grassy backyard and stepped into the mottled light of the orchards.

Her heart pounded in her chest, and her mouth went dry at the sight of the round tables with their crisp white tablecloths, wildflower arrangements, and gleaming white china. She could hardly bring herself to look at the townspeople filling every seat, turning to watch as she and the models neared.

Celie lifted her chin a notch and forced a confident smile. Esther Polino had had the right idea. The two of them should have stayed in the restroom. Her stomach rolled. Dear God, she simply wasn't cut out for this. If she didn't throw up, it'd be a miracle.

Matthew stood at the start of the runway, wearing a dark gray suit that had to be much too warm for the hot summer day. He had his arms folded and feet planted solidly over the grass he'd been cutting just the night before. Only a small nick on his chin where he'd cut himself shaving that morning suggested any hint of nerves. He was smiling, but the expression didn't quite reach his eyes.

The murmur of voices hushed. Celie glanced over her shoulder at the nervous but excited expressions on the women behind her, then she nodded at Matthew, who gave the signal. The music changed, and Celie gently urged Jill Lane forward.

The slender policewoman was wearing one of the first outfits Celie had created—a black pencil skirt and a patterned gray and olive blouse that in its last life had been a T-shirt. She'd tied a hand-knit gold scarf around Jill's neck. A pair of black boots—Celie's Jimmy Choos—finished off the outfit. Jill had her hands on her hips and swaggered down the grassy aisle with all the attitude of a Paris runway model. Celie could not have been prouder. Jill hit a pose at the end of the runway, and Benji fired off at least ten shots. People began applauding.

Mrs. Innetti went next in the yellow sundress outfit. She tottered off a little unsteadily in high heels that put her over the six-foot mark, but she seemed to pick up speed as she went.

Then it was Sally Netherlands's turn in the patterned scarf that had been turned into a wrap skirt, then Shirley Elliot who walked a perfectly straight line despite her lack of glasses, then Esther Polino who showed not one trace of nerves as she pranced down the runway in the tiered ruffle dress.

Click! Click! Click! More applause. More models marched down the runway, backs straight and chins held high. Lilac Westover received enthusiastic applause when she trotted out in the modified tuxedo.

Emily Taylor went next in a short black cocktail dress. With her long hair swept into an updo and the dress hugging her curves, she looked more beautiful than Celie had ever seen her. The audience seemed to think so, too. There were oohs and aahs, and somebody whistled. It wasn't Matthew—Celie was standing right next to him—but she didn't let herself look at his face either.

And then it was Kiera's turn.

Celie caught her breath at the sight of her friend. The dress looked as if someone had poured a bucket of green silk over her head and the fabric had magically molded itself to Kiera's slender body.

A hush fell over the crowd as Kiera stepped out, every inch of her five-foot-ten frame working. Before she'd reached the first table, everyone was standing, applauding. The noise only grew louder as Kiera prowled down the runway, seeming to see no one and to walk with a confidence that suggested she owned the runway. At the end of the runway, she struck a pose as Benji snapped off shot after shot.

Suddenly Celie didn't care that no one else would ever see this dress. All that mattered was that it represented everything good that had happened to her here at the orchards. Kiera stepped forward, the dress flowing around her long, slender legs. Celie remembered the breeze on her cheeks when she and Matthew had taken a carriage ride around the orchards. She hadn't realized it when she'd been sewing the dress, but she knew now every stitch had been sewn with love. Love of these orchards. Of June. Of Matthew.

Kiera beamed at Celie as she stepped off the runway, signaling the end to the fashion show. Now Celie, as designer, would lead the models for one final turn down the runway. Celie's feet seemed suddenly rooted to the spot, and her Jell-O knees were wobbling.

Jill nudged Celie's arm. "They're waiting."

"I know."

Matthew glanced down at her. His blue eyes crinkled at the corners. "You're getting a standing ovation, but you'd better get out there."

She looked down the long lane between the trees, saw people clapping, smiling. June and Jeremy stood shoulder to shoulder, applauding and motioning for her to come forward. She hesitated, understanding finally that it wasn't stage fright that kept her rooted to the spot. She simply didn't want the fashion show to end. She didn't want to go back to Centerville either.

"I don't want to go," she said.

"It's just stage fright." Matthew smiled in encouragement. "You can do it. They all loved your fashions."

She shook her head. "I mean I don't want to go—as in go back to Ohio." He still didn't seem to get it. She bunched her hands into fists and looked straight up at him. "Helping your mom with a canning business sounds pretty good."

He laughed. For a moment something very intense flashed in his blue eyes, and her heart did a long, slow turn in her chest. He wanted her to stay. She was sure of it. But then his jaw tightened in determination, and he shook his head. "You need to go. You need to get out there now," he clarified, pulling her forward.

She had a choice: walk with him willingly or risk being dragged across the grass. Celie lifted her chin and walked with him onto the runway. Forcing a smile to her stiff lips, she waved at the blur of faces in front of her.

Plain as day, she'd practically told him she loved him—right in front of who knew how many people—and the best he could do was say, *You need to go?* And then the not-so-romantic way he'd tugged her arm to get her moving.

Celie wanted to jerk away from Matthew, but he kept his fingers firmly wrapped around her hand. Wasn't he afraid that Emily Taylor would see him holding Celie's hand? Matthew would never have told Emily Taylor, *You need to get out there.*

An excited bark broke her thoughts. Ahead, Celie spotted Toaster, looking like a pirate king in a purple satin jacket with grommet closures. The small dog strained at his leash as Celie neared. June had the leash firmly wrapped around one hand. The other hand was holding onto Jeremy Taylor's hand. Celie swallowed a lump at the loving look June gave her.

It helped steady her and allowed her, moments later, to give James a genuine smile when she saw him.

James had his arm around his wife, Frieda, who was beautiful in a pale yellow silk shirt and patterned skirt—the very outfit Celie had designed for her birthday last May. And then her breath caught as she saw the tall, silver-haired man in gray Armani standing beside James. Her footsteps faltered, and she clutched Matthew's arm. "Matthew, it's him. It's George Marcus—my old boss."

Matthew glanced down at her. He had a pinched look about his mouth, and his eyes didn't quite hold her gaze. "I know."

"What's he doing here?"

"Right now he's applauding."

It was true. George Marcus was giving his signature three-beat clap. Celie's heart raced. How was this possible? Her gaze shot to James, beaming at her, and then back to George Marcus, who met her gaze and gave her a short, curt but unmistakable nod of approval.

"Breathe, Celie."

She gripped Matthew's hand more tightly and forced herself to exhale. The rest of the runway passed in a blur. She barely registered Benji taking shot after shot, and somehow she reached the beginning of the runway again. Everyone swarmed around them. Matthew stepped back as people rushed to congratulate her.

Chapter 28

The shears whispered through the fine threads of the black silk fabric as Celie concentrated on cutting the exact line of the pattern. At this phase, the dress looked like abstract art, a smattering of geometric shapes that shared nothing more in common than the fabric on which they lay. She freed a crescent-shaped piece that would become part of a bodice and laid it aside.

Straightening, she swept her bangs behind her ear. They'd grown long enough to stay there now, and she absently considered getting a new cut. She could afford it now. And get her nails done. While she was at it, she'd get a pedicure to go with the new Jimmy Choo peep-toe pumps. She was a full-fledged designer now. She still couldn't believe Libby Ellman was gone. The head designer had resigned. "To avoid being fired," George Marcus had explained after the Castoffs to Couture show had ended. "Our house does not steal designs," he explained and then smiling, had added, "We hire the designers who create the dresses we wish we had designed in the first place. Will you work for me?"

Celie freed a panel of the skirt next and put it aside. The job offer had been everything she'd wanted, and yet she wasn't nearly as happy to be back as she thought she'd be.

"Hey," a familiar voice said, and James popped into view. "Heard you're making a dress for Grace Bradley. You going to help her anchor the evening news, too?"

Celie set the scissors down. "Absolutely," she joked. "She'll interview people, and then I'll critique their clothing." James was balancing a large cheese Danish and two Styrofoam cups on a cardboard tray.

James set the tray down on another cutting table. "The Danish is for you. I told Frieda you've lost ten pounds since you've been back. She told me to invite you home this weekend. She'll make you fettuccine Alfredo." He handed her one of the cups. "Say good-bye to your cholesterol," he added cheerfully.

June liked to fatten up people—and animals, too, Celie thought with a pang.

She picked an edge off the Danish and nibbled it more for James's sake than out of hunger. "That's nice of her. I'm fine, though."

James made a scoffing noise. "You're not fine. You've got huge bags under your eyes, and you're white as a sheet. What time did you leave last night? Did you even leave?"

It was Lipton tea, and James had added a generous amount of sugar. She sipped it gratefully, welcoming its warmth. "Of course I left." She didn't tell him that she'd taken the last train out of Grand Central or that the bags under her eyes had nothing to do with working too hard. She just couldn't seem to sleep anymore. She'd toss and turn and end up at the small window in the bedroom, remembering another view in another house.

"It's Matthew, isn't it?" His voice gentled. "You really miss him, don't you?"

Celie stuck the lid back on her tea. "What are you talking about, James? This job was what I always wanted. This spring I'm going to Paris!" She remembered just in time to smile.

James wasn't fooled. "You should call him."

Call him after the way she'd practically thrown herself at him? She stood. "Thanks for your concern, James, but I really don't want to talk about it."

"Like I couldn't figure *that* out." James sipped his coffee placidly. "You practically bite my head off every time I bring up his name." He held his hand up as she started to protest. "Look, you're like a daughter to me—the daughter me and Frieda never had." He paused. "All I want is for you to be happy. Matthew said that you belonged here. I thought you did, too, but now I'm realizing that we both got it wrong."

Celie, who had started to move away, froze in her tracks. "What do you mean Matthew said I belonged here?"

James turned his cup slowly in his hands. "All he wanted, Celie, was to give you the choice."

"What are you talking about?"

"To get your old job back. We discussed it when he came here."

"He came here? Matthew?"

"Three times," James confirmed. "He sat in the lobby trying to get George Marcus to see him. Just sat there, holding your dress. Wouldn't leave until George saw him personally."

Celie searched James's eyes. "He did?"

"Absolutely. Nadine was supposed to call security, but she didn't. She kept telling Libby that someone was on the way." He grinned. "She always thought it was wrong the way Libby fired you."

"She shouldn't have done that. She could have lost her job!"

"Word kind of spread, Celie, what Matthew was doing. All your friends here conspired to get him into George's office. It took us two days, but we finally figured it out. Connie from maintenance pretended to be this rich buyer from Madrid and kept Libby on the telephone. Surhina intercepted George's two o'clock appointment and flirted with him in the conference room. You need to know, Celie, Milah came forward, as well, and told George how you covered for her singeing a dress." His eyes looked sad. "You should have told me what really happened."

Celie sank back onto the stool and put her head in her hands. June had offered to hang the green silk in her closet because it had more room. Now she realized she must have been helping Matthew. "I. . .I don't know what to say. I didn't know. You all did that for me?"

"Of course we did." James patted her shoulder. "You think Connie's forgotten the wedding dress you made for her daughter? Or who took the blame when Surhina broke Libby's sewing machine? Who went to court with Nadine over child support issues?"

Celie lifted her gaze. "Why didn't you tell me about this before?"

"Matthew asked me not to tell you. He thought it was better that way."

Matthew's face flashed through her mind. She felt the familiar pain and longing. She remembered standing with Matthew on the back porch the night after the fashion show. June had gone to bed, and they had discussed George's offer. He'd said, "If you don't take this job, Celie, you'll always wonder what you could have done."

She pushed Matthew's image away. "He just wanted to get rid of me."

"Celie." James's voice rang more sharply than she had ever heard it. "Are you blind as a bat? A man who spends three days sitting in the lobby even after Libby Ellman threatened to have him arrested—not to mention highly insulted his suit—was trying to get rid of you?" He raked his hand through his thin dark gray hair. "The only time that man looked beat was *after* George Marcus saw your dress and said he loved it."

Celie stood, sat down, then stood again. She paced the floor, pausing to look at James who apparently wasn't angry at her anymore. By the half smile on his face, he seemed fairly satisfied that he'd sent her emotions into a tailspin.

He wanted her to take the job but not because he wanted to get rid of her. Because it was what he thought she wanted more than anything.

She glanced at the clock, mentally calculating how long it would take her to get home, pack some clothes, and get her Honda.

Too long, she decided. She'd skip packing and simply drive. If she didn't hit traffic, she could be there by eight o'clock.

Chapter 29

Matthew was in his office working on invoices when the front doorbell rang. Toaster, who'd been sleeping in his lap, sprinted for the front door, barking his head off.

He frowned and pushed back his desk chair. Too late for a social call, he walked quickly to the door. June and Jeremy were on the road tonight—dinner and a movie. It was a beautiful October night, but accidents happened. The irony of him worrying about June being out on a date would have made him smile if he wasn't so worried.

The sight of Celie standing in the doorway hit him just like a punch to the stomach. He could only stand there, looking at her, aching to take her in his arms. He forced himself to stand so still it felt as if his body had turned to stone.

Toaster shot through the opening and jumped up on Celie's knees, shamelessly begging for her attention.

Matthew gripped the brass doorknob so tightly he thought he would crush it. "Hello, Celie."

"Matthew."

She looked thinner than he remembered—her collarbone more prominent—and there were purple shadows beneath her eyes. He pulled the door wider. "Come in."

She passed him on a pair of high-heeled shoes. Her perfume, the faintest hint of something floral, drifted past him as she crossed into the foyer. His heart beat hard at the sight of her once again in the house.

"June's out with Jeremy. A date." Matthew wondered if he had lost the power to speak a complete sentence. He tried again. "Can I get you something to eat or drink?"

Her smile seemed a little tight. "No thanks."

He frowned at the dog. "Toaster, will you stop? She already greeted you."

"It's okay, Matthew. I'm glad to see him, too."

"You want to sit in the living room while you wait for June?" Matthew folded his arms in what he hoped was a casual pose.

"Actually," Celie said, "I'm not here to see June."

"Well, Kiera's in Storrs, meeting Benji's family. Turns out the Batemans raise dairy cows. I don't think either Kiera or Benji has a farming bone in their body. They both want to live in New York City." He was rambling but couldn't seem to help himself.

"I know," Celie said. "I didn't come to see Kiera either." She paused, her eyes

242

dark and luminous as she looked up at him. "I came to see you, Matthew."

The October night was cool, but he felt himself start to perspire. He tried to swallow, but his throat was inexplicably parched. "Why?"

"James told me you were the one who convinced George Marcus to look at my dress—and give me my old job back." Celie pushed a strand of shiny hair behind her ear. He noticed it did not fall forward again. She shifted her weight, and it occurred to him she might be as nervous as he was.

"I...um...wanted to thank you for doing that."

He didn't want her thanks or for her visit to be motivated by gratitude. "You're welcome." Disappointment weighed over him, but he forced a smile to his lips. "You didn't have to come all this way to tell me that."

"I know. But I want to know why. Why would you do that, Matthew? Why would you go into New York City—a place you hate?"

Matthew shifted his weight. "I don't hate Manhattan. And I didn't want to let them get away with stealing your design. I figured if George Marcus saw your original, which I knew had to be better, he'd do the right thing, if he were honest. And if he wasn't honest, he had to know we were going to fight him legally."

"You'd do that for me?"

"Of course."

Go ahead and tell her, something deep inside him insisted. *Tell her how you really feel* His feet seemed to step forward of their own accord.

He stood within an arm's reach now, and all at once a deep calm came over him, as if all his questions had been asked and answered. The fears and doubts were replaced with a quiet certainty.

"Celie, I wanted to give you what you wanted, what you deserve, because...I love you." He looked deeply into her eyes. "I'm in love with you."

Celie's cheeks turned red. Her eyes shone as she looked up at him.

"I'm in love with you," Matthew repeated. "It almost killed me to let you go once. I promised myself if you came back I'd tell you how I felt." His heart thudded so loudly he wondered if he could even hear her response.

"I love you, too, Matthew."

He reached for her hands. To hear her say she loved him filled him with a joy beyond his wildest dreams. "I've loved you," he said, "from the moment you outran Happy the goat."

"I'm never going to live that down, am I?" Celie replied, but her eyes sparkled. She squeezed his hands. "I don't know when I started loving you, Matthew. It just took me awhile to figure it out." She shook her head ruefully. "We can thank Emily Taylor for part of that."

Matthew shook his head. "You were jealous?" He felt a rush of pleasure then the need to reassure her. "It's you, Celie, I want. Just you." The words seemed to release the last bit of weight that had been on his shoulders since the day of the fashion show. He got down on one knee. "You won't live an exciting life here, Celie, but it'll be a happy one. As happy as I can make it. Will you marry me?"

Her eyes went wide with shock, then a deep glow of happiness seemed to radiate from her. "I would be proud to be your wife. Yes, Matthew, I'll marry you."

"You won't have to give up your career. If you want to live in the city, we'll find a way to make that work. And if you want to stay here, I'll build you a sewing room on the back of the house. Whatever you want, Celie. I mean that."

"I want you," Celie said. "Now and forever. I want to grow old with you. I want to see you sitting under that quilt with our kids. Teaching them to be the kind of person you are."

Matthew didn't think he deserved that kind of praise, but he was determined to spend the rest of his life trying to live up to it. With God's help, maybe he could. He thought his heart would explode with joy when he put his arms around her. Such a tiny woman, and yet she fit so perfectly against him. He could feel her heart beating, a strong and steady pulse against his chest.

He'd always thought home was this orchard, this land where two generations of his family had lived. Looking down into Celie's beautiful brown eyes, he realized there was a whole other kind of belonging.

Epilogue

A year and a half later

H old still, Celie. Your veil is slipping." Linda Donovan's hands were cold but steady as she adjusted the lace. "There." She smiled tearfully into her daughter's face. "I love you so much."

"I'm so glad you're here." Celie blinked back her own tears as she wrapped her mother into another hug. "I love you, too."

Click. Click. Click. Celie lost count as Benji Bateman fired off another round of photographic shots in rapid succession. She could feel her mother's heart pounding beneath the taffeta folds of her navy dress. "I'm so happy for you," her mother whispered. "To find love is such a blessing."

"You sure you aren't disappointed about me not working in Manhattan?" Celie hadn't meant the question to slip out, but now that it had, she couldn't simply will it back.

Her mother shook her head. "All I've ever wanted was for you to be happy. Didn't you know that?"

"But you've made so many sacrifices."

"You're special, Celie. I wanted the world to see that. But as far as what you do with your gifts, that's up to you and God. I'll be proud of you no matter what."

"Keep talking," Benji instructed, clicking away. "Pretend I'm not here. Can you move a little to your left, Celie?"

Celie sighed and did as he asked.

"You're going to thank him after you see the photos." Kiera adjusted one of the backlights. "I didn't remember half of what happened at my wedding until I saw the photos."

Benji and Kiera mirrored happy grins. "You two are a walking advertisement for marriage," Celie said.

"You'll see for yourself how wonderful marriage can be," Kiera promised. "I've never seen Matthew so excited and nervous in my entire life. He's checked the air pressure in the truck's tires at least twice."

"But we're flying to Paris for the honeymoon," Celie said.

Kiera laughed. "You have to drive to the airport first. He has three routes to Bradley planned in case of traffic. What can I say? The man's in love."

And so was she.

Someone knocked softly on the bedroom door, and June's smiling face appeared in the crack. "It's almost time. . . . Oh, Celie," she whispered reverently. "You're so beautiful."

"June!" Celie waved her inside. "Let me see you." June stepped into the room, her silk chiffon skirt rustling. Toaster's head peeked out from beneath the fullness of the skirt. Kiera grabbed him just before the small dog jumped up on Celie.

"Put the dog down," Celie said. "He's fine." She paused as she took in June's outfit. "You look amazing!" Celie clapped her hands together in delight.

"It should. You sewed it." June winked. "Toastie likes his pretty little lilac suit, too. Don't you, Toastie?" At the sound of his name, the dog trotted back to June. "But you, Celie,"—June put her hand on her heart—"are beautiful beyond words."

Benji fired off more shots as Celie hugged June. When she finally stepped back, she had to wipe the tears from her cheeks. "June. . .thank you so much for all you've done for me. For welcoming me into your home and into your family."

June's throat worked for a moment. "You, honey. We should be thanking you. You've brought a whole new light into our house and into our lives. I couldn't love you more if you were my own daughter. I thank God for the day you stepped into our lives."

Unshed tears turned Celie's world blurry. A happy kind of blurry, though.

"You're going to ruin your eye makeup, Celie, if you don't stop crying," Kiera said. "Someone hand me a tissue please." She then proceeded to dry her own eyes. Celie couldn't help laughing, which was probably exactly what Kiera had intended.

"We'd better get going," June said. "We'll make Matthew a nervous wreck if we're late."

"Not just yet." Celie took Kiera's hand on one side and her mother's on the other. Her mother reached for June's hand, and soon everyone had formed almost a full circle. Everyone but Benji.

"Put your camera down," Kiera ordered her husband, who placidly continued photographing June's and Linda's joined hands.

"Someone has to record this," Benji protested. "Someone has to keep their emotions in check."

"We don't need a camera to remember this," June said, breaking her link to reach out to him. "We need you."

With the circle complete, Celie closed her eyes. "Heavenly Father," she said, "thank You for this beautiful day, for Matthew, June, Kiera, Benji, my parents, and everyone here today. I don't know what heaven will look like, but it's got to look a lot like this house and farm. Thank You, Father, for all the blessings you've sent us—especially the ones we don't always recognize as blessings."

When she finished, there was a big sniffle, and Benji said, "Would someone please hand me a Kleenex?"

It was a short walk to the spot in the grandfather grove—the very same spot where they'd had their fashion show. Neither her mom nor June had allowed her to see the decorations until now. The sight of the tulle bows and white gossamer ribbons hanging from the old trees almost took her breath away.

Matthew waited for her at the end of the aisle formed between the grandfather apple trees. He stood tall and very straight in a pinstripe charcoal gray suit that fit his frame perfectly. His face lit up when he saw her. The whole world seemed to fall away from her. All she wanted was waiting for her at the end of the tree-lined aisle.

She clutched her bouquet of gardenias and ordered herself not to cry. A gentle breeze touched her cheek, like a caress, and brought with it the faintest odor of apples. They were still on the trees, small clusters no larger than grapes, part of a cycle she was just beginning to understand.

The speakers crackled slightly, emitted a high-pitched ringing noise, then settled into the clear notes of the sonata she and Matthew had selected. People stood as Jeremy, resplendent in a light gray suit with a lavender bow, escorted June slowly down the grassy aisle. Toaster seemed to understand the importance of the occasion and walked solemnly at June's side with his head held high.

Her mother went next, then Celie was watching Kiera's back moving away from her. Kiera in the green silk dress—the one that relaunched both their careers and, even more importantly, helped bring her and Matthew back together.

The music paused, and the sound system gave another ominous crackle before starting the notes to Wagner's traditional march. Everyone stood. They were all there, everyone she loved, and she could see their faces shining with joy. Matthew waited for her, his arms at his side, his feet firmly planted on the close-cropped lawn. Matthew, who would stand strong with her no matter what problems came their way.

She suddenly couldn't wait to get down the aisle to be with him, to speak the vows that would bind them together. She linked her arm through her father's and smiled up into his familiar craggy profile. "Let's go."

He smiled, patted her fingers once, and then they stepped forward.

A STILL, SMALL VOICE

Dedication

Special thanks to JoAnne Simmons, editor extraordinaire, for her unfailing encouragement and support. She's believed in me from day one, laughed at places in the book where I hoped she would, and gave me free rein to create. I am so thankful for you. I'm also very grateful to Rachel Overton and April Frazier for their excellent editorial work. They both worked tirelessly to bring the manuscript to the highest level possible. Additional thanks to the rest of the Barbour team who shepherded the book through its many stages of publication and distribution. You all are the best!

Chapter 1

I'll think about it," Mrs. Madison said.

Jamie King kept her smile firmly in place. In real estate, a client saying, *I'll think about it*, was like a date going poorly and then ending with, *I'll call you.*

"What's the next house on the list?" Mrs. Madison flicked an invisible thread off the gray lapel of her jacket.

"There isn't anything else." Jamie kept smiling. "Have I mentioned the Brazilian cherry hardwood floors? The Viking appliances?"

During the past two weeks, Mrs. Madison had been inexhaustible in her quest for the perfect Connecticut home for herself and her husband, Fish, a retired Wall Street executive. They'd selected Greenwich—one of the most affluent and prestigious towns within commuting range of New York City—because Fish's best friend was a member of the Indian Harbor Yacht Club.

"Maybe we should go back to the little fixer-upper," stated Mrs. Madison.

The "little fixer-upper" was a 1.3 million dollar, 2,500-square-foot Cape Cod in Old Greenwich. "That one sold last week." Jamie placed her Realtor's card on top of the black granite countertop and gathered her car keys. Her feet ached in the darling but painfully high-heeled Ferragamo boots. She hadn't eaten since breakfast, and she felt the beginning of a headache. "I'll call you if a new listing comes available."

"Oh no," Mrs. Madison protested. "Fish will be so disappointed if I don't find something." She smiled, but there was a hard glint in her eye. "There's still a few hours of daylight. Could we start from the beginning?"

It was dark by the time Jamie got back to her apartment building. She longed for a cup of chai tea as she walked across the marble foyer. She'd almost made it to the bank of elevators when she heard whistling coming from the mail alcove.

She stopped in her tracks. It was a little after five o'clock. Wilson never came this late. She looked around. There wasn't time to make a run for it. A moment later, the still-whistling mailman appeared around the corner.

"Oh good, Jamie," he greeted her. "Perfect timing. Your box is so full it's about to explode. Let me get your mail for you."

"Thanks, Wilson, but I'll get it later."

"Hold on a second—I've got my key right here."

Jamie shifted her weight and looked unhappily at the elevators. Avoiding the mailman and letting her mail accumulate—had it really come to this? She thought of her bills. Yeah, it had.

"Here you go." Wilson pressed a stack into her hands. She nearly groaned at the top letter staring at her—the one from Miss Porter's. Another notice about Ivy's unpaid tuition bill, no doubt.

"Thanks, Wilson. You take care. I think we're supposed to get some sleet tonight."

"Sure will. See you tomorrow."

Jamie stepped onto the elevator and pushed the button for the fifth floor. She'd have to call Ivy's school tomorrow and explain that she was waiting for a commission check. Miss Porter's wasn't the sort of boarding school for people who juggled bills and asked for payment extensions. Practically all the families who sent their children there had tons of money and social connections. Kids who graduated from Miss Porter's regularly went to Ivy League schools.

She'd have to juggle a couple of other bills and work out a payment plan with the school, then she'd call every client who'd ever expressed an interest in buying real estate. So what if December was the worst month of the year to be in real estate? She'd bring Jaya a box of Godiva, which might coax her into sending a few leads her way. She'd even venture into the morgue—the shelves in the basement filled with boxes of old, expired listings.

She'd been in tough times and gotten through. She would again.

❧

Grayson Westler was fixing the split seat on the chairlift with duct tape when the call came. "Gray," his father's gravelly voice said through the receiver, "you better come straighten things out."

The last time Gray had heard those words his dad had backed over the No Parking sign in the space between CVS and the Silver Shears beauty salon. The time before that, his father had taken out the landscaping in front of Talbots.

Gray gripped the cell phone tighter. "You're okay, right?"

"Oh yeah, but I need you to come get me."

"Where are you?" Gray was already walking to the parking lot, fumbling with his free hand for the keys to the Jeep.

"Danbury—at the movie theater," his dad stated matter-of-factly, as if he went there all the time. If you'd asked Gray an hour ago where his father was, Gray would have said he was in the ski shop sharpening the edges of the rental skis—not at the multiplex in Danbury.

The Jeep bounced over the washed-out ruts in the dirt parking lot. His father wouldn't even watch the DVDs Gray brought home from the video store. He always complained either there was too much violence or people were mumbling and he couldn't hear them.

Gray made the drive down I-84 West in record time. He didn't have a hard time finding his dad at the movie theater. The blinking red lights of twin security cars drew him like a beacon.

He found his father standing between two uniformed security guards. Something inside him relaxed slightly at the sight of his dad's familiar stooped frame and shiny bald head. "Dad!"

"Gray." His father's face relaxed for a moment, then tightened as he turned back to the security guards. "My son's here. Can I go now? Or are you going to arrest me? If you do, I'll warn you, I'm retired military. No jury in America would convict me. You'd end up looking like blooming idiots."

"Dad," Gray interrupted. "What's going on?"

"Your father hit two cars," one of the security officers replied. He had short black hair, chapped lips, and the blotchy complexion of someone who'd been standing in the cold for a long time. Chapped-lip Guy exchanged amused looks with the other guard. "We watched him do it."

The second security officer was a tall kid with a skinny goatee. "He backed into a car in one row, then hit the other one when he went forward."

"The spot was too small," his dad grumbled.

"When your father showed us his driver's license, we saw it had expired." Chapped-lip Guy gave Gray a sympathetic smile. "My uncle used to sneak out from the nursing home all the time, so I understand the situation. I told Norman here that if someone would come get him and he paid for the repairs to the other cars, we wouldn't make a big deal out of it."

"I am not feebleminded." His father's face flushed. "And I don't live in a nursing home."

"Dad." Gray shot his father a warning look. Arguing with the officer wouldn't make things any better. He turned to Chapped-lip Guy, who seemed more in charge. "That's nice of you," he said.

"We probably should wait for the drivers of both those cars to come out of the movies," his dad grumbled. "Give them our insurance information in person."

That could mean at least an hour. Gray checked his watch. Halle was due home at five o'clock. Rush hour was about to start, so if they didn't leave soon, he'd be late. He could text her—his daughter would rather give up oxygen than give up her cell phone—but he'd worry anyway. She was old enough to babysit, but he didn't think a thirteen-year-old should arrive home to a dark, empty house.

"How about we leave a note on the windshield with our phone number and insurance information?" Gray glanced at the bumper of a silver Volkswagen. It had a few scratches but nothing serious. Hopefully the car his dad had backed into also had minimal damage.

With the information exchanged, Gray and his father headed home. It started to rain as they pulled onto I-84. Gray's grip on the steering wheel tightened. Great. How was he supposed to make snow in this weather? Farther north, all this was probably snow. Mount Tom was opening next Saturday, and Killington, Stowe, and Mad River Glen had all been open since Thanksgiving. Not only that, but Mrs. Dodges, the woman who cooked breakfast for the B&B, had asked for time off to help a sick relative in Virginia. Finding a replacement on such short notice was going to be difficult. Plus, he'd have to ask Tony to drive back to Danbury with him tomorrow to retrieve his dad's car.

Next to him, his father misinterpreted Gray's silence. "I'm sorry," he mumbled.

Gray shot him a sideways look. "No big deal. But why were you here anyway?"

"To catch the four o'clock showing of *Sand-Castle Dreaming*."

"A chick flick?"

"It had a good review."

"If you wanted to go to the movies, you should have told me. You don't have a valid driver's license."

"I would have my license," his dad pointed out, "if you would drive me to the motor vehicles department and let me get it renewed."

"And I would do that," Gray replied, "if I had any confidence that you wouldn't go around hitting other people's cars."

His father made a noise of disgust. "There's nothing wrong with my driving."

Gray pumped the brakes lightly as a car slipped into his lane. "Before I take you to the DMV, I want you to go to the optometrist and get your eyes checked. We'll get you a physical while we're at it."

"There's nothing wrong with my eyes or any other part of me."

"Please stop sneaking off in the car until we get you checked, and you've got to stop telling everyone you were in the military to get out of stuff."

"I *was* in the military," his father replied smugly. "Army reserves. And I was more than willing to go to Korea and fight for my country. I'd join the army today, if they'd take me. I could do it, too, Gray. I could drive a tank. You don't have to be young to drive a tank."

Gray squirted the windshield with fluid. The world blurred as the wipers swept across the glass. His father was winding up for his death speech—about how he didn't want to end up in a nursing home or attached to some machine in a hospital. He wanted to die while he was still useful. His dad would say that he would rather ski himself off a cliff than become a burden to Gray. He said this no matter how many times Gray tried to assure him it would never be like that.

Gray changed lanes as the traffic slowed. He could still make it back in time for Halle. He wouldn't meet her bus—she'd trained him not to do anything vaguely parental within sight of her peers—but he would have the house lights on and water heating for hot chocolate. He wondered how she'd done on her algebra test and if her friend Ella had been asked to the winter dance by Jackson Brennen, as Halle had been predicting would happen. He wondered if she'd have a lot of homework and if she'd worn the rain poncho he'd forced into her book bag early this morning. And he wondered when wondering about these things had become second nature to him.

Chapter 2

S orry, baby," Jamie apologized as she eased her Lexus over yet another rut in what was more of a mud pit than a parking lot.

Welcome to Pilgrim's Peak.

She pushed her sunglasses into place and walked toward the gray, barn-like structure that crouched in the shadow of the mountains. Her gaze took in the blistered paint and the shingles peeling like a bad sunburn on the roof. The place looked in even worse condition than it had in the pictures she'd unearthed from the file in the morgue. No wonder Mr. Westler had sounded so eager to meet with her. He probably couldn't wait to unload the place.

She bought a weekend pass from a teenage girl at the lift ticket window and asked for directions to the bunny hill. She'd gotten the impression from Mr. Westler that he wouldn't even consider listing the place with someone who didn't love skiing. Jamie had never skied before, but hoped to impress Mr. Westler.

Sticking the lift ticket to the zipper of her new, fur-trimmed parka, Jamie hefted her skis—rented, but color coordinated with her parka—onto her left shoulder. They were awkward to carry and had been even more awkward to fit in her car, but she'd wanted to show up looking as if she were serious about skiing. The guy in the rental shop in Greenwich had promised these Rossignols would do it. As she followed a snow-crusted path to the other side of the building, she hoped he was right.

Pilgrim's Peak loomed in front of her, a tall mountain with trails of white cut through dense pines. A handful of skiers traversed a fairly steep pitch, moving slowly and gracefully. It didn't look that hard. The instructional video she'd rented also had been encouragingly simple. She'd watched Robert Redford in *Downhill Racer* for additional inspiration.

Sitting on the bench of a slightly wobbly picnic table, she put on her boots. They weighed a million pounds. As she lurched to her skis, she comforted herself with the thought that if she got this listing, she'd be able to pay off a lot of her bills and buy herself a pair of cute Manolo Blahniks.

Lurching her way across the snowy ground, Jamie headed for Looking Glass, also known as the bunny slope. She was panting by the time she reached it and paused to catch her breath. The slope was mostly scattered with small kids.

"Your first time on skis?"

Jamie looked down. A cute little girl in a pink ski suit stood next to her. "Yeah." Was it that obvious?

"Thought so." The girl turned to her equally miniature friend. "Better stand back. She looks like she's going to fall."

Gee thanks. Jamie watched the two of them slide past her, giggling as they effortlessly glided toward the chair lift—which wasn't a chair lift at all, but more of a towing machine.

Jamie was sure Robert Redford had sat down on his way to the top of the mountain. Probably this kind of lift was outdated and more evidence of the ski hill's financial fragility. She wished she had seen this on the Internet photos. She could have used it in her afternoon presentation.

Moving only slightly faster than a snail, Jamie covered the distance between herself and the antique-looking lift machine. Not only did it not have a comfortable chair to sit in, but it had a scary-looking J-shaped metal bar that went behind a skier's hips. The kids didn't seem to mind it, though. They rode stoically up the hill, their young faces comfortably blank like commuters on a train to Manhattan.

Jamie shuffled into the lift line. Before she knew it, the kid running the machine was yelling at her to hurry up and get in position. She tried, but her Frankenstein lurch wasn't fast enough and the boy ended up stopping the lift completely. "Don't sit on the bar," the kid advised. "Just lean forward and let it push you up the hill. You ready?"

The little five-year-olds could do it, and so could she. Jamie nodded. The kid released her. The next thing she knew, she was getting an enormous shove in the rear end. She clutched the rope cable for dear life as the bar pushed her up the hill.

"That's good," the kid called after her. "Keep standing."

This better be worth it. She kept her gaze fixed on the munchkin in front of her and tried to keep her feet in the ruts made by the other skiers. She was doing pretty well, but then the J-bar slowed and the metal bar slipped to a spot above her knees. Before she could decide what to do about this, the machine started up again. The J-bar took out her knees, and Jamie fell. She slid on her stomach to the bottom of the hill.

On her next attempt to master the J-bar, she fell again. On her third try, she managed to catch the J-bar thing as she fell onto her stomach. Clutching it like a trapeze bar, she let it slowly drag her up the hill.

"Let go!" someone shouted.

Let go? Jamie grimly ignored the cold, mushy snow forcing its way down the neck of her parka. Her arms already ached, and she closed her eyes to concentrate better. It couldn't be that much farther to the top. She only hoped that her bindings wouldn't release before she got there.

The machine stopped completely, but Jamie wasn't fooled. It was crafty—and merely waiting for her to relax her death grip before it lurched forward. She set her jaw. The moment lengthened.

"You have to let go," someone was saying right in her ear. Jamie opened one eye. A gorgeous mountain man with dark brown eyes, shaggy brown hair, and a hint of razor stubble peered down at her.

Jamie opened the other eye. Mountain Man continued to loom over her, looking even more solid and mountainly now that she was looking at him with both eyes. He was smiling at her with very even, very white teeth. "It's not safe to let the machine drag you," he said. "You could twist a knee or something."

She shifted. Twisting a knee didn't sound very good, but neither did sliding to the bottom of the ski hill and having to start the whole process again. "I'll be fine. We're close to the top, right?"

"Not even halfway." His voice softened a little. "Let me help you."

"Just give me a second," Jamie said, trying to get a foothold with her skis. She didn't need help, even if it came from a cute ski instructor. That's what he had to be—his red jacket said SKI SCHOOL in lettering across his impressively broad chest. He had unbelievable eyes; the irises were a rich, chocolate color.

She might not need his help, but Jamie recognized the need to let go of the J-bar. The second she did, however, she began to slide. Mountain Man grabbed her hands before she slid out of his range. "I can do this," she insisted, trying to figure out how to stand up when she was still on her stomach and her skis prevented her from bringing her knees under her.

The next thing she knew, Mountain Man scooped her under the armpits and set her gently on her feet. "Maybe you don't need to go all the way to the top," Mountain Man stated tactfully. "Maybe you should try skiing to the bottom of the hill from this point."

Jamie brushed snow from the front of her coat and tried not to lose her balance In the process. She didn't want to seem helpless in front of Mountain Man, even if she was. "I'll be fine," she said.

"You know how to snowplow, right?"

"I've seen *Downhill Racer* twice."

He laughed. "That old classic? You might want to take some lessons."

"Maybe," Jamie agreed vaguely. She remembered the reason she'd come out to the hill in the first place—to gain information. "Have you worked here a long time?"

"Yeah." He glanced over his shoulder at a group of munchkins obviously waiting for him. "Look, I've got to get back to the ski school." He hesitated. "Make a big V with your skis—kind of like a pizza-slice shape. It's called a snowplow and will get you down the hill safely."

Jamie wished he'd asked her to go have a hot chocolate with him instead of giving her ski pointers, then gave herself a mental head smack. He was a thirty something ski instructor. Probably one of those guys who lived at home with his parents and wanted nothing more from life than a good pair of skis and a snowy mountain.

With a smile and a wave, Mountain Man skied off, effortlessly gliding across the trail. She watched him go until she was in danger of being caught looking at him, then began her snowplow to the bottom of the bunny slope.

Chapter 3

At 4:55 p.m. Jamie made her way down the long, narrow corridor that led to the ski hill's administrative offices. She paused in front of the door marked MANAGER to calm her heart, which was knocking so hard against her ribs she could barely hear herself think.

She smoothed her wool sweater over the black ski pants. Fortunately they seemed none the worse for wear after getting dragged up the bunny slope. She rapped her knuckles on the wood. *Be confident,* she ordered herself. *Smile like you're the most successful agent in Connecticut and people will believe it's true.*

"Come in," a deep voice said.

She lifted her chin a notch and stepped into the room. "Hello," Jamie said. "Thank you for meeting. . ." The rest of her sentence died on her lips. Mountain Man sat behind an oversized laminated desk cluttered with stacks of papers. He had on a pair of frameless reading glasses, and his brown hair looked comfortably rumpled as he stared back at her.

"You're Mr. Westler?" Jamie couldn't keep the surprise out of her voice.

"And you're the woman from the bunny slope."

Jamie plastered on the confident smile, but her knees were shaking. "Nice to meet you."

"Grayson Westler," he said and extended his hand. "Glad to see you in one piece."

"Guess my survival instincts kicked in." Jamie felt other instincts kicking in as she shook the hand Grayson offered her.

Grayson motioned her to a chair across from him. "Now, how can I help you?"

Jamie handed him a business card. "Well, as we discussed on the telephone last week, I'm a Realtor from the Whitestone Agency in Greenwich. I've come to discuss the proposal I put together to list your property."

"List my property?" Grayson frowned. "Hold on. Why do you think I'm interested in selling?"

The room seemed to grow hotter. "We discussed this last week on the phone," Jamie reminded him gently. "You said it was a great idea."

"I don't think we ever spoke on the phone," Grayson said.

Uh-oh. Jamie clutched her hands together. Was this some kind of cruel joke? Had she dialed the wrong number and spent an hour talking with some stranger with a very warped sense of humor? She groaned inwardly at the thought of all the personal questions she'd answered. "I spoke with someone who said his name was Mr. Westler. Not only that, but obviously my name was in your appointment book."

"Oh. You must have spoken with my father. He, well. . ." Grayson raked his fingers through his hair. "I'm sorry, but I'm not interested in selling. I'm afraid you've come all this way for nothing."

Jamie's stomach gave an unhappy lurch. If she didn't get this listing, it was doubtful she'd be able to keep Ivy at Miss Porter's. *Forget Ivy's education,* she thought. *If you don't do something fast, you're going to be worrying about how to feed her.*

She pulled a slim portfolio out of her satchel. "Well, as long as I'm here, why don't I go over a few things with you?"

Grayson's dark brows pulled together. "I don't think that will be necessary."

Jamie's stomach tightened into a knot. Sometimes people said they weren't interested in selling, but they changed their minds when the price was right. "Well, it never hurts to know what your property is worth, does it?"

Grayson's voice grew colder. "I'm very aware of the value of this land."

"You've probably had a bank appraisal," Jamie argued. She was practically steaming inside her wool ski sweater. "However, that's not the only value of your property. Given the location of your land and the growing market for people who want a rustic landscape, I estimate your land is worth. . ." She paused, then named a number. "That could be low. Condos are an option, too. Here, just look. . . ."

He shook his head. "You need to leave."

She was sweating harder now. "Your major competition is coming from Mount Southington and Otis Ridge. Both of these ski hills are within a thirty-minute drive of Pilgrim's Peak. Both of these hills have more trails, more uphill lift capacity, and more amenities. They market their hills with advertising campaigns and attractive, easy-to-use Web sites." Jamie paused. "I've done my homework, Mr. Westler, and everything I've learned tells me these other ski hills are attracting a lot more business than yours." She held his gaze despite the dark set to his jaw. "It's always better to choose to sell than be forced to sell."

"This meeting just ended."

Jamie figured she had about five seconds before he threw her out. "You'll be out of business in five years at the rate you're going. The table on page three shows inflation versus your business growth."

"Have a nice day." Grayson pointed toward the door with all the warmth of the Grim Reaper.

"Just think about it. . . ."

"I won't."

It was over. She saw it in his eyes. She stood slowly, burdened by the weight of failure that lay over her shoulders like a stone blanket. "You have my card." She paused at the door, trying not to hope for a last-minute miracle. "Thank you for your time."

She stepped into the hallway. A medium-sized man with a slightly stooped frame and glossy bald head was hovering nearby. "All things considered, that went pretty well," he said. He followed her down the hallway. "Gray just has to get used to the idea. You can't change the brand of coffee you give him in the morning without hearing about it all day."

Jamie stopped walking. "Who are you?"

"Norman Westler." He extended a gnarled hand.

"Oh. You're the Mr. Westler who spoke to me on the phone."

"Call me Norman," the old guy said.

Jamie knew she should be irritated that Norman had led her on a wild-goose chase, but looking into his gentle brown eyes she just didn't have the heart. "Well, Norman," she said, "nice to meet you." She checked her watch and debated whether the traffic would be worse on the Merritt or I-95.

"You gave a very nice presentation," Norman said. "He shouldn't have cut you off like that. I'm going to have to talk to him about it."

"Oh, I'm used to it." Jamie decided to take Route 8 to the Merritt.

"I remember when we almost listed this place five years ago. A tall woman came here. She had big hair and an attitude—a real battle-ax. Her name was Theodora Roses."

"Oh—I know her. She's retired now," Jamie said.

Norman snorted. "Didn't like her much. But I give her credit," he said. "Must have come back here at least three times before Gray decided to let her draw up the paperwork." Behind his oversized glasses, his brown eyes looked at her intently. "My son is stubborn, but not stupid."

Jamie's eyes narrowed.

"He has a business degree from the University of Vermont. Graduated magna cum laude. You don't get that for your looks."

Jamie tapped her boot absently on the floor and ignored the voice that said she'd give Grayson Westler summa cum laude for looks. "So what are you saying?"

"Maybe you should stay a couple of days and work on him." Norman held her gaze steadily. "I think with a little more encouragement he might come around. Personally, I'm ready to retire to Cape Canaveral in Florida."

Grayson Westler didn't seem like the kind of man who would change his mind easily, but something inside her was telling her to stay. *What do you have to go back to?* it argued. *An empty apartment and a stack of bills you can't pay?* Maybe it wouldn't hurt to give it another day. She'd packed an overnight case, and obviously this Norman guy was firmly on her side.

"So what do you think it would take," Jamie said slowly, "to change Grayson's mind?"

Norman smiled. "Well, for starters, I'd take some private lessons with him. That way you can get to know him a little better. He's not a bad guy."

Building a relationship made sense. "I could do that," Jamie agreed. "But I'd need a motel to stay overnight. Could you recommend one?"

"I can do better than that," Norman declared, positively beaming now. "You can stay with us right next door. Normally we don't open our B&B until next week—but as long as you don't mind roughing it a bit, I'd be glad to make an exception."

Jamie hoped he'd give her a good price, but was too proud to ask. She held out her hand. "Looks like we've got ourselves a deal."

∽

The wind gusted at the top of the mountain. Gray leaned his weight against the top of his ski boots and hoped the rest of the junior team would hurry. Evan, Christopher, and Derrick were already there, and he was impatient to start the practice.

"Hey, Mr. Westler," Whitney Clarke skied up to him, followed by Steffie Newbanks.

Gray hid his irritation as the minutes dragged past. He'd told Halle over and over that just because she had talent it didn't mean she could show up late at practice. Last year the junior ski team had come in dead last at all the club races, and this year everyone had agreed to try harder.

"Sorry, Dad," Halle's skis sprayed him with snow as she came to a clean swish-stop beside him. Ella, following, wasn't nearly as graceful and nearly plowed into Steffie.

Gray gave Halle a look that said he wasn't too happy with her late appearance. "Okay, everyone," he began. "Let's get started. We're working on carving turns today."

He gave the rest of the instructions and then skied to a good vantage point. The boys went first. Evan caught an edge on the first turn and wiped out. Christopher had technique but wasn't aggressive enough, and Derrick. . .well, Derrick stood at the top of the hill talking to the girls.

Gray had had this problem at the last practice. His junior ski team seemed to prefer talking to skiing. He briefly considered separating the boys from the girls, but knew he didn't have time to work with two groups.

Finally, Derrick pushed off with Steffie not too far behind him. Steffie had nice form, but lacked confidence. "Good job," he said as both kids slid to a stop beside him. "But bend your knees more."

"Thanks," Steffie mumbled, eyes on the ground.

Whitney went next, with Ella just a few turns behind. Gray made mental notes as behind them Halle started her descent.

His heart swelled up with pride at the sight of his daughter navigating the trail with sharp, clean turns. If only Lonna could see Halle now. Their daughter not only had inherited her thick, curly hair, but also her grace on skis. Lonna had sacrificed her skiing dreams when she became a mother. Gray intended to do everything he could to make sure Halle had the opportunity to go as far as her talent would take her.

A moment later, the kids clustered around him, their faces red-cheeked from cold. "That was good," he said. "But we can do better. All of you need to bend your knees more and use your edges. When we start doing slalom courses, it'll make the difference between making or missing a gate." He paused. "Got it?" He glanced at their faces. "Okay, let's finish the rest of this run and try it again."

He pushed off his skis just as Halle said, "Oh, Ella. Don't worry. Jackson will ask you. He's just waiting for the perfect moment. . . ."

Boys. Dating. Boyfriends. Gray skied the fall line along the edge of the trail. He and Lonna had been barely teenagers when they'd met, then the day she turned sixteen he asked her to the movies. He let his skis accelerate and felt the rush of cold air on his face. Neither of them had ever dated anyone else; they hadn't wanted to. He prayed Halle wouldn't follow in his and Lonna's footsteps—falling in love so young and then getting married before they finished college. While he wouldn't change anything about his life, he realized he wanted something different for his daughter.

Please, God, he prayed, *let her be a kid a little while longer.*

Chapter 4

Jamie signed the guest book at the registration desk. The B&B had potential—high ceilings, lots of interesting wood detail, and beautiful, although scarred, hardwood floors. But the house needed fresh paint, and there was a sizable chew hole in the red wool carpet in the foyer. The chewer of the hole soon became apparent as a golden retriever trotted down the stairs. The dog had a sock dangling from its mouth.

"Meet Boomer," Norman said. "Looks like he brought you a present."

Boomer pushed the soggy sock into her hands. Jamie wrinkled her nose and let the sock fall to the ground. Boomer immediately picked it up and patiently pushed it into her hands again.

"We're going to put you in the Duchess Room. It's on the second floor and has its own bath." He handed her the room key. "You might want to make sure you keep your door closed, otherwise Boomer will come inside and steal your underwear and socks."

"I'll be careful," Jamie promised. She followed Norman up the stairs to a door with the number two hanging crookedly on it.

"Dinner's at 7:30. I'm cooking spaghetti."

"Oh, I couldn't impose. . . ."

"It's no imposition." Norman winked. "Let's just say it's a chance to get to know each other better."

Translation: a marketing opportunity. Jamie relaxed. "In that case, I'd love to."

The Duchess Room featured a queen-sized brass bed that needed a good polishing, a maple dresser with a slightly cloudy mirror, and a bookcase with an assortment of paperbacks. A tour of the bathroom netted a white-tiled floor, white fixtures, and a shower curtain with pictures of grinning Cheshire cats. Just what was it with all the *Alice in Wonderland* references?

The view from the room—the magnificent mountains, although too dark to properly admire—now *that* she could sell.

The house had not been included in the original listing, and she decided to factor it into a new proposal for Grayson, should he show any sign about changing his mind in selling.

Her cell phone rang. She smiled as she recognized the number. "Hey, Ivy, what's up?"

"Hi, Mom, guess what?"

"What?"

"Quinn Meyers invited me to spend Christmas break at their condo in

Aspen!" The rapture in her daughter's voice came clearly through the receiver. "Can I go, Mom? Can I go with her?"

Jamie felt her palms start to sweat. A ski vacation sounded expensive. At the same time, she knew she had specifically chosen Miss Porter's so her daughter could develop social connections. "Absolutely. It sounds like fun."

"It's going to be so cool," Ivy enthused. "And she's only asking me. Not any of the other girls."

"Really? That's great, honey."

"We're going sleigh riding on Christmas Day, right after a huge brunch!"

It started to sink in that she and Ivy would not be spending Christmas together. She wanted to ask if Ivy had thought about this and decided she probably didn't want to know the answer.

"Quinn said to bring a bikini for the hot tub. My old one is kinda worn. Could I get another this weekend?"

Jamie sighed. "Of course."

"And could you call Mrs. Meyers tonight and let her know?"

"Sure." Jamie pressed the receiver more tightly to her ear.

"You doing okay otherwise?"

"Yeah. Look, Dara wants me to show her how to do this thing on her iPod. I gotta go."

"I love you, baby," Jamie whispered but wasn't sure Ivy heard. The phone already had gone dead in her hands.

∽

"You're doing really great, Halle." Gray pushed open the door and stepped into the welcoming heat of the house.

"The last run you had I timed you at just over a minute." He shrugged out of his jacket and bent to loosen the laces of his boots. "That's close to your best time, and the snow is pretty heavy."

Halle added her parka to the coatrack beside his. "I was thinking about my electives next year." She paused. "When I go to high school, I might want to take band. Ella says they need people to play the french horn."

Gray frowned. "I don't know, Halle. Our family isn't very musical." It hadn't been lost on him the way people turned around and looked at them in church when they sang.

"If I start taking lessons now," Halle said pleasantly, but firmly, "I might be able to play in the high school band. Ella's brother says sometimes they march beginner players if it's an instrument they really want in the show."

Gray rubbed his cold hands on his jeans. "I don't think you'll have time to do the ski team and something like band in high school." The pink bow of his daughter's mouth flattened with disappointment. "It doesn't mean no," he quickly added. "It just means we need to talk some more about this."

A clicking noise on the wooden steps caught his attention.

Boomer came clattering down the stairs, wagging his tail, a sock hanging from his mouth. "You stealing another one of my socks?" he asked fondly.

"Hey," a woman's voice said from the top of the stairs. "That's mine."

Gray stiffened as he recognized the woman—the Realtor lady from Greenwich. The B&B wasn't even open for business yet. His gaze took in her heart-shaped face and very long, very straight brown hair. She held his gaze steadily. He remembered the kick in his stomach he'd felt when those big blue eyes had blinked up at him from the snowy tracks of the J-bar. He steeled his resolve as Realtor Lady trotted down the stairs.

"Thank you." She held the sock with clothespin fingers. "You stay out of my suitcase, Boomer." She didn't sound angry, though, and the golden thumped the floor with his tail and looked absurdly happy.

"What are you doing here?" Gray asked.

Her chin lifted a fraction. "Your father invited me."

"Who is she?" Halle asked, and Gray registered something like awe in her voice.

"Later, Halle," he said. He turned back to Realtor Lady. "We're not open to the public."

She smiled, oozing charm he would not let himself feel. "Norman already told me that. I don't need much—but if it's going to be too much of an inconvenience, I'll find another place."

Gray shifted his weight. He didn't want her staying with them, but Motel 9 was the closest place. He didn't like the idea of her staying there either. However, if she as much as opened her mouth about selling Pilgrim's Peak, he'd drive her there himself. "You can stay, but don't expect the Ritz."

Her full lips formed an amused twist. "That shouldn't be too hard."

"Boomer, no!" Halle pulled back the golden just as Boomer started nosing the fringe on Realtor Lady's boots. "Go find a tennis ball," she said. The dog trotted off with his nose to the ground, tail wagging.

He realized introductions had to be made. "This is my daughter, Halle. Halle, this is Miss King."

Jamie gave Halle a warm smile and extended her hand.

"Please call me Jamie."

"Miss King," Gray corrected.

At five foot six, his daughter and Realtor Lady stood almost the same height. Something in his chest tightened as he watched his daughter staring at this woman as if she were a movie star.

"Is that a Juicy Couture charm bracelet?"

"Halle," Gray said in warning. He hated it when his daughter asked personal questions. And he wasn't exactly thrilled either, that she was interested in Juicy Fruit—no, Juicy Couture—bracelets.

"Yes." Jamie smiled and held the bracelet up for closer examination.

"It's *so* cute."

He was spared any further conversation about jewelry as his father hollered, "Supper's ready!"

Inside the kitchen his dad was emptying a large pot of pasta into a colander in the kitchen sink. Wiping the steam from his glasses, he blinked at Gray in pleasure. "Ah, I see you've met our guest. Why don't you get Jamie something to drink with dinner, Gray?"

"Water's fine," Jamie said quickly. "I'll get it if you point me to the glasses."

"I've got it." Gray stepped toward the cabinets and pulled out the first glass he saw.

"You'd better make it a taller one," Halle said as Norman walked into the dining room with the bowl of pasta. "Grandpa's meatballs are usually pretty crunchy."

~

The meatballs looked fine, but when she bit down on one, it was as hard as a golf ball. She slid it to the other side of her mouth and tried again with more force. It cracked open, spreading an unpleasant taste in her mouth. Jamie ignored Grayson's smirk as she washed it down with a long drink of water. Wiping her mouth with a napkin, she smiled at Norman. "Usually my dinner comes out of the microwave, so getting a home-cooked meal is a real treat."

She enjoyed the blush of pleasure that rose on Norman's cheeks and ignored the dark look Grayson shot her. She did, however, slip Boomer a meatball and hid the others in her napkin.

After dinner they cleaned up the dishes and walked into the family room. Norman settled into a leather recliner. Jamie sat on a plump, leather couch and picked up a skiing magazine.

Over the top of the page, she watched Gray crumple newspaper to start a fire in the stone fireplace. In front of her, Halle arranged an assortment of folders and textbooks on a badly scarred coffee table.

Jamie turned a page. Ivy had always taken her homework straight to her room. From an early age, she'd encouraged organization and independence. She heard the tear of a match and then the soft, whooshing noise as the crumpled newspaper caught flame in the fireplace.

"I have so much homework," Halle grumbled. "Want me to tell you what it is?"

Jamie set the magazine down. "Sure."

"Okay." Halle rattled off an impressive list.

"You're in public or private school?"

Halle snorted. "Public, of course."

"I thought only private school gave out so much work." Jamie stretched her tired legs toward the fire, which just now began to crackle. Behind her she could feel the cold December night seeping through the thick walls of the old house. "My daughter, Ivy, is in the eighth grade."

Grayson's head swung around. "You have a daughter?"

Instinctively she hid her left hand under the magazine so he wouldn't see the absence of a ring on her fourth finger. Despite the pride and love she felt for Ivy, she also felt the familiar stigma of the circumstances of her daughter's birth. "Yeah," she said, meeting his gaze. "She's at a boarding school in Farmington— Miss Porter's. It's a college prep school."

Halle and Grayson exchanged looks. Jamie couldn't tell if they were impressed with the school or slightly horrified that her daughter did not live with her.

"I've heard of it," Grayson said. "It's a great school."

An expensive one, too, which reminded Jamie of her need for a commission check. She shifted in the chair, wondering the best way to transition the subject from boarding school to her market analysis. "This is a nice house," she said casually. "How many square feet?"

"It's not for sale," Grayson replied firmly.

From the recliner, Norman's eyes popped open. "Maybe you should hear her out, Gray."

Grayson shook his head. "There's no need."

Norman's bushy eyebrows lifted. "I've been thinking about Cape Canaveral, Florida. I've been thinking it might be nice to live near the military base. Probably there wouldn't be so much driving I'd have to do."

"Is this what it's about, Dad? Your license renewal? Make the appointment with the doctor, and then we'll talk."

Norman's cheeks flushed. "There's nothing wrong with my eyes, ears, or anything else about me. I'm just saying, Gray, maybe you should hear her out. Hiding from the truth doesn't change things."

"The truth is we're fine." Grayson's jaw tightened further. "I have no interest in selling—today, tomorrow, or next year."

"She's right about the numbers. I was listening at the door, so I know what she said."

"You shouldn't be eavesdropping behind closed doors."

"I wouldn't have to eavesdrop if you'd leave the door open." Norman turned to Jamie. "I'd like to hear more about your daughter."

She blinked at the rapid change in topic. Why was Norman so interested in her daughter? She tried to read his face and was even more confused when he winked.

"What's she look like?" Norman prompted gently.

"Well," Jamie began. "She's about my height and has olive-colored skin and darker-colored hair."

"Is she in the band?" Halle asked.

"No. She's on the debate team and likes to ski." She saw the interest in Grayson's eyes. "She's an expert skier."

"Our school has this awesome band that goes to Carnegie Hall. You have to make Wind Ensemble, but by senior year, most kids make it."

"Homework, Halle," Grayson interrupted.

"Mrs. Hayes gives way too much algebra homework. I have, like, fifty problems—and she doesn't explain *anything*."

"Let me look." Grayson scooted next to her and bent over the math book, giving Jamie a nice view of his shaggy brown hair—all natural no doubt, no salon highlights and no hours of styling. "Okay," he said at last. "Look at the formula. M equals y^2 minus y^1 divided by x^2 minus x^1."

"Huh? What's M?" Halle's nose wrinkled in confusion.

"The rate of change."

As Grayson started to explain, Jamie thought he might have been speaking another language. She was pretty sure they hadn't taught this advanced algebra when she went to eighth grade. And in high school, she'd barely gotten Cs in math. Of course, she'd been more interested in wondering if Devon Brown had noticed her new sweater, the way she was wearing her hair, her new shade of lip gloss—if he'd noticed anything about her. Anything at all.

Eager to escape these thoughts, Jamie settled back with the magazine. A short time later, she heard a very light popping noise, like a cork coming out of a bottle.

"Boom," Halle said. Hunching her shoulders, she pulled her turtleneck over her nose.

"Fire in the hole!" Norman yelled. He tucked his face into his red thermal shirt and looked braced, as if the ceiling were about to fall down on them.

Jamie was puzzled. Just as she turned to Grayson for an explanation, the most awful odor she had ever smelled permeated the room. "Ugh," she gasped involuntarily. Impossibly, it seemed to come in waves. She tried not to breathe, but could only hold her breath for so long. In his chair, Norman was shaking with laughter.

"Boomer." Grayson's voice was thick with disgust as he addressed the dog in front of the hearth. Looking up, he said, "Okay, who fed him the meatballs?"

Jamie raised her hand. "It was me. I didn't know."

"It's how Boomer got his name," Halle informed her happily. "If he eats anything besides his dog food, Boomer, well, *booms*."

"The silent ones are even worse. I'm thinking the military should study Boomer's gas," Norman commented, his voice muffled from under his shirt. "Drop a canister of that, and you'd have instant surrender."

"Enough, Dad," Grayson said in warning. "Come on, Boomer, let's put you outside for a moment." Grayson left the room with the dog at his side.

"How do you get your hair so straight, Miss King?" Halle asked when it was safe to come out from under her shirt. "I've tried to flatiron mine, but it never comes out very well."

"Well, tell me how you do it and what products you use." Before Jamie knew it, she was answering a multitude of hair and beauty questions and agreeing to straighten Halle's hair after the girl finished her homework.

Jamie didn't get to bed until late. Pulling the down comforter high under her chin, she tried to ignore the scratching noise coming from the vicinity of the closet. She really hoped whatever was making that noise wasn't chewing on her brand-new camel hair après ski boots.

Instead of the noise, she thought about Grayson and Halle crouched by the fireplace, their heads close together, their shoulders nearly touching. It was easy to see they had none of that awful awkwardness Jamie sometimes felt with Ivy. They probably never had that slight hesitation before they hugged each other to say hello or good-bye. She pulled the covers a little higher under her chin. Maybe it was different with fathers and daughters.

More scratching noises. Too loud to ignore. Jamie took a deep breath and fumbled with the light switch. She heard a low whine and realized she wasn't dealing with a mouse—and the sounds weren't coming from the closet either. She exhaled, felt her teeth set in irritation, and marched to the bedroom door.

"Go away, mutt," she whispered. Boomer wagged his feathered tail hopefully. "I mean it," she said. The golden grinned up at her, deep kindness in his amber-colored eyes. Jamie had wanted a dog when she was growing up, but her mother had preferred cats. Her feet were freezing, and the dog wasn't going away, so she opened the door a little wider.

"Don't you dare steal my socks—or do any booming," she warned the golden, who trotted into the room and then bounded right onto the queen-sized bed. Jamie started to push the dog off the bed and realized she didn't have the heart. Besides, he'd make a great foot warmer.

The last thing she heard before she fell asleep was the dog's snoring blending with the odd creaks and wheezy groans of the old house.

Chapter 5

Arriving early at the mountain the next morning, Jamie decided to take a couple of practice runs before her private lesson with Grayson. She braced herself for the J-bar's mighty shove and then remembered to lean forward and let the machine push her up the hill. She felt very accomplished when she reached the top without falling.

Norman had given her some pointers at breakfast, so when Jamie shuffled over to the beginning of the trail, she carefully arranged her legs into the snowplow position. *Keep pushing the backs of your skis apart,* Norman had coached, *and you'll be able to control your speed.*

He'd been exaggerating a bit about the control part, Jamie discovered a moment later. She was skiing down the mountain at a pretty good clip—but still standing—even though the snow was a lot lumpier than it looked. Then she saw the snaking line of the ski school just in front of her. "Look out!" she yelled.

The little kids didn't alter their course—or maybe they were like her, getting hijacked by their skis and couldn't. Jamie saw only one solution. She closed her eyes and threw her body to the side. Her bindings popped, and the next thing she knew, she was on her back and sliding headfirst down the mountain like a human torpedo.

She'd barely stopped sliding when Grayson loomed over her. "That was interesting."

"Interesting?" Jamie sputtered. She sat up and checked to see if everything still worked. "I almost kill myself, and you think it's *interesting?*"

"You look fine to me," Grayson said. "And at least you're near the bottom."

So she was—and it looked like the ski school was standing safely in line for the J-bar. Jamie took the hand he offered and let him help her to her feet.

"Guess our first lesson will be turning," Grayson said dryly.

Jamie thought the first lesson should be about empathy—his—then remembered he was a potential client. So, without any further comment, she followed Grayson to the J-bar. She made it to the top without an incident, and when she turned around to see if he was impressed, she nearly got hit by an empty J-bar swinging its way down the hill.

"You need to ski out of the path of the J-bar more quickly," Grayson lectured.

She had to bite her lip to refrain from telling him that getting knocked unconscious by the J-bar might be preferable to spending the next thirty minutes learning to ski.

"We need to work on your wedge turns," Grayson continued as they moved to the start of the trail. "I want you to follow me as closely as you can and copy my movements. Pay particular attention to the way I bend my knees into the turn and then straighten as I come out of it."

"Okay." Jamie flashed her best smile. "By the way, did you have a chance to look at that proposal I gave you last night?"

His lips tightened. "When are you going to accept that I don't intend to sell this place?"

"Your father and I had an interesting conversation at breakfast. He told me about this really great ski hill in Massachusetts that had been operating for thirty years—Powder Ridge—and then it had one bad year, 1995." Jamie paused to let this sink in. "It went into bankruptcy and was sold piecemeal at auction. I'm sure you don't want to see the same thing happen here."

Grayson shook his head. "It won't. I won't let it. Now, do you want to take this lesson or not?"

Jamie lifted her chin. "Yes."

Grayson pushed gently off the lip of the hill and began to glide down the mountain, making his movements slow and deliberate. Jamie set her jaw and followed. She'd been a cheerleader in high school. Hopefully skiing was easier than making pyramids or doing a dozen back handsprings.

Grayson looked over his shoulder. "You're not following my turns," he pointed out. "You need to keep up with me."

She brought her skis together, sort of like the way Grayson was doing. Immediately she picked up speed. Grayson bent his knees, did some kind of tricky weight-shift thing, and turned. Jamie gamely bent, pushed hard on one ski, and twisted her body a little.

Grayson looked over his shoulder a second time. He nodded and picked up a little more speed. Jamie wasn't sure she could handle going any faster, but she wasn't about to ask him to slow down.

Her legs were shaking as she went into the next few turns. Surely he planned to stop and let her catch her breath. *And when he does,* she thought, *I'll hit him with a few numbers.* She hit a bump that Grayson had somehow missed. It put her off balance, and she missed a turn. She decided to let herself pick up speed so Grayson wouldn't lecture her about falling behind again. She pointed her skis downhill.

She let herself pick up a little too much speed, she realized moments later as she watched Gray's back rushing nearer and nearer. "Go faster," she yelled, but instead of immediately following her direction, he glanced back at her. She saw his mouth open in surprise, and then she slammed into him.

The next thing she knew, their skis tangled, and they were falling. She landed on top of him and heard his breath come out in a single whooshing noise, like a down cushion someone had sat upon too heavily. Her ski bindings didn't release, and when they finished sliding, she found herself on top of his chest with her knees bent and her skis sticking straight up in the air behind her.

He'd lost his hat and sunglasses in the fall, but at least he was breathing. "Sorry," she whispered. "Are you okay?"

"I've been better." He shifted, but Jamie's skis, anchored in the snow, kept them both firmly in place.

Some of his shaggy brown hair had fallen across his face, and the rest was a tousled pile in need of a good smoothing. Jamie registered these facts, just as she registered that she'd tackled and squashed a potential client. "I don't suppose," she said slowly, "that now would be a good time to discuss my proposal?"

∼

Jamie had always considered herself the kind of girl who made the best out of any situation. Trekking to the parking lot, she reviewed the positives of the past couple of days. She'd enjoyed meeting Norman and Halle, discovered that she liked skiing but really stunk at it, and had probably burned off enough calories in the past two days to fit into her favorite pair of skinny jeans.

She was still broke, of course, but she had the Coleman closing later in the afternoon, and while it wouldn't be enough to solve her financial dilemmas, it'd pay for Ivy's trip to Aspen. She'd juggle the rest of her bills. She was used to doing that.

She wasn't, however, used to losing her car. Frowning, she studied the place where she'd parked earlier that morning. There were track marks in the snow, but no cherry red Lexus. It wasn't anywhere else in the parking lot either. Jamie nibbled her lower lip and rebalanced the skis currently digging into her right shoulder. Woodbury, Connecticut, didn't seem like the kind of place where people stole cars, but other than one other possibility—which her mind refused to accept—she couldn't figure out what had happened.

With her skis on her shoulder and her head held high, she marched back to the lodge area to straighten things out.

She found an empty picnic table near the concession stand. Two cups of coffee and several calls later, Jamie confirmed her worst fears—her Lexus had been repossessed. Not only that, but when she'd tried to rent a car, the credit company declined her charge card. She was trying to figure out what to do when her cell phone rang.

She recognized Marla Coleman's voice instantly and sat up straighter. "Mrs. Coleman. I was just about to call you."

"There's been a change of plans," Mrs. Coleman announced in the same girlishly happy voice that disguised an interior core of steel. "Geoff has been promoted to the London office."

"Promoted? London?" Jamie echoed but with far less enthusiasm. "What about the Hamilton Avenue house this afternoon?"

"Cancel it," Mrs. Coleman said.

"But your deposit. . ."

"There's the transfer clause, remember? We wrote it into the contract. In the case of an international transfer, our offer is rescinded in full."

A few minutes later Jamie hung up and replaced the cell phone in her purse. Her nose started to prickle painfully on the inside, the way it always did right before she cried. She dug her fingernails into the palm of her hand. *Don't panic,* she ordered herself and felt her body ignore the command as a sick feeling spread through her stomach.

Breathing shallowly seemed to help with the nausea, but didn't eliminate it completely. She dug her fingernails even harder into her palms. She'd figure out something. She always did. Maybe there was a bus she could take back to Greenwich and. . .and what? She swallowed something bitter tasting. How was she going to show houses without a car? She slammed her palm against the top of the picnic table. *You will not feel sorry for yourself,* she ordered. *You will not let this break you.*

Her nose positively burned now, and her eyes felt like they were floating in acid. She thought of Ivy, and her neck bent under the weight of despair. She laid her head on the flat surface of the table. It smelled like greasy french fries and ketchup.

"Miss King?"

It was Grayson Westler's voice. She tried to summon some last vestige of pride and sit up, but her head weighed too much.

"Go away," she muttered.

The table moved slightly under her cheek as he settled himself across from her. "What's wrong?"

"Nothing."

"Then why is your face plastered to the top of my picnic table?"

"Because I like it there," Jamie said.

"Are you hurt?"

"Nope," Jamie said, wishing it were that simple. "Just broke."

She sneaked a peak at him. He'd unzipped his ski instructor's jacket, and his impressive mountain-man chest was on full display. She had a feeling a girl could have a good cry on those broad shoulders. Not that she was that kind of girl. Nope. Jamie King was like the Lone Ranger. Only she wasn't the Lone Ranger—she didn't have a Tonto and her white horse had been led off to the repossession barn.

"Would you like me to call someone?"

Jamie straightened wearily. She really needed to pull herself together. "How about a cab?"

Grayson shook his head, then it seemed to register why she might be asking for transportation. "Did something happen to your car?"

"Repossessed." Normally she'd never have admitted that, but it occurred to her that once she got transportation, she'd never see him again. Therefore, for once, she didn't need to expend the energy to make it look like she had it all under control. "And don't ask me about leasing another car because I've maxed out my credit card. I just lost a sale that I've been counting on to pay my rent next month, and I have a daughter about to get out of school for Christmas break, and I'm not even sure how I'm going to *feed* her."

"Oh," Grayson said uncomfortably.

"I haven't spoken with my family in almost fourteen years, and if my friends find out I'm broke, I'm going to be professionally ruined." Her eyes began to tear, but it felt great to let it out. Why stop now? "Who wants to buy a house from an agent who has to borrow the client's car to drive to the showing?" She swiped her cheeks, angry at the tears for falling.

"You're that broke?"

"Yes." Jamie blew her nose into the tissue Grayson handed her.

He was silent for a long time. When he glanced up, he had an unhappy twist to his mouth and a fairly deep line between his brows. "Look," he said. "The lady who cooks breakfast for our guests has to take the next couple of weeks off for personal reasons. I'm looking for a temporary replacement."

Jamie blinked. "You are?"

"Our bed-and-breakfast opens next week, and we need a cook for the breakfast part. It's probably a bad idea," he added.

"No," Jamie corrected. "It's a great idea. I can cook."

"It doesn't pay much," Gray added.

"Just throw in room and meals," Jamie said, thinking rapidly. "And lift tickets." Ivy could spend Christmas break at Pilgrim's Peak instead of Aspen. "I'll need a car. To pick up my daughter from school and get a few things from my apartment."

"You'll need to be able to cook."

"I can cook." She saw doubt flicker across his eyes. "How about I make breakfast tomorrow? If you like it, you give me the job." She read resigned acceptance in his eyes. "And ski lessons." She held her breath. She probably shouldn't have asked for the lessons, but asking for a little too much was the way she negotiated real estate closings. *If you don't ask,* she always told her clients, *you'll never know.* "I make all kinds of breakfast pastries—and an excellent cheese frittata."

"Miss King, you've got yourself a deal."

"It's Jamie," she said, shaking his hand. "And thank you. You won't be sorry."

Chapter 6

Jamie went all out for breakfast. The day before she had checked the pantry. It was pretty well stocked. She was up before dawn and in the kitchen baking three kinds of muffins, frying up sausages, cooking hash browns, and making her specialty dish—an asparagus, tomato, and fontina cheese frittata.

She held her breath as she set plates down in front of Norman and Grayson in the dining room. Norman took one bite and began to laugh. It wasn't the reaction Jamie had been hoping for, and she felt herself start to sweat. But then Norman looked at her with a huge smile on his face. "I would never have thought someone as pretty as you could cook."

Jamie shrugged modestly. "My Aunt Bea taught me all her recipes." She glanced at Grayson, who was reaching for a second muffin.

"Who's Aunt Bea?" Grayson cut the warm muffin open and slathered it with butter.

Norman interrupted. "Whoever she is, she's a genius."

"She was a really good family friend," Jamie said. Normally she would never have mentioned Aunt Bea—or anything about that time in her life—but since Grayson was taking her in, she figured she owed him some information. "I lived in Maine with her during my senior year in high school. Want some more hash browns, Norman?"

"Absolutely." Norman held out his plate. "I'd love to meet your Aunt Bea. Is she single?"

She felt Grayson's gaze watching her carefully. His sharp brown eyes told her it would be difficult, if not impossible, to lie to him. Not that she was a liar, but Jamie disliked personal questions.

"Sorry, Norman, but she's been dead nearly fourteen years."

"That's too bad," Norman said very gently. "I'm sure she's in a better place now."

"I hope so." Jamie wiped an invisible spot on the table.

"So you grew up in Maine?" Gray asked.

Jamie's hands froze. "No. I'm from Connecticut. Darien, actually." She could feel his gaze trying to put the pieces of the puzzle together. She could have saved him the trouble and just told him the reason she'd been sent to the farthest corner of Maine was that her parents didn't know anyone in Siberia who would take in their unmarried, pregnant daughter. Instead, she met his gaze steadily. "So do I have the job?"

"Are you kidding?" Norman chuckled. "If I were a little younger, I'd be proposing marriage about now."

"Dad." Grayson said, warning in his voice. "Remarks like that are considered harassment."

"It's okay," Jamie said. She was sweating, but in relief. "So I have the job?"

Grayson nodded. "Just until Mrs. Dodges returns on January fifth."

Perfect, Jamie wanted to say, then thought of Ivy. School was letting out in a few days. "What about the car?"

"You can have Sally," Norman offered. "She's old, but she's like me—indestructible. You'll have to get the keys from my son, however." He shot Grayson a dark look. "He's hidden them from me."

"His license expired," Grayson explained.

"And *somebody* won't drive me to the motor vehicles department to get it renewed."

"I could drive you," Jamie offered.

Norman instantly said, "Great!" At the same time Grayson practically shouted, "No. And you know why, Dad."

Jamie held her hands up in surrender. "You two decide. I've got a lot of work to do." She had to let the office know she'd be away for several weeks. Plus she needed more clothing from her apartment and to have her mail stopped. There was grocery shopping to do, and Ivy to call.

Reaching for her cup of coffee, Jamie took a big swallow and felt the liquid burn its way down her throat. Ivy wasn't going to be happy about this change of plans, but hopefully she'd understand. Jamie would point out the positives. Being a Realtor had taught her that people, for the most part, didn't care if a house was perfect. They were willing to overlook a busy street or a backyard slightly too small if they could picture themselves doing something pleasant—like hosting football parties or throwing family barbecues. All they needed sometimes were a few prompts, and Jamie was only too happy to provide them.

❧

Sally turned out to be a 1979 aquamarine Buick LeSabre. Its rust-stained body crouched as if sitting directly on its white-walled tires. The fenders were dented, and there was a fist-sized crack in the rear windshield covered with silver duct tape. "Isn't she a beauty?" Norman said proudly. "They don't make them like this anymore."

And there's a reason for that, Jamie thought as she squeezed the handle of the front door. It groaned, stuck, and then fell open at a funny angle. "What war did you say you drove this in?"

Norman laughed. He leaned through the driver's side window. "She likes oil, so when you get down to Greenwich, you might want to put a quart of 10W-30 in her."

Jamie nodded. She turned on the ignition. The engine whined, caught, and then the car backfired. Through the rearview mirror, she watched a cloud of black smoke wafting through the air. Norman was smiling like a benevolent parent, so apparently this was the norm. She shifted it into reverse. The car bucked so hard, she nearly hit her head on the steering wheel. Jamie set her jaw. A week ago she'd rather have died than be seen in a car like this one. Times changed, though. She wasn't exactly in a position to be choosy.

When she reached Miss Porter's, the only parking she could find was right in front of the quaint white Colonial-style house where Ivy lived. Heads turned as she pulled alongside the curb and parked next to a sleek black Lincoln Navigator.

Turning off the engine, Jamie braced herself as the engine went into the same theatrics as it had at her apartment—thumping, knocking, and emitting a sort of *ping-pong* sound under the hood. As the engine's gasps and coughs became more intermittent, she reached for her purse. With her head held high, Jamie marched up to the dormitory.

She found Ivy in her room, along with a small group of girls who were hugging and tearfully saying good-bye to each other. "Come on, Ivy," Jamie said, figuring she and Ivy should make a run for it before someone tried to tow old Sally to the junkyard.

Extracting Ivy from the dorm proved more difficult than Jamie had anticipated. Ivy's friends wouldn't let go of her, and they ended up following her to the car. All of them stood in the bright December sunshine staring at Sally's broad, rust-stained frame.

"Where's the Lexus?" Ivy asked.

"At the dealership, I think." Jamie opened the trunk and dumped Ivy's suitcase into the back. Standing on her tiptoes, she managed to clip Ivy's skis into the rack on top of the car. "You ready, Ivy?" She glanced over her shoulder at Ivy's friends and pulled out a megawatt smile. "You girls might want to stand back. Sally is a little temperamental."

She hustled Ivy into the car and started up Sally. The engine whined. Jamie gave it a little gas, and Sally backfired. The girls on the sidewalk gave a startled scream. Jamie shifted gears and braced herself for the forthcoming jolt. She ignored the startled look Ivy gave her. She also ignored the black cloud hanging in the air and the puddle of oil Sally left behind on the immaculate street.

"So," Jamie said brightly as they turned onto I-84 West. "How does it feel to be on Christmas break?"

"Right now," Ivy said, "it feels like we're sitting right on the road."

"Sally rides low," Jamie agreed.

"I like the Lexus much better."

Me, too, Jamie thought. "You ready to do some skiing? The house where we're staying is right next to the hill." She glanced sideways at Ivy, trying to gauge her mood.

"My friends said that Pilgrim's Peak is a dinky little ski hill."

Jamie kept her gaze on the road. At least they were talking. "It is small, but quaint." Okay. Quaint was a stretch, but what was she supposed to say? "You'll like it."

Ivy snorted.

"So those looked like nice girls," Jamie ventured. "Which one was Quinn?"

"The one who's best friends with Dara now—because Dara is going to Aspen with her."

"Oh." Jamie tried to think of something positive to say. "Well, at least you and I will be together for Christmas."

"Yeah," Ivy agreed, but Jamie knew the word had been punctuated with an eye roll.

She didn't object when Ivy pulled out her iPod and ended the need for further conversation. She watched the gray landscape flash past and remembered the friends she'd had at Ivy's age. Most had been fellow cheerleaders. She remembered how hard it had been to fit in with them—she had to wear the right clothes and have perfect hair and makeup. She also had to be seen at the right places with the right friends. Jamie sighed, knowing she'd made Ivy look bad to her friends. She resolved to make it up to Ivy and buy her something really great the moment she had enough money.

About forty minutes later, Jamie turned off the highway. "Before we get to Pilgrim's Peak, there are some things you should probably know."

"What?"

"Take your earphones off." Jamie pantomimed the request.

"The house is a little run-down," she explained. "But it has a lot of character. The Westlers are nice people, and you are going to love the daughter—she's your age and is a really sweet girl." Jamie almost warned Ivy to be equally sweet, but then decided if she did, Ivy might do the exact opposite.

A short time later she pulled down the long driveway to the house. "We're here," Jamie announced unnecessarily and a bit too cheerfully.

"You're kidding." The sight of the old Victorian had temporarily snapped Ivy out of her campaign of silence. "Does it even have plumbing, or do I have to use an outhouse?"

Jamie laughed as if Ivy had been joking. "It has plumbing." She hesitated. "And Grayson's working on the hot-water problem."

"Seriously? No hot water?" Ivy's eyes widened with horror. Jamie clutched the wheel tighter and parked the Buick. They sat in silence as the engine refused to die and bucked liked a determined bronco.

"It has hot water," Jamie assured her. "You just have to shower fast."

"Why don't I just find a stream somewhere?"

Sally's last death rattle faded. "You could, but it'd probably be frozen."

Her humor fell flat. Jamie felt defeat, like the cold, seeping into the car. She steeled her resolve and wrestled open the door. She hauled Ivy's suitcase out of the trunk. She'd leave the skis for later. "Oh, one more thing. You know how I told you that you couldn't go to Colorado because one of my sales fell through?"

Ivy nodded.

"Well, this is sort of a working vacation for me. While I'm trying to get this listing, I'll also be cooking breakfast for everyone." Jamie climbed the porch steps. "Ivy, you coming?"

"Mom? You're working as a cook?"

"Don't look so shocked."

"But you don't cook."

How could Ivy not remember Jamie making her chocolate-chip pancakes—or blueberry crepes? *Because,* a voice inside said, *you decided about ten years ago that cooking didn't fit the image of a successful, professional woman.* "Don't be silly," Jamie scolded. "Of course I can cook."

They started up the steps. Ivy paused to stare at a Christmas decoration of a snowman on skis. Its hips were wiggling back and forth. "Mom," Ivy said. "Please pinch me so I can wake up."

Norman greeted them when they stepped inside the house. He shook Ivy's hand. "Gray's been making powder, and we've got twelve trails open."

After a brief hesitation, Ivy said, "Great."

Jamie shot her a warning glance. "You'll love the mountain, Ivy. It's right next door to the house. You can practically walk to the chair lift." She was babbling, but couldn't seem to help it. Ivy was making her nervous. What kind of mother got nervous around her own child?

Norman winked at Ivy. "Gray's going to let some moguls form on White Rabbit. You'll like them."

Ivy, to her credit, managed a strained but appropriate show of excitement. "Great!"

Jamie led Ivy upstairs. As they walked into the Duchess Room, Boomer followed them inside, a sock trailing from his mouth. "He's welcoming us," Jamie explained as Ivy uncomfortably backed away from the dog. Jamie took the soggy gift from Boomer's mouth into the bathroom and laid it on the side of the tub to dry.

When she walked back into the bedroom, Ivy was standing in the same place she'd left her. "Mom, there's only one bed in here."

Jamie nodded. "I know. We're sharing."

Ivy sighed. "This just gets better and better."

Jamie turned away so Ivy wouldn't read the disappointment in her face. Maybe she should have stayed in Greenwich in the silent apartment. They would have had their separate, tastefully furnished bedrooms and wouldn't have to interact so much. It would have been a lot easier to pretend that everything was right between them.

Chapter 7

After the Westlers returned from church the next morning, Norman invited Jamie and Ivy to help pick out their Christmas tree. Jamie put down her shopping list. "Thanks, Norman, but we wouldn't want to intrude on your family time."

"Intrude?" Norman laughed. "You can referee." His gaze moved to Ivy, who was sitting on the sofa in front of the fireplace reading *The Call of the Wild*, or at least pretending to. Jamie hadn't seen her turn the page in the last five minutes. "Hey, Ivy," he said. "Ever cut down your Christmas tree?"

The girl lowered the book. "No. We have an artificial one."

"That's not a tree," Norman scoffed. "That's a coatrack." He stepped closer to her. "I'll show you a real Christmas tree. Get your coat."

"It's actually kind of fun picking it out," Halle added. She was eyeing Ivy's striped cashmere sweater appreciatively. "Dragging it home isn't so much fun."

"You drag it home? The store is that close?"

Norman laughed. "The store is in our backyard, Ivy. Just look out the window."

"And it's starting to snow!" Halle cried. She whipped out her cell phone and blasted off a text.

True enough, outside the glass fat white flakes were gently falling. Jamie wanted her daughter to participate, but feared anything she said would make Ivy do the exact opposite. She didn't think their relationship had been this bad at Thanksgiving. Looking back, Jamie realized they hadn't spent much quality time together. Ivy had slept late and then spent hours texting her friends.

"What do you say?" Norman pressed. "You want to go hunt for the perfect Christmas tree?"

Ivy looked less bored than before. She put aside the book.

"I guess."

Within minutes, Ivy and Jamie retrieved their coats and boots and joined the Westlers in the backyard. Grayson was wearing a black parka and carrying a rusty-looking saw in his hands.

"That saw looks serious," Jamie said as they all marched off across the frozen field. "The last time I bought a Christmas tree all I brought along was a charge card."

Grayson shot a glance at his father. "Don't think we can buy the kind of tree we're looking for."

"That's true," Norman agreed.

Ivy and Halle ran ahead. Boomer raced alongside, his golden coat already dotted with snow. When Jamie was little, her mother had told her that in every snowfall there was always one flake that tasted as sweet as sugar. If she ever caught this flake on her tongue, she could wish for whatever she wanted.

"Did you ever catch one?" Jamie had asked, completely buying the story, just as she'd accepted the existence of Santa Claus and the Easter Bunny.

"Oh yes," her mother had said. "Just once, though."

"And what did you wish for?"

Jamie remembered her mother's blue eyes resting on her, warm as a summer sky. "I wished for you," she'd said.

Jamie thought of this story every time it snowed. Even though it also made her a little sad, she'd told this story when Ivy was very little. In Jamie's version, Ivy was the child who had been wished for.

"Just what kind of tree are we looking for?" Jamie asked, picturing the towering, lush blue spruce her parents had always placed in the marble foyer.

"We'll know it when we see it," Grayson said cryptically.

"The girls are having fun together," Norman remarked. "It's nice for Halle to have Ivy's company. Usually it's just us old farts and her."

"Speak for yourself," Grayson said mildly.

Jamie admired their easy bantering. She and her parents had never teased each other the way Grayson and Norman did—and she didn't do it with Ivy either. She was always afraid Ivy would take what she said in a bad light and get her feelings hurt. Probably it was a guy thing, not something she had failed to do as a mom.

The woods were getting thicker now. They were almost at the base of the hills. Dozens of fragrant pines mixed with the skeletal limbs of hardwoods. Jamie spotted a tall, elegant tree with thick boughs. "How about that one?"

Grayson barely gave it a glance. "Nope."

"What about it don't you like?"

"Not enough personality," he replied.

"What do you mean, personality?" Jamie pushed aside a branch and crunched over the frozen ground after Grayson.

She couldn't help but feel that finding the right tree was a lot like finding the right house for a client. The better she understood the criteria, the easier it was to find the right match.

"Kind of hard to define," Grayson replied.

They tracked deeper into a cluster of pines. The snow was definitely sticking now. The trees already had a light dusting, and the vast gray sky seemed to hang right over them, looking like it was capable of snowing for days. In the distance the girls held out their arms and spun in the thickening fall of snow.

"Your daughter is lovely," Grayson commented.

Jamie glanced at him suspiciously. "Thank you."

"I was impressed to see her doing some homework this morning. She must be an excellent student."

Jamie wondered where the conversation was going. "She works hard for her grades."

"So does Halle," Grayson said. "But not on the second day of Christmas break." He laughed lightly as if this were amusing.

"Well, it's the exam schedule," Jamie said vaguely. "Ivy has four finals waiting for her after the break. I guess it's a good thing she didn't get to go to Aspen."

"She was going to Aspen?" They walked a few more steps. "Is that where her dad lives?"

So this was where the conversation was going. Jamie planted her feet. She waited until she had Grayson's gaze firmly locked within her own. "One of Ivy's friends from her school invited her," she said in a frosty tone. "Her dad isn't in the picture."

Jamie felt her cheeks heat as Grayson studied her face. She braced herself for further questions, but none came.

"Dad! Over here!"

Grayson turned at the sound of his daughter's voice. Jamie followed more slowly. She kind of wished she hadn't been so prickly. He'd invited her—a total stranger—into his home.

No wonder he was trying to understand her situation. She shouldn't have gone off like that.

When she caught up, Ivy and Halle were standing next to a skinny pine tree with a hook-shaped tip.

"I like it," Norman stated. "A tree with osteoporosis. Sort of like me."

Grayson tested the strength of the trunk. "It has potential, but let's keep looking."

Halle and Ivy ran deeper into the trees. Norman followed at a much slower pace and Boomer happily dragged a branch through the woods. Jamie ducked under a branch and stepped over some deadfall. "So you're looking for deformed trees?"

"We like to think of them as unique."

Jamie still didn't understand. "Why choose an ugly tree when there're so many beautiful ones all around?"

Grayson's boots crunched as he headed toward another smaller pine. "Not ugly, Jamie. Our trees have personality. And it's a family tradition. How do you and Ivy pick out your tree?"

"We go to the basement and bring the box to my apartment." It was a nice tree, a four-foot-tall blue spruce, perfectly shaped and prelit with perfectly spaced white lights. "We decorate it with red balls and sterling silver ornaments." Actually, Jamie was the only one who decorated it. Sometimes Ivy helped, but afterward Jamie would have to rearrange the decorations into a neat, symmetrical look.

"I'm sure it's very nice." He said it tactfully, but Jamie could tell he didn't think that at all.

"It is," she stated firmly.

From up ahead, Halle shouted, "We found it! Dad, come look!"

Halle, Ivy, and Norman stood in front of a medium-sized tree. At first Jamie didn't see what was so special about it, but then Norman moved to the side and she saw the center branch sticking out at least a foot longer than any of the others.

"It has a nose!" Halle cried. Out came her cell phone, and she snapped a photo. "See it?"

Grayson smiled. "It has definite personality. What do you think, Dad?"

"I like it," Norman said. He seemed a little out of breath and rubbed his arm as if it hurt.

"You okay, Norman?" Jamie moved closer to him.

"Oh sure," he said. "Old army wound. Got it in the Korean War. I drove a tank, you know."

"Dad," Grayson said. "I don't think they had tanks at Fort Myers, Florida."

Norman straightened as much as his bent frame would allow. "How do you think they train people to drive tanks, Gray? You think they just ship them off to war with a set of tank keys and say 'good luck'?"

"I'm just surprised I hadn't heard about you driving tanks at Fort Myers before," Grayson said.

"Well maybe I just don't like to go around bragging," Norman said. His breath came out in small white puffs, and he rubbed his arm again. "You don't know everything about my life."

"I want to hear more about the tanks," Ivy said, surprising Jamie with her show of interest and support. "How do you see where you're going?"

"A very good question," Norman said approvingly. "There's a little window with metal slats, just like in a knight's helmet. You can close the opening if someone shoots at you."

Grayson's eyes narrowed suspiciously. "You sure, Dad?"

"Absolutely," Norman said, meeting his gaze.

Grayson shook his head as if he didn't quite believe him, then stepped close to the base of the tree.

Jamie watched Grayson's arm move back and forth and listened to the metal teeth slice through the wood. Suddenly she was seventeen years old, seven months pregnant, and using a steak knife to saw a bough off the pine in Aunt Bea's backyard. The smell of sap was strong, and she remembered sawing and sawing until her fingers went numb and the ache of cold spread up her fingers. She hadn't let herself quit, though. She wasn't about to let her baby spend its first Christmas without a tree, and Aunt Bea was too old and too sick to go out and get one.

She'd stuck the branch in a glass vase, decorated it with tinfoil balls, and put it on the coffee table in front of the fireplace. She remembered sitting on Aunt Bea's cat-smelly couch and wrapping her arms around her swollen stomach.

Don't worry, baby, she thought. *I'm going to take great care of you. And next year we're going to have a real Christmas, with lots of presents and a beautiful tree with red balls and sterling silver decorations. I'm going to love you more than any kid in the world, and you're going to have a great life. I promise.*

Chapter 8

It would have been a lot easier just to drag the tree home himself, Gray decided as they neared the house. He held the base, Jamie and Ivy the front, and his dad and Halle had the middle. Every time they had to go around something, Jamie and Ivy would try to go different directions, then argue which way made more sense. If this wasn't bad enough, Norman complained nonstop that everyone was walking too fast, and Boomer kept trying to play tug-of-war with the branches. And then, when they were almost home, Halle realized she'd dropped her cell phone somewhere along the way, and they all had to go back and look for it.

Gray was relieved to get the tree home and into the family room. He was even more relieved when the fat trunk fit into the old metal stand.

"Let's put giant sunglasses on him," Halle said. "That'd look so cool."

"Him?" Gray turned the screws that held the tree in the base. "How do you know the tree is male?"

"Because he has a moustache," Halle said, shaking the pine bough of the limb that stuck out of the middle of the tree. "See, the pine needles are like whiskers."

"Hold on, Halle, it isn't properly secured." Gray gave the bolt a final twist and straightened. The tree fit perfectly into the corner of the family room. "Trees aren't girls or guys, they're just trees." He tested the trunk to make sure it was balanced. Out of the corner of his eye, he saw Ivy watching. She was a pretty girl, but all too often he'd noticed a petulant look around her mouth, especially whenever she addressed her mother. He wondered what sort of mother/daughter team he'd brought into the house—and if hiring Jamie King was going to turn out to be the worst mistake he'd made in a long time.

It was only for a couple of weeks, he reminded himself as he opened the plastic storage box and pulled out a strand of globe lights. Besides, he sympathized with her financial problems. He'd had a couple of bad years where he'd wondered if he was going to be able to hang on. Always God had provided, and the help had come in many forms. In all good conscience, he could not have turned Jamie King away.

"Anyone want some hot chocolate?" Norman asked.

"Me," Halle said.

"Me, too," Ivy chimed in.

"Then you'd better come help me make it," his dad said. "You know I can burn anything."

"That's true," Halle said. "One time he even burned cereal."

"It was oatmeal, Halle," Norman said, chuckling as if he was proud of the accomplishment. The three of them disappeared into the kitchen.

"You want some help?" Jamie stepped over Boomer, who was chewing a bone in his usual spot on the hearth rug.

"Sure." Gray climbed up on a chair and clipped the first bulb to the top of the tree. He handed the string of lights to Jamie, who wound it around the other side of the tree. He secured these lights, too. "You know the Madisons, Fieros, and Kemplers are checking in tomorrow afternoon, right?"

"Yes," Jamie said.

As Gray handed her the light strand, he brushed her skin by accident. A small, electric thrill moved through his fingertips. It was gone as quickly as it happened, and he told himself it had been nothing more than static electricity.

He'd dated other women since Lonna died, but there'd been a flatness to the whole experience he'd found discouraging. He'd taken them to dinner, movies, walks through the shops in town. Although he could find nothing wrong with the women, he always felt as if he were just going through the motions of dating. Part of him wasn't quite there.

"Breakfast starts at six a.m.," Gray stated, careful not to let their hands touch when the strands came back to him.

"Don't worry," Jamie flashed a bright smile up at him. "I'm doing raisin scones with honey butter, scrambled eggs with chives, and Canadian bacon—kind of a run-through for when the guests arrive."

"Maybe you should be in the restaurant business instead of real estate."

Jamie laughed. "As long as we only serve breakfast." She fished another set of lights from the storage bin and handed him the end. "Besides, I love being in real estate. Even though it doesn't seem like it right now, I'm really pretty good at it."

He stepped off the chair and passed her the string of lights. "You been doing it long?"

"For thirteen years," Jamie said, hooking lights along the branches in the back of the tree. "I started as a receptionist and worked my way up."

He couldn't help but do some mental math. That put her somewhere between thirty-one and thirty-five. Looking at her smooth, clear skin and long, glossy hair, he would have guessed her age to be younger than that.

"I was ten when I started," Jamie said and then laughed. "I'm kidding. I was eighteen."

"That's pretty young." Thirteen years. He did more calculations. She'd had a job and a baby. He wondered how she'd managed both. When he'd been eighteen, he was a freshman at college, dating Lonna, and working on a business degree. His most consuming thought—besides Lonna, of course—had been how to go even faster on the downhill racecourse at Stowe.

"How about you?" Jamie retrieved the smaller, twinkler lights from the box and handed them to him. "When did you start running Pilgrim's Peak?"

"Oh, pretty much right after college." He reached the protruding branch. It already had been wrapped with the red globe lights. "You think we should add more lights to Pinocchio's nose?"

Jamie put her hands on her hips and regarded the tree. "Better not. It might start to droop." She looped the strands around the lower branches. "You didn't consider doing anything else? Not that running Pilgrim's Peak isn't a great job."

Gray hesitated. Running Pilgrim's Peak, in truth, hadn't been his life's ambition. "Oh, for a while I thought about a racing career. I had some sponsors lined up, but then it just worked out better for me to come back to Pilgrim's Peak." The lights were finished now, but he made no move to step away from the tree and neither did Jamie.

"What happened, Grayson?"

Her eyes were soft and gentle on him. She had a beautiful face, but it was not her beauty that made it hard for him to look away from her. He sensed something fragile about her, a brokenness that she worked hard to hide. He would not have recognized it if it were not something he had seen in his own mirror.

"I got married my senior year in college. And then we had Halle." He paused. "When you have a baby, it changes everything."

~

A baby changes everything. The words echoed in Jamie's mind. She was glad when Norman, Halle, and Ivy carried a tray of hot drinks into the room. She took a hot mug and walked to a solitary spot by a large, frost-framed window.

She looked at the falling snow but saw the parking lot of the Darien YMCA. It was a warm May night, and Devon had just finished working out. They were holding hands, and he was asking her if she wanted to get a burger at McDonald's. She looked up at his perfect face and knew she couldn't put it off any longer. "Devon," she said. "I have to tell you something." She took a breath. "We're going to have a baby."

She flinched as his fingers tightened painfully around hers.

"What did you say?"

She tried to smile and felt the muscles in her cheek quiver. "I'm pregnant."

He let go of her hands to rub his face firmly, as he always did when he was thinking hard. She dug her fingernails into her palms and prayed that when he opened his mouth he'd say something about them being in this together.

"Are you sure?"

Jamie nodded.

"I'm eighteen years old," Devon said, "and leaving for Ohio State in a couple of months. I don't want to be a father." He drew his hand through the thick, dark hair she'd admired so often. "How do I even know it's mine?" He'd looked at her so coldly she'd actually shivered. "This changes everything, Jamie."

And it had.

Chapter 9

The guests couldn't check in before four o'clock. This gave Jamie almost an entire free day. She decided to spend as much of it as possible with Ivy. By ten o'clock they were in line at the double chair lift. She was a little nervous. Grayson had promised to teach her how to get on and off the lift, but he hadn't had time. She didn't want to embarrass herself in front of Ivy.

When it was their turn, Jamie skied into position. Just like Ivy, she watched over her shoulder as the chair came nearer and nearer. The attendant steadied it, but somehow it knocked into the back of her legs anyway. Jamie sat down with a *whoosh*, and then the chair rapidly propelled them upward.

"Mom," Ivy said. "Are you okay?" She pulled the safety bar into place.

"Yeah," Jamie replied, watching the ground get farther and farther away. "So, tell me about school. How's algebra going?"

"Good."

"And your English class?"

"Language arts. Good."

"And history. It's world geography, right?"

"It's U.S. history, but, Mom, you don't have to pretend you're interested." Ivy studied the ground.

"But I *am* interested. Look, I know you're upset with me about the Aspen trip. Trust me, if I could have afforded to send you, I would have."

This earned her a snort of disbelief. "You bought a new jacket and skis. There was enough money for that."

Jamie sucked in the cold air. She glanced at Ivy. How could a kid change so much in the space of a few months? And yet was it such a big change—or had she simply been closing her eyes for a long time and thinking that Ivy's snarky remarks and disrespectful attitude were just part of teenage angst?

"The skis and boots are rented. The jacket is new, but honey, when you're a real estate agent, you're not just selling property—you're selling yourself. You have to look right if you want people to take you seriously. Appearances matter."

Ivy made a snort that definitely wasn't agreement.

Jamie expelled a long, frosty plume. "People judge you by how you look. You know I'm right."

Ivy lapsed into silence. It grew steadily colder as they climbed the mountain. A sign attached to a rocky part of the cliff read PREPARE TO UNLOAD. At this point Jamie thought she might be ready to jump right out of the chair. She hated that things between her and Ivy felt so broken. Didn't Ivy know that everything

Jamie did in her life was for her?

Ivy lifted up the safety bar. Jamie's stomach started a free fall at the sight of the open air below her. Beside her, Ivy wiggled forward on the seat, and the chair lowered as Jamie's skis bumped down onto the snowy platform.

Standing, Ivy used her free hand to push herself away from the moving chair. Too late, Jamie realized she should do the same. The chair swung around the corner with Jamie still sitting on it. "Stop," she yelled.

A teenage boy with a bad case of acne stuck his head out of a hut on the platform. "Um, you okay?" he said.

"Yes," Jamie replied. "Can you back this thing up?" She glimpsed Ivy high tailing it down the trail underneath the lift line.

"Sorry," the kid said. "You'll have to ride the chair lift back down the hill."

Jamie started to argue and realized it would be pointless. She pulled the bar back into place and tried to ignore all the perplexed looks from people whom she passed on their way *up* the mountain. Finally, about six minutes later, she reached the base of the mountain and began the trip back to the top.

This time the minute Jamie's skis touched the snowy platform, she gave herself a mighty shove off the seat. Unfortunately, it sent her to the far edge of the ice-coated ramp. She panicked and crossed her ski tips. She crashed and took several people down with her.

"Sorry," Jamie apologized, trying to crawl out of the pileup but hampered by her skis, which were tangled with another skier's. She got her legs under her as a boy on a snowboard slid down the ramp just inches from her nose.

"Stop the lift," a familiar voice ordered.

As Jamie struggled to her feet, another skier knocked into her from behind. She felt the breath rush out of her as she was propelled forward. She rammed straight into Grayson, who caught her just before she crumpled. "Nice running into you," he said.

Jamie extracted herself from his grasp. She tried to come up with a snappy retort, but the best she could do was say, "Oh, Grayson, is everybody okay?"

"Everybody's fine." He smiled, and Jamie felt her heartbeat pick up speed. There was just something irresistible about him—like a big piece of red velvet cake with gobs of rich vanilla frosting. She knew it wasn't good for her, but it was impossible to look at it without wanting it.

"I have to find Ivy," she said, firmly ordering her thoughts to more acceptable channels. "You haven't seen her, have you?" She pointed to the nearest trail. "I saw her going down that one."

Grayson frowned. "That's White Rabbit. I don't want you taking that trail. I've let some moguls form on it."

So that's what you called those lumpy things that from the chair lift made the trail look like the surface of the moon. She'd probably kill herself—or someone else—if she tried that trail. By now Ivy probably was waiting at the base lodge for Jamie anyway. She sighed. "What's with all the *Alice in Wonderland* names?"

Grayson chuckled. "It was my dad's idea. My mom's name was Alice, and he wanted to honor her by naming all the trails after characters in the Lewis Carroll novel."

"That's so sweet," Jamie said, genuinely touched. She could easily picture Norman being that kind of a romantic. "Well, then," she said. "If you'll just point me to an easier trail, I'll be on my way."

"I don't like the idea of you taking your first run down a novice trail by yourself."

"In our last lesson you said I was ready for novice trails," Jamie reminded him.

"Hey, Dad!" Halle called, skiing up to them. "We're tired of waiting. You coming? Oh hi, Miss King."

Gray addressed his daughter. "You all go ahead. I'm going to see Miss King safely down the mountain."

"I'm fine," Jamie tried to wave him off. "Don't worry about me."

"Halle, please tell the others to take a warm-up run on Alice's Alley and then meet at the double chair lift in twenty minutes."

"Gray, seriously. I don't need a babysitter."

"It's a safety issue."

"You help everyone down the mountain their first time?"

"When I see someone who needs it, yes."

Her chin came up a notch. "And you think I'm one of those people?"

"Most people don't have trouble getting off the chair lift."

He had a point, so Jamie stopped arguing. He brought her to a trail called the Queen of Hearts. It wasn't nearly as wide as the Looking Glass, and it was steeper. She could barely control her speed and once or twice came perilously close to skiing into the pines. However, as Gray coached her from behind, they progressed farther and farther down the trail.

At one point, the trail leveled slightly, and she was able to enjoy the scent of the peppermint air and the sensation of gliding through the silent pines. She thought of Gray skiing behind her. In her mind he was Gray now—not Grayson Westler, the owner of the ski hill. Grayson was much too formal a name for a guy like Gray. Gray ate muffins in two bites and had eyes that could either be dark as coffee or light as amber. Gray radiated some vibe that made it impossible for him to go anywhere on the hill without at least a dozen kids chasing after him.

He also had a past which she knew nothing about. He had a child but wore no wedding ring. Wouldn't it be ironic, Jamie wondered, if it turned out that he had a life story similar to hers?

Skkkkkkk. The ice hissed under her feet. Suddenly Jamie's skis swung around like windshield wipers. She was on the ground in an eyeblink. Her bindings released, and her skis chased her down the slope. Grayson was at her side in a flash. "You okay?" His brown eyes assessed the situation.

Jamie lumbered to her feet and brushed the snow off her parka. "Yeah. I lost concentration for a moment."

He handed over her ski poles and one of her skis. The other had slid a little farther down the hill. Jamie was about to go and retrieve it when a skier flashed past. Jamie recognized the black and neon blue ski suit.

"Hey!" Gray yelled at the skier's rapidly retreating back. "Slow down!" He shook his head. "Some of these kids," he muttered, "have no clue how dangerous it is to bomb the hill like that. If I see that girl again, I'm giving her a warning. And if she does it again, I'll pull her ticket."

Jamie laughed without humor. "That kid was my daughter."

Gray's eyebrows pushed together. "Your daughter skis like that?"

"When she's trying to avoid me," Jamie said dryly.

Immediately she wished the words back. It made Ivy look bad in his eyes. He was probably judging her daughter, which was totally unfair. He had no clue about Ivy—how hard it had been for Ivy to grow up with no family other than Jamie. What it felt like to be rejected before Ivy was old enough to know what the word meant.

"She's probably just letting off some steam," Jamie added quickly. "Miss Porter's is a tough academic school, and Ivy is a straight-A student."

"You've got to tell her to slow down. If she runs into somebody going that fast, she could seriously hurt them."

Jamie nodded. "If it helps, she knows what she's doing."

"She looks like she's had some good training," Gray admitted.

Jamie felt herself relax slightly. "She has. Gary Blanco—up at Killington." It had cost a cool fortune, but Ivy's best friend's family had a condo there and she'd been invited to go nearly every weekend. Jamie made sure Ivy had gotten the best lessons and skied on the best equipment possible.

"Why didn't you take any lessons?"

Jamie shrugged. "Weekends are busy when you're a Realtor." Besides, there hadn't been enough money. More than once she'd stretched a box of macaroni and cheese because she couldn't afford anything else. But he didn't have to know that.

She wanted him to see her North Face ski jacket, the half-karat studs in her ears, the side-swept bangs that were the perfect length and style. She didn't want him to see the caramel highlights in her hair that needed a touch-up or know that the skis and boots were rented. She didn't want him looking too deeply into her eyes either.

If you hid your flaws well enough, she'd learned, you could almost forget they existed at all.

Chapter 10

Gray got Jamie safely down the rest of the trail. She wouldn't promise to stay on Looking Glass, which he would have liked, but there wasn't much he could do about that. Besides, plenty of beginners skied the intermediate trails, he reminded himself. She'd be fine. Still, he felt uneasy and promised himself to keep an eye out for her.

The juniors were waiting for him, per his request, at the double chair lift. He noticed Ivy standing beside Halle.

Gray skied up to them. "You want to ski with us, Ivy? We're going to run some gates on Alice's Alley."

"Is it a black diamond trail?"

"It's an intermediate trail, but if you want to ski fast, you need to do it with us."

Ivy shrugged and looked bored. "I guess."

A short time later, they were standing at the top of Alice's Alley. "Okay," Gray began. "We need to get ready for the first club race, which is only two weeks away. I've set a slalom course. You've skied one before, haven't you, Ivy?"

"It doesn't matter if you haven't," Ella said. "Most of us aren't very good." She shot Halle an apologetic glance. "Except for Halle."

"You're all good skiers," Gray said.

"Last year we came in dead last out of five teams." Whitney giggled as if this were funny.

"I had a bad knee, man," Derrick said.

"This year will be different," Gray promised. The skepticism remained on their faces. Gray couldn't really blame them. The other ski clubs had the benefit of starting their training earlier and having longer courses to practice on. They had larger pools of talent to pick from as well. "Okay. Keep the green gates on your left and the red gates on your right. Who wants to go first?"

Ivy raised her hand. Gray skied the course first. When he reached the finish line, he waved his hand to indicate he was ready. Ivy swung herself forward, and he clicked the stopwatch.

He'd known she was fast, but he wanted to see if she could turn. From the moment he saw her swing through the first gate he knew she was good. So good, in fact, he almost forgot to click the stopwatch when she sped past him.

Ivy's time, it turned out, was a half second better than Halle's. He was still thinking about it at the end of the afternoon when he walked into the ski shop. A half second was a lot of time. Ivy was on better ski equipment than Halle. A new pair of racing Rossignols would make a great Christmas present for Halle. Until then, he'd try changing the kind of wax on the bottom of Halle's skis. His dad might have some thoughts on that.

His dad was bent over the worktable, sharpening the edges of a pair of rental skis when he walked into the room. To his surprise, he saw Jamie working at the counter. She was laughing with a customer who was returning a pair of ski boots.

He walked over to her. "What are you doing?"

"I was taking a break from skiing and saw that Norman could use a little help." She began wiping down the countertops with a bottle of window cleaner. "I saw Ivy come down the hill with Halle. Thanks for including her."

"You shouldn't be behind the counter," Gray said. "It's for employees only."

"Oh, don't be stodgy," Norman said. "She's doing a fine job. Tell us about Ivy. She gonna join the junior ski team? You could use her, Gray. Last year we took a lot of ribbing for coming in last place."

Gray shrugged. "Ivy is welcome to join our team or just ski with us."

Jamie smiled. "I'm sure she'll be excited to be on the team." Her brows drew together. "But you'd better be the one to ask her, not me."

He nodded. "We ran some gates, and she had the fastest time." Gray found himself staring at the bare spot on the fourth finger of Jamie's left hand. He thought about his gold wedding band, carefully packed away in a box in the top drawer of his dresser, and wondered if she had a similar ring packed away. If she'd ever held it up to the light and looked through the opening at a future that no longer existed.

"Glad all those lessons paid off," Jamie said.

"It's more than lessons," Gray admitted. "It's God-given talent."

A mother and two sons walked to the counter to return their rental equipment. Out of curiosity he watched Jamie interact with them. She smiled a lot. And her brown hair was long, very straight, and shiny.

"And don't forget, if you're here, to join us for the Christmas Eve Torchlight Parade," Jamie told the family. "Every year on Christmas Eve Pilgrim's Peak offers free lift service to the top of the mountain. There's a brief nondenominational service at the trailhead, then everyone turns on their flashlight and skis to the bottom of the hill. Afterward, there's hot chocolate and doughnuts in the lodge."

The family asked to sign up. Gray turned to his dad. "How does she know about the Torchlight Parade?"

"I told her, sonny boy," his father replied happily. "She's been signing people up like crazy. I think we're getting more teenage boys than we've ever had. They take one look at her and get a glazed look in their eyes—sort of like the one you just had on your face."

"I did not," Gray stated firmly, but his dad only laughed.

～

Jamie and Ivy drove old Sally the short distance back to the B&B. "So," Jamie began as the car bounced slowly down the rutted driveway. "Did you have fun today? I heard you were the star of the Pilgrim's Peak junior ski team."

Ivy was busy texting. When she finished, she looked up and said, "What?"

Jamie repeated her comment.

"Oh." Ivy studied the keypad on her phone. "That isn't saying much."

"Well, did you have fun?"

"It was okay." Ivy's phone buzzed, signaling the arrival of a text message. This time Jamie waited until after Ivy had sent the message to speak.

"I'm sorry we didn't get to ski together," Jamie added, hoping Ivy would apologize for ditching her, but not being entirely surprised when her daughter's only response was the irritating clicking noise of her phone as she texted.

"How long are you going to do this, Ivy? Be angry at me?" Jamie turned onto the main road and then immediately put on her turn signal. "Because, frankly, it's getting a little boring."

Ivy sat in stony silence.

Jamie's gloved hands tightened on the wheel. "Say something. Argue with me. Agree with me. Just don't sit there like a bump on a log." Too late, Jamie recognized the phrase as one her mother had often used.

"Okay. What do you want me to say?"

"Who are you talking to? What are you saying?" Jamie tried not to sound as desperate as she felt.

"I'm talking to Quinn in Aspen."

"What's she saying?"

Silence.

Jamie pulled old Sally into a spot in front of the big Victorian. As the engine began its death throes, she studied the dark curtain of her daughter's hair. It was a few shades darker than her own, much closer to Devon's color. Ivy had his square jaw, too. Not that Ivy knew either of these things. Devon had been very clear that he wanted no part of Ivy's life, and Jamie didn't want to say or do anything that might encourage Ivy to seek him out.

Ivy concentrated fiercely on texting a message—likely something about her loser mom. Jamie wanted to reach across the bench seat, grab the cell phone, and throw it out the window. She imagined herself hugging her daughter until something in Ivy broke and she hugged Jamie back.

Jamie tapped the wheel instead and wondered how Gray would have handled this situation. Impossible to know. Halle was so sweet. Jamie couldn't imagine the curly haired brunette giving Gray a hard time about anything. If Halle had been in Ivy's position, she would have pitched in and helped with Jamie's chores. Why didn't Ivy?

Maybe because Jamie wasn't a very good parent. Her stomach clenched as she considered the possibility. She thought of the sacrifices she'd made and shook her head. No. It was a teenage thing, something that Ivy would outgrow. Her grip on the steering wheel eased.

Maybe if she pretended not to notice Ivy's sullenness, she wouldn't be reinforcing the behavior, and it would simply go away. She checked her hair in the rearview mirror and freshened her lipstick. Guests were due soon, and she wanted to make a good impression. "You ready to go inside?" She didn't expect a response, and she didn't get one.

Chapter 11

D ad," Halle said as she and Gray walked into the kitchen the next morning. "There's only fifteen hours left on the auction, and the bidding is still at a hundred dollars. The french horn is worth triple that."

Jamie was at the kitchen sink and up to her elbows in sudsy water as Gray and Halle walked into the room with their breakfast dishes. She was scrubbing an omelet pan and trying to remember if Aunt Bea had used vanilla or almond extract in the white chocolate drizzle she planned to use to top the raspberry scones the next morning.

"Hey, Jamie," Gray said. "Excellent breakfast."

She flashed him a grin. "Thanks."

"Dad," Halle said. "You want me to place a bid for you?"

"Halle," Gray said patiently. "How do you know the instrument is really as good as it seems? Buying something off the Internet sounds risky."

"Ella asked her brother to ask the band director to look at it. Dr. D said he knew the company selling it, and it's a good one."

Gray set his dish on the counter. "Wouldn't you rather have new skis?" Jamie smiled at the hopeful note in his voice. "There's a new generation of racing Rossignols that's just coming out."

"My old ones are just fine," Halle said. Jamie heard the firm but polite note in the girl's voice. She'd make a great real estate agent—relentless but polite. "Dad, I won't give up skiing, but I really want to do band. Ella's brother is going on a really cool trip to New York City."

"Taking cool trips is not a reason for wanting to join the band." Gray gave Jamie a look that said, *Help me.* Reaching for a dish towel, he began drying the omelet pan. "If you're on the ski team, you'll go to lots of really cool places. When your mother was in high school, she was the Eastern High School girls' giant slalom champion." He paused. "You're just as good, if not better, than she was."

Jamie accidentally shot herself with water from the sink hose at the mention of Halle's mother.

"I know, Dad," Halle said. A note of resignation crept into her voice. "It's just that band sounds like fun."

Jamie handed another soaking-wet dish to Gray. "Band does sound fun," she said. "The kids in band at my high school always looked like they were having a great time." She ignored the look of warning in Gray's eyes. "They rehearsed like crazy. Nobody worked harder than they did, but you could tell they all knew and liked each other."

"That's what I heard." Halle flashed a grateful smile at Jamie. "Were you, like, in the color guard or something?"

"A cheerleader," Jamie admitted.

Gray set the skillet in a drawer. "I'm sure band is a lot of fun, but, Halle, I want you to think about what you're giving up, really think about it, and pray about it before you make up your mind. Now, if you want a ride to the hill with me, you'd better go and get ready. I've got a nine o'clock lesson."

After Halle was out of earshot, Jamie turned off the faucet and wiped her hands on a dish towel. She felt like the last person on earth who should be giving parental advice, but something inside prompted her to speak. "You really want her to ski, don't you?"

"She's good." Gray refilled his coffee cup and leaned against the counter. "I don't think she understands just how good she is or what it could mean to her future."

Jamie nodded. "Maybe she'd be great in band, too."

"Unfortunately, tone deafness runs in the family. Things might not work out the way Halle thinks they will."

Jamie picked up a rag and began to wipe down the counter. "Things usually don't work out the way you think they will." Case in point: Look where she'd ended up.

"I know," Gray replied. "But I have the perspective of being a lot older. I'd hate to see her throw her talent away."

Jamie thought of the countless times she thought she'd known what was best for Ivy. She was beginning to understand, though, that enforcing her parental authority had come at a price. "I still think I'd go for the french horn. You can always invest in earplugs."

"I'd rather invest in my daughter," Gray replied. Picking his car keys off a rack, he walked stiffly out of the room.

Ivy skipped breakfast and left for the ski hill with Gray and Halle. Norman was nowhere to be found, and by nine thirty the guests had also cleared out. This left Jamie with an empty house and a head full of thoughts she wasn't sure she wanted to have.

She wandered about the downstairs, cleaning up and pausing to examine pictures or knickknacks as if she were an archeologist trying to piece together an ancient civilization by the artifacts left behind. She found a wedding photo and several photographs of a dark-haired woman with wide-set eyes and a generous smile. Gray's wife—the ski champion.

She'd also been a mother, probably only a few years older than Jamie had been. She wondered if having a baby had been exciting for her or if she'd been as scared as Jamie.

She smiled, remembering the hours she'd spent rehearsing the kind of mother she'd be. In the afternoons, while Aunt Bea slept, she'd go into the kitchen and bake some type of sweet bread to tempt the old woman's appetite.

"This is how you knead dough," she explained to her unborn baby, all the while imagining a daughter or son working beside her, laughing at the sticky dough, and getting flour everywhere.

Of course, it hadn't happened the way she'd thought. She'd been naive enough to imagine she would actually have time to bake with her child. Day care was a concept they hadn't taught in high school. Then again, even if they had, nothing could have prepared her for the physical wrench that had torn through her the first day—and every day after that—when she'd left Ivy at Small Blessings.

After she checked in with her office—no messages, no new listings, no surprise there—Jamie headed for the ski hill. She rode to the top of the mountain in the double chair lift next to a middle-aged man in a bulky blue snowsuit.

"So how's your day going?" Jamie gave him a friendly smile.

The man pulled the safety bar down, and the chair began to climb the hill. "Great. My kids are having a great time." He glanced sideways at her and looked quickly away, not returning the smile she gave him. "My wife is enjoying a day without kids. She homeschools them—all four of them."

"Oh," Jamie said. "That's got to be a lot of hard work."

The man seemed more than happy to discuss in detail just how much work homeschooling entailed. He seemed to insert "my wife" or "my wife and I" into every sentence and addressed the air straight in front of him. Jamie, at first, was amused. The guy must have mistaken her politeness for something more. But then it occurred to her that he might be picking up a vibe from her—some fragment of availability or, heaven forbid, particles of loneliness that clung to her like a dusting of snow.

She couldn't wait to dismount from the lift, and purposely headed in the opposite direction when they skied off. She followed a group of snowboarders who were headed for the Queen of Hearts. It was a good distance from the lift, and the snowboarders were soon out of sight. Jamie gamely continued poling across the top of the mountain. Soon Jamie started to sweat. She paused to catch her breath.

There wasn't another skier in sight, and the only noise was the huffing of her breath. Surrounded by pines and snow, Jamie thought the world looked pristine and perfect. She exhaled frosty plumes and watched them disappear. It was so still here. So peaceful. So *unspoiled*. She leaned her weight on her ski poles and felt the rapid *thump-thump-thump* of her heart.

I've been living above my means, she admitted. *I'm alienated from my family, and now even my daughter isn't talking to me.* She closed her eyes. *I can't do this anymore. I am so tired of worrying about things and trying to do everything by myself.*

She lifted her face to the vast gray sky. *I don't know what to do.*

A deep, cold wind sliced across the mountaintop. She heard the trees groan, then the world became still once more.

Something stirred deep in Jamie's heart. She looked around the woods. *Just who,* she thought, *am I talking to?*

Chapter 12

Jamie was standing on a chair helping Norman string lights around the windows in the lodge when Gray came in from teaching. Norman handed Gray the staple gun. "Help me out, Gray. Staple the cord while I go to the storage room and get the garlands."

He scurried off, leaving Jamie alone with Gray and the uncomfortable echoes of the discussion they'd had earlier that morning. She stretched the light cord higher on the wall and reached with her free hand for the staple gun.

"Let me do it," Gray said.

"I'm fine," Jamie said.

"I know," Gray said. "But I can reach more easily."

Jamie could feel the blood running out of her arm and her fingers turning weak from lack of circulation. "That might be true, but my line will be straighter than yours."

"How do you know?"

"Because I see your old staple holes. They're all over the place." She could fix them with a little putty and a can of paint.

"How do you know they're my holes?" Gray argued.

"Because Norman told me," Jamie said, smiling, although he couldn't see it. "He also told me about the time you stapled his sleeve to the wall."

"He moved his arm at the last minute."

"Which he said was a good thing."

She and Gray laughed, and it seemed to ease some of the tension between them. He was right about one thing, though. She needed his help to reach the top of the window. Reluctantly, she stepped off the chair and passed the staple gun to Gray. "Be careful," she warned. "I don't want to have to explain anything to Norman."

He got to work. She studied the powerful set of his shoulders and the sunlight glinting in his thick brown hair. The cut was a little shaggy, and his brown ski sweater had a small tear on the side seam. He'd never be the kind of guy who'd be comfortable with a sleek, short haircut or a button-down shirt of Egyptian cotton, but there was a solidness about him that Jamie found extremely appealing. Not that she was going to let herself get involved. Jamie King stood on her own two feet. Maybe she wasn't the Lone Ranger, but she wasn't dependent upon anyone either.

"Look," she said matter-of-factly. "About this morning, I'm sorry." She swallowed and pushed forward. "I'm the last person who should be giving you parental advice. You should give Halle the skis if you think that's best." She untangled another length of cord as Gray reached higher around the window.

He stapled another length into place. "Don't worry about it."

She could leave it at that, but something in her needed to explain. "I wouldn't have opened my mouth, but I started remembering what it was like when I was Halle's age." She focused her gaze out the window at the white mountain filling almost all the space her eye could see. "My parents had some pretty big expectations for me. I never felt like I could live up to them."

"I'm sure your parents only set high standards because they saw something good in you."

Jamie's lips twisted. If he only knew the irony of that statement. "Maybe," she agreed. "But it was hard, Gray. Always pushing myself, trying to be what they wanted. I wasn't nearly as academic as they would have liked, and if it hadn't been for a lot of private tumbling lessons and a very strict diet, I never would have made varsity cheerleader."

"Why didn't you just tell your parents you felt they were pushing you too hard?"

Jamie shrugged. "It was complicated. But the more I achieved, it seemed the higher I flew and the farther I'd have to fall."

He climbed off the chair and looked at her for a very long time. "I'm sorry that happened to you," he said. "But it's a different story with Halle."

"I know," Jamie said. "I've seen the two of you together. You've got a great relationship." She glanced over as Norman returned with a box overflowing with garlands. "Hey, Gray, here comes your dad." She felt exposed, as if she'd said too much about herself and was eager to lighten the moment. "Give me your arm. Let's pretend I stapled your sleeve to the wall."

∽

The next several days passed in a blur of activity. Before she knew it, it was Christmas Eve, and Jamie was helping Norman arrange the picnic tables in the après ski room. Although Jamie was looking forward to the Torchlight Parade, she was dreading Christmas Day. Always in the past she'd managed to give Ivy really great presents—a shopping trip to Manhattan or a makeover for Ivy's bedroom. One year she'd even leased her a Thoroughbred horse.

This year would be very different.

"A little more to the right," Norman instructed. "We still need to fit about two more tables under the windows for the buffet."

The picnic table scraped the floor as Jamie shoved it into place. Straightening, she rubbed the small of her back. Gray had wanted to help them, but the J-bar had broken down and he'd had to fix it. "Hold on, Norman," she said as he single-handedly tried to move another table. As she moved to help him, a burly guy in ski bibs and a red thermal shirt stepped in to help.

Jamie took Norman's arm and pulled him away. "Why don't you sit down for a moment?"

"Don't fuss," Norman said, but allowed her to lead him to a picnic bench.

"I'm not fussing," Jamie said. "I'm taking a break. With you."

"When I was in the army," Norman stated, mopping his brow with a hand-kerchief, "we did a lot tougher things. Like drive tanks."

"You get to sit down when you drive a tank," Jamie pointed out. "You want something to drink?"

Norman mopped his face and then stuck the crumbled handkerchief into the pocket of his jeans. "What time is it, Jamie?"

"Getting close to five o'clock."

Norman groaned. "People are coming in two hours. We still have to put out the tablecloths, hot water, cocoa packets, cups, napkins, doughnuts. I have to set up Santa's chair—it always goes right next to the Christmas tree in the corner—and Santa's bag is back at the house and isn't even ready. The torches haven't been checked. How did we get so late this year?"

Jamie studied the deep lines etched across Norman's freckled face. His brown eyes were full of worry. "Let me drive you back to the house," she offered. "You can get Santa's bag ready, and I'll take care of the rest."

He shook his head. "There's too much that still needs to be done."

"Don't worry," Jamie said, smiling. "I'll get it done. I know a lot about running open houses, remember?"

An hour and a half later, Jamie put her hands on her hips and admired the room. The picnic tables looked cheerful with their bright red tablecloths and centerpieces of fresh pine boughs and silver balls. She'd moved around some of the ornaments on the Christmas tree so people could see them better. Turning on the tree lights, she admired the shimmering pine, which was as perfect as she could make it.

All she needed was a chair for Santa. She dragged Gray's rolling office chair into place beside the tree and threw a red blanket with white fur trim over the seat. Giving one last look at the fire blazing in the stone fireplace and the lights blinking on the Christmas tree, she hurried to the lady's changing room to put on her ski clothes.

Norman hadn't returned from the house, and she didn't see him as she joined the crowd gathering just outside the lodge. She saw Gray passing out flashlights. He had a fur-trimmed Santa's hat anchored on his head with his ski goggles.

"Nice hat, Gray," she called.

"Thanks. Where's yours?" He grinned across the space between them.

Jamie touched her white headband. "Right here."

"I don't think Santa's helpers wear headbands," Gray admonished her.

"I don't think they wear ski parkas or goggles either," Jamie replied.

He laughed and then waved with his hands to get the crowd's attention. Cupping his hands together, he shouted over the roar of voices. "Time to head for the lifts."

A cheer went up, and a massive traffic jam formed as everyone skied over to the double chair lift. Jamie glimpsed Halle getting onto the lift with Gray and the two of them swinging up into the dark, frosty night. She glimpsed Ivy standing in line with Ella. Obviously Ivy didn't want to ride the lift with Jamie.

She ended up seated with a man who kept leaning over the back of the chair to talk to his wife and daughter who were riding in the chair behind theirs. She didn't try to engage him. Instead she thought about the upcoming service at the top of the mountain. She hadn't been to church in fourteen years. Hadn't thought she belonged. Her thoughts drifted far past the dark borders of the pines.

"Are you gaining weight, honey?" Jamie's mother commented as Jamie walked over to the glossy black Lincoln Continental. It was Sunday morning, and they were getting ready to go to church. "Bill? You think she should change into a different dress?"

Jamie ducked into the backseat before the critical gaze of her father turned to her. She'd been hiding the weight gain and the morning sickness for weeks now, praying for her parents to notice something was wrong and terrified at what would happen when they did.

"We're late," Jamie's father replied, getting into the driver's seat. "She's fine."

"You didn't look," Jamie's mother complained. "She's about to pop out of that dress."

Jamie wrapped her thin cardigan more tightly around herself. The July morning was hot, but the sweater was one of the few items she owned that didn't strain against the new curves of her body. She looked out the car window and wondered how much longer she could disguise herself. Her mother wanted to take her clothes shopping, and her friends wanted to know why she wouldn't go to the pool with them. She was so tired of making up excuses, of the fear inside that seemed to grow as steadily as the baby inside her.

"You need to put yourself on a diet," Jamie's mother said firmly. "You don't want people looking at you and wondering why such a pretty girl would let herself go like that."

Jamie shut her eyes and tried to squeeze back the tears that came so easily now. She'd been praying for answers but felt more alone than she'd ever been in her life. Devon, since that awful night in the YMCA parking lot, hadn't returned any of her calls. She hadn't told a single one of her friends either, and the burden of her secret felt increasingly like a weight she couldn't carry. Her mother was going on and on about the evils of carbohydrates and the importance of disciplined eating habits as they turned into the church's driveway.

As they passed three huge wooden crosses, Jamie looked at the center one and thought about Jesus, about how brave He'd been to be crucified for the sins of the world. She should be brave, too. Before she lost her nerve, she blurted out, "I'm not getting fat. I'm pregnant."

There was a moment of silence, then Jamie's mother turned around and looked at her. The gaze seemed to burn straight through the white cardigan and sundress. "Bill, turn the car around. Church is the last place we need to be right now." She smiled, but it scared Jamie more than reassured her. "Who else knows, Jamie?"

Jamie mumbled Devon's name. It wasn't as if they wouldn't guess. After all, he'd been her only boyfriend. She tried to read her mother's face in the silence that followed. She expected disappointment, shock, even anger. Her mother's calmness caught her off guard, and she felt hopeful that it wasn't going to be as bad as she'd feared.

Jamie gripped the cold safety bar more tightly as the lift chair traveled through the night. It hadn't been as bad as she'd feared. The weeks following her disclosure had been far worse.

The mountain felt about ten degrees colder at the top. Jamie tucked her chin into the warmth of her jacket and followed the crowd to the top of Alice's Alley. Over the top of heads she glimpsed Ivy, who was standing by herself at the edge of the trail. Pushing through the throng of people, Jamie shuffled over to her. "Hey," she said. "Look at the stars."

"Yeah," Ivy agreed. "This is so cool, Mom."

Jamie savored the fragile connection between them. "The night you were born was like this. Aunt Bea looked out the window and said every star was shining."

"She was weak from the chemotherapy," Ivy said, picking up the story. "But that night she was strong."

"Strong enough to drive me to the hospital and strong enough to hold my hand while you were being born. She was the first one to hold you, Ivy, besides the nurse and doctor. She loved you. I wish she could have known you."

"May I have your attention please," Gray's voice boomed through a megaphone. "In a few minutes, Reverend Thomas Blaymires is going to say a few words, then we're going to ski single file down the mountain." He gave them some safety pointers and promised to be at the end of the line if anyone needed help. He passed the megaphone to the reverend.

"Good evening," Reverend Blaymires began. "I'm honored to be with you on this Christmas Eve." He had a Bible in his hands. "From the book of Luke." He paused. " 'And there were shepherds living out in the fields nearby, keeping watch over their flocks at night. An angel of the Lord appeared to them. . . .' "

The stars seemed to hang right over her head, and the night air was as pure and cold as chilled water. Tears swelled in Jamie's eyes and turned to icy streaks on her cold cheeks. She wiped them away quickly before Ivy could see and ask why Jamie was crying. She bit her lip hard and willed away the grief that rose and swirled and clogged her throat. She was suddenly so cold and so raw inside, as if the reverend's words were a wind that sliced through her, reminding her painfully that she had been raised in a family that went to church, that heard the words from Luke every Christmas Eve, but that family was lost to her. Even the comfort she might have gotten from God was lost to her. One by circumstance, the other by choice.

She looked at Ivy. Her beautiful, shining girl. Even in the poor lighting cast by the trail lights hanging in the trees, Jamie could see the radiance in her daughter's face as she listened to the reverend's words. *How can I look at her and have regrets? Everything that's happened to me is worth it,* Jamie assured herself. *Everything?* a small voice inside asked. *Everything,* Jamie agreed firmly.

~

The reverend ended his reading. "Merry Christmas," he said. "May the love of God shine through you onto others. Amen." He turned on his flashlight, and everyone else did the same. The sudden light was blinding after standing in the darkness.

The first skier began to descend the mountain, followed by another, then another. Soon a string of lights was snaking its way down the hill. Flanked by the trail lights, their flashlights burned as bright as fire in the darkness.

Finally, it was Ivy's turn, then Jamie's. She clutched the flashlight in her left hand and held it up like a torch. It felt a little awkward to ski without her poles, but it also made her feel lighter and freer and strangely exhilarated, as if very little gravity held her onto the mountain, and if she wanted to, she could fly through the darkness and into the stars shining so brightly over the valley below.

The party was already under way by the time Jamie put away her skis and joined the others in the après ski room. There had to be at least two hundred people laughing and talking. Someone had brought out a karaoke machine, and above the roar of voices, a gray-haired woman with a very shaky soprano was belting out an enthusiastic "O Come All Ye Faithful."

Jamie poured herself a cup of hot chocolate and added a generous helping of marshmallows. She was thinking about going for a doughnut when a deep voice said, "You look very familiar to me. Have we met?"

She turned. A large, heavyset man with silver hair and ruddy cheeks was looking down at her. "Gus Peters?" She felt the skin on the back of her neck prickle with excitement. She held out her hand. "I'm Jamie King. We met at the Connecticut Home Seekers banquet last spring. I loved your keynote address."

His eyes lit up with recollection. "Of course. I never forget a beautiful face. Now tell me. What are you doing here? Business or pleasure?"

"A little of both. I'm vacationing with my daughter—she's on break from Miss Porter's." She sipped her hot chocolate as her mind whirled. "How about you?"

"I'm visiting the grandkids. They love the Torchlight Parade." His cell phone rang. "Excuse me, but I've got to take this call." He slipped off into the crowd.

Jamie watched his back until it disappeared. She had a top-notch land developer and Gray in the same room. If she could get them together, there was a chance she could turn the conversation to the topic of real estate. More specifically, the future of Pilgrim's Peak. Something inside told her Christmas Eve was not the right time to discuss this, but she decided to hunt down Gray.

She found him deep in conversation with a small group. Before she could get his attention, however, a gravelly voice called out, "Ho! Ho! Ho!" and Santa walked into the room. A golden retriever, wearing antlers and carrying a red tennis ball in its mouth, walked at his side. At least a dozen kids rushed forward crying, "Santa! Santa!"

"Ho! Ho! Ho!" Norman boomed, bending to hug the kids who nearly knocked him over as they swarmed him.

"Let Santa get to his chair," Gray said. "Then I think there's a small present for each of you." He lifted the red velvet bag from Norman's shoulder.

Norman—who had at least three pillows stuffed beneath his Santa suit—clumped over to the chair by the tree. When he sat, there was a great whooshing noise and a few down feathers flew out from beneath his coat. "Santa's molting," he said in a stage whisper.

Boomer ducked out of his antlers and trotted off to Halle, who was standing in line for a turn at the karaoke machine. A couple of the smaller kids ran after Boomer. Boomer dropped his ball and began happily licking the small faces around him.

"Oh no," Gray muttered and then called out, "Don't throw..."

The ball sailed out of the little boy's hands. Boomer took off like a shot, cutting a swath through the crowded room. People cried out as the dog ran between their legs, or knocked into their knees, or narrowly avoided bowling them over. The golden almost reached the tennis ball, but then someone kicked it. The ball rolled under the tree, and Boomer dove in after it. Jamie heard the ornaments jingle.

"Get away from the tree," Gray yelled, motioning with his arm.

Boomer emerged from beneath the limbs, tail wagging and tennis ball firmly in his jaws. He trotted safely away as the tree began to topple.

"Timber!" Norman shouted, moving away faster than Jamie had ever seen him move.

The tree fell to the side, landing squarely on the picnic table, squashing several boxes of doughnuts and toppling a plastic punch bowl. A river of ginger ale and grape juice gushed across the floor, carrying with it a variety of sprinkled, cream, and glazed doughnuts.

Everyone seemed to freeze in place. Even the karaoke singer paused as everyone stared at the Christmas tree on top of the refreshments table. Jamie looked at Gray. She thought about how upset her parents would have been if something like this had happened at one of their parties. Gray, however, began to laugh.

"You know what they say," Norman announced cheerfully. "It's not a Christmas party until the tree falls over."

Somebody started to applaud, and then everybody was talking at once, straightening the fallen tree and cleaning up the spilled punch. Jamie had just finished mopping the floor when Gray walked over to her. "You need any help?"

"Nope, almost finished." She straightened and pushed her bangs behind her ear. Out of the corner of her eye, she spotted Boomer. The dog had his head in a plastic garbage bag, which was slumped on the floor. She watched Boomer's head emerge with a squashed doughnut in his jaws. "Boomer digests doughnuts, right?"

Jamie met Gray's gaze, and they both laughed. "Can we open a window?" she asked. "I think Boomer is preparing to boom."

Chapter 13

It was snowing lightly on Christmas morning. Jamie let Boomer outside. The sun hadn't risen yet, but the porch lights illuminated a white veil of snow against a black velvet background. She hugged herself and smiled. A white Christmas in an old Victorian house surrounded by mountains and woods. It might not be Aspen, but it was lovely. No matter what Ivy said, some small part of her had to be glad she was here with Jamie.

She made coffee and was just putting a pan of sticky buns—Ivy's favorite—in the oven when Gray, Norman, and Halle walked into the kitchen. Halle was still in her pajamas and wearing a fluffy pink bathrobe. With her rumpled, thick hair and huge brown eyes, she looked more like a little kid than a teenager. "Merry Christmas, Halle," Jamie said and gave the girl a hug.

"One for me," Norman quipped. When Jamie gave him a squeeze, he kissed her cheek. "Merry Christmas, sweetheart," he said.

It seemed awkward to ignore Gray, so she hugged him lightly, too. "Merry Christmas, Gray."

His flannel shirt felt incredibly soft against her cheek in contrast to his chest, which was rock hard. Although she wanted to be impervious to the clean man scent that clung to him, she wasn't. When she let go of him, she hurried to the oven and pretended to be absorbed in adjusting the temperature.

"Can I open my stocking now?" Halle asked.

"Sure," Gray replied. He started to head for the family room, but stopped. "Come with us, Jamie."

She waved them off. "Oh, you guys go on. I've got a little more to do here."

"It's Christmas," Norman stated kindly. "We don't want you working all day in the kitchen."

"I know, but I still have some work to do on the buffet." Jamie wiped her hands on her apron. Probably the Westlers would rather open their gifts in private. Besides, Ivy was still sleeping, and it wouldn't be right to start Christmas without her.

"The buffet is perfect," Gray said.

"But the sticky buns. . ."

"Still need time to cook. Come on," Gray urged.

Jamie laughed as Gray took one of her hands and Halle the other and literally pulled her toward the family room. The tree with its funny branchlike nose was lit, and there were two stockings hanging from the mantel—one for Halle and the other for Boomer. Jamie's gaze settled on the Nativity scene on the top of the wooden mantel. Last night the manger had been empty, but this morning there was a tiny baby inside the straw.

"You okay?" Gray asked.

She smiled automatically, but something must have showed on her face because Norman patted her arm gently. "I know just how you feel. Every Christmas morning I feel like the luckiest man on the earth."

"Here's your bone, Boomer," Halle extracted a large knucklebone from the dog's stocking. Boomer politely wagged his tail and took it from the girl's hands.

As Jamie watched Halle lift her stocking, she realized she wanted Ivy to be there, too. She didn't have a lot of presents for her daughter, but she had filled a stocking with Ivy's favorite candy—Sour Patch Kids—and inexpensive beauty products she'd bought at the grocery store. She excused herself and hurried up the steps. "Ivy." She gently shook the girl's shoulder, which felt as thin as a fin under the blanket. "Wake up, honey. Merry Christmas."

Ivy turned and blinked sleepily at her. "What time is it?"

"Almost seven."

Ivy groaned and tried to pull the covers over her head.

"Halle, Norman, and Gray are starting to open presents. I thought you might like to be part of it."

The lump under the covers made another unintelligible sound.

"Come on, honey. You don't want to miss anything." She tugged at the covers, and when Ivy resisted her attempts, she increased her efforts until it was a tug-of-war match. Then, with a final wrench, Jamie pulled them free. Ivy lay on her back, glaring at her.

"It's snowing," Jamie said brightly to cover her dismay at Ivy's expression. "You should see how pretty it looks!"

"I'd rather sleep," Ivy said and snatched the blanket over her head.

Jamie's stomach tightened with the knowledge that Ivy wasn't excited about Christmas—or was it just that she wasn't excited about spending it with Jamie? Or was Ivy just a typical teenager who wanted to sleep? Jamie wasn't sure of anything anymore.

"I made sticky buns—your favorite. But I can't guarantee there'll be any left if you wait much longer." She moved to the door. "They're warm and gooey, with raisins and cinnamon and cream cheese frosting. . . ."

The figure groaned, but the covers moved. Jamie decided to take this as a good sign.

∾

Gray blinked as his dad fired off a shot with the camera. His father never asked anyone to pose and had an uncanny ability to sneak up and take the most unflattering picture of a person's life. His father never seemed to mind that he chopped off people's heads or caught them with their mouths hanging open.

"Grandpa!" Halle complained as his father pointed the camera at her. "I haven't done my hair yet."

"You don't need to. It's supposed to be a candid."

Gray looked up as Jamie came into the room. She had a tight look about the mouth, which his father immediately immortalized with the camera. She'd probably want to burn that picture. Gray gave her a sympathetic smile. "Is Ivy coming down?"

"I think so, but don't wait. It could be awhile."

Halle dove into her stocking. It contained the same things it did every year—a bottle of vitamins, wool socks, a giant chocolate bar, a stuffed animal, a book of Life Savers, and an orange at the toe. This year Gray had added a sterling silver ring that had belonged to Lonna. He watched Halle's eyes grow wide as she pulled it out of the box and held it to the light.

"It was your mother's," he said, although he was pretty sure she realized this. "I thought your finger might be big enough to wear it now."

She slipped it on the fourth finger of her right hand and held it up for him to admire. "Looks good," Gray said.

Halle held her hand out to Jamie. "It's beautiful, honey," Jamie said. "There's something small under the tree from me that might go with that."

Halle spotted Jamie's box immediately. She ripped the wrapping paper off and held up a sterling silver bracelet. "Oh my gosh," she cried. "It's beautiful. Thank you, Miss Jamie."

Gray almost corrected Halle, but stopped himself. He hadn't thought of Jamie as "Miss King" in days. If Halle wanted to call her "Miss Jamie," he didn't see the harm of it.

"You're welcome, honey." Jamie stood to hug her. Just as she put her arms around Halle, Ivy walked into the room.

"Merry Christmas, Ivy," Gray said, rising with the thought of giving her a hug, but then stopped at the look of hurt on Ivy's face. "We're just getting started."

"Merry Christmas, honey," Jamie stepped away from Halle. Her hands fluttered. "You want something to drink?"

"Coffee," Ivy said. "Black."

Jamie's lips twisted. "How about hot chocolate?"

"My friends and I walk to a coffee shop in Farmington all the time."

"I'll make her a cup." Gray winked at Jamie, hoping she would trust him. "It's a flavored coffee—decaf. You'll like it, Ivy."

When he came back into the room, Ivy was holding a jewelry box in her hand and wearing an unhappy expression. "What'd you get, Ivy?"

"Earrings," she said. "Just like my mom's."

He peeked into the velvet box. A pair of diamond studs winked back at him, and true enough, they looked exactly like the ones sitting in the lobes of Jamie's ears. "They're lovely," he said.

"Thanks."

Gray gave Jamie a sympathetic smile. He remembered the year he'd given

Halle the wrong American Girl doll. Polly? Molly? He'd felt like the worst parent in the world. But how could Ivy be disappointed with such a beautiful gift? He pondered the question as he reached beneath the tree. "Here's one with your name on it, Dad." He tossed his father a box.

"It's from me, Grandpa," Halle said.

His dad ripped off the paper. "A Chia Head!" He sounded as if nothing could have pleased him more, then he looked at Halle. "What's a Chia Head?"

"You water the head, and grass grows like hair, Grandpa," Halle explained. "Then you cut it with scissors to style it."

"I'll be a monkey's uncle," Norman said, turning the box slowly in his hands. "Too bad someone can't figure out the same thing for growing hair on people."

"They have, Dad," Gray said. "It's called Rogaine."

His father grinned. "And how would you know about Rogaine? Personal experience?" He winked at Jamie.

Gray ran his hand through his hair. "Nope. From the TV, Dad. Some of us actually stay awake for an entire program."

"Some of us don't care for the programs. There's either too much violence or people mumble and you can't understand them." He gestured to Halle. "There's something for you and something for Ivy under the tree."

Halle dove beneath the tree and found the gifts in about five seconds. The two girls sat next to each other on the rug and simultaneously ripped off the wrapping paper. "Oh Grandpa, it's beautiful," Halle cried out, holding up a brand-new sweater. "It's from my favorite store and is just the right size!"

"Good job, Dad."

His father nodded and winked at Jamie, leaving Gray no doubt as to who had picked out the sweater.

"Mr. Westler," Ivy said rather shyly, holding up leather ski gloves. "Thank you so much. I love them."

"They're racing gloves," his dad said proudly. "Thought they might come in handy for you."

After a brief break for breakfast, more presents were exchanged. Gray opened an electric razor from his father—and took some ribbing about needing to use it—a book from Halle written by a Christian author he particularly liked, and thick wool socks from Boomer.

Jamie opened up a box of chocolates from Norman. She also received a framed photo of Ivy smiling next to a big white sign that said MISS PORTER'S SCHOOL, FOUNDED 1843. Gray found himself wishing he'd bought Jamie a gift, especially when she handed him a tin of homemade chocolate peanut butter fudge.

"There's something else for you, Halle, behind the tree," Gray prompted after almost all the other gifts had been opened.

Halle dragged out the long, tall box he'd tucked behind the branches. He knew, though, from her expression that she'd seen it all along and had been waiting to open it. He found himself holding his breath as she examined the size and weight of the box.

"What do you think it is?" Gray was unable to resist asking.

"Skis?" Halle guessed.

"Open it," he pressed gently.

She did. Her nose wrinkled in confusion as she tore off the green and red paper and saw the brand name of a company that made ski racks for cars. "A ski rack, Dad?"

"What every girl needs," Gray said, trying not to smile.

Halle began to pull out the wads of tissue paper, then she found the leather case. "Is this. . . ?" Her face turned rapturous. "Oh, Dad. . .did you. . .?"

"I don't know," Gray said innocently, enjoying the light that had come into his daughter's eyes.

Halle's fingers clicked open the bindings as she pulled out the shiny brass horn. She looked over at him, rapturous. "You're kidding me. You got this? You went on eBay?"

"Go on," Gray urged. "You can actually hold it."

She took her time pulling it from the case, then held it reverently against her chest. "It's so beautiful," she said. "Thank you so, so much, Dad."

She studied every gleaming inch before bringing it to her mouth. Closing her eyes she took a deep breath and put her lips against the mouthpiece. Gray heard air passing through the instrument. Halle took another deep breath and tried again. This time she managed to produce a low, wheezy-sounding note that unexpectedly jumped several octaves. When she ran out of breath, she put the instrument down and looked at him triumphantly.

"That was great, honey," Gray said, struggling to sound sincere.

"Want to hear it again?" She already had the instrument to her lips and was summoning forth the breath needed to produce that awful sound again. He looked over at Jamie, who was smiling from ear to ear. His dad, however, was doing the only thing that made sense, and that was leaving the room.

"Where you going, Dad?" Gray asked.

His father glanced over his shoulder and grinned. "I'm going to get my bugle, sonny boy, so Halle and I can jam together."

Chapter 14

After lunch Gray, Halle, Ivy, and Jamie went for a walk. Norman stayed home to watch the Sugar Bowl on television. The snow was deeper than her boots, and Jamie felt like some sort of wilderness survivor as she stepped onto the road, which was no longer a road at all, but part of the scenic white landscape. "It's beautiful," she breathed. "Simply beautiful."

"And quiet," Grayson agreed, appearing by her side. "Blessedly quiet."

Jamie watched their two daughters, who had run a short distance ahead, plow through the unbroken path. They were purposely leaving long lines in the pristine blanket of snow. "You did the right thing, Grayson, giving her that french horn. Did you see her face?"

"Yeah," he said. "And did you hear the noise she made? It's lucky we don't live in Africa. Every mother elephant within hearing range would have come running."

Jamie laughed. "She'll get better."

"I thought a lot about what you told me," Gray admitted. "I don't ever want her to feel pressure to ski." He gave her a sideways glance. "However, her birthday is coming up in February, so I might give her an early present."

"French horn lessons, right?"

He laughed and bumped her shoulder playfully. "She'll get those, but she'll also be getting new skis."

Jamie laughed and bumped him back. "But no pressure to race, right?"

"When she skis on them," Gray stated with confidence, "she'll want to race."

Jamie didn't want to spoil Gray's daydream, but she wondered if he realized how much Halle was drawn to a world that had little to do with skiing. On more than one occasion the girl had pumped Jamie for tips on hair and makeup, and Halle's eyes lit up when she talked about band, especially the marching band, which she'd seen perform last fall.

They hiked to the ski lodge, which no longer looked slightly dilapidated. Under its thick coat of fresh snow, it seemed rustic and charming. Sturdy and inviting, it sat like a refuge beneath the huge, snowy mountain looming behind it.

"Dad!" Halle called and then flopped onto the snowy ground. "Look." She spread her arms and legs and made a snow angel. To Jamie's amazement, Ivy did the same thing. Before she thought too much about it, she flopped down and made a snow angel, too. Gray did the same, and soon the four of them were admiring the four imprints on the ground.

They wandered to the back of the lodge. It seemed strange to see the lift still, the cable carrying a line of snow up the mountain.

"Let's build a snowman," Halle suggested, already crouching to pack as much snow as she could into a ball. Ivy bent to help her.

Jamie snapped a photo with her cell phone of the two girls working together. Kneeling, she began to build her own snowman. Next to her, Gray did the same. His snowball was larger, but significantly lopsided.

"I see we're going for a snowman with personality."

Gray looked up. He had snowflakes on his dark eyelashes, and his nose was red from the cold. "And you're going for a miniature one."

"It will be smaller," Jamie agreed. "But perfectly shaped."

"Until someone steps on it," Gray teased.

"I would rather have someone step on my snowman than have it look like a Mr. Potato Head."

"Not everything has to look perfect, Mom," Ivy announced. "I like the way Mr. Westler's snowman looks."

The unexpected harshness of Ivy's words hurt. Jamie ducked her head before anyone saw, and she barely heard Gray tell Ivy to call him Mr. Grayson. Ivy didn't mean to sound so harsh, she tried to assure herself. Ivy was just at that age where everything Jamie did or said was wrong. She packed some snow onto the ball and hoped someday Ivy would appreciate and understand the choices Jamie had had to make.

Gray rolled his lopsided ball over to hers. "If we pool our talents," he suggested, "we could build a really nice snowman."

Jamie glanced up at him through the falling snow. She didn't want his pity, but it seemed churlish to refuse his offer. "Sure," she said. "Do you want to make a girl snowman or a boy snowman?"

Grayson cocked his head. "We're not shaping an anatomically correct snowman, are we?"

"Of course not," Jamie stated. "I just thought it would be nice to build a snow couple."

"We'll make the girl snowman," Halle cried. "I have an old pink scarf and some rhinestone buttons from my Halloween costume. We'll give her earrings, too."

"Want my diamond studs?" Ivy offered. Just as Jamie was about to lay down the law about that, Ivy turned to her, grinning. "I'm just kidding, Mom."

Jamie exhaled slowly. "You had me for a moment there."

"I know," Ivy said. "I couldn't resist it."

Her daughter gave her an impish grin—one Jamie recognized from years past—and then went back to work on the snow girl. Jamie stared at her daughter's back, appreciating for maybe the first time how her mother used to look at her sometimes, as if Jamie had arrived on earth straight from Mars.

About an hour later, Jamie stepped back to admire their snow boy. "He looks exactly like their snow girl," she commented to Gray, who was beginning to look a little bit like a snowman himself with all the falling snow that had collected on his shoulders.

"That's only because their snow girl is pretty muscular. Tomorrow we'll put a cowboy hat on ours, and he'll look a lot more macho." He turned to the girls who were huddled a short distance away and appeared to be whispering to each other. "Hey, girls, how about some hot chocolate?"

Instead of replying, Halle launched a snowball at him. Ivy threw one at Jamie, who quickly ducked behind the snow boy. Gray dropped to the ground and began forming snowballs as the girls pelted his stationary form.

"Gray," Jamie shouted. "Retreat!"

"Never!" He dodged one snowball and laughed as another exploded across his chest. "Okay," he said. "You asked for it." He launched a snowball at Halle, hitting her leg. He aimed a second ball at Ivy, who launched a ball at him at the same time. The two snowballs collided in midair.

Jamie scurried out, clutching two snowballs. She handed one to Gray and threw the other at Halle, missing by a mile. As Jamie rearmed, Ivy moved in and began pelting her with a seemingly endless supply of snowballs. Jamie's hat joined Gray's on the snowy ground. "Hey! That's cashmere!" Jamie said.

Ivy grinned. "I know."

"Okay. It's war now." Jamie straightened, clutching a snowball. Ivy also had one final ball in her hands. "Okay, then. On the count of three," Jamie said soberly. "One, two, three. . ." She closed her eyes and threw her snowball well to the side of her daughter. At the same time, an icy fist exploded across her face. She jerked back, wiping the clumps of snow from her eyes and cheeks.

"Game over," Gray announced. He positioned himself at Jamie's side. "You okay?"

Jamie's face burned from the cold. "I'm fine. No big deal."

"You can take a free shot at me," Ivy offered. "And I'll even stand close enough so you won't miss."

Jamie shook her head. "Don't worry about it, Ivy. I just need to check my contact lens."

"We can go inside the lodge," Gray suggested.

"You sure you're okay, Mom? Seriously. I thought you'd duck. Why didn't you?"

Because I never thought you'd aim for my head. "I don't know," Jamie said. "Been a long time since I was in a snowball fight."

Ivy hesitated, as if she might say something else, then ran to catch up with Halle.

Gray fell into step as they headed for the lodge. "You missed Ivy by a good six feet. You weren't even aiming for her, were you?" He was walking so close she could hear the whisper of his ski clothing chafing.

"Nope," Jamie admitted. "But don't tell her that. She'd only feel worse." But would she? Although she didn't want to admit it, Jamie knew the snowball to her head hadn't been an accident. Devon had been a terrific athlete, and so was

Ivy. She stopped just in front of the lodge. "How do you do it? The whole single-parent thing?"

Gray laughed. "You just haven't seen our less than perfect moments."

"Well, she's turning out great."

"So is Ivy."

Jamie glanced sideways at his face. "Are you serious?" Her face tingled from the cold, and she could feel snow melting uncomfortably down her neck.

"She hangs on every word my dad says, and the other day I saw her helping a novice skier who was having some trouble on White Rabbit."

Jamie thought about this. "Then why is she so awful to me? Everything is a battle. I don't see why she doesn't realize I'm trying to look out for her, not make her life miserable." She clenched her hands into fists. "What's your secret?"

"No secret," Grayson said. He opened the heavy wooden door to the lodge and stepped back to let her pass. "I pray for her constantly. Every single night I'm on my knees by the side of my bed."

"And God tells you what to do?" Jamie honestly wanted to know.

"Not in words, but I know He's listening and that helps."

Jamie paused in the door frame. "How do you know He's listening?"

"It's a feeling." The expression in Gray's eyes turned thoughtful. "It's like any relationship, I guess. The more time you spend with a person, the better you get to know him."

Jamie could feel the welcoming heat of the lodge contrasting with the coldness behind her. She needed help, but her situation was very different from Gray's. "What if a person did something wrong, but he or she is not entirely sorry for it either. Would God want a relationship with that kind of person?"

"Absolutely," Grayson replied. "God loves everyone. He hates sin, but He loves the sinner—and basically that's all of us. There's nothing He can't forgive, and no situation He can't change for His glory." He looked into her eyes. "You should tell that person not to be afraid to talk to God."

But what would she say? *Hello, God, it's me, Jamie King. You know—the girl who messed up about thirteen years ago. Do You think we could just look past that and move forward?*

Jamie shook her head. She didn't think prayers worked like that. Besides, her parents had kicked her out, and there was no reason to think God would want her either.

Chapter 15

The day after Christmas was one of the busiest days of the year at Pilgrim's Peak. By noon his dad had run out of rental equipment, and the Looking Glass was beginning to remind Gray of rush hour on I-84. The ski patrol had its hands full, and the extra three college kids he'd hired during the break as instructors were booked solid with lessons. He'd known this day would be jam-packed, and yet he'd gone ahead and scheduled a private lesson with Jamie King.

He'd asked her casually after dinner last night. "Hey, Jamie. One more present." Then he'd handed her a Christmas card. Inside it he'd included a handmade coupon for a ski lesson with today's date and time written on it.

Now here he was, standing beside the chairlift, his heart beating in anticipation. Since when did he look forward so much to giving a lesson? Since never, maybe. She skied up to him, and his heart gave a small, excited leap. As they settled into the chair lift, he found himself sitting a little closer and studying her profile for clues that might explain just what it was about her that he found so compelling.

She felt his gaze, turned, and said, "What are you looking at?"

Caught, he tried to laugh it off. "You looked so serious just then. I was trying to figure out what you were thinking."

"Oh," she said. "Just something about Ivy."

"What about her?" Almost against his will, his gaze lowered to her lips, and he wondered what it would be like to kiss her. The thought seemed to release something pleasantly heavy inside that flowed through his veins.

"Well," Jamie said at last. "I've been thinking of what you said yesterday. About spending more time with someone in order to strengthen a relationship." Her brow furrowed. "Can you teach me to giant slalom in a week?"

"What?" The question was so far from his own chain of thoughts it took him a few seconds to process it.

"I want to enter the interclub race."

"Jamie, you're making good progress, but running gates is going to be tough for a beginner."

Her chin lifted. "I can do tough."

"Two weeks ago you were getting dragged up the bunny hill by the J-bar."

"And I would have made it to the top if you hadn't insisted that I let go."

He shifted on the bench seat. "It takes time to develop the skills you need for a ski race."

"I can do it," Jamie argued. "All you have to do is ski around the gates and not fall down."

He laughed at the gross oversimplification. "Jamie, you have to be able to hold an edge when you turn, control your speed, and stop at the end of the race. You wouldn't believe how many people I've fished out of the safety net."

"If you don't want to help me, just say so."

"I'm not saying that," Gray hedged. The chair jostled them slightly as it rolled across a support tower. "Why all of a sudden is this race so important to you?"

"Because I have to find a way to connect with her before she goes back to Miss Porter's." He heard an unaccustomed vulnerability creep into her voice. "I think I'm losing her."

He thought about it. If she'd given him any other reason, he'd never have agreed, but this one he understood. Where would he and Halle be without a shared love of skiing? Besides, if he didn't help her, she'd do it anyway. "You'll have to ski more," he said, "to build up your leg strength. And you'll need to follow my instructions to the letter."

The small hut at the top of the hill came into sight. They dismounted without incident, and he brought her to the top of Alice's Alley. The first drop was the steepest, and he couldn't help a small glimmer of satisfaction at the way her lips thinned at the sight of the pitch.

"This is the hill we use for the race," he said. "Right now I only have three gates set, and they're a little farther down the hill. There will be twelve the day of the race, and they'll start at the top."

"I can do that," Jamie stated, but the way her gaze slid away from his, he knew she was a little afraid.

"We don't have to do this," he offered. "You can find another way to spend time with Ivy. You could take her to the Farmington mall or something."

Jamie shook her head. "It has to be this. It's the only way I'll earn her respect."

He held his breath as she pushed off the top of the hill. She skidded sideways on the first turn, but then recovered her balance. She'd improved considerably, but she still had a lot to learn. She struggled with the next turn, and he called out for her to unweight her uphill ski.

He insisted she rest just before they reached the area of the trail with the gates. Pulling up alongside her, Gray waited until her breathing slowed down.

"Okay," he said. "See those three gates down there? You want to ski as close as you can to them. You keep the green gates on your left side and the red ones on your right. I'll show you."

With a push of his ski poles, he headed down the hill. He kept his speed slow and exaggerated the up and down motion of the turns through the gates. Pausing at the side of the trail, he turned to watch her.

She picked up more speed than he would have liked, but managed to turn around the first gate. He held his breath as she headed toward the second gate, skied right past it, then gave a cute little wiggle turn and headed for the third gate, which she also gave a wide berth.

She skied toward him with her elbows out like wings. Her legs were too straight and her hips too bent. She had no form at all, but she looked so adorable that he didn't have the heart to correct her.

"How was that, coach?"

"Not bad," he said.

Her grin grew bigger. "Can we try it again?"

He nodded, firmly ignoring the small voice that said he'd be late for his next lesson. "Yup," he said. "Try and come a little closer to the gates next time. You missed the second gate."

"I know," Jamie agreed. "I would have missed the third, too, but I hit a bump, and it slowed me down enough to turn."

She beamed up at him. He looked at those full, rosy lips and thought about kissing her. It seemed a little less crazy than before. With a sinking feeling he realized it wouldn't be long before the thought of kissing her was not crazy at all.

Chapter 16

Jamie skied for several more hours before heading back to the house. Her lesson with Gray left her nearly light-headed with excitement. With a little more practice—and Gray's expert coaching—she was convinced she and Ivy would make a decent showing in the mother/daughter class in the ski race.

In the foyer, she checked the registration book. The Kilpatricks and Wongs had checked out, and the Banbridges, Gregorys, and Goldmans had checked in. A full house. She'd make her asparagus, tomato, and fontina cheese frittata for tomorrow morning. After a quick shower, she headed to the kitchen to help Norman with dinner.

When she stepped in the kitchen, she found him leaning heavily against the kitchen counter. "Norman," she said and hurried up to him. "Are you okay?"

"Oh sure," he replied, but he continued to lean on the counter and his face had a frightening grayish cast.

"Sit." Jamie helped him to a kitchen chair and studied him anxiously. "What happened?"

"I just got a little dizzy for a moment," Norman admitted. "I'm fine now."

"Your face barely has any color."

He waved away the hand she placed on his forehead. "Stop fussing. I'm fine."

"Maybe you ought to lie down," Jamie suggested. "I'll make dinner, and if you don't feel like coming downstairs, I'll bring a tray to your room."

Norman didn't seem to have the strength to argue. He leaned against her as she helped him to his room. She was surprised how thin and fragile he felt against her. She tucked him into his bed and pulled an extra blanket over him. As she turned to leave, he caught her wrist. "Listen," he said, "let's not mention this to Gray. With the club race coming up, the last thing he needs is to have me on his mind."

Jamie frowned. "I think he should know, Norman."

"Know what? That I got a little dizzy?"

She hesitated. "You almost passed out, Norman. Maybe you should see a doctor."

"They'll keep me waiting for hours in a room full of sick people," Norman stated firmly. "All I need is a little rest. Don't treat me like a child. I'm seventy-seven years old and a veteran of the Korean War. I may have lost my hair, but last time I looked, all my senses were present and accounted for."

He was getting agitated, so just to keep him calm Jamie agreed to do as he asked. If he wasn't better by dinner, however, she'd tell Gray.

Jamie was adding butter to a steaming pot of potatoes when Ivy, Halle, and Gray walked into the kitchen. Although they'd dropped their coats and boots in the mudroom, the clean, cold scent of the mountain still clung to them.

"Where's Dad?" Gray asked, setting his keys and wallet on the counter.

"Upstairs," Jamie replied, sticking a mixer into the pot. "Resting."

Gray frowned. "That isn't like him."

"Yeah, well. . ." The whirl of the beaters drowned out any further conversation, which was exactly what Jamie wanted. She watched the chunks of potato smooth and wondered if she should go back on her word to Norman. The decision was taken out of her hands a moment later when Jamie looked up and saw Norman in the doorway.

"Norman!" she said. "Glad you're feeling better."

"I was just about to explain to Gray here that the chili dog I had for lunch was talking to me." Norman gave her a slightly defiant look.

"You know chili dogs give you indigestion," Gray stated. "Why do you eat them?"

"Because they taste good."

Gray gave Norman a fond, but exasperated look. "You're impossible, Dad." He turned to Jamie. "You need any help?"

Jamie peeked at the chicken in the oven. "Nope. I'm all set. You've got about five minutes until dinner." She took off her apron and caught Gray's gaze lingering on her. There was a softness in his eyes she'd never seen before. He looked away quickly and left the room. Jamie stood still, watching the place he'd been. The heat of the oven warmed her back, but it couldn't account for the sudden heat in her cheeks or the breathless feeling that left her slightly light-headed and pleasantly tingly.

After dinner Norman asked if anyone wanted to play a board game.

"Which one?" Halle stacked two plates. "I kind of want to practice my instrument."

"Monopoly," Norman declared. "In honor of Jamie's profession."

"I don't know, Norman," Jamie said. "Maybe you should just take it easy. You barely ate anything."

"My digestion would benefit from a game of Monopoly," Norman stated firmly. Then in a much softer tone he added, "And maybe a little Mylanta."

After they cleaned the dishes and reset the dining room table for the breakfast buffet, all of them, including Boomer, marched into the family room.

"I want the dog piece," Halle declared, opening the playing board on the coffee table.

Jamie had never played Monopoly with Ivy before. They owned the game, but Jamie had always been either too busy or too tired to play. With a stab of guilt, she realized she should have made time. She hid the emotion under a confident smile. "You pick the next playing piece, sweetie."

Ivy rolled her eyes. "I'll be the Rolls-Royce."

"Jamie girl?" Norman prompted.

She picked up the first piece her hand fell on. "The iron." She pretended to iron her already perfectly straight hair. Halle laughed, but Ivy cringed.

"You be the shoe, Gray. I'll be the hat." Norman began handing out money.

"Hold on," Gray said. "I should be banker."

"Oh no. I'm always the banker." His father winked at Halle. "Maybe Halle should decide."

Halle grinned. "Grandpa is always banker, Dad."

Gray pretended to look crushed as he set the Chance and Community Chest cards on the board. "Okay," he said, "but I'm keeping a close eye on you, Dad." Then he grinned at Ivy. "You have to watch out for Mr. Westler—he cheats."

Ivy's eyes lit up, and she laughed.

"I don't cheat," Norman replied with dignity.

"You cheat, Dad," Gray said flatly. "Show me your sleeves."

Norman held out his arms for inspection. Halle and Ivy laughed as two five-hundred-dollar bills fell out of his sleeves. "Now how did those get there?" he asked innocently.

"My own father—a cheater." Gray sighed dramatically and almost, but not quite, hid a smile. "Tell you what, Dad. I'll let you get away with it this time, but the next time I catch you stealing from the bank you're going straight to jail."

"That's fine," Norman agreed. "Now let's get this game started before the next millennium comes."

Halle rolled the dice and the game began. By the time they'd all gone around the board a couple of times, Norman had talked Halle and Ivy into forming an alliance with him. Although Norman offered the same deal to Jamie, she turned to Gray and smiled. "How about making me a better offer?"

"Team with me and I'll give you another free ski lesson."

"That's not fair," Norman growled as Jamie shook Gray's hand.

"Sorry, Norman," Jamie said. "I need the lesson." It was more than that, but she kept this to herself.

After an hour, both sides were about equal. Norman's team had slightly more cash, but she and Gray had more properties.

"Gray," Norman said. "Would you mind getting me a glass of water from the kitchen?" He rubbed his stomach. "That chili dog is talking to me again."

"Jamie, please keep an eye on him," Gray warned and left the room.

"Jamie! Is that a mouse under that chair?" Norman pointed excitedly.

Jamie jerked her head around. She was terrified of anything that crawled. Fortunately, she didn't see any furry little rodent. "I think that's just a dust bunny." Something about the game board looked different—she didn't think all those extra houses on Norman's properties had been there before. Halle and Ivy were studiously not looking at her.

Despite the extra houses and a few properties that inexplicably ended in

Norman's possession, Jamie and Grayson soon found themselves winning. When Halle landed on Park Place, which belonged to Jamie, it nearly bankrupted Norman's team.

"You want to concede?" Gray began slowly counting out the cash Halle handed him.

"What do you think, girls? Should we admit defeat?"

"Probably," Ivy said. "We've got less than two hundred dollars."

Jamie yawned and dropped one of the dice. She leaned over to pick it up and saw paper money lying near Norman's battered sheepskin slippers. "Hey, Norman," she said. "You must have dropped some money." She handed him two five-hundred-dollar bills.

"How did those get there?" Norman's brow furrowed.

"As if you didn't know," Grayson stated. "I wouldn't be surprised if you were sitting on several other five-hundred-dollar bills."

The girls laughed excitedly. Jamie couldn't get over the look on Ivy's face. She was glowing with happiness and looked about five years younger.

"I'm not sitting on anything," Norman declared. "You can check if you like."

"I will. Stand up, Dad."

Norman did. "See? Totally innocent. You should be ashamed, Gray, for thinking otherwise."

Gray snorted. "And I suppose Boomer hid that money when nobody was looking." He turned to Jamie. "Did my father hide that money there when I went to get his water?"

"Nope," Jamie said. "He put extra houses on the board when you got his water." She enjoyed the look of mock displeasure on Gray's face and the sound of the girls' laughter.

"Come on, Dad, fess up. You put the money there."

"I didn't." Norman shook his head. "I'm innocent."

"So who did?" He scrutinized each face, and when he looked at her, Jamie burst out in guilty laughter.

"My mom is a cheater!" But the way Ivy said it, it didn't sound like a bad thing.

"Sabotage," Gray declared, shaking his head. "I give up. You all win." He didn't sound unhappy, though, and his eyes sparkled at her.

Norman gave his teammates a high five, then he beamed at Jamie. "You're quite a gal, Jamie." He turned to his son. "Isn't she?"

Gray looked up from putting away the game pieces. "She's something," he agreed and winked at Jamie. She thought she saw something tender in his eyes, but whatever he had been about to say was lost as Mrs. Banbridge, one of the guests, rapped on the french doors and asked if Jamie had any pastries left over from the morning.

Chapter 17

Could I please have your recipe for the lemon blueberry muffins?" Mrs. Banbridge asked. Although it was barely six thirty in the morning, Mrs. Banbridge was in full makeup and dressed for the ski slopes. The older woman and her husband hadn't been the first at the table either. Skiers, Jamie had discovered, were early risers. Well, the nonteenage ones, she amended.

Smiling, Jamie walked to the white-haired woman's side and replenished Mrs. Banbridge's cup with hot coffee. "Absolutely. It's not my recipe, though. It's my Aunt Bea's."

"If you're giving out recipes," Mr. Gregory said from the other end of the table, "please give my wife the one for that egg, cheese, and sausage casserole. You wouldn't have any left over from yesterday, would you?"

Jamie smiled at the wistful note in his voice. "I don't. But I'll make it tomorrow morning, and I'll be glad to give you the recipe." She raised her voice to address Mr. Banbridge who was hard of hearing. "More coffee, Mr. Banbridge? Gray says the weather's supposed to warm up this afternoon, so the skiing will be best earlier."

Mr. Banbridge held up his cup for a refill. "The powder's always best early." He gestured to his wife. "Hope it stays this good for the race on Saturday. Barbara and I are the oldest racers in the husband/wife race. We won it in 1975, you know."

"Only because Alice was eight months pregnant with Grayson and Norman wouldn't let her race." Mrs. Banbridge laughed. "How many years did Norman and Alice win that trophy?"

"At least ten," Mr. Banbridge said, pulling another muffin from the basket and cutting it open. "And then Gray and Lonna got married and continued the family tradition." He popped a piece of muffin in his mouth.

"Those two were simply unbeatable," Mrs. Banbridge said. "It's no wonder Halle is so talented. With those genes for skiing, she'd have to be." She glanced around the room and added casually, "Terrible shame what happened to Lonna, though."

Jamie kept her head down. "What happened?"

"Car accident." Mrs. Banbridge lowered her voice. "She hit a patch of black ice on I-84 and the car spun out of control, straight into the path of an eighteen-wheeler. Killed her instantly." She glanced around the room again and added softly, "Some witnesses said she was driving too fast."

Jamie's mind struggled to process the information even as questions bubbled up in her. How long ago? Had she been alone? And Gray. Her heart ached for him. She realized Mrs. Banbridge was waiting for her to comment. "It must have been awful," Jamie murmured.

"Oh it was," Mrs. Banbridge said. "If it wasn't for that little girl, I think Gray would have died from his grief. Shut himself up in the house for weeks." Her gaze grew troubled. "Norman about lost his mind trying to keep everything together—running the ski hill, teaching Gray's classes, and keeping the B&B open. It got so bad they almost sold this place." She shook her head. "Got themselves a Realtor and all but signed the paperwork."

Jamie cringed, thinking how hard she had pushed Gray to let her list the ski hill. No wonder he'd nearly thrown her out of his office that first day. Her hands were shaking a little as she picked up a coffee mug. "Why didn't he? Why didn't he sell?"

Mrs. Banbridge shrugged. "I don't really know. Darren and I were so glad, we didn't press for more." She patted Jamie's hand. "I don't go around telling just anybody that story, you know. You probably think I'm a gossipy old woman with nothing better to do than talk about somebody else's business."

"I don't think that at all," Jamie protested. But she was wondering why the older woman had decided to share the story with her.

Mrs. Banbridge gripped Jamie's arm with surprising strength. "I saw you all in the family room last night, playing Monopoly," the older woman said. "You were all laughing, and that dog was sleeping in front of the fire. I knew in my heart there was love there. There was a *family* there. Men don't always tell a woman the things she needs to know." She squeezed Jamie's arm. "Gray's special. Take good care of him. Now, do you use cream cheese in the recipe?"

Jamie was too stunned by Mrs. Banbridge's words and her own tangle of emotions to do anything but nod.

"Thought so," the old woman said and sipped her coffee with an unmistakable look of satisfaction stamped across her weathered features.

～

Mrs. Banbridge had it all wrong. Gray and Jamie weren't in love, and there had been two families playing Monopoly last night, not one. Jamie clicked her bindings into place and propelled herself toward the double chair lift. Her heart tugged, however, at the memory of all of them clustered around the coffee table in the family room, talking and laughing. She hadn't seen Ivy look so happy for a long time.

What if the thing Ivy needed most was a family? Gray's family? She imagined family game nights, long walks in the woods, and holidays with the big dining room table filled with people. *Hold on,* she warned herself. *Aren't you getting a little ahead of yourself? If you want to give Ivy a happy future, maybe you should be thinking about how you're going to pay her tuition at Miss Porter's.* She plunked herself down on the chair lift and tried to think about her job. She'd been neglecting it lately and resolved to check her messages more frequently as well as check new listings on the MLS.

At the top of the mountain, she headed for Mad Hatter. As usual, the trail was nearly empty. When she reached the trailhead, she paused, watching a few skiers and a lone snowboarder gracefully slide out of sight. She took a deep breath.

Are you there? She listened carefully to the white silence. *Can you hear me?* Not even a squirrel moved through the woods. *Idiot,* she thought, *who did you think was going to answer—God? And even if He did, what did you think He'd say? Hey, Jamie, great to see you. Let's talk.* She gripped her ski poles more tightly. No. If God were going to talk to her, He'd probably say something like, *Why didn't you listen to me? Why did you get into Devon Brown's Mustang that night? We both know I tried to stop you. I was the fear in your stomach, the dryness of your mouth, the crushing beat of your heart.*

"Stop it!" she cried. "How could I ever regret having Ivy?" Her voice rang out in the quiet forest. She was ashamed and fearful that someone might have overheard. She listened hard. In the distance she heard voices—but they weren't God's. Other skiers were approaching, and she didn't want to be seen standing at the top of the trail talking to herself. She pushed off, wanting to get away from her thoughts, away from the faint hope that God would hear the need in her heart.

At the bottom of the mountain, she spotted Ivy heading toward the double chair lift and hurried to catch up to her. "Hey," she called. "Wait up."

Ivy obediently paused long enough for Jamie to reach her.

"How's it going?"

"Fine."

"Where's Halle?"

"Back at the house practicing her french horn." Ivy crinkled her nose. "Mr. Grayson told her to practice when the guests weren't around."

Jamie made a sympathetic noise. "When I was in fifth grade, I wanted to play the clarinet. I squeaked that instrument so badly my mom made me practice in the basement with the door closed." She bit her lip. It only made things worse for Ivy to hear about the family that had never acknowledged her.

"You think your mother ever thinks about us?"

"I don't know. Maybe." Jamie inched her skis forward in the lift line, thinking she'd asked herself that same question hundreds of times.

"You think I'll ever meet either of your parents?"

Something in Ivy's voice made Jamie glance at her. Her stomach tightened at the barely disguised longing on her daughter's face. "Ivy, you know I really don't like to talk about my family."

"It's my family, too," Ivy stated, but her voice lacked conviction. "Maybe we should visit them sometime. You know, just show up at their doorstep."

Jamie shuddered. She remembered showing up at her parents' house uninvited with three-month-old Ivy in her arms. Her mother had backed away from the door with her hands pressed to her mouth, while Jamie stood on the welcome mat like a stranger. Her father, finally, had come to the door. He'd had a check in his hand and a pinched look to his mouth. Understanding just what that check represented, Jamie hadn't wanted to take it, but she'd needed the money. By then Aunt Bea was in hospice, and the bills had been accumulating. Jamie remembered the door closing and the sound of the lock snapping into place. Fortunately, Ivy would never remember that day. "I don't think so," she said very gently.

The chair lift swung around the turn. Two people took their seats, and as their chair lifted them into the air, Jamie and Ivy poled forward to catch the next one. A moment later they were seated and the chair was ascending the mountain.

"Are they so terrible?" Ivy asked. "How do you know they wouldn't be happy to see me?" She flipped her long, sleek ponytail. "I happen to be smart and good looking."

"You are," Jamie agreed, smiling, but beneath her daughter's bravado, she sensed a deep insecurity. "It's not anything about the way you look or anything you've done." Jamie hesitated. They'd gone over this more than once, but each time Ivy was less content with her answers. "Look, they're not awful. They just want their lives to run a certain way."

"We wouldn't try and run their lives." Ivy shot her a look packed with emotion. "I wouldn't, at least."

Jamie ignored the barb. She watched the skiers moving gracefully down the hill beneath the lift line. "Trust me, Ivy. We're better off without them."

"I'm the only girl at Miss Porter's who doesn't have siblings, a father, grandparents, stepparents. . .cousins. . .anything." She scowled fiercely at Jamie. "I'm like an alien."

Jamie shook her head. "You're not an alien." More softly she added, "And you've got me."

"You shut me down every time I ask about my father or your family." Bitterness and resignation hung in the air like frosty breath.

Because I'm trying to protect you. Jamie's cheeks burned despite the cold air. "I love you, Ivy. I've done what I thought was right."

They were close to the mountain, and Jamie knew time was running out. "Hey, listen," she said. "I've been wanting to talk to you about the club race. I've spoken to Gray, and he's agreed to let us join the Pilgrim's Peak race team so you and I can go in the mother/daughter race this Saturday." She gave Ivy a big smile. "I've been practicing, and I think we can make a decent showing."

Ivy shifted on the seat. "You're kidding, right?"

"I think it'd be fun." She gave Ivy the encouraging smile she used on her most reluctant clients.

"I don't think so," Ivy said.

"Why not? I've been practicing, and there was only one time I missed a gate. I won't be the best skier out there, but I won't embarrass you."

The sign instructing skiers to raise the safety bar flashed past them. "Because I don't want to. That's why."

"How about we ski down the race trail together and then we talk about this some more?" Jamie kept her gaze on Ivy's unrelenting profile. "You'll see how much better I've gotten. I can even get off the chair lift now." She was joking, of course, but Ivy didn't laugh or smile or even roll her eyes.

"Mom," Ivy said sharply. "Why don't you ever listen to what I want?"

The skiers in front of them were unloading, and there was no time to answer. Ivy took off the minute her skis hit the packed snow. She immediately headed down the trail, her slender body tucked for speed. Jamie could only watch her go, filled with the sad realization that whatever was broken between them might be beyond her ability to fix.

Chapter 18

Jamie," Gray yelled. "Slow down!" What was wrong with her today? She was skiing faster than usual—almost recklessly. She'd wiped out a couple of times already, and it hadn't slowed her down one bit. She maneuvered a gate, taking it at an angle that would have been impressive if he'd had any faith at all that she was in control.

In the next instant, it happened. She hooked a ski on the inside of the gate. The pole gave, but not before it knocked her off balance. Both bindings popped, and she crashed to the ground.

An adrenaline rush shot through his body. Before he even thought about it, he launched himself uphill. Her bindings had released, but people broke bones or tore tendons in their knees all the time. His heart thumped. "Jamie!"

She sat up slowly and began brushing snow from her parka. "I'm okay," she said but winced when she said it.

He continued to sidestep up the hill as quickly as he could. "Don't move until I get there," he ordered.

When he reached her side, he scanned her for any sign of injury. Other than a pretty good amount of snow clinging to her clothing and her hair, she looked fine. Suddenly it was much easier to breathe. "What were you thinking?" He helped her to her feet and brushed some snow from her parka. "Didn't you hear me tell you to slow down?"

"I thought I could do it."

"You thought you could do it?" Gray slapped at the snow a little harder than necessary, but he couldn't seem to help himself. "Do you realize if your binding hadn't popped quickly enough, you'd be looking at a spiral fracture?"

"Fortunately, I'm fine," Jamie snapped. "Stop being a worrywart."

"I'll stop being a worrywart when you start showing some common sense." Gray glared down at her, thinking he'd like to shake some sense into her.

"You don't like my skiing, don't watch." Her eyes flashed defiance.

He set his jaw. If she wanted a fight, she'd get one. "Fine," he said. "I'm pulling your ticket. You don't listen, and I'm not going to stand here and watch you get hurt. That wasn't part of our deal."

"Fine," she snapped. "It's what you wanted anyway."

"Is isn't what I wanted." He slid a few feet backward and was about to swing his skis around when he thought he saw her face crumple. It occurred to him through his haze of anger that she was about to cry. "Jamie?"

"Keep going!" she thundered. "Just like everyone else."

"I'm not like everyone else!" he yelled back and began to sidestep back up the hill. She saw him coming and tried to put her skis back on, but there was snow under one of the bindings. She stepped harder and harder onto the back of the binding, but it refused to close.

"You want to tell me what's going on?" He felt some of his anger evaporating at the sight of her whaling on the poor ski.

"I'm done," Jamie snapped. She gave up on the ski and started to walk away. Her boots punched holes into the snow.

He grabbed her arm. "We have one disagreement, and you're done? I thought there was more to you than that."

"You were wrong." She tried to shrug off his grasp, but he tightened his fingers. "Let go of me!"

"Not until I understand what's going on."

"I told you. I'm quitting the race."

"Half the ski hill heard that, but I'm still waiting to hear why."

"It doesn't matter."

"It matters to me."

Someone uphill yelled for them to clear the course. Gray scooped up Jamie's skis and stepped to the side. She trailed behind him silently, and when he glanced over his shoulder, he saw the uncharacteristic slump of her shoulders.

They'd barely reached the edge of the trail when a group of snowboarders sped through the gates. He heard the edges of their boards slice through the snow, but kept his gaze on Jamie's face. She was doing it again. Melting some part of him that warned him not to get too involved. Maybe it was his sanity. He didn't understand how one minute he'd be furious with her, and now all he wanted to do was take her into his arms. "Just for the record," he said, "I'm pulling your lift ticket, not walking away from you."

She glanced up, surprise in her eyes. "Yes you were. You were skiing backward down the hill and picking up speed."

"That was before," Gray said. "I'm not moving now. I'm very stationary. It'd probably take a Sno-Cat to move me right now."

She made a sound that could have been either a laugh or a cry. He touched her arm, and she turned toward him, searching his eyes and looking more miserable than he could ever remember seeing her.

"I'm sorry," she said at last. "You're right. I was being reckless. I just didn't care if I got hurt or not."

"Well, I do."

"Ivy and I had an argument," Jamie admitted. "She hated the idea of the mother/daughter race." She laughed a little bitterly. "She can't wait to go back to Miss Porter's and get away from me."

"She's a teenager," Gray stated. "She doesn't really know what she wants."

Jamie shook her head. "My whole life I've tried to give her the best of everything so she'd feel good about herself and not miss having a dad." She hesitated.

"I can't do that anymore, Gray. I'm not even sure I can afford to keep her at Miss Porter's." She looked at him, and his heart ached at the despair in her eyes. "She hates me, Gray. I thought this mother/daughter race would help bring us together, but obviously it isn't going to happen. I've tried everything in my power, and it hasn't worked." She paused. "I don't know what else to do."

Gray remembered when Lonna died. He'd been overwhelmed by even the smallest decision, and his grief had been crushing, as if he were lying under a boulder and could barely draw a breath. He remembered crying out to God, begging Him for the strength to love Halle when everything inside felt broken. "Talk to God, Jamie. I know He can help."

"I don't think God wants anything to do with me."

"What makes you say that?"

Jamie's gaze followed another group of skiers speeding down the slope. "There was a time in my life when I really needed Him and He wasn't there."

"Maybe He was, but you couldn't see it."

Jamie's lips tightened. "I don't think so."

"When Lonna died, I wanted to be angry with Him and to blame Him," Gray admitted. "Every time I looked at Halle, I thought about all the things Lonna would never see—Halle's first date, Halle's graduation from high school, what college she'd go to, what she would look like on her wedding day. The face of our first grandchild." He felt himself teeter on the edge of something dark and painful and pushed forward. "It was like I was dead on the inside, Jamie, and there was nothing for me to give anyone. Not God, not my father—not even Halle. I couldn't let her grow up that way. I knew I had a choice—to stay angry at God and turn from Him, or I could turn to Him." He sighed. "He helped me put my life back together, and He can help you do the same. Whatever you've done, Jamie, it isn't greater than His love for you."

∽

"Whatever you've done, Jamie, it isn't greater than His love for you." Gray's words continued to resonate in her mind. She barely tasted the pizza Gray had had delivered and skipped dessert entirely, preferring to escape to her room. Standing by the darkened window, she looked blankly into the night and thought about what Gray had said about faith. When Ivy came into the room, Jamie found their silence unbearable and took refuge in a long shower. Even with the water pounding over her, she found herself wondering what her life would have been like if she'd turned to God instead of running away from Him. Would it have made a difference? And if so, could it make a difference now?

She put on her pajamas and bathrobe and wound her long hair into a towel.

In the bedroom, Ivy lay under the covers listening to her iPod. "Ivy, can I talk to you?"

No reply. Jamie reached over and unplugged Ivy's ears. "Can we talk, please?"

Ivy shrugged. "Whatever."

Jamie released a breath she hadn't known she was holding. She studied her daughter's full lips, so reminiscent of Devon's, and her large blue eyes, the mirror of her own. "We need to talk about this afternoon," she began.

Ivy pulled her knees up, turning the comforter into a tent. She looked ready to disappear into the folds of the covers at any second. *It's no use,* Jamie thought. *She hates me. This is hopeless.*

Just ask God. Jamie could almost hear Gray's deep voice urging her not to be afraid. She feared it was hopeless, and yet something insisted she try. She closed her eyes. *If You can hear me, I need Your help to reach my daughter. And if You don't want to do it for me, please do it for Ivy. She's blameless in all this.*

"I know you don't want to go in the mother/daughter race," Jamie said. "I'm not going to fight you on that. But something you said to me on the chair lift really bothered me. You said I never listen to what you want. Is that how you really feel?"

Ivy pleated the top edge of the comforter and avoided Jamie's gaze. "Yeah."

"But I give you everything you want," Jamie said.

"Just forget it. Whenever I try and talk to you, all you do is tell me why I'm wrong."

Jamie mentally counted to ten. "I'm sorry. Let's try it again."

"Oh, what's the point?" Ivy asked bitterly. "You really don't care."

"Of course I do." Jamie's stomach tightened into a hard lump. Just as she'd feared, God wasn't going to help her. Ivy had made up her mind to leave her—just like Devon and her parents had so many years ago. It was only a matter of time. She steadied the towel wrapped around her wet hair. She wanted—no needed— to look at her face in the mirror and see if there was anything visible that would explain just what it was about her that was so unacceptable. So unlovable.

"Okay," Ivy said. "I wanted to go to Aspen for Christmas. First you said yes, then you said no. I think you only wanted me to come to Connecticut so you wouldn't look like a bad parent to Mr. Grayson."

Jamie's hand went to her mouth. "Oh no, honey. Never that. I told you, it was the money thing. The Coleman sale fell through, and I couldn't swing it."

Ivy's eyes flashed. "You managed to swing diamond earrings for me for Christmas."

Jamie's hands automatically went to her earlobes, although she'd taken out the studs before she'd showered. She took a breath, hating what needed to be said next. "I gave you my diamond studs and bought myself a pair of cubic zirconias so no one would know."

Ivy seemed to shrink as the realization sank in. "But Mom. You love those earrings. I remember how proud you were when you bought them."

"I love you more," Jamie stated. "And I wanted you to have a really great Christmas gift. I still do. As soon as I can swing it, we'll pick out something more your taste."

Ivy shook her head. "No. It's okay. I didn't know. I thought you wanted me to look exactly like you. To be your clone."

Jamie winced at the choice of words. "I don't want you to be anything but my daughter."

"That's the trouble," Ivy said sadly. "I'm not just your daughter. I have a father and grandparents and who knows, maybe aunts and uncles and cousins." Her voice thickened as she visibly struggled to keep control of herself. "Why can't you tell me about them? Aren't I good enough for them?"

Jamie placed her hand on the tent pole that was Ivy's knee and felt the bony contour through the thick comforter. *What words, God? What words? If I say the wrong ones, I'll just make things worse.* "You're better than all of them put together." Jamie drew a shaky breath. "I don't like to talk about them because I don't want you to know them. They'll only hurt you, Ivy, just like they did me."

"Whatever happened," Ivy said flatly, "I want to know. I want to stop wondering if my dad is a secret agent or if we're in the witness protection program."

"We're not in the witness protection program, and your dad is not a spy—at least he wasn't when I knew him."

"Then who was he? What did he look like?" Ivy's voice cracked a bit. "I want to know his full name—and if he knew about me. If he ever saw me or. . .held me."

Jamie looked away from the vulnerability in her daughter's eyes. How much of the truth could Ivy handle? Her gaze moved to the brass door handle. Everything inside wanted to bolt out the door, run into the night and away from this conversation. She gripped her cold hands together. *I can't give her what she needs, God.*

Her gaze returned to Ivy, who was watching her intently. Jamie feared the judgment in those eyes. She wasn't prepared for the compassion in her daughter's voice as Ivy lifted the down comforter as much as Jamie's presence on the bed would allow. "You're shaking, Mom. It's warmer under the covers."

Jamie crawled into the bed. She heard the radiator's hiss and felt the heat coming off Ivy's body. When Ivy was a baby, the two of them used to cuddle in bed like this, keeping each other warm through the long Maine winter.

What Ivy needed to hear didn't start there, though. Jamie wound Ivy's hair around her index finger and began the story her daughter had waited thirteen years to hear.

Chapter 19

Jamie was serving breakfast in the dining room the next morning when Ivy walked in. It was just after six and way earlier than her daughter usually made an appearance. "Is everything okay?"

Ivy nodded, muttered a nearly incoherent good morning to the guests, and grabbed a lemon cheesecake muffin with the crumble topping. Jamie pretended not to notice her daughter's gaze following her as she moved about the room. When she went into the kitchen to refill the coffeepot, Ivy followed her.

"Look," Ivy said to Jamie's back. "I've been thinking. If it really means a lot to you for us to enter the mother/daughter race, I'll do it."

Jamie nearly dropped the coffeepot. She composed her face before she turned. "Only if you really want to do it." She realized immediately Ivy was wearing the diamond earrings. Her breath caught in her chest. Instinct, however, warned her to play it cool.

"Whatever," Ivy said and began to pick apart the muffin with her fingers. "If you want, maybe we could practice on the course this afternoon. I could give you some pointers."

With her free hand Jamie picked up a recipe card she had begun writing earlier that morning and slipped it into the pocket of her apron. She hoped Ivy didn't see how hard her hand was shaking. "Okay," she said. "I'll be ready to go about nine o'clock."

After Ivy left, Jamie leaned against the counters. Had her daughter actually suggested they spend some time together? She closed her eyes. *Thank You,* she said. *Now please help me not to blow it.*

She heard Gray's voice coming from the dining room. Opening her eyes, she set the coffeepot down and hurried out of the kitchen. She couldn't wait to give him the exciting news.

∼

Gray was thrilled to hear Ivy had decided to partner with Jamie in the mother/daughter race. He was less thrilled with Halle, who was late to practice later that afternoon. He searched the top of the mountain for her. With the interclub race just days away, every moment of practice time was valuable. Besides, it wasn't fair to the other kids who were waiting to get started.

"Sorry, Dad," Halle said, shushing to a stop just inches from the tips of his skis. "I was practicing scales."

"I don't want to hear any excuses," Gray said coldly and watched the sparkle die in his daughter's eyes. He ignored the urge to say something encouraging to her. "Today we're practicing our starts." He climbed up the snowy start gate he'd created and demonstrated how the kids should do it. "Just like that." He gestured to the tall, lanky teenager next to him. "You try it, Chris."

The boy took his place at the top of the embankment Gray had created with the Sno-Cat. Chris began to slide back and forth as Gray began the countdown.

"Great," he yelled as the boy sped out of the makeshift gate.

He let all the other kids go, but held Halle back. Watching her take her place in the starting gate, he remained silent. She signaled her readiness, but Gray couldn't start the countdown. *Did you know, Halle,* he wanted to say, *that your mother once dreamed about trying out for the U.S. ski team? But then she had you—and she gave up those dreams because she didn't want to leave you. She never complained, not once, but I knew deep inside there was a part of her that wondered what could have been. She used to hold you off the ground and swing you gently side to side, like you were skiing. "This is our Olympic baby," she'd say. "Our gold-medal girl."*

"Dad?" Halle prompted.

He looked at his daughter and saw Lonna's face at that age. Young, strong, bursting with confidence and desire to show the world just how good she was. Lonna whispering dreams about the mountains they'd ski and the races they'd win. Lonna laughing as he warned her to be careful the snowy afternoon she'd gone out to buy Halle's favorite cookies—Social Tea Biscuits—for a make-believe tea party. Lonna pale and still beautiful in the clothing he'd picked out for her funeral service.

"Halle," he started and then didn't quite know what to say.

"I'm really sorry about being late, Dad. It won't happen again."

"I know," he said. "You ready?"

She nodded.

"Okay, then." He counted down and watched her launch herself out of the starting gate. She flashed past him in a tight tuck, and he watched her back grow smaller as she sped down the hill.

Gray braced himself against a piercing, cold gust. The wind was always strongest on this part of the mountain. Harder to handle was the thought that the dreams he'd held on to so tightly might be long gone, and if he opened his fingers he'd find his hands were as empty as those of a magician who had successfully performed a disappearing coin trick.

New Year's Eve arrived on the heels of some uncharacteristically warm weather. Despite his best efforts, Gray watched the sun erode the snow base, and patches of straggly grass and mud appeared in the places worn thin by skiers. Business dropped off, especially when he had to close several trails in order to concentrate his snow-making efforts on the main ones. Gray couldn't stop thinking how one bad year had put Powder Ridge out of business. The thought of seeing Pilgrim's Peak on the auction block haunted him.

The rain began falling lightly at dusk. Gray was in no mood for the party, which already was in full swing when he walked into the family room. Norman stuck a silly hat on him and pulled him toward the front of the room. "We're playing charades," he said. "Hurry up, Gray. Our team could use you. The theme is movies, and Jamie's team is killing us."

Gray shrugged off his father's arm. It was supposed to rain all night and all the next day. Then, if this wasn't bad enough, the temperature was supposed to drop below freezing tomorrow night. The hill was going to be like skiing down a glacier. "No thanks, Dad," he said. He picked a slice of pizza off the buffet table.

"Window!" Jamie shouted. "*Rear Window!*"

Gray felt a draft of air. It was coming from a window Mrs. Banbridge had cracked open. She appeared to be shooing something through the narrow opening. Her team seated on the couch had fallen into speculative silence.

"Fire!" Mrs. Gregory finally yelled. "*Towering Inferno!*"

Mrs. Banbridge shook her head and opened the window wider.

"I think she's trying to climb out the window," Mr. Gregory stated. He pulled his moustache. "*Escape from Alcatraz*," he shouted.

Gray grinned as Mrs. Banbridge pretended the cold air coming in from the window was powerful enough to knock her backward. She struggled against an invisible wind that was trying to blow her backward. "*Ghost*," Halle shouted.

"*The Mist,*" Ivy yelled.

Mrs. Banbridge stopped struggling against the wind and started laughing. After a moment she walked over to the draperies and wrapped one around herself. "*The Mummy,*" Jamie called out. Ivy and Halle burst out laughing.

As Mrs. Banbridge pantomimed throwing random things out the window, Gray's gaze traveled to the back of the couch. Jamie's long, sleek ponytail bobbed with laughter as Mrs. Banbridge lost her grip on a plastic cup and sent it sailing into the darkness.

Crossing the room, he stopped in front of the couch and told Halle to scoot over a bit. Seating himself next to Jamie, Gray established himself as part of their team. A log popped in the fireplace, and Mrs. Banbridge resumed waving at everybody as Dr. Goldman, who was on the other team, gave them a five-second warning.

"*Gone with the Wind,*" Gray yelled, as surprised as anyone else to find the words coming from him.

Mrs. Banbridge nodded and beamed at him as the other team good-naturedly protested his involvement. Gray glanced sideways at Jamie, who was smiling in delight at him.

She was warm and soft against his side, and she smelled like cinnamon. Something deep inside him started to relax. The sound of the rain disappeared in the voices as Mr. Gregory took his turn in front of the fireplace. Gray looked into Jamie's face, and suddenly the New Year was filled with possibilities he would never have imagined existed a month ago.

Chapter 20

A light rain continued to fall on New Year's Day. Jamie stayed inside and thought she'd lose her mind with Ivy peppering questions at her. Why couldn't they drive down to Greenwich and drop in on her parents? Could Ivy call them herself and then hang up when they answered? Could Jamie give Ivy her credit card number so Ivy could hire an Internet service that would help her locate Devon?

Jamie stayed busy in the kitchen, answering with monosyllables—mostly noes—and reminding Ivy that the interclub race was the next day and that she couldn't very well leave Gray and Norman to do all the work.

"You're putting me off again," Ivy stated.

"And you're getting on my nerves." Jamie smashed an egg against the side of the bowl so hard the yolk dripped down the outside edge. "I told you, you've got to give me time to figure things out."

"You've had thirteen years to figure it out," Ivy said. "I can't wait any longer."

Jamie pushed back a strand of hair and met her daughter's determined gaze. "You have to wait until after the interclub race."

"You promise?"

"Only if you understand they might not be the grandparents you want."

Ivy held out her hand. "Deal."

After lunch, when the rain finally stopped, Jamie escaped to Pilgrim's Peak with Norman. They carried boxes of office supplies toward the lodge. "Careful," Jamie warned. The temperature was dropping, and already she could feel a thin layer of ice forming in the parking lot. She glanced uneasily at the glassy coating on the limbs of trees and power lines. "Will we still be able to have the ski race tomorrow?"

"Oh sure," Norman said, picking his way over the semifrozen ground. "Gray'll break up the ice on the mountain with the Sno-Cat. The hill will be fast," he warned in his gravelly voice, "but it won't stop anyone from coming."

His prediction turned out to be completely accurate. Despite icy roads and frigid weather, by seven o'clock the next morning the ski lodge was packed. Jamie could hardly hear herself think in the low roar of voices. She handed out dozens of numbered racing bibs as Norman provided a running commentary on the PA system.

A few hours later, new volunteers arrived to give Jamie and Norman a break. Although Norman refused to give up the microphone, he urged Jamie to find a good spot on Alice's Alley to watch the races. "If you hurry," he explained, "you'll be in time to see Ivy and Halle."

Jamie hurried to the chair lift. As it carried her up the mountain, she heard the crowd cheer each time a skier completed the course. Norman's voice boomed out the time. When she dismounted at the top, she hurried to Alice's Alley.

Gray had warned her about the corn snow—the little nubs of ice that had been formed by the Sno-Cat—but Jamie hadn't realized just how hard it would be to turn and control her speed. She found herself struggling with her wedge turns and nearly skiing into another spectator as she sought free space along the orange safety net.

A girl in a silver bodysuit and bowl-shaped helmet flashed past. Jamie heard the girl's skis hiss across the ice as she maneuvered around a gate.

Jamie's cold hands tightened into fists as racer after racer sped through the course. There were a few wipeouts, one poor child missed a gate, and another had a false start. Her heart began to race when she spotted her daughter at the top of the hill.

"Go, Ivy," Jamie murmured as her gaze followed her daughter. "Go, Ivy," she said more loudly as Ivy picked up speed. "Go, Ivy!" Jamie screamed at the top of her lungs as her daughter neared, then blasted past. Ivy finished the final turn and held a tight tuck as she crossed under the finish line.

Then Halle was coming down the course at full speed. Jamie had never seen her ski full-out. Even knowing as little as she did about skiing, she could tell Halle was in a class by herself. Smooth and graceful, her skis barely seemed to touch the snow.

"Go, Halle!" Jamie bellowed as the girl rocketed past her. Unable to stay where she was for a second longer, Jamie skied down the rest of the mountain. She found Halle and Ivy among the crowd of spectators and competitors milling about the finish line. The girls were hugging each other and jumping up and down.

"Ivy's had the best time so far!" Halle cried out when she saw Jamie.

Ivy had beaten Halle? She looked at her daughter's face for confirmation. "Only by, like, a tenth of a second," Ivy said, trying and failing to appear as if this were no big deal.

"We're in first and second place!" both girls said in unison.

Jamie opened her arms. "Girls, I am so proud of you both." They were as tall as Jamie, and yet both their heads folded into her neck as if they were much smaller and younger.

"Okay, Mom," Ivy said, drawing back. "Halle and I want to watch the rest of the junior race."

The two girls disappeared into the crowd. Jamie brought Norman a hot chocolate and a pastry. He seemed in good spirits and brushed off her offer to help. "Just go have fun," he said. "But be careful."

Jamie went back outside to watch the rest of the junior team races. The girls' race continued for another hour, but Ivy's and Halle's times held. Two other girls on their team also had good times, and by lunch Norman was announcing that the Pilgrim's Peak junior girls had won their division. Jamie couldn't wait to see Gray's face.

Before she knew it, it was midafternoon and time for the mother/daughter race. Jamie rode the lift to the top of the hill with Ivy, who could not seem to sit still on the bench seat. "Don't worry about going fast on the course," Ivy coached. "My time will more than make up for yours. Just don't DQ."

Jamie knew DQ meant disqualify. "Don't worry," Jamie said. "If I have to slide on my back to the finish line, I will."

"Gate eight is the worst," Ivy said. "It's the one closest to the safety net, so you have to turn pretty sharply—and there's a lot of ice around it. You'll probably want to slow down before that gate."

"Right," Jamie agreed.

"Remember, Mom, after the last gate the race isn't finished. You should go into a low tuck until you cross the finish line. Races are won or lost in a hundredth of a second."

"Okay." Jamie smiled. Ivy was really into this racing thing. Just as she'd hoped, it was bringing them together. "This is fun, huh?"

"Yeah," Ivy agreed. "I've been thinking. You know how you said you wanted to wait until you weren't broke to introduce me to my grandparents? Well, if we won the race together, you would feel more confident and I wouldn't have to wait for you to start selling houses again."

The thought was so awful it was almost funny. She pictured both of them standing outside her parents' front door. "Hello," Jamie would say when one of them answered the bell. "This is for you." And she'd hand them an enormous golden trophy. "Can we be part of your life again?"

They'd nearly reached the top of the mountain, so Jamie lifted the safety bar. "Let's just get through this race."

The wind seemed to slice right through Jamie's parka as she and Ivy skied to the start of Alice's Alley. Over the heads of racers she spotted Gray at the starting gate. He had his arm raised like a flag and was about to send the next racer down the course. His face looked red and chapped from the extreme cold.

There were about twelve teams in the mother/daughter race. They ranged in size and shape, but most of them had skintight racing suits that said they'd done this before. Jamie looked at the grooves cut into the snow by the other skiers and felt slightly sick. None of the other skiers looked like they struggled with wedge turns.

Soon Gray called Ivy's number. Jamie gave her daughter a quick hug for luck, and almost immediately she was watching the back of her daughter speed down the hill. The crowd cheered and cowbells rang as Ivy leaned hard into the first gate.

When it was Jamie's turn, she lined up at the starting gate. Her heart was going full tilt, and her legs shook. Gray raised his arm. "Jamie? You ready?"

Jamie swallowed. The hill suddenly looked a lot steeper. She glanced at Gray and saw the tight, worried line of his mouth. She didn't trust herself to speak, so she just nodded.

He spoke into a radio and then began to count down. "Three. . .two. . . one. . . Go!"

Jamie hurled her body forward. At the same time, the wind gusted, pushing her forward. In the blink of an eye, she went from standstill to full speed. The crowd yelled encouragement as she headed for the first gate.

Easy, she cautioned herself as she flew down the icy course. The snow felt like hard little balls of packed ice under her skis. Cold air slashed her cheeks. Even behind the protective shield of her helmet, her eyes began to tear. She reached the first set of gates and aimed for the second. They came up quickly.

She swung a little wide after the second gate, but corrected herself in time to take the third, fourth, and fifth gates. She'd never skied so fast in her life, and it was both exhilarating and terrifying. More of the course flashed under her skis. She made no effort to check her speed. She'd either finish the course or crash. And then she glimpsed the eighth set of gates. They were straddling a large patch of ice.

Her skis made a shrill *ssssss* sound. She felt her downhill ski begin to skid out from under her. She threw her arms up for balance. She hit the side of the plastic gate, and her ski poles flew out of her hands. *Oh God,* she screamed in her head. *Help me.* She braced herself for a fall that didn't come. Instead, somehow she remained balanced—one leg in the air and arms straight out to the side— and then miraculously she was off the ice and heading straight for the next set of gates.

She cut the next turns as tightly as she dared. Several times her skis chattered over icy chunks of snow, and once she came scarily close to the orange safety net holding back the spectators. But then the finish line was in sight, and she was streaking toward it, crouched over just like Ivy had instructed, and then she flashed under it. She straightened and forced her tired legs into a snowplow position before she plowed into the safety net.

Halle and Ivy rushed out to congratulate her. Both girls enveloped her in hugs as she struggled to catch her breath.

"Mom!" Ivy cried. "I can't believe how fast you went!"

"That makes two of us," Jamie panted. "I was never so scared in my life."

"You scared me, too, Miss Jamie."

"Gate eight," Jamie said. "I don't know what happened."

"You looked like you were doing this really weird yoga pose," Ivy declared, hugging her. "I seriously thought you were going to crash, but you didn't! You're amazing!"

Jamie realized she was still shaking from head to foot. Norman's voice came over the loudspeaker. "Ladies and gentlemen," he said. His voice shook with excitement. "I'm pleased to announce a blistering time of one minute two seconds!"

"That's the fastest mom's time yet!" Halle began to jump up and down. "And since Ivy had the fastest daughter time, you guys may be the winners!"

Jamie glanced at Ivy's glowing eyes and small but proud smile. It was worth that nerve-racking run down the mountain to see her daughter looking at her like that. A man she didn't recognize handed her her ski poles, and she smiled her thanks.

They moved aside as another racer sped across the finish line. A muscular woman in a blue and red racing suit hooted with laughter. "That was insane," she said. "And so much fun!" A chunky girl with a striped hat and scarf rushed out to give her a hug. Jamie watched the two embrace and smiled. Nothing like the fear of crashing on an icy slalom course to bring people together.

She waited for Norman to announce the woman's time. It seemed to be taking longer than usual, and she wondered if there had been some kind of complication. The silence stretched on and on. People began to murmur and look around. Jamie turned to Halle, who shrugged. "Maybe there's something wrong with the speaker system," she suggested.

Jamie nodded. That made sense. But then an unfamiliar voice boomed over the loudspeaker. "EMTs to the announcer's booth immediately!"

Chapter 21

Gray prayed. Jamie drove. When she pulled up in front of the emergency room at the Waterbury Hospital, he barely waited for the car to stop before jumping out. Pushing open the sliding double doors, he ran to the front desk.

"I'm looking for my father, Norman Westler. He came by ambulance. Probably arrived about a half hour ago."

"Let me see." A heavyset woman with black hair scraped into a painfully tight bun hit a few keys on a laptop computer. "He's in exam room three. I'll show you."

Gray followed the woman down a hallway lined with curtained-off examination rooms. He found his father lying on a bed with all sorts of electrodes hooked to his chest and an IV snaking out of his arm. His father's face was ashen.

"Dad." Gray reached his father's side in two steps. He peered into Norman's red-rimmed eyes, which looked painfully exposed without the thick lenses of his glasses. "What happened?"

"It was like an elephant was sitting on my chest," Norman replied, sounding subdued, but nonetheless alive and kicking. "And it hurt so bad I passed out. The next thing I knew the paramedics were strapping me to a stretcher."

A young man with a long skinny black braid walked into the examination area. "I'm Henry," he said to Gray, but his eyes were taking in the numbers on the monitors and he had a needle and syringe in his hands. "I'm the nurse helping to care for Mr. Westler."

"I'm his son, Grayson Westler. What's going on?"

"He's already had some nitroglycerin, and now I'm giving your father a shot of morphine. It'll help with the pain and with the workload on his heart."

"His heart?" Gray felt his own skip a couple of beats. "You think he's had a heart attack?"

"The doctor will want to talk to you about that." He turned to Norman. "How are you feeling, Mr. Westler?"

"Like I never should have had that chili dog at lunch."

Henry laughed, but his brown eyes were serious. "What time did you eat?"

"About noon."

Gray rolled a stool closer to the bed and sat near his father's head. If Henry was asking about the food his dad had eaten, he was probably thinking surgery. *Oh God,* he thought. *No.* "He probably had at least two chili dogs," Gray added.

"And french fries and a soda. Maybe a chocolate pudding."

"It was an ice-cream sandwich," Norman corrected. "And a pastry."

"I'll let the doctor know." Henry left the room.

Gray stared down at his father's shiny bald head. He hoped it was the fluorescent lights that painted an unhealthy cast to his dad's skin color. He tried to warm his dad's cold fingers, but his own were barely warmer. "You're going to be okay, Dad. They're going to take good care of you here."

"I'm not afraid to die." A look of pain crossed his features. "If it's my time, I'm ready to go to Jesus."

Gray rubbed his dad's hand gently. "You're not going to Jesus today."

"How do you know?"

"You're still here."

Norman smiled a little. "Today's not over." He shifted in the bed. "Don't let them hook me to any life-support machine, Gray. Promise? And my will, it's in a wooden box in my closet."

"Okay, Dad," Gray agreed just to soothe him. "Just rest."

Gray looked up as a beanpole of a man in green surgical scrubs walked into the room. He had a clipboard in his hands and a very serious look on his face. "I'm Dr. Gabriel York. I'm a cardiologist. Your father has had a heart attack, and we need to perform an angioplasty in order to open one of the arteries in his heart."

Gray swallowed, taking in the information. More doctors entered the room—a female anesthesiologist and another doctor who introduced himself as the ER admitting doctor. They gathered information from Gray as yet another person entered the room and thrust some papers into his dad's hand to sign. Before Gray could truly take in what was happening, they whisked his dad off to the operating room. After they left, Gray stared at the empty space where his father had been and prayed.

∼

Jamie looked up as Gray walked into the waiting room. His face looked ill with worry. She tried to smile reassuringly as he picked his way across the room, but her lips trembled. "Is he okay?"

"They've taken him to surgery," Gray explained. "We need to go to the fourth floor."

On the way, Gray explained in a tight voice that his father was having a heart attack and the doctors were performing an angioplasty in order to prevent further damage to his heart. Although Gray said this operation was very common, it sounded serious, and Jamie had to fight to keep the fear from showing on her face.

The surgical waiting room was empty. She and Gray dropped onto side-by-side chairs. She curled her fingers around his. "He's a strong man, Gray. He'll pull through this."

Gray nodded and gripped her hand a little tighter. He stared for a little while at the TV monitor, which was turned to CNN but had no sound. After a short time he bowed his head and closed his eyes. She realized he must be praying.

She thought about it and then closed her eyes. *Lord, there's this man, Norman Westler, and he's in surgery right now, and he needs Your help. Please don't let him die. Let him get better. Gray needs You, too, God. His hand's like ice.*

It seemed like forever, but then a tall, painfully thin man in surgical scrubs popped out from behind a closed door and marched toward them in long, unhurried strides. Jamie struggled to read his face.

"It went very well," the doctor said, holding out a cloudy-looking X-ray. "We were able to restore blood flow, but we'll have to run some more tests before we understand the extent of the damage." He pointed to the lower right chamber of the heart. "See this discolored area? It's deterioration. I suspect your father has been experiencing symptoms for some time now."

Gray frowned at the X-ray. "So you're saying this is not a new problem."

"No. Has your dad been complaining of shortness of breath, chest pain, pain in his arms, or dizziness?"

"I don't think so," Gray said. At the same time Jamie said, "Yes."

She glanced at Gray's surprised face and turned back to the doctor. "I saw him one night get dizzy. It went away after he rested."

Gray's eyes narrowed. "When was this?"

"A few days ago. The night we played Monopoly."

"Did he complain of chest pain or nausea?" the doctor asked.

"He said his stomach was a little upset. He didn't eat much dinner. Remember, Gray?"

Gray shook his head. "No. He's seemed perfectly fine to me."

"The key to surviving a heart attack is getting the proper treatment as soon as possible," the doctor said gravely. "Restoring the blood flow is critical."

Gray had a lot of questions. Jamie began writing things down for him on a scrap of paper so he could go over it later. It all seemed complicated—just the terminology was confusing—and after the doctor drew several diagrams, it became clear the doctor was trying to tell them he feared Norman was in the early stages of heart failure.

"Will he need a heart transplant?" Jamie asked and saw her own fear mirrored in Gray's eyes.

"It's too soon to tell," the doctor said.

When Norman woke up, a surgical nurse brought Gray back to the recovery area to see him, and several hours later he was taken to a room. Jamie was frightened by the bluish tint to his lips and fingernails and the paleness of his skin. Monitors flashing unfathomable information flanked him. He had an IV dripping into his arm and an oxygen tube fastened under his nose. His eyes were closed, but when Jamie squeezed his hand, she felt him grasp her fingers a little harder. She bent low so she could whisper for his ear alone. "I love you, Norman."

She and Gray didn't speak much on the way back to the house. Gray drove. His gaze, fixed on the road, discouraged conversation, and Jamie felt a lump of guilt settle directly on her vocal cords. She should have mentioned the dizzy spell to Gray. And if this wasn't enough, she feared her reckless trip down the ski hill had triggered Norman's heart attack. When she tried to apologize to Gray, he cut her off, claiming his dad's condition was not her fault.

Halle and Ivy raced out to greet them the minute Gray parked the Jeep in front of the house. Gray barely got out of the car before Halle launched herself into his arms and buried her head in his shoulder. "Shhh," Gray said in a low, soothing voice. "Grandpa is okay. He's resting now."

Ivy's eyes were large and luminous beneath the porch lights. "What's wrong with him, Mom?" she asked. "Is Mr. Westler going to be okay?"

"I think so," Jamie replied. Glancing over the top of Ivy's head, she watched Gray stroke the back of Halle's head and saw Halle's back shake with sobs.

"Grandpa had a heart attack," Gray said gently, "and he has to stay in the hospital for a few days for some tests."

Jamie put her arm across the top of Ivy's shoulders. "Come on, let's go inside. Did you and Halle get something to eat?"

"No," Ivy said. "We weren't hungry." She stared at Halle and Gray for a long moment, and it occurred to Jamie that their grief was foreign to her daughter. Ivy had never been close to anyone they'd known who'd died or had faced a life-threatening illness. She had no idea how scary and painful it could be. Jamie studied her daughter's eyes a little more closely and realized she had it all wrong. Just because Ivy had never known her father or grandparents didn't mean she was incapable of mourning their loss.

Chapter 22

Norman grew stronger, but as the doctor had suspected, there was irreversible damage to the heart. It was not immediately life threatening or bad enough to put him on the list for a heart transplant, but it was life-changing. For the rest of his life, he would have to remain on a very strict diet and exercise plan and take medications—"Horse pills," Norman called them.

On Sunday afternoon, Jamie drove Ivy back to Miss Porter's school in old Sally. When they reached Ivy's dormitory, Jamie turned off the engine. Over the knocks and rattles of the old car, she hugged her daughter. "I love you," she said.

Ivy murmured something like, "You, too." She drew back. "You're not going to forget about me meeting my grandparents, are you?"

"Of course not," Jamie promised. "When things settle down a bit, I'll call them."

Ivy started to open the car door and then stopped. "You're not going to call them, are you? There's always going to be some reason why you can't."

Jamie reminded herself to be patient, although a part of her felt a little irritated with Ivy. The last two days had been rough, and she was tired. "Of course I'm going to call them. You have to trust me, Ivy."

"When?" Ivy pressed. "When will you call them?"

Jamie bit her tongue before she spoke. "Soon." She held her hand to ward off Ivy's next question. "It depends on how Norman and Gray are doing."

Ivy shook her head rapidly back and forth. "My real grandpa could have a heart attack, just like Mr. Westler, and he could die. I wouldn't even get to know him." She wrenched open the car door. "Maybe he's already dead."

"Look," Jamie said flatly. "You know what my parents did—I would think you would have a little loyalty to me." She saw the look of disgust on Ivy's face just before her daughter slammed the door shut.

Jamie marched to the back of the car. She hauled out Ivy's suitcase and ski bag. She set these on the sidewalk and freed Ivy's skis from the rack atop the car. "When you're up in your room cataloging all the things I've done wrong, just remember that I was the one who stuck around. I was the one who loved you—who still loves you."

"I'm sorry," Ivy said. "I know. . . . It's just. . ."

Jamie put her arms around Ivy. "Hard," she finished. "But we'll figure this out together."

Ivy wriggled out from Jamie's arms. "Are you mad at me?"

"No. Are you mad at me?"

"No," Ivy said. "But you'll call this week, right?"

Jamie sighed. Ivy had no idea how much work was waiting for Jamie back at the office or what she was asking Jamie to do. "Ivy, please," she said, then relented. "I'll try." She started to roll Ivy's suitcase toward the house, but Ivy's hand on her arm stopped her. "It's okay, Mom. I've got it."

"You've got the skis and ski bag." Jamie took another step toward the building.

"Mom!" Ivy said sharply. When Jamie turned around, she added, "I can do both. You ought to get going." Then she whispered, "Old Sally is leaking oil on the road. It's embarrassing."

Jamie hurried back to the car just as a white Infiniti pulled to the curb. A well-groomed woman stepped out. For a moment their eyes met. Jamie watched the gaze of the other woman slide away from her, the way someone might glance away from a homeless person.

Jamie slammed the old Buick's door. Turning the key, she punched the gas. "Make Norman proud," she said. The Buick backfired as if it were expelling a cannonball, and a large black cloud blocked the view out the rear window. Jamie started to laugh as she roared away from the curb.

$\sim$

They brought Norman home on Monday. Gray wanted to take his dad straight to the house, but Norman insisted on going to the ski lodge. He intended to get back to work in the rental shop, but Gray put his foot down. They began to argue, but Jamie stepped in and negotiated a compromise. They would take Norman to the ski hill, but only if he agreed to settle in a comfortable chair in front of the lodge windows.

"You want some tea?" Jamie asked as she pulled a woolen throw higher on Norman's lap. "A piece of fruit?"

"I want a chili dog," Norman stated. At the look on her face, he added, "I'm joking. The two of you get going." He pointed a knobby finger at Gray. "You've got lessons to teach and a hill to run. And you,"—he pointed to Jamie—"I want to see you coming down Alice's Alley, hopefully slower than the last time I saw you."

Jamie felt herself cringe, although Norman had assured her that she hadn't caused his heart attack.

"I'm teasing," Norman said. "The two of you have to stop wearing funeral faces. Shoo. Get going."

Gray said, "I don't have any lessons scheduled today. Besides, Dad, I'd really like to hang out with you."

"Don't take this wrong," Norman growled, "but I'd rather be alone. I just want to sit here with the sun on my face and nobody telling me what to do—or trying to stick another needle into me."

"Dad," Gray said gently. "You just got home. At least let one of us stay until you get settled." Gray glanced at Jamie, who nodded in agreement.

"No," Norman thundered and turned an alarming shade of red. "I'd rather ski myself off a cliff than be treated as an invalid."

"Gray," Jamie said, laying her hand on his tense arm. "Maybe we better do what he says."

"She's right," Norman said. "Besides, the best medicine would be knowing the two of you are on the hill having fun. Alice and I made some great memories on that hill. You two should, too." He winked at Gray.

After Gray asked Doreen Mosley, who was working in the concession stand, to keep an eye on his dad, he and Jamie headed to the locker rooms to change. She worried about leaving Norman alone, but thought it would be okay if it was only for a short time. She understood, too, that Norman needed to exert his independence.

She met Gray at the double chair lift. The line wasn't long, and soon the two of them were at treetop level and climbing higher. After spending so much time at the hospital, the air smelled incredibly fresh and healthy to them. The heat of the sun contrasted with the freezing temperatures, and the bulk of Gray seated on the bench beside her warmed something deep inside.

"He's arguing and being bossy," Gray said. "I think that's a good sign."

"Yeah," Jamie agreed. "But maybe after this run, we should check on him."

Gray nodded. "Good idea." He glanced at her. "I haven't thanked you enough for all you've done for us, Jamie. I don't know how I would have gotten through the last week without you."

"I'm glad I was here," Jamie replied. "And I wouldn't have been here if you hadn't taken in me and Ivy. You're a good man, Gray."

They rode in silence and then, very casually as if he were only stretching, Gray laid his arm over the back of the bench seat. Jamie's heart started to beat a little faster. Equally casually, as if she were merely shifting into a more comfortable position, she leaned into the curve of his arm.

Neither said anything, but Jamie wondered if his heart was beating as fast as hers. She could hardly breathe, and all she could think about was how good it felt to sit so close to him, how strong his body felt and how perfectly she fit into the crook of his arm.

She lifted her face and found him looking down at her, a soft, searching expression in his brown eyes. She didn't resist when he bent his head and kissed her. It was over in a flash, but Jamie saw something serious in his eyes as he pulled away from her.

"You don't know how long I've wanted to do that," he said.

The wind shook the lift lightly. Jamie felt the chill right through her parka. "Gray," she said. "I like you a lot, but tomorrow. . .I'm going back to Greenwich. My job," she said. "I can't take any more time off."

This was true, but it was only part of the reason. They rolled over another support tower, and the top of the mountain came into view. The snow-covered ground and trees braced against the wind seemed to mirror something lonely and empty in her heart.

"Greenwich and Woodbury are just a little over an hour apart. I'd really like to see you again."

"Me, too, but..." Jamie struggled to put something in words that she really didn't fully understand herself. "I need to figure some things out first. Alone." She said the last word gently, but watched Gray's features tighten.

The lift reached the top of the mountain, and Jamie skied off the chair next to Gray. Although they moved out of the way of the lift line, it was unnecessary. The hilltop was empty. A cold wind whipped across the peak, stinging her cheeks. Jamie's nose started to run, and she wiped it with a tissue, thinking she must look awful. *Talk to him,* something said. She wanted to ignore the voice— did Gray really need to hear the awful story? Yet she sensed it would be a mistake to ignore such a strong feeling.

"When I was growing up," she began, "I was the girl who got straight As, made varsity cheerleader, and played Mary in the church's Nativity play, but all I wanted was my parents to see me—not my achievements. I wanted them to love me unconditionally. At the same time, I was afraid not to be the daughter they wanted.

"There was this boy on the football team—Devon Brown. He held the high school record for scoring touchdowns. He was also a rebel—the kind of kid who talked back to teachers when they deserved it and wore his hair twice as long as he was supposed to." She glanced up at Gray's eyes to see if he'd figured out where this whole story was going and if his opinion of her already was changing. "I wanted to be like him. I didn't want to care what the world thought about me. I thought I could be a different person with him.

"So I pursued him," Jamie continued. "At every game I cheered louder than anybody else for him. I decorated his locker and made up personal holidays in his name. I wore the clothes I thought he'd like and flirted until he noticed me. We started going out, and just like I hoped, I began feeling a bit like a rebel."

She was getting to the part of the story she dreaded most. "One night Devon asked if I wanted to drive to the beach. I knew from the way he said it and the look in his eye that it was going to be more than that. I thought it would be the final piece of finding myself."

She could almost hear the sound of Devon's car door slamming shut behind her, and the rumble of the motor as they drove away from her parents' house. They'd parked in a lonely spot where they could see the black water of the Atlantic rippling in the moonlight. She'd felt fear, cold as the hand Devon placed on her neck, wash over her. *"I love you, baby,"* he'd said.

"Devon didn't want to be a father, and my parents didn't want to be grandparents, so they sent me to live with Aunt Bea in Maine. They said I was beyond their help and should beg for God's forgiveness." She looked Gray straight in the eye. "I've loved Ivy since before she was born. How was I supposed to tell God that I wish I hadn't gotten into that car with Devon Brown? If I hadn't done that, I wouldn't have her."

Gray's eyes held the kindest expression she had ever seen. "There are no accidental children—they're all designed by the Lord. I don't think God would want the circumstances of Ivy's birth to keep you from having a relationship with Him. He doesn't focus on sin."

"I can't ask for His forgiveness," Jamie said sadly, "because I'm not sorry for what I did. If I didn't get in that car, I wouldn't have Ivy. Don't you see?"

"I think if you spent time with the Lord and got to know Him more deeply, you would think differently. God loves you unconditionally," Gray said. "He wants no walls between you. I don't think you do either."

Many times in Jamie's life she'd felt herself reaching out for God, then jerking her hand back. Wanting His love but fearing she didn't deserve it. She flexed her cold fingers and shifted her weight against the top of her boots. This was all true, but if she were honest—truly honest with herself—she'd admit it wasn't just fear of rejection that kept her from God. Part of her hadn't wanted to give up control of her life to anyone. She'd wanted her parents and the whole world to see that Jamie King could make it on her own. What she saw now, however, was how foolish she'd been.

She looked at Gray, at the gentleness in his dark eyes and the tousled brown hair framing his suntanned face. He'd lost his wife, almost his father, and a bad year of weather could cripple him financially. Yet there was an inner core of strength about him. She remembered the expression on his face as he'd sat beside his father's hospital bed praying, and she felt something inside her start to give.

"Jamie," Gray prompted gently "What are you thinking?"

About you, she thought. *About what it must feel like to have such a strong faith and how I'm scared that I'll never be like that.* "We should get going," she said at last. "Norman needs you, and I have to start packing. I'm leaving tomorrow, remember?"

He tugged gently on her scarf. "Yes, but you don't have to. You could stay and run the B&B. Mrs. Dodges could help my dad in the ski shop."

Jamie understood he wasn't just talking about a job. He was talking about them. Their future. Her heart started to race. She stared at his lips, wondering what it might be like to kiss him and knowing instinctively that it would be overwhelming. She could feel parts of herself dissolving just thinking about it. It was tempting, but there wasn't just herself to consider.

"Thanks, Gray," she managed to reply, "but I wouldn't be able to keep Ivy in private school. She deserves a chance to get the best education I can give her."

"Maybe you deserve something, too," Gray said. "A chance to be happy. Maybe it's time you stopped punishing yourself for something that happened a long time ago. I understand if you want to go back to Greenwich, but it doesn't mean what we started here has to end."

It made perfect sense, and it wasn't as if she didn't want the same thing, too. The longing for him to put his arms around her was an ache so strong it was nearly unbearable. At the same time, she cringed at the thought of him seeing the apartment she couldn't afford and learning about her maxed-out credit cards. He deserved better than the messed-up life she had to offer.

She could change, though. Straighten out her life. All she needed was a little more time. One good sale could turn everything around. Two sales and she'd be debt free. The market really heated up in the spring, and by then she might have other things figured out, too—like Ivy's obsession with meeting Jamie's parents.

For his own sake, she needed to make Gray understand she wasn't saying no—just not now. She took a deep breath of icy air and began to speak. It was hard, but not impossible, to move past the look of hurt and disappointment that formed in Gray's dark brown eyes.

Chapter 23

Her apartment felt cold and empty. Jamie kicked off her Ferragamos at the door and pulled her suitcase through the plush white carpeting. She turned up the heat, but continued to wander about her apartment, touching things, trying to feel a sense of homecoming.

She changed into a dark gray pantsuit and spent forty-five minutes fussing with her hair and makeup. When she got into old Sally, she had every intention of going straight to work. However, she surprised herself by driving right past the office building.

She had a vague idea of going to Todd's Point to walk the beach or picking up some groceries at the A&P, but when she spotted the mottled gray stones of an old Methodist church, the car seemed to turn into the parking lot of its own accord.

The church was empty, and she settled herself into a hard-backed pew. The light through the stained glass illuminated an image of Jesus on the cross. She thought about Him, about how much He had suffered and yet how much He loved. She remembered all the prayers of her youth—*make me a cheerleader, make me blonder, thinner. Make Devon love me.* When had she ever closed her eyes and given herself to Him? Putting her face in her hands, she let the tears fall.

She wasn't sure how long she sat there, but when she looked up a man in blue jeans and a shirt with a black collar was standing next to her. He had deep-set blue eyes and a wreath of gray hair around a shiny bald scalp. Jamie wiped her eyes self-consciously. "I'm sorry," she said.

"It's all right."

His voice was deep and comforting. Jamie felt as if she could tell him anything and his eyes would still shine with the same deep kindness. "I've made a mess of things," she said. "I need to change."

He nodded sympathetically. "You've come to the right place," he said.

⁓

The stately brick colonial had not changed in the years since Jamie had last seen it. The azalea bushes grew the same height along the front of the house; the shutters gleamed the same glossy black; and the same winter mix of holly, juniper, and ivy grew in the oversized concrete planters flanking the brick walkway.

Jamie's fingers trembled as they hovered above the doorbell. She bit her lower lip and reminded herself that she wasn't seventeen anymore.

The long slow chimes drifted softly through the double doors. *Stop it heart,* she ordered. *Stop racing. It's distracting.* A moment later the door opened. Her father's lanky frame filled the wedge of space. One glance at his powder blue cashmere sweater and pressed wool slacks and Jamie felt swept back in time. She tried to smile and failed. "Hello, Dad."

"Jamie," he said quietly. "Come in."

She recognized the Chippendale table in the foyer. The glossy black-framed mirror hanging over it was new, as was the trendy zebra-print fabric on the old camelback sofa in the living room.

"Let's go in my office." Her dad gestured to the room immediately to their right.

"Is Mom home?" She winced at the hopeful note in her voice.

"No."

Jamie kept her back straight as she followed her dad into his office. She settled herself into a hunter green leather chair. Her father took a seat behind a glossy, key-holed desk and pulled out a yellow legal pad as if he intended to take notes on their meeting.

She moistened her dry lips. "Dad," she said, "I'm here to ask a favor."

He nodded as if he had expected no less. "How much?" Before she even replied, the drawer to his desk opened, and he pulled out a checkbook.

His words stung—as they'd been meant to. "I'm not here for money." She clenched the strap of her purse. "I'm here for Ivy, your granddaughter, remember?"

"I remember," her father echoed quietly.

Jamie pulled out Ivy's most recent school portrait and laid it on her father's desk. "She wants to meet you and Mom."

Her dad removed his glasses, studied the lenses for spots, and then replaced them. Only after this agonizingly slow process did he pick up the photo. "So this is the child."

Her father's face could have been made of granite for all the emotion he displayed. He had aged, though. Jamie saw it in the deepening grooves in his face and the receding line of his silver hair. "She has his coloring," he said without looking up. "But your features."

"Ivy's a straight-A student at Miss Porter's School. Her debate team went to state last year, and she just won her age category in an interclub ski race." There were other things she could tell him—the way Ivy's eyes lit up when she laughed, the sweetness of her voice when she sang in the shower, how her nose curled in a cute way when she stuck her toes in cold pool water.

"Miss Porter's, you say?"

"This is her first year."

"Ed Nickelson has a granddaughter going there. Shelly. You know her?"

Jamie shook her head. Truth was, she barely knew Ivy's friends.

"It's an expensive school," her father said. "You must be doing well to send her there."

"I'm a Realtor," she said. The rest wasn't any of his business. "So what do you think? Do you want to meet her?" She held her breath, hoping he would and terrified for the same reason.

"I'll have to talk about this with your mother." He seemed to hesitate and then added, "You look good, Jamie."

How could he hesitate? How could he not jump on this opportunity? Here she was, offering him the most precious gift he could ever receive and all he could say was she looked good? Jamie felt her temper rise. Why was she so surprised? At the heart of things, he was a selfish person—a man with a moral code so rigid he could not bring himself to forgive his only child.

She curled the strap of her purse tightly. "One thing, Dad. If you decide to meet her, I want to be very clear that you will do nothing, say nothing that could in any way hurt Ivy more than you have already."

His face remained impassive. "Hurt her? At the time, Jamie, your mother and I did what we thought was best for you and the baby." His face softened. "You couldn't stay here—people would have made your life miserable. And the child, she would have been labeled."

Jamie felt the blood rush to her face. "You think being disowned was so much better?" She shook her head. "You weren't afraid for me or Ivy—you were afraid for yourselves. We would have been an embarrassment to you."

He took off his glasses and raked his hands through the thin strands of his silver hair. "I won't deny that we thought about that. It wasn't the deciding factor, though. We felt if you realized how hard it would be to be a single parent, you'd give the baby up for adoption. We thought the child would be better off with an older, married couple."

"You were wrong," Jamie said, rising to her feet.

Her father's gaze was steady, but she saw a sheen of perspiration on his forehead. "Don't think it's been easy for us either. Don't think we haven't suffered because of what we did."

Jamie set her business card on the desk. "I'm sorry for that, and I'm sorry that Ivy wants to meet you, but here we are." She looked around at the stacks of legal books on the dark wood of the built-in shelves and knew her father saw things in black or white, right or wrong. "Call me when you and Mom make a decision."

She was too upset to drive straight home. Instead she headed for the Methodist church. The choir was singing when she walked into the chapel. She slipped into a pew and bowed her head, thinking some hurts were too deep to be healed and feeling like she'd failed. She dreaded telling Ivy about the meeting. After a few moments, the reverend joined her on the bench. He sat quietly next to her, studied her face, and asked, "How'd it go?"

Jamie shrugged. "Okay, I guess. He said he'd have to think about it."

He nodded. "Let me pray for you."

"Thank you," she said. Joining hands with the minister, she looked steadily into his eyes. It took a moment to work the words past the lump in her throat. "I feel so broken," she admitted. "Everything hurts."

His grip tightened. "You're not alone."

Her cell phone rang on her way home. When she saw the Connecticut number, her heart began to race, and she pulled over to the side of the road. "Jamie King," she answered crisply.

"It's your father," her dad said.

She felt her muscles go rigid. A terrible fear crept along her spine. She couldn't bear it if he disappointed Ivy.

"You left your gloves," he said.

"Oh." Her heart sank. He could keep the gloves.

"You can come pick them up on Sunday," her father said. "If you like, you could stay for lunch. And bring the girl—Ivy—if she can get away from school."

"I'll check with her," Jamie replied calmly as if her heart wasn't firmly lodged in her throat and every muscle hadn't gone limp. "But it'll probably be fine. Would you like us to bring something?"

There was a long pause and then her father said, "No, just yourselves." His voice gave nothing away, and he quickly hung up. Afterward Jamie stared at her cell phone and realized they had not set a time. She pictured her dad sitting at his desk realizing the same thing and trying to decide what to do about it. She wondered if his hands were shaking as hard as hers right now.

Chapter 24

Where'd you hide my car keys, Gray?" Norman asked. "I want to take Sally for a spin."

Gray had come into the ski shop on the pretext of needing a wrench to fix one of the mountain bikes. It was April and soon people would be coming to Pilgrim's Peak to bike the ski trails. Mostly, though, he wanted to check on his father. "I've got some free time. Where do you want to go?"

His dad's brows pushed together. "Stop treating me like an invalid, checking up on me every two minutes."

Gray grinned. "It's been two hours since I saw you at breakfast. Besides, I need a sprocket wrench."

Norman retrieved the tool from a drawer. "I want to drive. I have a clean bill of health from the doctor. I'm even legal, remember?"

How could Gray forget the trip to the motor vehicles department? While waiting in line, his dad had flirted with a woman with a swooping eagle tattooed to her shoulder, and the minute Norman found out she liked bikes, he'd invited her to Pilgrim's Peak. Fortunately for Gray, it turned out she liked motorcycles and not mountain bikes, and she had turned him down.

"I know you want to drive," Gray said, "but I haven't put any oil in Sally recently, and I don't think we have any in the garage."

In truth, he was afraid to go anywhere near the car. When Jamie had returned it several weeks ago, it'd held the very faintest trace of her perfume. He'd sat in the Buick like a lovesick teenager, breathing her in and wondering if she ever intended to come back.

"I'm sure there's enough oil to get me to a gas station." Norman picked up a file and began rubbing the tool against the edge of a ski. Even though it would be months before anyone rented skis, he liked to spend the off-season getting the equipment in perfect condition. "I don't know how much time I've got," he stated flatly.

"According to the doctor, if you stay away from the chili dogs and doughnuts, you'll be here for years." Gray studied the plank floors worn into the color of dirt by hundreds, maybe thousands of ski boots clumping across them. "If you want to drive somewhere, at least let me come with you."

His dad snorted. "You'll only slow me down."

Gray laughed. "What are you talking about?"

His father's face looked thinner, and there were lingering shadows beneath his eyes that hadn't gone away since his heart attack. "The only thing I really care about is you, Gray, and Halle. I'm not going to be here forever you know."

Not another death speech. Gray willed himself to listen patiently.

"Before I die, I want to make sure you'll be happy."

"Dad," Gray interrupted, despite himself. "Halle and I are fine. And you're going to be here for a long, long time."

His dad banged the file onto the worktable. "And when Halle goes off to college, what are you going to do, Gray? Rattle around this ski hill like a ghost? Now give me my car keys and let me get to work."

"Work, Dad?"

"Finding you a wife. We made good progress with Jamie—and to be honest, I was a little disappointed on how that turned out—but since she doesn't seem to be the right one for you, we have to keep looking."

Gray flinched. The mention of Jamie's name could do that to him. Then his brain registered the last part of the sentence. "Dad, I don't need you to find me a wife."

"Obviously you do. Now, Gray, you didn't like the women at Talbots, the beauty salon, or the movie theater. I'm thinking of taking Boomer to the new dog-grooming place in Southbury. I'll stake out the waiting room and call if I see someone promising."

His dad was joking. Gray rubbed his eyes. When his father's face came back into focus, Gray saw the same look of concern in his dad's brown eyes. "You're serious," he said.

"Of course. Usually women who like animals are caring people. I don't know why I didn't think of this sooner."

It was all starting to make horrifying sense now. "Dad, tell me all those so-called car accidents weren't attempts to set me up with women?"

"How else was I going to delay the girls long enough for you to see them?"

"You could have hurt someone." Gray raked his hands through his hair. "Not to mention you inconvenienced everyone, damaged a lot of cars, and nearly gave me a heart attack every time you called and said you'd been in an accident." Gray studied his dad's stoic features. "You're not even sorry you made a mess of things."

"Love is messy," his dad stated gravely. "Get over it, Gray. Now tell me where you hid the keys."

Gray shook his head. If he had to, he'd bury those keys in the backyard. "Not until I'm sure you aren't going to drive into some poor woman's car."

"I will when you stop waiting for love to show up on your front doorstep." His father's gravelly voice sharpened. "Because it looks like God tried that once—and I don't think He's going to do it again."

Gray's face burned. He clenched his jaw to keep from saying something he'd regret later. Turning, he stormed out of the room, his work boots echoing in the empty building. His dad thought he knew everything, but he knew nothing. Nothing at all.

Gray shoved the door to the ski lodge open and stepped into the strong April sun. He'd given Jamie months, and she still hadn't called. The cloudless blue sky taunted him, and he kicked a rock that had the nerve to get in his way. He glanced at the near-empty parking lot. His dad was right about one thing— he highly doubted Jamie King was going to show up on his doorstep again.

His gaze remained on his Jeep. Nope. Jamie King might not show up on his doorstep, but there was nothing keeping him from showing up on hers.

It didn't take long to find her address—he wasn't without computer skills. By late afternoon, he found himself in the parking lot of a high-rise apartment building in Old Greenwich. There was a Hertz moving truck parked in the front. His stomach clenched at the sight of Jamie standing beside it.

She was standing next to a powerfully built man with dark hair and olive-colored skin. The guy said something that made Jamie laugh. Something about the guy seemed familiar. Gray clenched his fists as the brawny guy gave Jamie a kiss on the cheek.

"That ought to do it," Brawny Guy said. "We'll see you at the new place."

"Thanks, Devon," Jamie said.

Gray's heart sank as the reason Jamie hadn't called became clear to him. He felt like an idiot. Mending relationships had obviously included a renewed one with Ivy's father. He turned to leave, hoping she wouldn't see him.

～

The shape of the back was right and so was the color of the hair, but the cut was wrong. It was much too short. She squinted her eyes. Gray?

"Gray!" The man didn't stop. She started running, caught up to him, and grabbed his arm, half expecting herself to be wrong.

Gray turned around, and the expression on his face chilled her to the bone. She released him. "Is Norman okay?"

"He and Halle are fine."

Jamie looked at him, confused. He'd cut his hair since the last time she'd seen him, and his jaw was clean-shaven. He seemed thinner, too, and his eyes were guarded. "I don't understand," she said.

He shrugged. "I came to see you, but I can tell this isn't the right time." He clicked his remote, and the locks popped open. "Good luck with the move, Jamie."

"I owe you a phone call," she admitted, studying the tense line of his mouth. "I was going to call you from my new place."

His mouth twisted. "You don't owe me anything. Look, I know you need to get going. You don't want to keep Devon waiting."

Jamie put her hand on his arm. His muscles felt as tight as steel cables. "He's just helping me move."

"You don't need to explain anything to me." Gray pulled the car door open and climbed onto the seat.

"Look," Jamie said, hauling uselessly at his arm. "I don't want you to go away thinking there's something between me and Devon when there isn't. He's just trying to make up for the past."

Gray's eyebrows lifted. "Looks like he's succeeding."

Jamie pressed closer to the car. She wanted to yank the keys out of his hands. "Gray, don't. He's Ivy's father, and that's it."

"He kissed you," Gray said flatly.

"Devon kisses everyone—that's just him." Jamie looked in his eyes and wondered how to make him believe her. "Gray, he's only in my life again because of Ivy. She needs to know him. I'm not interested in him or anyone else." She paused and registered the disbelieving twist of his lips. "I'm only interested in you."

The air went very still around them. "Then why haven't you called me? Why did you drop off Sally without even seeing me?"

To her dismay, Jamie's throat started to tighten. "I couldn't."

"Why not?"

She bit her lower lip. "Because I was afraid if I saw you or talked to you, I wouldn't be able to stay away from you. I told you, when I came to you, I wanted things to be as perfect as I could make them."

He looked at her for a long time, then the seat creaked as he stepped out of the driver's seat. He folded his arms and gazed sternly down at her. "You have to stop thinking everything has to be perfect," Gray said. "Because it's never going to happen. There's always going to be some problem, some obstacle that gets in the way, and that's called life. People who love each other should go through these things together."

"I'm not talking about a clogged sink," Jamie said, afraid to focus on his last sentence. "I'm talking about financial debt. I'm talking about a daughter who is very confused about who she is."

"You have some challenges," Gray agreed. "But if you didn't have them, I never would have met you."

She told him about the beautiful old church she had accidentally found and the reverend who had talked her into coming back for Sunday service. The message had been about forgiveness, and Jamie had cried when she realized how much she was hurting herself and Ivy by not forgiving the people who had hurt her.

"I'm coming to see that I was wrong about a lot of things, Gray. Most of all for not trusting God. I didn't think He could forgive me, much less love me. I'm still trying to wrap my mind around that concept." She shook her head. "All these years I stayed away from Him, but He was still watching out for me. How could I not see that?"

"You see it now."

"I have a long way to go and so much to learn."

"We all do. But we don't have to go through things alone."

Jamie shook her head. They were starting to talk in circles. "Sometimes you do."

"Does that mean I have to have everything in my life in perfect order before you could love me? Does Halle have to be able to play a perfect set of scales on the french horn, or does my dad have to pass his next physical?"

"Of course not." Jamie was horrified to think he might believe that.

"And you don't either." Gray lifted her fingers and kissed them gently. "I've missed you, Jamie, and I don't want to miss another day without you in it. I wake up thinking about you, and all day I wonder what you're doing. I go to bed thinking about you. I want to start a life with you today. Right here. Right now."

She searched her heart for answers. The truth was, she didn't want to turn Gray away. It didn't mean she'd stop struggling to change her life or get side-tracked in her desire to build a relationship with God. Learning about the Lord was going to be a lifelong journey—a journey she wanted to take with Gray at her side. "If you really mean that," Jamie said, "then I could really use your help moving my couch into my new place." She started to tell him about the great view of the Mianus River and then said, "It's a basement apartment and much cheaper. I'm on a budget now."

"I'll help you move—today and when you're ready to come back to Pilgrim's Peak."

Jamie started to smile. "You sure you aren't just wanting my lemon blueberry muffins?"

"No," Gray said gravely. "I like the lemon cheesecake ones with the crumble topping much better."

"As long as we're clear," Jamie said, savoring the expression in his eyes, which she knew had nothing to do with muffins. "And if I were to agree to start seeing you again, would the arrangement include private ski lessons?"

"As many as you want."

"In that case," Jamie said, smiling, "I think I might want a lifetime of them."

Gray's eyes crinkled. He smiled as he tilted his head toward her. "I think that could be arranged."

Chapter 25

Jamie lifted her veil over the back of the seat. Beside her, Ivy pulled down the safety bar as the chair lift swept them into the crisp February afternoon. The white gossamer fabric streamed behind them like a flag as they started up the mountain. A white parka and ski pants weren't exactly the wedding outfit Jamie had once imagined herself wearing, but it felt right. Better than right, actually. Perfect.

"You nervous, Mom?"

"A little," Jamie admitted. "Don't ski too close to me after the ceremony. I might run into you by accident."

Ivy made a face. "You're not going to run into anyone, Mom."

She'd only been joking, but Ivy had missed it completely. Jamie studied her daughter's lovely profile. "What? What aren't you telling me?"

"It's stupid." Ivy sighed.

"Please, Ivy. Tell me. I want this to be a happy day." She twisted to see Ivy's face better. "You are happy, aren't you?"

"Of course." Ivy studied the tips of her skis. "But I still don't know what to call them—the Mr. Westlers."

"I thought you were going to call Gray, 'Dad,' and Norman, 'Grandpa.'"

Ivy waggled her skis. "I know, but I've been thinking, it's going to be confusing having multiple dads and grandpas."

Jamie smiled and patted Ivy's leg. "It's a good problem to have, isn't it?"

"But it's weird, too, to think of you moving to Woodbury and living at Pilgrim's Peak."

"I know," Jamie said, holding her veil as a strong wind rocked the chair lift in the same spot it always did. "But I'll be closer to Farmington, and it'll be easier to see you." She grinned. "If you want me to, that is."

Two bright spots of color appeared in Ivy's pale face. Her face morphed into a series of expressions before her lips formed any words at all. "Well, I'm kinda thinking I might not want to stay at Miss Porter's. I'm kinda thinking I might want to train with Mr. Grayson and start going to some more ski races. It would be easier to do that if I lived with you," Ivy said.

"You could do that," Jamie said eagerly. "I'd love for you to do that."

"I'm not quite sure," Ivy said. "I don't think Woodbury is going to have teachers as good as Miss Porter's, and I don't want to leave my friends. I really want to go to a good college, maybe Yale or Princeton."

"Woodbury High is a great school," Jamie said. "You could go there and still get into a good school."

"I don't know," Ivy said. "Part of me wants to stay at Miss Porter's and. . ."

"What?" Jamie asked. To her dismay, she saw Ivy's lips tremble and her eyes fill with tears.

"Part of me wants to stay here. I'm kinda scared you're going to forget about me if I don't."

"Oh honey," Jamie said, hugging her as much as the narrow seat would allow. "I could never forget about you—I love you so much. I always have, and I always will. Nothing can change that. Nothing."

"You'll have Gray and Halle. You'll be a family without me, and you'll have all these inside jokes I won't understand."

"Ivy," Jamie said. "Nobody in the world could ever replace you or make me love you less. Do you love me less because you're starting to get to know your father and your grandparents?"

Ivy shook her head. "No, but they aren't coming to live with us."

They never really went away, did they? The old hurts and deep fears. They popped up like moles in that silly arcade game. As soon as you bopped one on the head, another mole popped up in another place. She linked her arm through Ivy's and wiggled closer on the bench seat.

"If you want to want to change your mind and go to Woodbury, you're welcome to do it. You know I would love it."

"But then Grandma and Grandpa King will be disappointed, and they've offered to pay half of my tuition. I should stay at Miss Porter's."

Jamie patted her daughter's leg. "Helping you financially is their way of saying they love you. You should do what you think will make you the happiest." She paused as a skier passing beneath them stopped to shout his congratulations. "Let's both pray about it. I haven't always asked for the Lord's guidance, and I've made a lot of mistakes because of that."

Ivy pointed to the glittering diamond in her ear. "I love you, Mom. When we get off the lift, I want to give you the diamonds as a wedding gift—they're the best thing I have to give you."

"You're the best gift," Jamie said and started to cry. When they reached the top of the mountain, Ivy practically had to haul her out of the lift seat and down the ramp. Ivy solemnly wiped her cheeks with a tissue and then threaded the studs through Jamie's earlobes. "You're perfect now," Ivy declared.

Gray waited at the top of Alice's Alley next to Reverend Blaymires. Halle stood at his side, next to Norman, who had driven to the top of the mountain in the Sno-Cat. Nearby, a group of the Westlers' closest friends hovered nearby, ready to witness the ceremony and then ski down the hill with them. Jamie waved at Jaya and Misty who had driven up from Greenwich. Standing beside them looking very out of place were Jamie's parents. Her mother's feet had to be freezing in her stylish but impractical leather boots. She smiled, though, when she saw Jamie. Her father gave her a curt nod. She believed this was supposed to mean approval but she wasn't quite sure. It was hard to tell with her parents, but their presence was another step forward in their relationship.

Jamie's gaze returned to Gray and stayed there. Framed by the immense blue sky, it almost looked as if he waited for her on the edge of the world. Of course this wasn't true—she'd skied this trail enough to know that even though the trail couldn't be seen until you skied right up to it, it was there. She thought faith was like that—sometimes you couldn't see very far ahead or know exactly where it was leading you, but it was always there, a never-ending path for all who cared to walk it.

Jamie squeezed Ivy's hand, gave thanks to God, and glided steadily toward her future.

Epilogue

Jamie powered up the video camera as the Woodbury Royals marching band took the field for the half-time show. She scanned the sea of blue and black uniforms for Halle's slender form. Fortunately, there were only three french horn players and the other two were tall guys.

"There she is, Gray!" Jamie zoomed in on Halle's face. "You see her?"

"Yeah, she's on the forty-yard line," Gray said calmly, but he was leaning forward on the bleachers, and his body radiated energy.

"Can't she wear a different colored plume on her hat so she's easier to see?" Norman complained. He was proudly wearing a Woodbury Royals marching band sweatshirt under his Woodbury Royals Windbreaker.

The show started with a melody led by the flutes and clarinets, then the brass and drums kicked in and the stadium resonated with the power of the full band. Jamie trained the camera on Halle, but lost her in a band-wide shuffle that sorted itself in an eyeblink into an enormous winged formation. Jamie pulled the camera back for a wider angle.

"They're great," Norman said loudly, applauding as the color guard threw bright blue and white flags into the air, catching them as the band belted out the music. "They should march at the Rose Bowl—or the White House."

Jamie's throat tightened as the band effortlessly shifted formations. She wished Ivy were there to see the show, but hoped she was having fun with Jamie's parents in Manhattan. Ivy'd be back tomorrow morning. Gray and the girls planned to go running together in order to get in shape for the coming ski season. Ivy planned to try out for the Chargers—Woodbury High's ski team. Ivy was determined to qualify for the varsity team by having the fastest time. Her daughter also planned to graduate at the top of her class—a feat the guidance counselor felt was well within Ivy's capabilities. Jamie was just glad that Ivy was happy with the transfer of schools and her new life in Woodbury.

The tempo of the music changed. In the center of the field, a lone trumpet player stepped forward. His silver instrument gleamed under the stadium lights as he pointed the instrument upward and played a flawless solo.

"And he's just a sophomore," Norman said. "That kid is amazing. He never misses a note."

The rest of the band kicked in. Jamie strained to hear the notes of the french horns. Halle, surprisingly, was developing a talent that continued to astound and thrill them all. Before Jamie knew it, the performance finished, and the band members marched proudly off the field. Turning off the camera, Jamie slipped her hand into Gray's. "That was awesome! Even better than last week."

"You say that every week," Gray pointed out, but he was smiling.

"And I mean it every week." Jamie smiled as the football team returned to the field.

They were well into the third quarter when Gray touched her arm. "Look," he said. "The kid who played the trumpet solo is climbing up on the band director's platform."

Jamie had never seen anyone but the band director on top of the ladder. The boy was very tall, thin, and blond. He had a megaphone in his hands and a determined look on his face. When he reached the top of the platform, a sudden hush fell over the entire band. "Halle Westler," the boy's voice boomed over the megaphone. "Will you go to homecoming with me?"

Gray shot her a frozen, panicked look before returning his gaze to the boy on the platform. "Did you hear that?"

Norman laughed gleefully. "It's starting," he said. "Thank God I'm here to see it."

Halle stood up and handed someone her instrument and her hat. She bounded down the bleacher steps with her long ponytail bouncing behind her. She reached the blond boy, who had climbed down the ladder just in time to meet her. Jamie peered around the man in front of her for a better view. She watched her stepdaughter walk into the boy's arms. "I think that's a yes," she said.

"I can see that," Gray said dryly. "I don't think I'm ready for this."

"I don't think that matters," Norman said and thumped Gray's back. "I give that kid a lot of credit," he said. "Not just anyone could ask a girl out in front of everyone like that." He gave Jamie a nod. "I approve."

"Dad," Gray protested. "You don't even know the kid."

"Some things you know in your heart. Besides, Halle's been hoping for this."

"How do you know?"

"I eavesdropped. How else am I supposed to find out anything interesting?"

"Dad," Gray said. "You're awful."

Norman just laughed. "It wasn't my fault. I was napping in my chair, and when I woke up she was talking to Ivy about this boy who plays trumpet."

Jamie smiled, but most of her attention was on Halle and the blond boy. They were still standing at the base of the director's ladder. Halle's lips moved as the boy looked down, smiling. They were so young and vulnerable. She ached to hold them both in her hands and watch over them so neither of them ever hurt the other. Just for a second, she saw a glimmer of the girl she had been, standing off to the side, almost lost in the shadows, watching.

She felt her heart tug. That girl had been so lonely, so lost, and so unhappy. That girl had tried to hide her pain and be somebody she wasn't. She wished she could go back in time and tell her that everything was going to be all right. She'd put her arms around this girl and whisper the words that Jamie wished she'd understood so many years ago.

God loves you. He loves you unconditionally, and He will never leave you.

The girl disappeared as Halle and the boy climbed back into the stands. Gray slipped his arm across the back of Jamie's shoulders. She leaned against his side and settled back to watch the rest of the game.

Jamie's Lemon Blueberry Muffins

(Makes 9 jumbo or 12 regular-sized muffins)

4 ounces cream cheese
1 teaspoon lemon juice
Zest of ½ lemon
1 teaspoon vanilla extract
2 cups flour
¾ cup sugar (1 cup if you like very sweet muffins)
1½ teaspoons baking powder
½ teaspoon baking soda
2 eggs
½ cup milk
¼ cup canola oil
1 cup fresh blueberries

Preheat oven to 350 degrees. In blender, mix cream cheese, lemon juice, lemon zest, and vanilla until smooth. In separate bowl combine flour, sugar, baking powder, and baking soda. Slowly add dry ingredients to the cream cheese mix in blender. Add eggs, milk, and canola oil. With a spoon, fold in blueberries. Fill muffin cups. Bake for 35 minutes.

A Letter to Our Readers

Dear Readers:

In order that we might better contribute to your reading enjoyment, we would appreciate you taking a few minutes to respond to the following questions. When completed, please return to the following: Fiction Editor, Barbour Publishing, Inc., P.O. Box 719, Uhrichsville, OH 44683.

1. Did you enjoy reading *Connecticut Weddings* by Kim O'Brien?
   - ❑ Very much. I would like to see more books like this.
   - ❑ Moderately—I would have enjoyed it more if _____
   _____
   _____

2. What influenced your decision to purchase this book? (Check those that apply.)
   - ❑ Cover ❑ Back cover copy ❑ Title ❑ Price
   - ❑ Friends ❑ Publicity ❑ Other

3. Which story was your favorite?
   - ❑ *Leap of Faith*   ❑ *A Still, Small Voice*
   - ❑ *A Whole New Light*

4. Please check your age range:
   - ❑ Under 18   ❑ 18–24   ❑ 25–34
   - ❑ 35–45   ❑ 46–55   ❑ Over 55

5. How many hours per week do you read? _____

Name _____

Occupation _____

Address _____

City_____ State_____ Zip_____

E-mail _____